Exit Katrina

R. CHRIS LINK

Dennis,
 To a great friend and coworker I always enjoyed working with; as well as a true Christian brother. All the best!

Chris Link 12/20/16

Exit Katrina

Front cover photograph reproduced and edited by permission from Shawn Alladio of K38 Rescue. I am in awe of the incredible work she and her team accomplish.

www.shawnalladio.com

This is a work of fiction. Names, characters, places, and incidents are products of the author's imagination or are used fictitiously and are not to be construed as real. Any resemblance to actual events, locales, organizations, or persons, living or dead is entirely coincidental.

No part of this book may be used or reproduced in any manner whatsoever without written permission, except in the case of brief quotations embodied in critical articles and reviews.

Copyright © 2016 R. Chris Link

All rights reserved.

ISBN: 069279283X
ISBN-13: 978-0692792834 (OzLink Works)

DEDICATION

To Mom, the one most responsible for my love of reading,
and to my Dad who I miss more than I can say.

CONTENTS

Acknowledgements i
Prologue 1
Stranger in the Rain 4
Jimmy Dean 14
Missing 26
Playing Catch 33
Letters & Phone Calls 42
Get a Job 52
Tested 59
Private Investigation 67
Magic Candle 74
Looking Back 83
Fishing Story 95
Preparing to Leave 105
Hattiesburg 111
Butterflies & Bees 117
Sicily 125
Online Strangers 138
Into the City 148
New Leads 161
Thanksgiving 174
Connected By Poetry 183
Falling 194
Adoption 205
Out Of Body 219
Death & Trauma 224
Recuperation 232
Twice Born 243
Snow Falls 253
Confrontation 263
Confession 272
Closure 281
Epilogue 286

ACKNOWLEDGMENTS

To Peg and Dylan for patiently giving me the time and space to let the imaginary become more tangible than the real.

Special thanks to Tammy Hugger for providing editing and support in great measure.

To the families of Katrina's dead and still missing.

For he beholdeth himself, and goeth his way, and straightway forgetteth what manner of man he was.
— James 1:24 —

PROLOGUE

NEW ORLEANS, LA – AUGUST 2005

The world had broken. Lake Ponchartrain raged through the ruptured 17th Street Canal levee as if to entomb the city below the surface of the Gulf of Mexico.

A lone man floundered through the rising eddies bordering the tumbling flood. He cried out in frustration, unable to keep pace with a child's inflatable pool, twisting and turning as it careened along on top of the churning water, pummeled by the wind and rain of a category 3 hurricane. Peeking out over the top edge, a frightened, tiny girl with cornrow braids in a wet red t-shirt, frantically clung to the inside of the makeshift raft. Hope diminished; the distance between them was steadily growing.

Abandoned houses and backyard debris blocked his progress. A submerged chain-link fence caught his shirt, pulling him under before ripping away. The great mass of water relentlessly spread outward and rose ever higher, forcing him to skirt farther away from the treacherous center of the flow. He anxiously kept an eye on the girl as his arms wind-milled, ragged breath now coming in gulps. The water continued to rise until his feet could no longer reach the bottom; it was either sink, swim or tread water.

A bobbing propane tank blocked his view, and by the time he pushed by, he had lost sight of her altogether. Was she still afloat?

Even if she was, how long could she possibly ride out the turbulent water? Desperation and dread gripped his mind.

Through the gauntlet of houses, he glimpsed her again, still hurtling along in the distance. Then, impossibly—in this flat city—she headed straight toward a high knoll of ground rising up to split the current.

Now less than a hundred yards away, he caught sight of two people standing on the south end of the high ground, near a wire cage protecting electric power transformers. A man in a rescue vest joined the two, all of them wading into the water to catch the makeshift raft. Deeply fatigued, he dog-paddled through drifting debris toward a nearby house. Retching into the flotsam, he somehow kept his head above the surface. With the last of his remaining strength, he grabbed outside stairs leading to a second floor and crawled up, away from the water, resting a few minutes to catch his breath before sliding back into the churning water to continue.

He worked his way around the house by grasping the wooden railing of a wrap-around porch. The blowing rain calmed long enough for him to glimpse the little girl on top of the knoll, wet braids as black as shoe polish, clutching her rescuer every bit as tightly as she had hung on to the inflatable pool. It was hard for him to believe that she had managed to stay inside. She was going to be okay.

He grabbed the top of the porch rail and dragged himself up and over. The floor was under water, but one of the columns supported him. He wept in exhaustion and relief for the rescued girl, and in sorrow for a man he'd seen disappear under the water. He started to yell to let them know he was there, but then did not, though he hardly knew why. They hadn't noticed him. Maybe the rain had hidden him. Their eyes had only been on the girl.

He sat on the porch rail arguing with himself, long after he heard them leave in a boat from the other side of the mound. Finally, he swam through the water to the knoll across the flooded road. He climbed to the top, turning in circles to view the surrounding flood in amazement.

After a few minutes, he entered the water once again, swimming from house to house, away from the center of the flow. He lost any sense of time. Exhaustion and the nightmarish surroundings plagued his mind. He slowly worked back around to where he had left the car. A dog's forlorn howl echoed through the houses as he struggled on alone, through the doomed city in the heart of the storm.

CHAPTER 1 – STRANGER IN THE RAIN
BENFORD, TN – SEPTEMBER 2005

Maggie Young ran out of Simmons Hardware, embarrassed at hearing Bart's laughter following her through the closing door. She would take his teasing if it meant staying dry. Slamming her door as she hopped in the front seat, a gust of wind forcefully shook her car. Immediately, rain fell from the swollen sky above. She backed out and headed east, slowing only for Deputy Jones' fat beagle, out of his pen and making his rounds, as meticulous as a paper route. Lightning pierced a dark wall of clouds in her rearview mirror.

She had only driven a few blocks when, between swings of the windshield wipers, she made out a lanky man trotting down the shoulder of the road, duffle bag bouncing on his back. He skirted a section of missing sidewalk in front of a derelict gas station to head for the dry car wash next door. Maggie followed slowly, guessing he was trying to make it to one of the empty bays to wait out the rain.

He turned a hooded head without slowing his easy jog, as though listening to the tires swishing on the wet pavement to detect how closely her car followed. Maggie fought back a girly urge to swerve through the puddle beside him—give him a good spraying. *That's what I would have done to Tom.* And with that thought, she realized the man's easy, athletic movements reminded her of her deceased husband when he had been young.

Of course, there were a million reminders of Tom in Benford, but never another man. Maggie had no idea who he was. Still, she was curious enough to follow him as he turned into the shelter of the car wash. She drove the car next to the opening of the first bay and rolled down the passenger window.

Maggie was unsure of what she expected. The man laid the duffle on the concrete without hurry, pulling the hood of his windbreaker back and unzipping the front as he turned around. A cheerless smile climbed his face to replace the wary frown. She guessed he had judged that a woman in an old station wagon was not likely to be trouble. Now that he was hoodless and facing her, she realized he was older than she had guessed—maybe in his early 40s.

"Escaping from Katrina?" she shouted through the sound of the rain on the metal car wash roof.

He shrugged and nodded, glancing up at the rain and then down at his boots, "I don't suppose I've quite gotten away from her yet," he hollered back.

Maggie's focus broke from his blue eyes to travel down a long frame. Water-soaked boots and jean bottoms stood squarely beside a stained duffle. It occurred to her that even with the horrific loss of life and property, one of the most maddening things that hurricane battered evacuees must have endured was constant, wet feet.

He stepped closer to the open car window, staying just out of reach of the falling water peppering the car and metal roof of the car wash. It was so loud; they were unable to understand each other. Maggie reached to roll the window back up part way, but the rain lessened as soon as she touched the switch. "Do you need a ride somewhere?"

"I'm heading north."

"North from—"

"Trying to find a place to work and live for a while before I go back home."

"Where is home?"

"New Orleans—a little place in Gentilly." His short statements seemed devised to hold back a longer explanation. His pronunciation didn't ring native to her ear—New Awyuns or New Orleeuns. His accent didn't sound Southern at all for that matter. Maggie suspected that he must have moved there within the last few years.

Maggie had sometimes spoken before thinking for most of her 54 years. She obeyed the same notion this day. "Why don't you come and dry out at my place? I'll fix you something to eat. You can rest and figure out what you're going to do next." Even as she spoke, she realized it was probably not smart. Her adventurous, kindness constantly got her in trouble with Rod and James, her grown boys who had left Benford to live in bigger and busier places in North Carolina and Minnesota. They often complained about her extravagant view of Christian charity. She added this to an existing long list of events she would be careful to not mention in their next conversations on the phone.

Her voice trailed off with the next thought. What would the girls at church say? Her face must have betrayed her sudden misgiving; the man now appeared hesitant and doubtful behind the curtain of water dripping from the eaves. Deep weariness and something even more unsettling peered out from his dark eyes. Running fingers back through his hair, he raised his eyebrows, reminding Maggie of little boys in her classroom trying to appear to be grown up.

"Ma'am, I appreciate you asking, but I don't want to be any trouble. I can hang out here and catch a ride after the rain stops."

He had indeed given her a chance to escape her offer, but Maggie's mouth continued to operate on its own; "Now look, this rain isn't supposed to quit very soon. Get in the car." Straight-line lightning skewered the ground to the north as if in emphatic agreement. She had spoken with what Tom used to call her "teacher's voice." He had claimed years in the classroom had given her voice almost supernatural powers of command and persuasion. Put on your teacher's voice he would say to her whenever a crowd needed to come to attention or the situation called for someone to take charge.

The stranger gave in and opened the rear door to toss his duffle in the back seat. Maggie reached over, threw open the passenger door, and he dived through the rain into the front seat, closing the door behind him as she raised the electric windows.

"Nice car," he said, all wet and grinning, as he looked around the interior of the car.

"1979 Caprice Wagon Estate."

"White with Woody sides—classic."

"You don't think it looks like a hearse?"

"Nah." He looked around the interior. "Well, maybe it's big enough for a hearse, "he said, smiling.

Maggie turned the wipers on high, pulled out on the empty road and headed home, trying to ignore second thoughts about picking up a stranger. She would never have given him a ride if he hadn't reminded her of Tom. Maggie was accustomed to helping people, and it was a hard rain, but still—one didn't give rides to hitchhikers. She had done what she had done. No use regretting it now.

"By the way, I'm Maggie Young," she said as they neared the edge of town, turning onto the street that ran by her house.

"Jonas... Bays," he answered in a broken, two-part manner.

Was it Jonah or Jonas? Maggie wasn't sure she'd heard correctly. The thought of a Jonah escaping from a storm threatened to trigger an inappropriate giggle. "You did say Jonas, right?"

Jonas sat back with an inaudible sigh. "Yes. That's my name."

The long pause had caused Maggie to expect more. She looked over at him, observant and questioning. Wandering down the road 500 miles from New Orleans, he had somehow kept a tidy neatness about himself. He was close-shaven. His clothes, while well worn, didn't appear dirty. As wet as his clothing and bag were, the interior of the car only smelled of the rain. They drove the last few blocks in awkward silence. Jonas appeared to be uneasy. She supposed that was understandable. There was no telling what he had been through during the recent past. Her cheer evaporated.

News from New Orleans and other coastal towns, from Texas to Alabama, had been sobering over the last few weeks. Surrounding states were beginning to witness the human aftermath. Jonas wasn't the only refugee from the Gulf making his way to central Tennessee. Local churches in Benford had cooperated to prepare a shelter in the First Baptist gymnasium. They were taking in some of the transfers from early, primary shelters in Texas and Louisiana. Retired for one year and wanting to stay busy, Maggie had volunteered.

Questions about Jonas weighed on her mind, but Maggie thought they could wait. She switched on the headlights when the sky grew darker. The rain was now blowing horizontally across the road, making it difficult to see the landscape outside the windows of the car. Impressionist glimpses of the hay fields and barns to the West showed a mixture of single-family houses and hobby farms. She struggled to see the road in the wet darkness, but the way home was so familiar, Maggie thought she could almost find her way home blindfolded.

The white fence in front of her house glowed out of the cloud-covered gloom as she turned into the drive. Maggie considered stopping by the side entrance to the house, but because of the rain, she continued to the 3-car garage, pushed the opener, and drove into the left bay. Bright lights came on with the opening of the door.

"We're home," she said as she slid out of the driver's side. Jonas opened his door, looking around at the interior. A well-maintained 80s era white Chevy Pickup sat in the next bay over, covered in dust. In the third bay was a zero-turn radius mower. White pegboards displayed meticulously placed tools, but they too were dusty. Spider webs intersected corners and angles between the ceiling and wall. Maggie had the unusual experience of seeing her place through a visitor's eyes. She thought the garage still looked well taken care of, the dust only revealing a lack of use in the recent past.

"You know," she said, shutting the car door, "there's an apartment above this garage. My late husband used to camp out here sometimes, and my boys are partial to it when they come home. It will be a quieter place for you to rest. I'll show you around and then you can come over to the house later for dinner."

She led him upstairs and made sure he knew where the shower and towels were before grabbing an umbrella from a coat rack on the wall and hurrying back downstairs and out through the storm to the house. Slamming the door in the utility room, she realized she had forgotten to bring in the bags from the car. She decided to get them later after it quit raining—maybe even call Jonas in the apartment to have him carry the bags when he came for dinner.

Later, as Maggie was preparing their meal, she reflected on how quietly and carefully he had taken everything in, glancing at her often to give her that sad smile. It came to her that she already trusted him, for no good reason—no reason but that he somehow reminded her of Tom. Not that he looked like him. *No*, she thought, *he didn't look like Tom at all.*

Jonas woke to sunlight warming his face, lighting the back of his eyelids to a soft yellow-orange. The vague vestiges of a dream lingered, disturbing enough to resist returning to sleep. The same dream. He doubted he would ever be free of it. A part of him didn't want to be free—accepted that it was deserved. He opened his eyes to stare at a vaulted oak ceiling, trying to remember where he was.

A phone began ringing on a nearby end table. When he was finally able to get the receiver to his ear, Maggie's voice sang, "Jonas?" As his mind started to come out of the haze, he was able to cough out a hello into the phone. Maggie's voice was annoyingly cheerful and awake like she was thrilled just to be talking.

"Were you sleeping? I forgot to tell you about the telephone. Of course, you found it, or you wouldn't have answered. Sorry to wake you, but dinner is almost ready. You are going to eat, aren't you?"

All the time she was talking, he was still trying to clear his mind enough to answer her first question. "Uh, yes. I mean... I was sleeping. But yes, ma'am." He paused again. "I'm sorry," he apologized. "I'm afraid I'm not making much sense."

She tried to be patient but finally treated him like she treated most men—like they were one of her boys. "Well, you're going to have to get rid of that ma'am business. It's Maggie. Wash up and come on over to the house and let's eat. Oh, and please bring in the bags out of my car?"

Jonas did as he had been told.

The storm had apparently passed, he noticed as he left the garage. The sky was clear and the late afternoon sun was dropping in the west. His watch read 7:05 p.m. He guessed he had slept for about 4 hours. He glanced in surprise at a large oak tree uprooted in the backyard—tree roots now reaching for the sky like the legs of a dead armadillo on the side of a road. Surely, the storm had not been that bad. Still, it seemed possible; he had slept soundly for the first time in many days. Maybe he had slept through such a storm, but scrutiny revealed leaves that had withered over the course of several days. The tree hadn't fallen today.

When he knocked, Maggie opened the door, smiling and humming a tune, wiping her hands on an apron already stained with flour. She was clearly pleased. She derived much pleasure from cooking a meal for others, even more in enjoying it with them.

"We're going to eat in the kitchen; I hope you don't mind."

"Ma'am, I'm grateful—" He let his words trail off when he saw the stern look on her face.

"It's Maggie," she reminded him once again. "It's very similar to what you have been calling me. Starts with the same two letters—shouldn't be that difficult." Maggie's wink let Jonas know she wasn't actually annoyed with him.

"Maggie," he repeated, sitting at the table where she had set a place for him. "I am grateful, but you sure didn't have to cook like this for me."

The savory aroma overpowered his inclination to leave. Was that fresh baked bread coming out of the oven? Maggie cut off three slices with an electric knife, placed them in a cloth-shrouded basket and brought it with her to the table. She set the last items on the table, plopped down in the chair around the corner of the table, pulled one foot and leg under her, and said, "I'll say grace."

Without waiting for any comment, she bowed her head and began, "Father—"

Jonas didn't bow his head or close his eyes. He respected people's need for religion. He had used the concept of a higher power himself, as long as it had been useful, and then set it aside as a tool he would hopefully never need to use again.

He took the opportunity to look closely at this extraordinary woman. Her face was striking—aged yes, but still very attractive, especially her smile. Her hair was shoulder length, varying shades of silver and charcoal. The front swept down in a wave, breaking across the corner of her eye to sweep on around over her ear. Her eyebrows were defined, but not plucked into extinction. The wrinkles around her eyes and forehead spoke to him of laughter and real pain, not toxins and worry.

Upon closing her eyes, her lips had pursed into a smile, as if she and God had a little private joke going. A parade of expressions continued throughout the prayer, displays of concern and joy. *If there actually is a God listening,* Jonas thought, *he must be learning as much from watching her face as he is from her words.* He didn't pay attention to much else of what she said until—

"And God, please bless my new friend, Jonas, who has certainly been through far too much, and yet has joined me in this meal today. Please bless this food. Amen."

The simple request at the end surprised and touched him. In the attempt to keep his face a mask, he forgot to quit staring.

"Jonas," she exclaimed, "did you have your eyes open the whole time?"

Maggie didn't exactly accuse him of staring at her, but her jade colored eyes, under arched eyelids flashed at him like a circus knife thrower, landing much too close for comfort. He had been caught, open-eyed, emotions as transparent as if he were still a small boy.

He attempted to cover it by making it all about the prayer. "I'm not a religious man, Maggie. No offense," he added quickly.

"None taken. I should probably apologize to you. I sometimes treat adults like they are kids in my classroom."

"So, you're a teacher?"

"Retired just last year. It still seems strange not to have returned to school this month."

They talked while they ate, or rather, Maggie spoke and Jonas listened. She told him about her late husband Tom dying two summers ago, a heart attack out on his John Deere tractor. She glared out the window at the machine shed while admitting that she irrationally blamed the tractor because it gave her a place to target her anger. He listened quietly and examined her eyes to measure the pain, but she seemed to have taken it in stride, other than to say he had died too young, "just like a man to not pay attention to his own body." Then she told him about Rod and James, now in their early 30s, both of them having left home for college, then moving out of state to follow careers. Rod was a sales manager for a pharmaceutical company headquartered in St. Paul, Minnesota. James was an associate pastor of an Episcopal church in Raleigh, North Carolina.

"High church," Maggie said, raising her eyebrows at Jonas. He wasn't sure he knew what she meant by the phrase but figured it must have something to do with ecclesiastical class structure, one of the many things he disliked about Christians. She noticed his uncomfortable quietness. "What about you? Do you have family?"

Jonas had expected the question. He surveyed the rehearsed answers in his mind that somehow never came out very smoothly. Jonas was a poor liar who felt like he had little choice. "I lost my family," he murmured, looking at his hands, repeatedly opening and closing overlapping fingers.

Questions and thoughts crossed Maggie's face. He knew it was blatantly apparent to her that he wasn't opening up. She seemed about to ask further questions, but all that came out was, "I am so sorry."

Jonas finally broke a pregnant silence, changing the subject to ask her about the tree down in the backyard. Maggie told him several thunderstorms had recently swept through the area, one becoming a tornado that took down the oak. It had been a precision surgery, knocking over many trees in the vicinity but leaving buildings and houses standing, all but a dilapidated trailer house that had been transformed into a pigsty.

"This particular trailer actually housed pigs. It had two front doors, torn off their hinges. The wind must have filled it like a balloon and sent it flying. The pigs escaped harm. Evidently, they stayed out in the wallow during the storm."

Jonas smirked. "I guess all the people who have vowed, 'when pigs fly' dodged a bullet there."

Maggie laughed. "You're right. Be careful what you call impossible." She chuckled again. "Anyway, I called Jim Turner to cut up the tree, but he's on the Mississippi coast helping with the cleanup. Everybody else I know is still removing their own downed trees and other debris from the storms."

Jonas considered this. "If you have a chainsaw, I could cut it up for you." He looked out the window at the beginnings of twilight. "But I don't suppose I have time to finish it tonight."

"Tomorrow is fine. There are two chainsaws in the garage," she said. "It's going to be a big job. Are you certain that you want to do it? Of course, I'd pay you," she added.

Jonas tried to find words to argue, but Maggie didn't give him a chance.

"It's too late for you to get another place to stay tonight. No one is using the garage apartment, so you might as well stay there. I'll be glad to have the tree cut up."

As Maggie replayed the events of the day before falling asleep, she admitted to herself that she was happy that she had taken the risk. She was glad for the company, even if he was a sad stranger who vaguely reminded her of her deceased husband.

CHAPTER 2 – JIMMY DEAN
BENFORD, TN – SEPTEMBER 2005

The heat arrived with the momentum of a train the next morning, quickly erasing any trace of the rain from the day before. Jonas had risen while it was still dark to examine the chainsaws and tools in the garage below. Maggie's husband Tom had been a neat and organized man. The saws appeared to be in good condition. A big Stihl didn't seem to have been used much; the smaller McCulloch was older, but well maintained. He found chain files in a small tool chest on the bench by the saws, 2-cycle and bar oil on a higher shelf. By the time the sky had started growing light, he had already sharpened the blades and topped off the saws with fluids.

Jonas was taking a closer look at the tree, vowing to begin before the day became too hot when Maggie saw him and came outside. She had been puttering around since before 5:00 a.m., worrying about what her guest might need. She brought out the key to the hated John Deere and told him where to find it and the flatbed trailer in the equipment shed. He mentioned having some concern about putting ruts in the yard with the tractor and trailer, but Maggie stomped around and assured him the ground was dry enough.

They had a short discussion about his shoe and clothing sizes. Jonas assumed Maggie was getting ready to push off some of Tom's old stuff on him. Then, she mentioned glasses and gloves. Jonas was amazed. Maggie was as bright and energetic at dawn as she had be the day before, leading him back to the garage to point out the gloves and eye and ear protection.

Jonas looked forward to the work distracting him from the days of dreary reflection that had held him captive on his journey. Within a half hour, he had fetched the tractor and trailer, fired up the McCulloch and started cutting the limbs and tops from the trunk.

The first time Jonas stopped to put in more gas and sharpen the blade, Maggie brought out coffee, water, and blueberry muffins. The second time, he glanced up to find her waving at him as she backed the station wagon out of the garage. "I'll be back with lunch," she hollered. "Have to do my Saturday shopping." Jonas smiled helplessly and nodded. If he had to be around other people, it was good to be with someone who took care of most of the talking for both of them.

The problem was, he realized, he genuinely liked Maggie. He just didn't want any personal attachments. If he hung around here much longer, he might risk forming a relationship, even if he didn't have a clear idea of what the nature of it would be. He put those thoughts aside and returned to the tree. As the saws sang through the wood, the tree began to disappear as if he was a slow motion magician. It was satisfying work.

At one point, when he had shut off the saw to load wood on the trailer with the John Deere's front-end loader, he noticed a boy peeking through the fence between the yard and the barn. Later, the boy was sitting on the top rail. He waved shyly and swatted at a fly. Jonas waved back. He continued cutting on the tree but still glimpsed the boy out of the corner of his eye, alternately climbing on the fence and throwing some ground-fall apples he had picked up.

After several apples had made short flights to roll across the pasture, he shut off the saw and shouted, "Hey! Hey!"

The boy stopped in mid-throw, dropped the apple and hollered back. "What? Whad-ja say?"

"Come here," demanded Jonas, unwilling to engage in a shouting ied his cut-off jeans that were at least a size too big y quickly dropped around his hips again when he ith his dirty t-shirt bottom and started trotting ..., toward Jonas. His feet hit the ground with much more force than was necessary, knees bending at odd angles, blonde hair swimming across his face like curtains in front of an open window.

"Whad-ja say?" he asked again when he got closer.

"Why are you throwing those apples? Mrs.—" Jonas trailed off, realizing he had already forgotten her last name. "Maggie might not want you throwing apples all over her field."

The boy considered this with such a surprised face, it made Jonas reconsider. Why did he care if the kid moved apples from one place on the ground to another, especially apples full of worms and ants and stuff? He began to wish he had stayed quiet when he noticed that the boy was staring at the ground, kicking at fallen sticks with the toe of a worn-out sneaker.

As Jonas was about to say something about it being okay, the blonde head shot up, eyes bright as if an idea was shining through. "Well, Mizzzz Young said I could have some apples when I come over, and I was tryin' to hit the barn."

Jonas turned his head away to smile to himself. None of the apples had landed anywhere near the barn. The boy couldn't throw worth a lick, but it amused Jonas how he had stuck up for himself without showing any disrespect. He guessed this conversation could wander in many directions based on how it had started. The day was quickly becoming hot.

"What's your name, son?"

"Jimmy Dean Rogers." The boy frowned at Jonas and asked, "Are you the tree sturgeon?"

Jonas laughed. "No, I'm not the tree sturgeon. I'm doing some work for Mrs. Young this morning. Look, Jimmy Dean, I've enjoyed talking to you, but I need to get back to work. If Mrs. Young doesn't mind you playing here, then it's OK with me. But please stay away from where I'm cutting. It isn't safe." Jonas followed Jimmy Dean's gaze to the flooded hole where the roots had been and recognized he was imagining making it into a swimming hole or pond.

Jimmy Dean tore his eyes away reluctantly. "What's your name, mister?"

"The name is Jonas. Now, I have to get back to work. I'll talk to you again some other time."

Finally, the boy appeared satisfied. "OK, Jonas. I'll be catchin' ya later," he said, jumping over a branch to run back toward the apple tree. Once there, he jumped at a low-hanging apple that was barely within reach, grabbed it on the second attempt and bit into it as he climbed over the fence. Jonas watched his progress long enough to see that his destination was a white bungalow across the field behind the barn.

Jonas started the saw again and resumed cutting. He switched over to the Stihl to segment the trunk, hauling the pieces out to the barn to split later. Jonas considered how to move the root wad and stump, but in the meantime, Maggie would want the twigs and sawdust cleaned up. He was heading to the garage to locate a rake when the station wagon showed back up.

Maggie jumped out, gazed at the back yard, opened her eyes wide and dropped her jaw in astonishment. "Wow!" she exclaimed. "How did you get that huge tree cut up so fast?" Maggie gazed into the blue eyes of this tall, unassuming man, standing there covered with sawdust, searching his brain for an answer once again.

He finally stuttered, "I... I'm not quite done. I still have the stump to take out. I dumped the wood out by the barn. I still have to split the big pieces and stack the whole thing. Besides, I had some help from your neighbor, Jimmy Dean."

Maggie laughed. "So you have met the little rascal, have you?" She chuckled again, "I'm sure he was a big help."

She went around to the back of the station wagon, and opened the back, crammed full of packages. Jonas started to help her carry them in, but she shooed him away. "No-no, you've done enough right now. I'm sure you're hungry. I can carry these bags. Go shake the sawdust off and wash your hands. I have lunch. It'll take me a sec. We'll eat on the deck."

"He asked me if I was the tree sturgeon," grinned Jonas before he took a bite from the fried chicken wing.

They had been discussing Jimmy Dean Rogers who was now tacking across the field like a sailboat in a headwind. His changes in direction every few feet took him to rocks and sticks to throw at targets along the way. Jonas noticed the thrown rocks were no more accurate than the apples had been.

"Yeah, he might have got that from talking to me the other day. I told him I was going to have to hire a tree surgeon to remove it from my yard."

"Use the gate," Maggie hollered at Jimmy Dean, who was apparently getting ready to climb the fence again.

The "gate" was an angled walkthrough, another 50 feet closer to the garage. Gangly boots and knees hit the ground with aggravation at the need to travel an extra hundred feet, although he had already covered a football field and a half to get to the yard. Maggie winked at Jonas who smiled in return.

"Are you hungry, Mr. Rogers?" she asked after he had slipped through the walkthrough.

"Yes, ma'am," Jimmy Dean hollered.

"Well, help my time," she exclaimed. "Why does everyone insist on calling me ma'am these days?"

Jimmy Dean bound up the steps but was met by Maggie who insisted he go inside to wash his hands.

Outside again, Maggie inspected his hands. "I'm afraid we started without you." This was lost on the boy who was busy helping himself. "I've already said grace," she told him after he had already filled his mouth and taken a drink of lemonade. Jonas had not escaped grace or mention of his own presence to God once again, but this time, he had kept his eyes shut.

Maggie had once again outdone herself with the meal as far as Jonas was concerned. "Bosh," she said when he mentioned it. "Everything's from the deli: the fried chicken, potato salad, and the coleslaw."

"'Maters are from the garden," disagreed Jimmy Dean.

"The tomatoes are indeed from the garden," articulated Maggie precisely. "And so are the radishes, cucumbers, and onions."

Maggie had never quit teaching after retiring, at least when children were around, and Jimmy Dean was often around. They enjoyed the lunch and each other's company, even if the day was becoming fiercely hot.

"Jonas, do you want more iced tea?" Maggie asked, as she stepped into a pair of flip-flops and headed toward the kitchen.

"Yes, thank you," he replied.

Maggie disappeared through the French doors and Jonas turned to the boy. "So JD, how old are you?"

"Ten."

"Ten. Are you in the fifth grade then?"

"Yep. I'm in Mrs. Hooper's class." Jimmy Dean was squinting and scrunching his face in puzzlement again. "Uhm, why did you call me JD?"

"J for Jimmy and D for Dean. I thought it might be easier. Do you mind if I call you JD, or do you want me to use your real name?"

"There's a girl in my class that has a nickname," he said, squirming around in the patio chair, putting one leg over the arm. "Her real name is Kathy, but everybody calls her Kit."

"What about you? Do you have a nickname?"

"Uh-nope," he said. "You can call me JD," he conceded, not appearing particularly happy about it.

"Nah," Jonas said. "I like Jimmy Dean better anyway. Jimmy Dean, it is."

Maggie came back and leaned out of the French doors holding a pitcher of tea. "You know what? Let's go inside. Grab some bowls and bring them in."

They had soon carried all of the dinnerware into the kitchen and deposited them on the spacious counters. It was much cooler in the air conditioning inside. Maggie went to a back porch, dug in a freezer and returned to the kitchen, carrying a carton of ice cream. She pulled three bowls from the cabinet. "I know Jimmy Dean will want some ice cream. What about you, Jonas?"

"If Jimmy Dean is having ice cream, then I'm having ice cream," he declared.

Maggie winked at Jonas as she dipped out a couple of big scoops for each of them and then herself.

After the ice cream, Maggie turned on the radio in the kitchen. "Mind if we listen to the Cardinals?"

"Are they on TV, asked Jimmy Dean?"

"You know I'd rather listen to them on the radio."

The radio was already tuned to the right station, the Cardinals' announcer Mike Shannon talking about David Eckstein being a sparkplug for the team. Maggie nodded her head. "I like Eckstein," she said. "He hustles."

Jonas looked over at the boy who was trying to make his spoon into a catapult. "Hey Jimmy Dean, do you like baseball?"

"Yeah, I guess," he replied.

"Do you play on a team?"

"Yep, but I don't play for the Cardinals. I'm a Cubs. I mean... I'm on the Cubs."

Maggie rolled her eyes at the mention of this despised name but then explained, "It's his little league team. Every 9-10 year-old team has a major league name: Cardinals, Cubs, Reds—"

Jonas was interested. "What position do you play?"

Jimmy Dean appeared to be ready to talk about something else. He had his head back, teetering in his chair, making funny noises. Maggie closed her mouth on something she had started to say. She gave Jonas a significant look. Jonas remembered the apple and rock throwing performance from earlier and understood. The boy was probably riding the pine. From the way he was now acting, it hurt.

Jonas doubtfully asked Jimmy Dean if he wanted to play catch. To his surprise, the boy was excited. While Jimmy Dean was making the trip across the field to retrieve his glove and a baseball, Jonas looked for a glove. Maggie told Jonas to look for one of her son James' old ball gloves which she thought was somewhere in the garage. Jonas found an old Rawlings infielder's glove in a closet upstairs. When he carried it outside, Jimmy Dean was already standing on the asphalt drive, tossing a ball in the air, missing it every time. Jonas searched the surroundings for a convenient backstop. He finally settled on the barn in the field. He didn't want to risk damage to the garage, nor did he feel like chasing balls all over the yard.

Jimmy Dean's glove was a cheap synthetic glove, probably from Kmart. Not only did it have no shape, Jonas knew it never would. Out at the barn, he backed against the wall. He asked the boy to throw the ball, which he did with enthusiasm. The ball smacked the barn wall at least ten feet away. Jonas walked over, picked it up and threw it back. Jimmy Dean predictably missed the ball, running twenty feet to retrieve it. This process continued, usually with the same results.

Eventually, Jonas suggested they change gloves and move closer. At about 10 ft., using the well broken in Rawlings, Jimmy Dean finally caught the ball. Jonas had been patient the whole time, but with this success, he stopped, held onto the ball a few seconds, nodded his head slowly and smiled. The quiet praise was not lost on Jimmy Dean. He started throwing a bit more accurately and caught several more balls. Jonas decided it was good to quit while they were ahead, so they headed back up to the garage to get a drink.

Jonas was quiet, reflecting on all that had happened in the last 24 hours, but his young friend was filling the silence.

"I like this glove. I can catch a whole bunch better with it. Don't you think so, Jonas?" He paused to catch his breath before taking off with another excited sentence. "Hey, do you wanna play catch again sometime? Maybe after Mrs. Young helps me with my homework next week."

"Well son, I don't know if I'll be here much longer. Maggie helped me get out of the storm last night. I thought I'd help her out with the tree to pay her back. But I may have to leave tomorrow."

Jonas had said it gently, but Jimmy Dean's eyes fell. He dropped the glove without another word, took his own glove and ball from Jonas's hands, and wheeled around to head home. For the first time all day, the kid didn't pick up anything to throw or find anything to kick. He walked with his head down and didn't look back.

"That boy has had almost everything and everyone taken away from him, or in the case of his sorry daddy, simply up and left."

"Maggie, I'm sorry. I didn't know."

"I know you didn't. It isn't your fault. I'm explaining—feeling sad for Jimmy Dean. He's a good kid, Jonas—somewhat rare in a way. He's always been genuinely happy for other kids, even when they have things he doesn't, or beat him out of a starting spot on a team. I'd like to see him get the prize, experience some favor for a change. And... I guess I'm feeling a little sorry for myself as well."

Jonas gazed at Maggie, who had been so kind—incredible in so many ways. She had asked him to come back in the house to discuss his immediate plans. He had told her he planned to leave, probably in the morning. After that, he had shared his last conversation with Jimmy Dean, not leaving out the boy's disappointment.

Maggie sat cross-legged in padded wicker armchair on the screened porch, sun haloed around her, hair in her eyes, appearing to him as she must have looked years earlier, a young girl with pouting lips. He felt empty. Why? Why did he always disappoint? There was something in his manner that raised people's expectations too high.

As if she had read his thoughts, Maggie broke the silence. "I don't mean to be presumptuous, but why are you leaving? Have I been too pushy? What makes you want to move along?"

"Maggie. No, it's not you! When you gave me a ride yesterday, I was leaving Benford. I didn't imagine there would be much opportunity to work in this small town. You have enough refugees with the Red Cross shelter. It's somewhat hard to explain, but I'd rather settle in a place that won't categorize me as a victim—as someone who needs charity. I finished cleaning up the tree. It won't be difficult for you to find someone to bring in the top soil for the hole. I'm sorry if I gave you the wrong impression or seemed to promise—" His voice trailed off in embarrassment, as she appeared genuinely distressed over what he was saying.

"Okay. Don't apologize. I did presume too much." Maggie considered her toes for a few moments, uncurled her legs and stood up. She walked over to the patio table, smiled and grabbed his hand, pulling him up to stand. "Well, come inside anyway. I want to show you something."

On the kitchen table were several bags from her morning shopping trip. She pulled men's jeans and shirts out of bags, as well as underwear, socks, and a box with a pair of work boots. Jonas was speechless. Her questions about his clothing sizes had not had anything to do with her husband Tom's clothing.

"Listen, I know you think you need to leave, but I still want you to have these clothes. It's nothing, really. And I still need to pay you for the tree."

Jonas picked up the boots, gave them a once over, and sat down in one of the kitchen chairs. He slowly began to lace the eyelets, keeping his eyes down to gain control over his emotions. His throat was too tight to speak. Pulling the boots onto his stocking feet, he tightened the laces and stood up. He had always fully appreciated a new pair of good boots.

He gazed into Maggie's eyes, searching for a reason, "How can I accept all of this? It's too much, and I don't deserve it. Why are you doing this for someone you don't even know?"

"You're a good man. You care about the quality of your work. You're patient with Jimmy Dean. I know how exasperating he can be." She sat down in a chair across the table.

I'm not a good man. Clouds in his mind darkened his vision. *How could I have so lost my way?*

Maggie's eyes narrowed intently. Her voice took on that same firmness which demanded his attention. "Before you go, I want to say a few things more. I would never try to tell you what to do, but maybe I can give you a hand up. Maybe you can help me out at the same time. There is work to be done here. Since Tom died, I haven't been able to maintain everything. I have the apartment, which isn't being used. We could work out something, maybe a few hours a week for room and board."

Before he had said a word, she continued, "And that's not all. I'm guessing you are wrong about finding work. I think folks around here might accept you. I don't know what your job history is like, but based on what I have observed, I'm certain I know some people who will hire you immediately. She paused for breath. "Whatever your concerns are, I'm sure we can work something out."

She made coffee, got out picture albums full of Tom and the boys, pictures of her and Tom's parents, grandparents, and extended family. There were sepia and black and white prints from the 30s - 50s, Polaroids and fading 110s from the 60s, and 35mm prints from more recent days. They talked about her family, both aware that Jonas was still saying almost nothing about himself. He knew she had noticed his own reticence. She was one of those people who was infinitely patient, no matter what his demeanor was. Jonas, against his better judgment, felt his defenses falling, the promise of the past day extending into the future becoming a strong appeal.

"It's lucky for me that you happened to be driving by in the rain yesterday," he exclaimed.

"I'm not so sure that I *just happened* to be driving by," Maggie replied thoughtfully.

Jonas wasn't sure what she was suggesting. A quizzical frown occupied his face, but Maggie smiled back innocently.

"I had better let you go to bed," he announced finally, picking up the bags to carry them to the garage.

"Are you going to stay at least another day?"

"I don't know; I guess so."

"Will you go to church with me tomorrow morning?"

He felt dread rise inside, but closed his eyes, hearing himself say, "Oh Maggie, I don't want to. But yeah, if you want."

Maggie gave him a quick hug and then he was out the door wondering why he had been unable to say no to this woman.

CHAPTER 3 - MISSING
ST. JUDE, MO – SEPTEMBER 2005

Kate Mitchell was worrying a swivel stool back and forth in front of a drafting table in the newspaper office when Delbert came in from the City Hall next door. She spun 90 degrees to stare into his eyes and immediately knew it was the worst. Her eyes dropped from his sad, florid expression to focus on unflattering details, his uniform shirt, damp with sweat and testing the buttons, the way his belt buckle faced the floor on a belly now frozen in place because he had noticed her despair. She made a constricted keening the poor deputy couldn't deal with.

Mandy was already at her side, holding her up. She felt Kate's ribs sticking through her knit top like slats on a ladder back chair. Kate buried her face in Mandy's shoulder and began to sob.

Mandy rescued him. "Come back later, Delbert." Delbert didn't hesitate, escaping back through the front door, moving much more quickly than he had first entered.

Mandy held her as she rocked softly repeating her name, "Katie… Katie." There was nothing else to say.

Kate and Mandy sat together in a small conference room in the City Hall, holding each other's hands while Delbert read the details from his notes. He had been in contact with the New Orleans Police

Department, accomplishing little in the weeks following Katrina. He had reported Daniel missing, and answered basic questions about Daniel's identity before being passed from one officer to another. The voice on the phone today had been different. Detective Arceneaux's acquisition of the case had produced quick results. She had quickly linked Daniel to his abandoned rental car, and the story told by a 7-year old girl who had been rescued in Lakeview on August 29, the day Katrina ravaged New Orleans.

Delbert read this part of his notes with some enthusiasm. *Sicily Jackson and her father Joe drove "to a better place"* (Delbert raised two quoting fingers on both hands) *on the morning of August 29 after the front edge of the hurricane had passed. They were in the area where the 17th Street Canal levee broke over a two-block area. Joe wanted to leave New Orleans before, but their old car wouldn't start. The "distillator"* (again with the quotes) *had been broken. Then it got fixed. The little girl didn't know why they had driven into the water. It was just there. The water had raised their car from the street and planted it against a tree. The flash flood swept Joe away while he was trying to pull Sicily from the car.*

Delbert paused and looked up. "Detective Arceneaux said this next part is a mystery to her." Delbert nodded his head with eyebrows and shoulders raised to let them know he was mystified as well. He began to read again.

Sicily said she was still in the car when an angel showed up. They both went into the rushing flood to escape the vehicle, but the angel put her into a child's inflatable pool that was floating by. After getting her inside the pool, he went under and didn't come back up. Sicily clung to the top of the pool until two teens plucked her from the water. They were all then rescued by first responders.

Two police officers had been responding to a call in the area when they witnessed the massive rush of water into the city from the 17th Street Levee breach. Fortunately, they were still on the south side of the flood and were able to escape the water by driving south to I610. They then joined rescue efforts in the area and so were aware of Sicily's rescue. One of the two subsequently left his job and New Orleans altogether, but his partner corroborated the story and passed the story on to Detective Arceneaux.

The break came days later when volunteer searchers, on a suggestion from Detective Arceneaux, were looking through receding waters a few blocks west of the rescue location. They reported the license plate numbers of two cars abandoned in the middle of a street divided by a strip of Live Oaks. The '78 Oldsmobile was registered to Joseph Jackson, Sicily's father. Twenty yards to the north on the same street was a 2005 Ford Taurus, identified later as a Hertz Rental, leased to Daniel Mitchell of St. Jude, Missouri on August 22, 2005.

"Detective Arceneaux thinks that Sicily's Angel could very well have been Daniel." Delbert was quick to add, "But she doesn't know. It's all circumstantial right now."

Delbert was more comfortable talking about details than he was giving bad news, especially to Kate. They had been friends since Kindergarten—had graduated from the same 1984 class at St. Jude High School. Like all of the other boys, he'd had a crush on her at one time or another. Delbert knew she considered him a close friend, but she had always been smarter and more mature, stronger in an indefinable way, as though she knew how life truly was and they were just bungling along, trying to figure it out. A part of him relished the unusual situation; this time, he was the knowledgeable one.

"Detective Arceneaux told me she wanted to ask you a few questions. The police in New Orleans are still overwhelmed with the aftermath of Katrina. She said she would call you within a few days, but she also told me you could call her whenever you wanted."

Kate seemed to be quietly considering this. Delbert watched her sitting there so quietly, hands folded, tear-glazed eyes gazing at the tabletop. She was an attractive woman, but the last three years had taken a toll. She was now so thin. The beginnings of lines were discernible on her forehead and around her eyes. Grief, he thought, and now it's only going to get worse.

"I need to go down there," she exclaimed.

"Kate, you can't go to New Orleans," argued Mandy. "It's too dangerous right now."

Delbert agreed. "She's right. Now isn't the time. Call Detective Arceneaux before going. She sounds like she'll cooperate, but I don't know how she'll react if you simply show up."

The three of them sat quietly. Delbert wondered what Kate was thinking. Was she rehearsing her side of a conversation with an unknown detective who would question her about everything? How would Mandy deal with Kate being gone from the Guardian if she took off to New Orleans? Mostly, Delbert thought about Daniel not obeying the evacuation order before the hurricane.

"Why was Daniel still in New Orleans?" he muttered aloud.

He regretted bringing it up, but an appropriate way to rephrase the question would not come to mind. Kate closed her eyes, seemingly resigned to the problem.

"Kate?" Mandy asked.

Kate leaned back in the chair and sighed.

"I don't know—not really. I mean... I talked to Daniel on the phone on the Friday before Katrina. What would that be, the 25th?" She paused. "Doesn't matter," she said under her breath. "Anyway, I talked to him on Friday evening. I thought that maybe he had been drinking. We didn't talk long. He was supposed to fly home that day, yet here he was calling me from New Orleans later on the same evening." Kate paused for long seconds again, as though she was having a difficult time collecting her thoughts.

"Okay," she sighed again. "You two know Daniel and I haven't been getting along for a while. Actually, it's been a long time." She didn't say the words, but Delbert knew Kate meant not since David died. David, their seven-year-old son, their only child, had died three years before from being hit by a car that failed to stop for the flashing red lights and stop sign of his school bus. It had broken both of them.

"So our conversation was … it was short. I was short. I wasn't actually listening." She squeezed her eyes in concentration as if to make her memory clearer. "Daniel said he had decided not to fly out on Friday. He had met someone—someone at the conference, I guess."

Delbert was a bit shocked to hear this. He noticed the same

reaction on Mandy's face.

Kate saw their reaction. "No, no. Not that. He said he had talked for a long time with—I don't know—I think it was with someone he was working with. This other guy was helping some people who were trying to leave the city. So... Danny was going to stay to help him the next morning, and then they were going to drive out of New Orleans on Saturday or Sunday. I guess he was going to keep his rental car." She began to cry again. "But I couldn't reach his cell on Saturday, Sunday or Monday," she sobbed. "I haven't talked to him since."

"Kate, did he mention the other man's name? If we could locate him—" Delbert was still hoping for a quick and easy resolution. Listening to Detective Arceneaux tell about the overwhelming number of unidentified corpses had been discouraging.

Kate seemed to be trying to recall the conversation for long moments, head down, and eyes closed, running fingers through her hair as if to massage the memory out, but finally she responded. "He didn't mention a name. I'm certain of it. I assumed it was someone he had met during the conference. I think that's all he said. Something like, 'I talked for a long time with a man I recently met.'"

Delbert left to get some coffee, but when he returned, Mandy and Kate were leaving. Mandy told Delbert she was going to drive Kate home. Delbert agreed to drive Kate's car home for her. He told them he would have one of the other deputies follow him out to pick him up. Kate surprised Delbert by hugging him before she slipped through the door. The big deputy stood there, feeling the wet spot on his shirt, over his teddy bear heart, thinking it might break.

Later, after she had repeatedly told Mandy that she would be okay—alone with the lonely house and not knowing what to do—Kate called her parents.

"Hello."

"It's Kate, Mom."

"Oh, hi Hon. Are you all right? Have you heard from Daniel yet?"

Why had she become a stranger to herself when she talked to her mother? As if an outside observer, she wondered at this cold person who now communicated without emotion. "No, Delbert spoke with a New Orleans detective today. They believe he might have drowned, saving a little girl when one of the levees broke."

"Oh, Kate," her mother cried. "When?"

"The day of the hurricane. They don't know for sure. They haven't found him. They're assuming. Guessing. His rental car was found close to the car the little girl was swept from."

"But if they haven't found him, there's still a chance, right?"

Kate had long ago lost patience with her mother's inclination to search for the silver lining in all situations. She cut her off quickly and continued.

"Mom, I haven't heard from him in three weeks. He said he was going to leave the city before the hurricane. I know Daniel. He would have called that day if he had been able, the next day at the latest."

"Well, Kate—"

"Mom, listen to me. The little girl—her name is Sicily—told rescue workers and the police that an angel put her in an inflatable kid's pool. It must have come from a backyard that had flooded nearby. And then he must have gone under himself before she was rescued."

"Kate, I don't know—hold on. Here, your dad wants to speak to you."

She calmly repeated it all again. Kate knew her father would grasp every bit of it immediately. He would, even before the story had ended, make plans and attempt to control the situation as he always did. Bill had been infallible for most of her life, but he'd been unable to fix it when David died, and it was only the most recent defeat to understand she had no faith in his ability to change this reality either.

"Kate, we're not going to accept this," he asserted. "I'll go with you to New Orleans in a few days. We'll find out what we can. There are other possibilities. Maybe he's in a hospital. Maybe Daniel even has amnesia."

She knew better than to argue with his calm rationality. "Okay,

Dad."

"Sweetheart," his voice softened, "this isn't the time to give up. We don't know much yet."

"I know." she conceded quietly.

"Do you want me to come get you? You could stay here for a few days."

"No, Dad. I need to take care of things at home and at the paper if I'm going to take off work for a while. I'll call you again after I've talked to the detective in New Orleans."

"Call us tomorrow, Kate. We need to know you are all right."

"Goodnight, Dad. Tell Mom not to worry."

"Night, Katie. We love you."

Kate sat on the sofa for a long time with closed eyes, as the darkness of the encroaching evening enveloped her. The silent house was foreboding, almost seeming accusatory. She finally opened her eyes and reached into her purse for the number Delbert had written. She opened her cell phone and punched in the number.

"New Orleans Police Department," answered a bored voice.

"Is Detective Arceneaux there?"

"Detective Arceneaux is off-duty. May I direct your call to her voice mail?"

"No. No. I'll call back later. Thank you."

The frustration and pain had grown until it out-weighed what remaining strength she had held in reserve. She felt control slip away. With rage, she would never have shown in front of anyone else, she began to wail, face buried in the sofa, beating and flailing against the cushions. She cursed the police in New Orleans. She cursed New Orleans. She cursed the hurricane, and finally she began to curse Daniel. She screamed at him as though he were standing in front of her. Daniel! You've been trying to check out for three years, and you finally found a way, didn't you? Does saving someone make amends? It doesn't! It does not! And I don't... I will not forgive you.

Kate lay back on the sofa and surrendered to a black night that seemed it might never end.

CHAPTER 4 – PLAYING CATCH
BENFORD, TN – SEPTEMBER 2005

Jonas sat up in bed, early on a foggy Sunday morning. The temperature had dropped so much the night before, the warm earth released its moisture to coalesce in the cold air. He gazed out the window, distinguishing little except for subtle silhouettes of trees bordering the road at the edge of the property.

He remembered his promise to go to church with Maggie and sighed. He did not want to be around people. He didn't even know what kind of church she attended. Was he in for fire and brimstone, or something a little more sedate and liturgical? Her "high church" label for her son, the minister, made him assume she preferred something more spontaneous. It mattered little to him. Either way, he didn't want anything to do with the God of his last several weeks. Unfortunately, he could think of no excuse that seemed valid other than saying no. Noticing the packages on the dinette again, he thought, *At least I have some decent clothes to wear.*

Maggie was her usual enthusiastic self in the car, commenting on the sun lighting the misty landscape in mystery and soft monochrome hues. She directed him along a rectangular path along nearby streets until they were in front of the bungalow across the pasture behind her house. She had to park on the street. A white, beat-up 4-wheel drive Ford—one wheel deep in the ditch and three wheels out—was blocking the driveway.

Before Maggie was able to get out of the car, Jimmy Dean came running out the front door, hair slicked down, in obvious hand-me-downs, huge, clunky black Sketchers, a faded t-shirt, and chinos that were too long and too big around at the waist. Maggie must have called ahead because the boy was already standing outside. He opened the back door of the wagon and threw in a huge, black Bible, and climbed in before slamming the door.

"Hey Jonas," he said excitedly. Apparently, Jimmy Dean had forgotten the glum feelings from the day before, as if he had forgiven Jonas, simply for still being there.

Jonas glanced back. "Lookin' spiffy there, Jimmy Dean," he said, before noticing a large red mark on the boy's cheek. He stared, frowning before turning back as Maggie put the car in gear.

"You're lookin' kind of spiffy yourself," pointed out Maggie as she turned the car around in the street.

"Yeah, you're lookin' spiffy too, Jonas," hollered Jimmy Dean from the back seat. "Mom is mad at Bo again. She said he's not allowed back in the house. He got his truck stuck in the ditch. Hey Jonas, do you want to play catch again today?"

Maggie shot Jonas a look, but he was lost in thought. She quit trying to get his attention and concentrated on steering the boat of a station wagon into town. Jimmy Dean maintained a steady commentary on everything he saw out the windows of the car. "It's awful foggy outside. Boy, that's a big diesel. Did you see, Jonas? It's got two trailers. Hey, Mrs. Young, Junior's out of his pen again."

They skirted the square and turned into a parking lot behind a brick and glass sign that announced to the world that this was the Evangel Chapel Family Life Center.

Jimmy Dean jumped out of the back seat, grabbed his fifty-pound Bible and hollered, "See ya later Mrs. Young. See ya later Jonas." He somehow got the Sketchers both headed in the same direction and bounded across the parking lot and into a brick addition.

Jonas followed Maggie into a separate door where they encountered a long wide hallway full of curious people. Jonas had to endure introductions, handshakes, and "we're glad to have you here's." Maggie introduced one grave, smartly dressed man as her husband Tom's business partner. Bill Anderson watched Maggie's guest intently. Jonas had the distinct impression that the gaze was intelligent and suspicious. Maggie mentioned Katrina several times. He also noticed some quizzical, raised eyebrows among several of the other people, and he imagined his presence might spawn some un-Christian gossip among the saints.

Maggie led him into a large, sun-filled room crammed with tables and chairs. There were nonstop introductions and handshakes. Finally, he and Maggie sat down at a table across from a young woman who smiled so steadily at Jonas, he wondered if he had made an error with grooming. He carefully composed his face into a noncommittal smile and made plans to leave it glued that way. Someone brought him a cup of coffee, and mercifully, the teacher stood up, adjusted his tie and announced the class would begin with prayer.

The teacher introduced the lesson with background information regarding the Sermon on the Mount and the meaning of the word 'beatitude.' Jonas's attention wandered from the teacher's voice as he surveyed the people in the class. Many of them appeared to be barely listening. He tried not to judge these people, but he didn't understand them. He recognized the need to belong to something. He had a basic acceptance of the benefits of spirituality and believing in a higher power, having had first-hand experience with that. But why be so tied to an old-fashioned way of thinking that they sacrificed beautiful weekend days like this to worry over the same ancient book, week after week, year after year?

"Blessed are those who mourn for they will be comforted," read an energetic young man at the next table. This brought Jonas's attention back to the present. He wanted to hear one of them explain precisely how they believed comfort comes to those who mourned.

The teacher mentioned everyone suffered from loss. In the process of mourning, people are reminded that only God satisfies. *But how?* One of the women in the class mentioned in her darkest times, God had always been there to give her peace and comfort.

Another man reasoned that loss got people's attention and made them more willing to listen to God. "Will you trust me and let me use your grief as a gift that will transform you into a person who comforts others?"

Jonas was abruptly angry. Had these people actually experienced grief themselves? Was God speaking to him? If so, it was only to say that He intended to harass Jonas's every move, even after he had lost hope and had nothing left. Agonizing images played across the walls of his mind, flooded houses of sickness and death haunting the present.

Anger and despair washed over him, leaving him weak. His mind automatically recoiled, protecting him by taking him to a neutral place. Then, looking up, he saw Maggie watching him. He realized that his carefully composed facial expression had melted away. He had let his guard down. He was exposed. A consuming desire to run pulled at him, but he slowly returned the smiling mask to his face and ignored her concerned expression.

The very thing Jonas had feared about attending church had occurred within a few minutes, and then it was over. For the rest of that Sabbath morning at the Evangel Chapel Family Life Center, he carefully ignored the teaching and preaching, and any memories that dared intrude.

Jimmy Dean was back at Maggie's house for Sunday dinner. The three of them ate roast beef, potatoes, and carrots in silence. Maggie had noticed Jonas turn inward, and she respectfully gave him space. Jimmy Dean had tried to get him to talk on the way home, but soon quit after *yes*, *no*, and *hmm* were the only replies.

The slow cooker had worked its magic, turning the meat and

vegetables into something ambrosial. Jonas was comforted out of his reverie.

"Maggie, this is unbelievably good. You are an excellent cook."

The other two brightened at this utterance. Jimmy Dean tried out the new word he had learned earlier in the morning. He scrunched his forehead and eyes, not sure if he quite had the meaning down, "She's kinda spiffy, ain't she, Jonas?"

Jonas glanced at Maggie. Her smile was open and kind. She was older than he was, but he had to admit, she was a beautiful woman with qualities beyond her ability to cook. He felt he didn't deserve to be sitting in her company. Wondering why she had taken the chance to help a total stranger, he felt guilty just for being on the receiving end of her generosity.

"You bet, buddy. Maggie's pretty—" Jonas had intended to say more and wished he'd said less. There seemed to be no good way to continue, and then too much time had gone by. It was too awkward to go on.

He was embarrassed, but it was Maggie who blushed. "You guys are silly. I threw this together in the crockpot." Maggie busied herself by being their server, bus boy, and dinner partner as if to bury her own embarrassment. She handled it all so smoothly it was almost unnoticeable. It seemed to Jonas that little made her happier than serving. He supposed she missed her husband, and probably her boys more than she would admit to herself. It was obvious that she cared deeply for little Jimmy Dean Rogers. He also had to admit that despite his own closed ways, she seemed to like him. It felt real. She wasn't phony about anything.

He couldn't know that she intuitively sensed God's pull on his life. Had he known, he would have been gone in the morning, like a rabbit at the first sound of a predator.

Maggie looked out the window later to check on the boys. Jonas and Jimmy Dean were tossing a baseball around down by the barn. Jimmy Dean was still missing about as many balls as he caught, but he cheerfully chased after them with small explosions of energy. She noticed Jonas's mouth curl into a grin at the boy's exuberance.

Later, Maggie glanced out again to see Jonas hanging an old red saddle pad on the wall of the barn. She was curious but confused until she noticed him lifting his left knee, falling forward, swiveling to the left and stepping at the same time his right arm came swinging up and over in an arc. He had Jimmy Dean imitate his strange movement, patiently correcting him and repeating the exercise repeatedly until he was satisfied. It finally dawned on her that he was teaching the boy how to pitch.

When she returned to the window to look again, Jonas had backed away from the barn wall and was now performing the same pitching motion with a baseball in his hand. The ball smacked the saddle pad, producing a little dust volcano. Then it was Jimmy Dean's turn. The ball didn't hit the saddle pad, but Maggie was surprised at how well he had thrown it. Jonas demonstrated the throw again. Plunk! The dust erupted. Then Jimmy Dean missed again, throwing the ball harder but into the dirt.

Later in the afternoon, when the boys were no longer in sight, Maggie went outside to find the two of them still together. Looking toward the garage, she observed Jonas with a pile of old boards. Jimmy Dean had climbed to the top to balance on one leg.

"What are you guys doing?"

"We're buildin' a seej injun," hollered Jimmy Dean.

Maggie walked over to where they were working. "What did you say you were doing?"

"We're building a siege engine," repeated Jimmy Dean, trying to articulate another new word for the day.

"It's going to be a small trebuchet which is a type of medieval siege engine. It's similar to a catapult," Jonas explained. "I hope you don't mind me using this old lumber I found down by the barn."

"No, I don't mind. But you guys should be careful." She frowned at Jimmy Dean. "How did you get that big scrape on your jaw?"

The phrase "siege engine" triggered a motherly instinct in her. The boy wasn't answering her. She started to ask him again when another thought came to her, "What are you guys going to throw with this catapult?"

Jonas shrugged. "Oh, probably a baseball. We promise not to break any windows," he added, smirking. "Right, Jimmy Dean?"

"Yeah, we promise."

Jimmy Dean Rogers was having the time of his life.

After Jimmy Dean had taken the shortcut across the field to go home, Jonas went to the house to find out what chores Maggie wanted to be done around the house the next morning. They had coffee on the deck. Before Jonas could ask about household projects, Maggie surprised him with some news. Bill Anderson, her husband Tom's old business partner, had phoned. He wanted Jonas to come down to the plant the next morning to talk about a job. Jonas stared across the patio table suspiciously.

"So, you're telling me Bill Anderson, who I met at church this morning—and knows nothing about me—called to offer me a job?"

"No, he called to find out and understand what was going on. He's only looking out for me. I told him about how handy you were. So, he said he wants you to come down to the plant to talk about a job. I'm not sure what he has in mind, but he wouldn't have you come if he didn't have something available."

"And you didn't ask him to find something for me?"

Maggie showed annoyance with her reply. "I promise you I did not ask Bill to give you a job, but so what if I had? I assure you Bill doesn't do *anything* he doesn't want to do."

Jonas considered it. He would have preferred handyman work at Maggie's for a while, and not attract attention to himself. But he couldn't think of a good excuse for not considering what Bill Anderson had in mind. Jonas suspected Tom's old business partner only wanted to interrogate the stranger living in Maggie's garage. Jonas didn't like it but considered that he didn't have much choice. It would seem strange if he refused.

"OK. I'm sorry. I'll go tomorrow morning if you tell me how to get there." He paused. "Oh, and I guess I need a ride."

"Drive Tom's pickup. You have a driver's license, right?

Jonas nodded.

"You know, Bill is a good guy. He's probably concerned about me, but that's only right. If the situation were reversed, Tom would have done the same thing."

Jonas nodded again in acceptance.

They sat there in the late afternoon, enjoying the breeze and the setting sun. The phone rang from inside the house. Maggie stood, motioning for Jonas to follow her. She wasn't on the phone long. He overheard something about a club meeting later in the week. Then she took Jonas into a room that appeared to double as a family room and library. There were several large bookshelves filled with books.

"I thought you might want some entertainment besides the little television in the garage apartment. Do you like to read?"

The closest shelf was full of war and military non-fiction near the top, other non-fiction, and biographies below. Jonas scanned the titles, gradually moving to the next set of oak shelves built into the wall around a brick fireplace. Here he found the shelves dominated by literary fiction: Faulkner, Welty, Hemingway and much more. A few books tempted him, but he moved on across the fireplace, and his eye landed on a book of poetry by Robert Frost. He pulled the book from the shelf and opened it to a small poem titled "The Question":

> *A voice said, Look me in the stars*
> *And tell me truly, men of earth,*
> *If all the soul-and-body scars*
> *Were not too much to pay for birth.*

"I'll take this one with me."

"You like poetry or just Frost?" Maggie's furrowed brow suggested surprise.

"No. I mean... I don't know," said Jonas matter-of-factly.

"I'd be very interested in talking to you about either one."

Jonas didn't reply. His mind had traveled to people in another place and time.

"Well, take it with you. I know where you live," she laughed.

Jonas managed a fleeting smile. As he was leaving to go to the garage, he stopped outside the door and turned. "Maggie, what is it with Jimmy Dean's mom? Why is he here all the time?"

Holding the door open, leaning against the frame, Maggie shook her head and sighed. "Jess is a wild one. Always was boy crazy. Her lively imagination transforms bad boys like Bo, the one she recently kicked out, into some sort of prize. He's typical of the men she seems drawn to. She'll let him come right back. He's all about partying and finding trouble—hardly the best influence on Jimmy Dean."

Jonas was thinking about the mark on the boy's face. He knew it hadn't happened while they were playing catch the day before. "Did you see the place on Jimmy Dean's cheek?"

Maggie's eyes narrowed in concentration. "I did notice it. Why? Do you suspect Bo?"

"I don't know what to think. I honestly didn't like the way it looked."

Maggie stared at nothing as if considering. "Maybe the boy fell down. He *is* a bit awkward."

Jonas nodded reluctantly in answer, but he noticed that Maggie still looked concerned.

She continued. "I've never seen any signs of abuse before. If so, it must have been Bo. I know Jess loves Jimmy Dean. She works at taking good care of him. She chuckled. "I'm sure Jimmy Dean has told her all about *you*."

CHAPTER 5 – LETTERS & PHONE CALLS
ST. JUDE, MO – SEPTEMBER 2005

Kate waited for Bud Kreilik at K&L Chemical Engineering Group in Chesterfield, MO. Sophie, Bud's devoted administrative assistant for the last fifteen years, had been looking out at the parking lot for the UPS truck when Kate unexpectedly drove up. Sophie greeted and hugged her as she led Kate into Bud's office. Kate was grateful for the support. The potent reminders of Daniel's workplace had her feeling fragile.

Placing a chair so their knees were almost touching, Sophie gazed into her what Kate knew were red-rimmed eyes. She instinctively gave herself to the older woman's care, trusting one who had often been a source of comfort after David had died, and Daniel had retreated into silence.

"What have you learned about Daniel?" Sophie quietly asked, squeezing Kate's hand. The question freed a sudden unrestricted flow of tears. Sophie dabbed at Kate's cheeks with tissues. "Oh Hon, it's going to be all right."

Kate tried to form words. She had determined not to break down—to stay in control. Desperately, she reached into herself for coldness, for anger—anything to allow her to escape the embrace of despair.

After brooding over the news about Daniel from New Orleans, she had spent a horrific Saturday night warring with a swarm of negative thoughts. Lying between sleep and wakefulness, Kate never felt like she had slept yet was never able to construct a meaningful purpose or plan. It was late Sunday morning before she rose, feeling no better. She called Mandy to tell her she was going to Daniel's office in Chesterfield on Monday, and so was not coming in to work at the paper. She spent the rest of the day in restless, abortive pursuits. Television repulsed her. Words lacked meaning or significance when she read. Knowing her anger towards Daniel was irrational had changed nothing. She immersed herself in the emotion because it was easier to face than the depression.

Remembering the anger now, she reached for it. Anger compounded. It was not a stretch to be angry with Bud for sending Daniel to New Orleans in the first place. By the time Bud arrived at his office after a morning meeting, Kate was back in control. Anger jerked at the leash, but the weeping was gone.

Bud Kreilick was a short, squat powerhouse who had turned innovative chemical engineering processes into a successful family owned business. Kreilick Chemical Engineering had become K&L Chemical Engineering Group after acquiring LowEng, an older, established company in the St. Louis area. Finding Kate and Sophie in his office, he leaned on the edge of his desk to listen with a close frown.

Daniel Mitchell had been his star during the first several years of his employment. He had lost his energetic edge after his only son David had died three years ago, but he was still a very competent and robust engineer. After listening to Kate describe what Delbert had learned from Detective Arceneaux in New Orleans, Bud was having a difficult time assimilating Daniel behaving so compulsively that he ignored a mandatory city evacuation. This was completely out of character with the thoughtful, buttoned-down man he knew.

"Katie, I don't get this. I talked to Fred Albiel with Pearl

Petroleum, the company we do business with in New Orleans. He was at the ACAE conference and attended some of the same workshops. He said that Daniel told him on Thursday that he was going to fly out the next morning. Why stay there with a hurricane on the way?"

An agonized Kate shook her head while Sophie held her hand. "I don't know, Bud. I talked to him on Friday night. Daniel said he met someone at the conference. He was going to stay an extra day to help this man. Then they were going to drive out of the city on Sunday in the rental car. I was angry. I guess I didn't listen as carefully as I should have."

"But the car was obviously still there on Monday, the day of the hurricane. Something caused them not to leave on Sunday." Bud was talking out loud as he pondered everything—his usual method of working out problems. "No way they wanted to ride it out. Something must have kept them from leaving."

The office was silent while the three of them considered.

"You haven't had a chance to talk to the detective?" asked Bud.

"Detective Arceneaux? No, I called and left a message. She hasn't called me back yet. I'll try again this afternoon."

"Kate, call me when you find out more. I'll ask Fred at Pearl if there is anything he might have forgotten to mention. Maybe he noticed Daniel talking with somebody at the conference." His eyes lit up. "I know. I'll get a list of attendees from the organizers. If Daniel's friend was another person who didn't fly home on time, we might be able to figure out who it was."

Kate smiled. "Great idea," she replied. "When you get the list, please email a copy to Detective Arceneaux at the New Orleans Police Department."

Bud was not one to jump to conclusions from scant evidence, but he thought the abandoned rental car was bad news. Still, he knew Kate needed a glimmer of hope. As long as there were hundreds of missing persons, thousands of refugees, and no conclusive evidence, there was hope. Missing people were found all the time. That hope was exactly what he promised Kate with all the force of his character—a man used to swaying others with his will.

Bud's confidence actually had improved Kate's outlook. Nevertheless, it was only minutes later—sitting in her car in the parking lot—Kate's emotional pendulum had swung back to fearing the worst. Anger had become her medication of choice, her mind searching incessantly for new targets. She had intended to stop by her parents' house before heading home, but an idea gripped her; she was immediately on her cell phone making a call.

Directory assistance found and dialed a number for her. Kate made her request to the correctional facility employee on the other end of the line. After being denied, she resolutely made the request once again, but the bureaucrat was insistent; all visitors must complete a formal application to be included on a prisoner's list. The review and background check required time. For her to visit the prison today was out of the question.

Kate was frustrated once again. Evidently, in her universe, even anger demanded a level of patience that she lacked. She was sick of the unending obstacles. She drove home above the speed limit and immediately went into her office to type a letter she had written in her mind while driving.

> Andrew Jenks
> Missouri Eastern Correctional Center
> 18701 US Highway 66
> Pacific, MO 63069-3525
>
> Andrew,
>
> You have requested several times over the last few months for my husband and me to come speak with you. I can only guess you wish to express regret or ask for forgiveness for what you have done. There will be no forgiveness from me.
>
> I actually considered coming to visit you today, and would have,

had the process not required so much time. I don't waste time, so instead I am sending this letter. It will be the last. Do not bother replying because any letter I receive from you will be disposed of immediately.

You killed my son, David. What you did also indirectly killed my husband, Daniel. He too is now dead. I want you to know this: Daniel died, saving the life of a child. You lived, destroying the life of my son and husband.

You will not get the chance to destroy me.

Kate Mitchell

Kate typed it without hesitation, finishing in a few minutes. After the printer spit it out, she started to put it into an envelope, but her phone interrupted.

"Mrs. Mitchel? I'm Detective Arceneaux from the New Orleans Police Department. Your number was given to me by Deputy Delbert Scott, and you also left a message on my voice mail." The detective's voice displayed an accent that Kate was unable to identify, competing as it was with background noise and ringing telephones.

"Oh yes, Detective Arceneaux. Thank you for calling. Delbert said you wanted to talk to me."

"Do you have time to answer questions now, or should I call back at another time?"

"No, please. Now is a good time." Now that she had the detective on the line, Kate was eager to speak with her. "I'd like to call you something other than Detective."

"Sure. Not a problem. Call me Sara. I'm glad that I'm finally talking with you, Kate. I'd like to start out with some basic information about your husband. Deputy Scott gave me much of this information and sent a photo, but I want to go over it to make sure we have everything correct. Is that okay?"

Kate agreed, and they went over the details: 6'2", 180 lbs., short-cropped black hair, and blue eyes. Kate filled in a few more details that didn't quite match a category: square eyebrows, cleft chin, and lanky frame with square shoulders. She also gave her a detail that wouldn't show on the photo—Daniel's left big toe pointed inward slightly from being broken when he was a boy.

There were more details to go over, including Daniel's purpose for being in New Orleans, when he had arrived, the hotel he had stayed in and the conference he had attended. She told her about Daniel's employer, her morning meeting with Bud, and that he would be sending Sara a list of the conference attendees that could be cross-referenced with the existing database of missing persons.

Sara asked about Kate's relationship with Daniel, so she told her about their last phone conversation. She let the detective know that—while her relationship with her husband had been strained—she did not believe he was missing for any other reason than something unexpected had happened related to the hurricane.

Finally, she told her about their son David—what the tragedy had done to the both of them. "Daniel didn't know how to handle it, and he didn't know how to help *me* take care of it." Her thoughts evolved as she spoke them aloud. "Sara, the story the little girl told? Well, it does sound like something Daniel would do. It doesn't surprise me that he would have chosen to save someone at the risk of his own life. After David's accident, he said more than once that he wished he could take David's place." The detective heard Kate's quiet sobs and gave her a moment to recover.

"I'm sorry," Kate said. "Is there anything else you would like to know?"

"Does Daniel have any other family he might have contacted?" Sara asked. "A parent or a brother maybe—?"

Kate couldn't help but be annoyed at this question. Was the detective suggesting Daniel might have left her? "Listen, he would have contacted me if he could have. I'm not trying to hide anything. Yes, John and Debra Mitchell, his adoptive parents, live in Des Moines. He doesn't have a lot of contact with them, but I've spoken to them on the phone. They haven't heard from him."

Sara wasn't exactly apologetic, but she explained. "I hope you understand that I had to ask. So no siblings, right?"

"No other family," Kate said.

Kate gave the detective Daniel's parents' phone number. They agreed to keep each other up-to-date with new information. Kate asked about coming to New Orleans, but the detective was adamant that the city was still too chaotic and dangerous for her to visit in person. She let Kate know that the authorities had already been comparing Daniel's picture and description with the inventory of recovered bodies. The FBI was getting involved with the process of identifying corpses. Sara warned Kate that this would probably take months due to the difficulty of working with fingerprints and DNA evidence from bodies, often in a deteriorated condition.

Kate noticed that the detective had never promised the hope of a good outcome. She *had* conveyed her competence and promised the investigation would continue as quickly as possible. Kate thanked her for calling and the effort they were putting into finding Daniel during a tough time.

After the call ended, she no longer felt the complete darkness of the last 48 hours. Grabbing the letter to Jenks, she left for the post office in town. Kate sat behind the wheel of her car in the post office parking lot for a while... hesitating. Jenks was serving time in prison for vehicular homicide. It was only partial justice, but she was now beginning to doubt her letter would cause him more punishment than ignoring him. She was getting out of the car when Mandy pulled up in her white Wrangler.

"Hey, I thought you were going to the city today."

"Already been there and back."

Mandy's scrutiny of Kate made her self-conscious. Mandy was also glancing at the letter in her hand. Kate noticed how much better she felt—more in control. She no longer felt like she was in a separate place from her body, but still, she made the letter and envelope disappear within the other hand tucked behind her.

"How did it go? What are you doing?"

"It went fine. I talked with Bud. He's going to follow up with the company in New Orleans that Daniel was working with—find out if someone there might know something. And I talked with Detective Sara Arceneaux on the phone. She must be Creole, Cajun, something—a very noticeable accent—but she was kind and very thorough. I feel better about that."

Mandy hopped out of the Jeep. "Good! At least you have someone capable on that end that you can talk with. So... did you discuss visiting New Orleans?"

Kate bit her lower lip. "That's the tough part. She said the city was too chaotic for me to visit right now. They are still searching for bodies. Can you believe there is still standing water? I doubt going will do much good until they aren't so swamped. No pun intended."

Mandy let out a sigh of relief. "Look, I know how much you want to find out what happened. We all do. But I'm glad you aren't going yet. So, what are you doing now, picking up the mail?" She glanced at Kate's arms curling behind her back.

Kate pursed her lips and then exploded, "Okay, you know me too well. I fired off a letter to Jenks and came down to mail it. None of this would have happened without him—none of it. Daniel wouldn't have been in New Orleans doing—*throwing up her hands*—God knows what because he's lost and doesn't know who he is anymore."

As she tossed her arms in the air, the letter slipped from her fingers, blew open from a gust of wind, lifted into the air like a paper airplane, and tumbled across the parking lot. Kate and Mandy gave chase, almost reaching it several times before Kate finally jumped on it with both feet. Her face red with the effort, she grabbed the letter with the envelope and tore them into pieces. Kate noticed Mandy was studying her in shock. She laughed, and then they were both laughing. They were almost quiet when Kate squeezed out, "That'll show him." They laughed until the tears ran.

"What's the joke?" hollered Bernie, the insurance agent from in front of his office next door.

"A horse walks into a bar!" Mandy hollered back without a hitch.

"And the bartender says, 'Why the long face?'" replied Kate.

"Ooh, that's baa-ad," said Bernie, shaking his head.

Kate raised an eyebrow. "No, there was no sheep there, Bernie," she said, winking at Mandy.

Bernie stood there trying to figure it out. The women wiped eyes, got themselves under control, and climbed in their respective vehicles.

Mandy yelled through the passenger window of Kate's car, "Your girls on the Puzzled Poet are worried about you. You'd better let them know you're okay."

Kate waved as she backed out and left. "I'll be at work tomorrow," she called out through the car window as she drove away.

Kate had been neglecting her regular contribution of critique and original works to Puzzled Poet, the collective blog she managed with four other regional authors. What was worse, she had even been neglecting to contact her partners. After Mandy had mentioned it in town, Kate knew it was time to tell them she was planning time away from the group.

There were enough other contributors to keep the blog active and vibrant. After scanning through the last three weeks of unopened emails and RSS feeds on her computer, Kate comprehended they were mostly upset about her lack of communication. She had bluntly and abruptly informed them of Daniel's disappearance by email, and then ignored all subsequent attempts at contact. She decided to call each one independently.

Her blog partners were understandably stunned at the latest news but relieved she was coping with the dreadful situation. She called Beth last, the writer who had first recruited her participation on the blog. She wanted to make sure Beth understood she was not permanently pulling away from the blog. She promised to stay in contact and to read updates at least once a week. Finally, she wrote an explanatory note to readers and posted it to the blog. It said nothing about Daniel.

CHAPTER 6 – GET A JOB
BENFORD, TN – SEPTEMBER 2005

Jonas was dreaming. In waking moments, he was mostly successful at keeping his mind compartmentalized. Unwanted memories remained locked away. But when he slept, his mind's gatekeepers seemed to relax as well. The doors were thrown open, and the ordered institution became a chaotic asylum.

The dream was a closed loop, a needle hitting a scratch in the vinyl and jumping back a groove to play the same passage repeatedly. Riding the Canal Street trolley to the New Orleans City Park was ridiculously impossible. Every time he boarded the trolley, he headed north on Canal St., only to end up right back at the river end of Canal St.

A band across the street was playing Dixieland, and he noticed the somber-faced trombone player was just a kid. The band was movin' and blowin' and every time the players dipped their horns, the end of the trombone slide hit the sidewalk. *Bang!* It made him cringe. He needed to get across the street to tell the kid he was damaging the slide, but his legs wouldn't move. *Bang!* He woke up.

Struggling to get his eyes open to enter the conscious world, he squinted as first golden light filtered through the back window. He glanced at the clock. 6:10. *Bang!* He swung his legs off the bed, trudging over to the window to look out at what had made the noise.

Well, I'll be. Down by the barn in front of the old hanging saddle pad, Jimmy Dean was picking up a baseball at the foot of the wall.

"Jimmy Dean ... Son. What were you doing out there at the barn so early?"

"I was practicin', ma'am."

"Well, I know that. What I mean is... why were you practicing so *early?*"

Through a mouthful of pancake and syrup, Jimmy Dean raised his eyebrows and nodded thoughtfully, "Because Jonas said I needed to."

"Don't talk with your mouth full," warned Maggie good-naturedly. "I swear, if you don't take smaller mouthfuls, you'll asphyxiate yourself, and then you'll be sorry."

Jimmy Dean had a visceral, comic reaction to unknown words. He laughed at "asphyxiate" before taking a big swig of orange juice. Jonas was sitting across the table from the two, enjoying the banter, more than just a little pleased the boy was taking baseball so seriously.

"You're going to get us both in trouble, Jimmy Dean. I said you needed to practice. I didn't mean that you needed to wake up earlier than the rooster."

The boy finished drinking his orange juice, seemingly unconcerned about being in the middle of a conversation. He slid off his chair and ran around the table to sit next to Jonas, who was still finishing off his last slice of bacon. "What're you goin' to do today, Jonas?"

Jonas was all business. "I am going to apply for a job. I'm going to fix the leaky water spigot behind the house. And then I'm going to split the wood I cut the other day—that is—if Maggie doesn't mind."

He peered over at Maggie, perceiving she was clearly pleased. "Sounds good to me." She stood, picking up plates and silverware while announcing, "I am going to the Baptist Church to help organize the gym for the hurricane refugees coming this week."

Jonas was startled. "It's odd. I've only been here two days.

Thinking about Katrina again actually surprised me. What day are they coming?"

"The bus is supposed to arrive on Wednesday." She shook her head and sighed, "We have a lot to get done."

Jonas rose from the table and lightly punched Jimmy Dean's shoulder. "Pay attention in school. You have to work hard at your studies, or there won't be any baseball lessons."

Jimmy Dean jumped up and ran for the door. "I will. I gotta go get ready for the bus." He shot out the door and jumped off the deck, clearing every step to make a stumbling landing, catching himself before falling, and was off across the yard.

"That boy." Maggie shook her head, but she was chuckling.

Jonas found Benford Fabrication north of town, within sight of the bridge over the Duck River, exactly as Maggie had said. The old Chevy ran smooth, feeling surprisingly tight as he shifted down to turn into the parking lot. Once again, he felt a measure of respect for Maggie's deceased husband. Everything Tom had owned exhibited quality and care.

He found a space in the visitor parking. Nearby stood a landscaped brick office building attached to a large, gold metal manufacturing plant and warehouse. At the counter inside the foyer, a cheerful receptionist, who appeared to be barely out of high school, saw him immediately and asked, "May I help you?"

Jonas gave her his name and she smiled in recognition. "Bill said you were coming by. Fill out this application first. Then he'll talk with you before we do anything else." Jonas read the nameplate sitting on her desk, filing it away in his mind for future use. Brandi led him into a small windowed conference room across the hall from the greeting area. He noticed the informal way she talked about her boss. There was a relaxed atmosphere in the office. Another secretary smiled, and a busy supervisor greeted him while he was still in the hallway. Happy people at work. It was a good sign.

Jonas had prepared for the application and the possibility that he might interview the night before. Deliberating carefully about how to present his educational background and work history, he had written the details down to copy onto the job application the next day. He left most of his former employers off of the application. They would lead to too many questions. And as much as it bothered him, he had to lie on at least one question.

Brandi checked on him often, and he soon handed her the completed application. She told him Bill was still in a meeting. "Are you ready to take a test?"

"What kind of test?" he asked.

It's a mechanical aptitude test we give maintenance workers and fabricators. You'll have to take it before you get hired anyway."

"Sure."

He might as well be doing something rather than simply sitting there waiting, Jonas thought. The test was straightforward, and he spent the next half-hour answering questions about fundamental physics, machines, and tools in the workplace. Enjoying the test, Jonas worked quickly. He was almost at the end before he considered that perhaps he should have purposely made a few mistakes. He contemplated several answers for a few minutes and then finished, making one change.

Brandi left with his test and was gone for another 15 minutes. The second hand on the wall clock repeated its jerky, circular route. Jonas counted the ceiling tiles, estimated the area of the room and was considering finding a restroom when Bill Anderson walked in, followed by a balding man with a mechanic's stained and hardened hands.

Bill introduced Jonas to Harlan Schmidt, the Maintenance Department Manager. They shook hands and sat down, both company men sitting across the table from Jonas. He recognized this was probably the interview, forcing himself to breathe evenly and relax.

Bill spoke first, explaining Harlan was planning to retire in a few months. They had other people in the maintenance department who could probably move into the manager's role, but they still needed at least one additional staff member.

While he was talking, Harlan looked over his completed application and the test results. Jonas was unable to make out what he was looking at but didn't want to stare. Finally, Bill asked him if he had any questions before they asked *him* a few questions.

Jonas asked what type of products the fabrication plant produced, explaining he had not been in the area long enough to research the business. Bill nodded.

"We build industrial switchgear—everything from small boxes to wall panels. Maintenance is similar to what you might find in most other industrial plants, but we have a large number of welders and other specialized metal fabrication equipment. We build the enclosures from metal stock, and do all the painting and wiring here as well."

Jonas nodded understanding. "I'd be happy to answer any questions you gentlemen want to ask."

Jonas felt he was walking a thin line with Bill. He wanted to appear relaxed enough to show confidence in his ability to do the job, but not so comfortable in speaking with management that it was inconsistent with the information on his application. His work history noted no supervisory experience. The application did list a few specialized industrial skills and certifications. Bill's first question demonstrated that he might be distrustful.

"Did you know you didn't miss any questions on the Bennett assessment, Jonas?"

"*But they weren't all correct,*" Jonas thought and came very close to saying so before swallowing his words. Jonas's eyes narrowed slightly before returning to normal. He was quiet for a moment before asking, "The test? No. But I guess I've always been pretty good at taking tests."

"I guess so. Is this the first time we've had a perfect score, Harlan?" asked Bill.

Harlan wasn't happy with the question. "No. Jackie Freeman didn't miss any." Jackie, one of their lead technicians, often challenged existing methods and policies. Harlan didn't necessarily consider the perfect score a positive sign.

Jonas was a little shook up. Bill seemed suspicious. Was he suspicious because of the test, the lack of a relevant work history on the application, or was he only concerned about Maggie?

Bill conducted a standard interview. "Why do you want to work here?" was typical, but struck him as a silly question for a Katrina victim who needed a job. Harlan asked Jonas to expand on his experience with welders, hydraulic and electrical systems and preventive maintenance schedules. Jonas cruised through this part of the interview. When asked about his work experience, he explained that his most recent employer in the New Orleans area had been struggling before the hurricane, and he doubted the business would restart soon, if at all. His employer before that had gone out of business.

Bill talked for a while about the importance of the maintenance department to continuous production and the organization as a whole, and then he indicated the interview was over. He and Harlan left for a few minutes before Bill returned and told Jonas he was offering him a job that would pay $12.52/hr, during a temporary, probationary period. His performance would be reviewed after 90 days. If acceptable, he could expect to become a full-time employee, receive full benefits and the opportunity for a significant raise.

Jonas agreed, and they shook hands. Bill asked him to be there the next morning at 6:30 a.m. He showed every sign of being genuinely happy that Jonas would be working there. After he had left the interview, Brandi made copies of his Louisiana Driver's License and his water stained social security card and had him fill out an I9 and other paperwork. As she was handing his cards back, she glanced at his driver's license. "You know you actually look younger than you do in that picture. What's your secret?"

Taken aback, Jonas paused before mumbling, "Walking 500 miles, I guess."

Brandi's look said she didn't know whether to take him seriously.

He was surprised to be outside in less than three hours. Climbing in the pickup to head to town, he pulled out to leave when a beat-up, white Ford pickup shot past in the parking lot aisle, raising a dusty cloud and narrowly missing Jonas's front bumper. The driver clutched the steering wheel with his left hand while lifting his right with the middle finger extended. Jonas wasn't sure, but it looked like the pickup that sat in front of Jimmy Dean's house.

CHAPTER 7 - TESTED
BENFORD, TN – OCTOBER 2005

At Simmons Hardware, Bart, the owner, pushed two threaded rods, a paper bag with assorted faucet hardware, a seal kit, and the splitting wedge across the counter, coming around to walk with Jonas to the front door. The century-old hardwood floor creaked agreeably under their feet. Jonas took it all in, enjoying the decades' old atmosphere of the place. Bart was pointing through the front window across the square to a white storefront with a dark green awning.

White Copperplate Gothic script intersecting a notched gear design on the building's front window announced the restaurant name: *The Sprocket*. Bart sounded a little envious when he said, "I suppose Maggie suggested that you go there for lunch."

"She said it was the best place in town."

"Yes. Might as well say it's the *only* place in town. They have great food. And they have something else."

"Atmosphere?"

"People. Friends. I have a mind to join you."

Jonas glanced at the storeowner's sweep over. He surprised himself by asking, "Well, why don't you? I'd be glad for the company."

Bart only mulled this over briefly before blurting out, "I think I will. Give me a second." He went to the back of the store before returning with a brooding girl with spiked black hair and a scowl, which said she disapproved of the plan. "My sister Blanche's daughter Kayla," Bart explained as they left the store. "She's allergic to everything—but mostly work."

"Hey look, that tightwad Bart's spending his hard earned money!" hollered a florid-faced banker in a white shirt and tie too small for his neck, as Jonas followed Bart through the door of the café.

"Better'n given' it to the bank," said Bart. The Sprocket was almost full of people even though it was only 11:15 a.m. After he and Jonas had sat at a small table in the middle, between a row of booths and a long counter with stools, the room-wide conversation continued. Martha, the cafe's owner, came to the table with glasses of ice water. Jonas ordered the Rueben. Bart was busy talking. Jonas raised his eyebrows to her and nodded his head towards Bart, but Martha said, "Oh don't worry about Bart. He always orders the same thing. Do you want anything else to drink besides the water?"

"I'd like a coffee too if you don't mind."

"Good heavens! You just ordered the 'xact same lunch Bart always gets. Are you a long lost son-a-his?"

Bart overheard this last part and interrupted himself mid-sentence to spout, "Martha, are you already giving this boy the 3rd degree? This is Jonas. He's Maggie's new boarder."

Any eye not already turned their way now took a closer look at the stranger sitting at Bart's table. Jonas suffered their quiet gaze. Martha headed back to the kitchen, and the murmur of voices continued. Jonas absorbed his surroundings without noticeably staring. There was nothing special about the décor, except the walls were covered with the largest assortment of sprockets he had ever set eyes on—bicycle and motorcycle chain rings and hubs, old industrial spoke gears, and even some that looked more like a saw blade than a sprocket.

Martha noticed his line of sight when she brought the Reubens. "Now I know you're gonna ask, so I'll just tell ya; my husband Leroy loved the Jetsons when he was a kid. Still does. He always wanted to start a company like Spacely Sprockets. Instead, he opened this." She waved graceful arms and fingers at the wall as if she were a ballet dancer.

Jonas smirked. "Leroy?"

"That's right. And yes, he wanted to change his name to Elroy."

"He always has been Elroy," snorted Bart as Martha headed to her next table.

Bart had dropped out of the communal conversation to make the comment, and then he concentrated on eating. Jonas was thinking about Bart having automatically put the hardware he'd bought on Maggie's tab.

"Maggie told you I was coming to the store?"

"Yeah, she called this morning. Said you'd be by to get some supplies."

"What else did she say?"

Bart glanced up from his plate to gauge Jonas's face. "Listen, you can't have a better friend than Maggie. Folks around here are curious, but they mean well for the most part. If she accepts you, then they'll accept you."

Bart paused to fork a pile of kraut that had fallen from the sandwich. He continued to stare at his plate, and his voice grew quiet. "But if you or anyone else did anything to hurt her, you couldn't put enough miles between you and this place."

When Bart stared at Jonas after this short speech, Jonas held his gaze. Bart's face was either a grin or a grimace, but his eyes were hard and severe. *This little man with the Barney Fife comb-over had some fire to him.* Jonas thought he might be sweet on Maggie too. Now that he considered it, Bart probably wasn't the only man in town who had an eye for Maggie. He'd have to tread carefully.

"Actually," Jonas said. "I am glad to hear it. It says something positive about the people in this town." With that, he grinned. Bart couldn't help but laugh.

The two men walked back across the town square to the Chevy

sitting in front of the hardware store. Jonas told Bart he had enjoyed lunch, but it would probably be his last chance to eat there during the week since he was starting to work at the plant the next day.

Bart was staring straight through the front window of his store. He frowned and stomped his way to the door, mumbling moodily, "That girl. No one is minding the store." Jonas allowed himself a grin and got in the truck to head to Maggie's place. There was a pile of wood waiting.

Jonas replaced a worn out seal on the leaky faucet before splitting the wood piled down by the barn. He expected the green wood to fly apart quickly, but he needed to use the new wedge more often than he had expected. Jonas wasn't quite done when Maggie got home. Anxious to talk to her about the new job, he still finished up before heading back to his apartment to shower.

After cleaning up, he came outside to find Jimmy Dean breathing hard and waiting expectantly with the ball gloves. The talk with Maggie would have to wait even longer.

"How long have you been here, Jimmy Dean?"

"Just got here."

"What did you do—run all the way?"

"Huh-uh. I rode the bus."

"Why are you out of breath?"

"Well, I ran from *my* house."

Back down through the pasture grass to the barn, they marched, the sweet smell of the split oak in the air. They played catch for a few minutes. Jonas noticed the boy was now throwing the ball within catching distance most of the time. He had him throw at the saddle pad a few times, allowing him to concentrate more on Jimmy Dean's throwing motion.

He actually didn't look too bad, except for palming the ball and throwing stiff-armed. They worked together for about a half hour holding the ball across the seams and tossing it with just fingers and wrist. Jonas appreciated that his pupil was willing to learn, and didn't get bored easily.

A cowbell ringing back on the deck interrupted them. Maggie was at the house, motioning for them to come. On the way to the house, Jimmy Dean continued a steady stream of questions. "I'm startin' to throw better, ain't I Jonas?"

"Yep. You sure are, bud."

"How do baseballs get the threads?"

"Those are seams. Baseballs are sewn together with thread."

"Who taught you to throw a baseball?"

"Huh. I'm not sure. Probably from watching older kids play. You *are* throwing better. You just need to keep practicing."

"Dinner time," Maggie said cheerfully as they got closer. "Are you boys hungry?"

Jimmy Dean took off toward the deck, and Jonas made a mental note to help him work on running too, or he would never beat out a throw to first base, not to mention all the foot, ankle and knee problems he would endure later in life. He had all the grace of a giraffe.

The house had a butter, garlic, and tomato smell. Maggie announced that they were having spaghetti with brats, garlic bread, salad, and maybe some ice cream if Jimmy Dean finished his salad. The boy frowned. Jonas noticed and said, "Boy, you don't know how good you got it. Maggie is an excellent cook, and it is awfully nice of her to cook for us. It seems to me that getting the ice cream is worth eating the salad."

As they were sitting at the table, Maggie asked impatiently, "Well, what happened at the plant today? Did they offer you a job? I've been wondering all day."

Jonas noticed that Jimmy Dean's eyes were big as saucers wanting to know too, so he smiled and told his story dramatically, "Well ..." He paused with his eyes going back and forth between the two. "They took me into a special room. They made me sit there for a long time. But a lovely lady brought me coffee." He paused again to move a fork to the other side of his plate and said nothing.

"Then what happened?" hollered Jimmy Dean, shaking the hair out of his eyes.

"Oh yeah, I forgot what I was talking about," fibbed Jonas. "Well... then they made me take a test."

"They made you take a test?" asked Jimmy Dean in disbelief. "Why did they make you take a test?"

Maggie was grinning as she served the pasta and started to spoon on the sauce.

"Yes, I had to take a test, but it wasn't difficult because I knew most of the answers."

"Why do old people have to take tests?" Jimmy Dean didn't appear willing to let the issue go.

"Are you calling me old, boy?"

"Oh for crying out loud," Maggie complained. "Did you get the job or not? The sauce is going to get cold."

"I got the job," Jonas finally admitted, grinning at the other two.

"Praise the Lord," exclaimed Maggie and continued right on saying grace. "Thank you, God, that Jonas passed his test. Please help Jimmy Dean remember the answers on his next test … and bless the spaghetti too. Thank you, Lord, for your wonderful blessings and provisions. Amen."

"Amen," hollered Jimmy Dean.

Jonas added a grudging "Amen" before looking at Jimmy Dean. "By the way, young man, why didn't you bring any books? I was serious when I said there would not be any baseball unless you keep up with your homework."

"Ain't got no homework tonight." Jimmy Dean was trying to fork his spaghetti.

"I don't have *any* homework tonight," corrected Maggie as she showed him how to load his fork with a spoon and a twirl.

As it turned out, Jimmy Dean ate all of his salad, along with all of his spaghetti, and they all had vanilla ice cream with chocolate syrup.

After Jimmy Dean had gone home, Maggie and Jonas discussed

his plans, now that he had a job. "Look, I know a man likes to be independent. I wouldn't blame you if you wanted a different place." She repeated that she liked their current arrangement. Jonas was welcome to stay in the apartment above the garage.

Jonas nodded. "Maggie, I like it here very much. I just … I just don't know what to say. It's too much—the cooking and everything. It's like a free bed and breakfast. And even driving the pickup." He threw up his hands in exasperation, not knowing what to say further.

"But look at the work you have done. Listen, if we're both happy with the situation, why worry about it?"

Jonas drew a breath, held it in for a second, and then let it out in a long sigh before giving in. "Okay. I do like it here. I just don't know if I'll be staying."

"I'll let you know if I'm unhappy, or things need to change. Okay? I'd have to hire somebody to take care of what you have been doing. What you're doing for Jimmy Dean—that means even more to me."

Jonas pondered the situation. "But I insist on paying for gas. I'll keep the truck serviced. Oh, and I want to get internet service to be aware of what is happening in New Orleans. I suppose I could go to the library, but it would have to be on the weekends since I'm working." He kept thinking aloud. "I can buy a used computer. I still have some cash and will get a paycheck in two weeks."

Maggie went to a closet on the other side of the room and pulled a black nylon laptop case off a shelf. "Here, I never use it. I bought it to use out on the deck, but the sun and all the flies bothered me. I just didn't enjoy using it outside like I thought I would. It has wireless so you can probably hook into my route thing. At least that's what they told me at the store. Is that what it's called?" she asked sheepishly.

"A router," he replied. "Maggie, I can get my own."

"Nonsense. I never liked using the thing. You might as well use it. I still use my Dell over there." She pointed to a desk with an LCD monitor showing on top.

She pushed the laptop case across the table and patted his hands as he reached for it. "I'm so glad this has worked out. I know you probably don't want to hear this but… God actually is good. He has something is store for you. I feel it."

He was halfway out the door when Maggie asked one more question, "Did you read any more poems last night?"

Jonas stopped and nodded. "Yeah. Frost again. If I remember right, it was called 'Revelation'."

"Oooooh," Maggie sang out. "We'll have to talk."

Jonas frowned. "I don't know what there is to talk about. I agree with Frost. If there is a God, he's hiding a little too well for me. He needs to speak up." Before she answered, he was out the door.

CHAPTER 8 – PRIVATE INVESTIGATION
ST. JUDE, MO – OCTOBER 2005

The leaves on the maples in the little park across from the Weekly Record were at the height of indecision, still holding onto green while experimenting with shades of yellow and orange. Mandy was wandering around town with her Nikon, looking for one perfect scene to become the color photo on Thursday's front page. Kate was proofing an article on the newly proposed city well when her cell phone vibrated underneath the scattered papers on her desk. She pilfered through the pile until she found it and glanced at the caller name on the screen. It was an unknown number with an 832 area code. Kate hurriedly answered before the phone went to voice mail.

"Kate?"

"Yes. She paused, trying to place the voice. "Oh, is this Detective Arceneaux?"

The detective hadn't phoned for almost two weeks. Kate had lost patience and called the NOPD twice. On both occasions, the person on the other end informed her bluntly that the detective was not in the office.

"Well, actually I'm just Sara Arceneaux at the moment. I'm no longer with the police. In fact, I'm not even in New Orleans. Didn't anyone from NOPD call to let you know?"

"No!" Kate was stunned. All of her contact with NOPD had been with Sara. What now? "What happened? Where are you at?"

"I just moved to Hattiesburg, Mississippi—staying with my sister—still hoping to find a position with the police department here. So much has happened in the last week. Things weren't always pleasant for me with the department even before Katrina. They're impossible now. The city is chaotic, and the NOPD isn't much better. I didn't think my living space was still safe."

"Where were you living? Surely not in one of the flooded areas."

"No, I wasn't even working out of the 3rd District where your husband's car was found. I was assigned to document and organize reported missing person cases—not even making a dent. Every policeman still in the city is worn out and depressed. They had us staying in rooms on the Ecstasy, a docked Carnival cruise ship. As nice as it was, the little room was no holiday, especially since I was always being harassed. Don't get me wrong; I had it much better than most."

Kate was beginning to realize that her perspective of events in New Orleans had been terribly inaccurate and incomplete. "But Sara, who was harassing you?"

"A dirty cop. With all the chaos, there is no one keeping Detective Manson in line. He was making life hell for me. Central Command hasn't been in control since Katrina. Manson has used the opportunity to do whatever he wants. Nothing I can do about it. I'm sorry to tell you this because I know you're going to have to deal with him."

The news devastated Kate. She struggled over what to say. Until this moment, she had only been considering her own situation. After the last two abrupt conversations with the NOPD, and now this added knowledge about a rogue detective, she dreaded attempting to contact them again. "I'm sorry Sara," she said helplessly. "You've been helpful to me."

"It was my job. "You know what—when you call the NOPD, don't ask for Manson. Don't mention me either. Ask for Lieutenant Grayling. Let him know NOPD hasn't contacted you since you last talked to me. Tell him you're upset about it."

Kate wrote the name down and was about to ask Sara to tell her about the Lieutenant, but Sara wasn't finished.

"Kate—Listen. I didn't just call to let you know I had left New Orleans. I have two more pieces of information for you. You know the ACEA conference attendee list you had your husband's boss email to me. Well, I compared that list with the list of missing persons from Katrina. There were two matches. Of course one was your husband, Daniel, but another man's name appeared on both lists as well."

It took a moment for the significance of this to sink in. As soon as Kate understood this might be Daniel's friend, she was out of the chair, around the desk, and running for the front of the newspaper office. She jumped up and down in front of the window looking out over the street. "I love you! Can you give me the name?"

Sara laughed over the phone. "I can give you more than that, girl. I have a name, address, and telephone number. And get this—he made it home from New Orleans. Are you ready to write?"

Kate spun and skipped to the desk, kicking over a trashcan on the way and banging her knee. "Ah, oh, darn! Sorry, sorry. OK, I'm ready." She kept moaning as she grabbed a pen and legal pad.

Sara laughed again. "Are you sure you're OK?"

"Yes, yes. Go ahead."

"All right, here it is. Joe Conroy; 131 Sterling Dr; Adrian, Michigan." Sara followed with the phone number and a light warning. "Kate, go easy. I don't know what he's been through, but I'd say there is a good chance—"

"I understand. Believe me, I know."

"Well Sweetie, I'm glad I could share some good news for once. That's been a very rare thing for me, lately."

"I'm so sorry. I don't know how you did it. It must have been horrible—" Kate's voice died as she abruptly remembered. "But wait, you said you had two pieces of information."

"Oh yeah, I forgot. I do have something else. Well, I don't know how you'll feel about this, but I'll just tell you. I also found Sicily Jackson. Do you remember the little girl who was rescued?"

"The girl Daniel might have saved, right?"

The news puzzled Kate. In fact, she wasn't sure just what she was feeling. She was glad the girl had been rescued. There was no doubt about that. Nevertheless, she couldn't help but be reluctant to think about her, about what might have happened.

"I was worried about her and decided to follow up. She's here in Hattiesburg, living with a foster family. I have her counselor's name and telephone number."

"OK. Give it to me. I'll write it down too."

Sara gave Kate the address and reminded her to write down Lt. Grayling's name. They talked for a while longer. Sara said she was going to share an apartment with her sister until she found work. She was hoping for a position in law enforcement. She offered to help Kate when she visited New Orleans, letting her know that Hattiesburg was a good base for visiting the beleaguered city.

They also exchanged personal email addresses so that Sara could forward the conference list to Kate. It hadn't occurred to her to get the list from Bud. Now, it seemed obvious to email everybody on the list. It would take work and might be a long shot, but if Mr. Conroy didn't know anything relevant, maybe one of the other presenters or attendees would.

"Sara, I'd like to pay you for what you have done on your own. You've been working on your own time."

"If I don't find a job soon, I might have to become a Private Eye," Sara said with a dismissive snort. "Let's just see what happens. Hopefully, this will generate some leads."

"Okay, but I'm going to pay you."

Sara didn't reply to this statement, so Kate said goodbye, thanking her once again.

"Hello."

"Hello, this is Kate Mitchell calling from St. Jude, MO. May I speak with Joe Conroy please?"

Kate was trying to remain calm, but her excitement was evident in her voice. Mandy sat close with another of the cordless house phones listening in. Both of them had a legal pad to record details.

The woman's voice on the other end was articulate but sounded rehearsed and frightened. "Joe can't come to the phone now. May I have your name again? And your number, please? I'll have him return your call, or perhaps I can help?"

"Oh yes, of course." Kate was almost desperate to keep her on the line. "My name is Kate Mitchell." Kate followed with her home phone number and her cell phone number. "I'm calling because my husband Daniel was in New Orleans during Katrina, and is missing. He was at the same conference Mr. Conroy attended. I received word that Mr. Conroy had survived the hurricane. I was hoping to speak with him to confirm if he might have met Daniel or possibly—"

Kate was talking very fast. Her emotions washed over her until she found herself unable to continue. There was silence on the other end for several seconds until the same voice said flatly, "Please wait a moment. I'll be right back."

Kate was glad for the time to regain control. The phone was silent. Had the unknown woman set the phone down and left? The two covered their mouthpieces, and Kate whispered, asking if the line was still live. Mandy nodded yes. They listened again.

"Hello."

Both pairs of eyes grew wide. "Is this Mr. Conroy? Joe Conroy?" asked Kate.

"Yes. Your husband was in New Orleans at the conference?"

"Yes, and you were there too?"

"I was. What is your husband's name?"

"Daniel. Daniel Mitchell."

The phone was quiet. "Hmm. The name doesn't ring a bell. Was he a presenter or a conference attendee?"

"No, he wasn't a presenter. He attended as a representative from K&L Chemical Engineering in Chesterfield, Missouri."

Joe sounded doubtful. "Oh, I'm sorry. I don't believe I met him, but I can't be sure. There were a lot of people at that conference. I didn't meet or talk to many people there."

He sounded as if he were trying to end the conversation. Maggie did not intend to let him off so easily. "Listen, Joe? My husband's boss was able to obtain a list of attendees included in the conference booklet. I'd like to email you a scan of the list and a picture of Daniel." Kate paused before broaching the subject she assumed Joe might be avoiding. "The thing is... Daniel was still in New Orleans during the hurricane. He called me two days before, and said he had met someone—I'm assuming at the conference—and the two of them were going to drive out the next day. He said something about them helping some people. I just thought—"

Joe interrupted her at this point. "Oh, I understand; you presume this other man was me because I was missing as well. But no, that's just not what happened. I mean, I'm definitely not who you're looking for. I had something different happen entirely."

And he doesn't want to talk about it, thought Kate, miserable once again. "Mr. Conroy, I know this is difficult for you. I'm just trying my best to find Daniel. May I please just send you the pictures so you can at least tell me if you saw him at the conference? Anything you say might help."

Joe gave his yahoo address, promising to reply if the pictures revealed anything. Maggie thanked him. She and Mandy were about to hang up when his wife's voice was back, shaky and weak, but determined. "He wasn't there," she said.

Kate and Mandy searched each other's eyes with puzzled frowns. "Who?" Kate asked. "Who wasn't there?"

"My husband, Joe." Kate and Mandy could barely make out Joe's voice in the background saying something incomprehensible. But Mrs. Conroy didn't stop talking. "Joe wasn't in New Orleans. He was with his girlfriend. Obviously, you need to know the truth." With that, she hung up.

Dead end. Yet, it wasn't entirely a dead end. Kate had more than

150 names on a list of conference attendees and presenters. At least one of them had to remember Daniel. Surely at least one of those few knew something that would help lead to the truth.

Mandy had the same idea. "We have our work cut out for us. I'll prepare a database like we use at the office. You start writing the letter. I'll do the mail merge so we can send them all out at once."

Kate was glad there were still things to do, actions to take. What she had to avoid at all cost was to find herself in a place where there was nothing left to do and no desire to do it.

CHAPTER 9 – MAGIC CANDLE
BENFORD, TN – OCTOBER 2005

A blue cloud of profanity was emerging from the bottom of the pickup when Maggie walked through the garage door carrying a large red thermos and some plastic cups. She glared at Jonas standing by the open hood on the passenger side. Then her eyes took in Jimmy Dean who was sitting on a hydraulic floor jack, slowly rolling it back and forth. Both of them looked like they had been caught smoking in the boy's room.

The disembodied growling voice continued from underneath the truck. "I'm telling you there is no way on God's green earth that putting a candle on this bolt manufactured in the pits of hell is going to cause it to relieve itself from this sorry, rusted excuse for what used to be an exhaust manifold."

"I'm just telling you that's what I read on the internet," Jonas said.

"The internet," sneered Harlan. "Well, that's where you went wrong. Why don't you have any penetrating solvents in this—Ow! Son of a—"

"Is that you, Harlan Schmidt?" Maggie had walked around Jonas and was peering at a pair of work boots sticking out from under the front of the truck. "Well?" she demanded again.

"Yes, ma'am," answered Harlan sheepishly, though he made no move to roll out on the mechanic's creeper.

"Are you unaware there are impressionable ears in this garage?" asked Maggie, glancing at Jimmy Dean who had now quit rolling back and forth, but hadn't stopped squirming.

"Yes, ma'am. I mean no, ma'am."

Jimmy Dean figured that Maggie was mad about Harlan's cussin', but she didn't know he heard a whole lot worse at home, especially when Bo was the once talking, and it was directed at him. This was different. Maybe Harlan shouldn't say all that and get so mad, but he knew Harlan didn't mean anything nasty by it. He couldn't get enough of listening to these two men work and talk.

"Come out from under there, Harlan. I've got some lemonade for you boys, and it sounds like you could use a break."

Harlan rolled out from under the Chevy, and Jonas gave him a hand to stand up. His face was still red from frustration and embarrassment, but Maggie smiled as though nothing had occurred. Having been a teacher for many years, she was adept at alternating negative and positive reinforcement. He quickly forgot he had been in trouble with her. After pouring the lemonade, Maggie headed back to the house without any explanation. Jimmy Dean stayed in the garage, unconsciously mimicking how the men stood and moved.

Harlan took his lemonade, leaned against the workbench and frowned at the face of the Chevy. "I'd like to get this da-gone manifold swapped out this evening, so we can go fishing in the morning."

Jonas and Harlan had been planning a fishing trip on the Duck River. The two had found they worked well together at the plant—so well, in fact, Harlan was beginning to be sorry he was retiring soon. Jonas was anxious to go fishing too, but when the Chevy developed the ratty sounding exhaust leak, he told Harlan he probably ought to spend Saturday working on it. Harlan had convinced him the two of them could finish it quickly on Friday evening and still go fishing in the morning. It was a good plan until one of the bolts refused to come loose.

"Did you try the impact wrench?"

"No. This impact wrench won't run slow enough to just bump it," said Harlan. "I'm 'fraid it would round the corners. I guess I'll drive home and get my impact and some penetrating fluid."

Jonas didn't seem quite ready to give up on his idea. "I know you think it's stupid, but what's the harm in trying the candle thing? Let's just try it once before you go driving off."

Harlan scratched the back of his head and rolled his eyes at Jimmy Dean. "I declare. He ain't gonna give up on the candle is he?"

"No sir," said Jimmy Dean sharply, as if he was about to salute.

"Well, what are we going to heat the dang thing with, and where are we gonna to get a candle?"

Jonas pulled a propane torch off a shelf and screwed on the bottle. Just as he had handed the torch to Harlan, Maggie appeared back from the house with a small votive candle. "Will this do?"

Harlan showed signs of being provoked, and dangerously close to beginning another cussing fit. "Maggie, you'll have to ask our man Jonas about that because he's the one wanting to cast this black alchemical spell. For all I know, it might have to be a white candle from the thwarted wedding of a runaway bride."

Jimmie Dean snorted. "Thwarted," he repeated, giggling.

"I never knew you had such a prodigious manner with words, Harlan." Maggie frowned and smiled at once as if she didn't know whether to be repulsed or impressed with the ornery old man.

"Oh that's nothing," Jonas said. "With you present, Maggie, we're getting the Reader's Digest condensed version."

"I can only imagine," Maggie replied dryly.

Jonas tried for a moment of levity. "The candle will work okay. When the heated bolt contracts, it will draw the wax from the candle in around the threads. That, plus the expansion and contraction of the bolt should help break it loose as well."

"What does contract mean?" asked Jimmy Dean as Harlan rolled back under the truck with the torch, a striker, and the candle.

"The word contract means become smaller," answered Maggie.

Jonas nodded. "Yeah, that's right. It may be hard for you to believe, but when something like a metal bolt gets hot, it actually gets bigger. That's what the word 'expand' means. Then when it cools, it becomes smaller. That's what we mean by 'contract.'"

Jimmy Dean's face screwed into a frown. "How does it get bigger?"

Jonas risked attempting an explanation. "The atoms that make up the steel in the bolt become more energetic when it's heated. They start moving faster and pushing away from each other. Sorta like hmmm, like—"

"Like a roomful of mental patients before they take their meds," hollered Harlan from underneath the truck.

Maggie threw out her hands in surrender.

"There's no cure for him," grinned Jonas.

Jimmy Dean laughed. This was the funniest thing yet. He'd never been in as much trouble with Maggie as Harlan, and he was an old guy.

"Here goes nothing," growled the doubtful voice from below. The next sound was the striker followed by the whoosh of burning propane. The whoosh ended with a short silence, then a grunt of effort followed by, "Well, I'll be da—"

"Harlan!" scolded an exasperated Maggie.

"I think we're going fishing tomorrow," said Jonas to an ecstatic Jimmy Dean.

The men finished replacing the exhaust manifold in short order after removing the offending bolt. Maggie asked Harlan to stay for dinner, which he said he was happy to do, "bein's my wife Betty ain't much of a cook." Maggie shot him a look but sighed instead of arguing. Jonas drove Jimmy Dean home in the dark to make sure his mother was okay with the boy staying the night at Maggie's so they could get up early to go fishing the next morning.

Jonas went with Jimmy Dean into the bungalow and stood just inside the front door of a small living room, lit by a TV in the corner. Greasy, black hair escaped from a dirty cap on a man slouching in a beat-up recliner. He was watching wrestling on the WWE Smackdown, nursing a beer and cigarette. *This must be Bo,* Jonas thought. The man didn't bother to acknowledge the boy or Jonas, or even look their way. Jonas realized that he was the driver of the old Ford pickup sitting outside, the same one that had just missed him in the factory parking lot.

Jimmy Dean went hollering through the house, "Mom, mom!"

Jonas stood, frowning at the man who was ignoring them. When had ordinary, decent conduct become so rare with country folk? The man finally glanced long enough to notice Jonas's eyes on him and snarled, "What are you starin' at?"

Jonas said nothing, but neither did he glance away. In fact, his eyes seemed to grow cold as they intensified their focus on Bo. Remembering Jimmy Dean's bruise, he was now sure where it had come from. He thought of Jess, Jimmy Dean's mom and wondered, h*ow can some women be this bad at picking men?* Bo was the man who had flipped him the bird in the factory parking lot. Harlan had told him later that Bo had been stealing copper wire, fired on the same day Jonas was hired. Jonas was just now connecting it all in his mind.

Before either man said anything further, Jimmy Dean and Jess came down the hall, toting a kid's sleeping bag and a backpack.

"He ain't got a fishin' pole," Jess said as she came over to stand next to Jonas.

"Jonas and Harlan got extras, Mom," said Jimmy Dean.

Jonas almost corrected the boy's grammar as Maggie often did, but caught his tongue. Correcting grammar in this house would be unending, and Bosephus in the recliner wouldn't accept it well. The scowl on his face said he didn't like the way Jess was squirming against Jonas.

Jonas recognized that Jess was probably a woman who only knew one way to deal with men, and that was to flirt. Every gesture was suggestive. She was attractive, but hardness had already set in around her eyes and mouth. Partying, booze—maybe something more. He hoped for Jimmy Dean's sake that it wasn't something harder.

"We'll take care of him, Jess," he said, turning to leave. She followed them out to the truck, reminding Jimmy Dean of all the stuff he had in his backpack.

"Don't forget to brush your teeth." Jess kissed his cheek through the truck window. She stared past Jimmy Dean, over at Jonas in a manner that was hard for him to interpret. It could have been thanks, or maybe something else he didn't want to have to deal with.

"Why were you so adamant the candle method was nonsense?" Maggie asked Harlan across the table.

"I don't know. The candle made the whole thing sound like some sort of witchy, superstitious, mountain folklore."

"I guess you never get too old to learn a new trick?"

"Are you saying that I have reached old age?" he sputtered.

Jonas snorted. "Are you saying you haven't?"

They were all having a good time talking, and eating some delicious lasagna and garlic bread Maggie had put in the oven. She liked to make lasagna in advance and keep it in the freezer for having guests over on short notice. Jonas reflected over the previous few weeks of great cooking, guessing he had probably gained at least 10 pounds even though he had continued to work hard.

"It's funny how an early wrong assumption can throw one completely off track," Maggie said seriously.

The two men's eyes met. "She's talking to you, not me," said Jonas with a smirk.

"I'm not so sure," Harlan said. "Perhaps you are making an arbitrary, mistaken assumption. What about it Maggie, are we still talking about my erroneous rejection of the paraffin injection fastener ejection method?"

"Good heavens, Harlan. The two of you are a great match. You have as much of a surplus of words as Jonas has a scarcity. Yes, I was still talking about the candle. If the candle's paraffin was in a different form, you might have considered its lubricant qualities. As it was, all you appreciated was its use in... in what, mystical events, weddings, séances? What is paraffin anyway?"

"It's an alkene, a saturated hydrocarbon," said Jonas. They all turned their heads his way in puzzlement. Even Jimmy Dean was bug-eyed.

"What?" asked Jonas, noticing their surprise. "It's just one of those trivial bits of information I happen to know."

Maggie was trying desperately to get back to her point. "What I'm saying is... if you make an early, wrong assumption, it can make a perfectly reasonable idea seem ridiculous."

Jonas had experienced enough serious discussions with Maggie to know what she was driving at. While it was true he had not been back to church with her, he had, unbeknownst to her, been reading a Bible along with the poetry. As far as he was concerned, he was reading it with more of an open mind than her peers at the building with a steeple.

So, Maggie believes I have made some wrong basic assumptions about God. It annoyed him that she wouldn't just let him be. Nevertheless, he said nothing. Annoyed or not, he would eventually consider her words as he always did. For now, he just wanted to spend some time relaxing with friends.

"Point taken, Maggie. Now, not to change the subject or anything but I promised Jimmy Dean I'd show him how to play cribbage. The cards and board are in the library. We could play partners with four."

"I'm assuming by *four* that you want us all to play?" asked Harlan. "I hate to disappoint you compadre, but this old man needs a few winks and a nod to get up early and go fishing in the morning. It's going to have to be *three*."

"Make that *two*. I have to bake cookies, muffins, and cake tonight for the bake sale at church tomorrow," added Maggie.

Jonas got the attention of Jimmy Dean with his eyes and raised his eyebrows. "Well son, I guess it's just you and me. We probably need to turn in early ourselves. Grab your gear. We'll head on over to the apartment."

As they were leaving, Jonas was already explaining to Jimmy Dean,

"In this game, the number 15 is very important."

Not long after beginning their second game of cribbage in Jonas's apartment, Jimmy Dean said, "Jonas, I get why the number 15 is important, so now can you tell me why the board is shaped like a 29?"

Jimmy Dean had asked the same question when they first got the board out to play. Jonas had told him that he'd have to learn the rules before he could understand the answer. He knew Jimmy Dean wouldn't forget to ask again. "Okay. You remember how we count the points in our hands, right? Well, 29 points are the most points possible in a hand."

"How do you get that many points?"

"It hardly ever happens. You have to have three 5s and a Jack in your hand. The other 5 has to be turned up when the cut is made. You get 16 points for all the combinations of 15 and 12 more points for having the set of four 5s. That's 28 points. Can you figure out where the 29th point comes from?"

Jimmy Dean thought about it and shook his head. "I can't think of it."

"Okay, think about this," Jonas said, smiling. "Remember the Jack in your hand? If it is the Jack of hearts and the 5 card from the cut is the 5 of hearts— Jonas cocked his head and grinned. Now, do you remember?"

Jimmy Dean's face lit up. "Nobs."

This was Jimmy Dean's favorite rule of the game. "One point for his nob, and two for his heels."

"That's right, Jimmy Dean. Good job remembering that."

"Have you ever got 29 points, Jonas?" asked Jimmy Dean.

"No, I never have, son. You don't have to have a perfect hand to win the game."

A little later, when Jonas was the dealer, Jimmy Dean was taking a long time to discard two cards for the crib. He was frowning in concentration.

"What's wrong?" asked Jonas.

"I can't decide which cards to get rid of. I don't want to get rid of any of the cards," Jimmy Dean said.

"You don't want to give me any good cards?"

Jimmy Dean shook his head in surprise. "No, I don't mind you gettin' good cards. I would just have a really good score if I could keep them all."

Jonas was impressed. Jimmy Dean wasn't even trying to keep him from getting points. He wanted Jonas to do well too. Being generous was his nature in most things, and yet Jonas knew it wasn't the way Jimmy Dean looked at baseball. When they listened to games on the radio, the kid cheered louder for strikeouts than he did for home runs.

"Jimmy Dean?"

"Yeah."

"Don't ever play cards for money."

"Why not, Jonas?"

"Because you're too nice, kid. And that's not a bad thing, okay?"

"Okay, Jonas."

"And Jimmy Dean?"

"Yeah."

"It can be hard to make a decision when you have several good choices. That's how life is sometimes." Jonas paused. "But that's a whole lot better than not having any good choices. All too often, life can be like that too."

Jimmy Dean smiled at that. He put his 5 card in Jonas's crib and kept a double run. Maybe, just maybe, Jonas would get his first 29.

CHAPTER 10 - LOOKING BACK
ST. JUDE, MO – OCTOBER 2005

Kate rose before dawn to go for a ride. She had taken the horses out of the pasture and put them in their barn stalls the night before, examining them carefully to be certain they hadn't harmed themselves with silly mischief over the previous weeks. She had been feeling guilty about not spending time with them other than to feed and make sure they were standing upright.

Neither Doc nor Jethro had shoes on—hadn't had for over a year. The farrier came out every seven weeks to trim their hooves, just to even them out. It was while examining their feet that Kate had the notion of going for a ride the next morning.

She fed the horses after dressing, and then went back inside to have some toast and coffee. When the sun began to climb the sky, Kate returned to the barn to saddle up. She was leading Doc, her buckskin gelding out of the barn when she glanced at Jethro pushing at his stall door, apparently ready to go. "No Jethro, it is too much trouble to take you. We won't be long."

The little Morgan talked to her in a low rumbling nicker. He pled his case the whole time she was saddling Doc. Sighing, she left Doc tied outside to come in with a halter and lead rope for Jethro. "Okay, you win," she said to the black, little gelding. "But you'd better behave yourself. I'm not going to drag you around."

Kate rode Doc, ponying Jethro through the gate behind the barn and into the pasture beyond, allowing a draw to funnel her into the beginnings of the wet weather creek bed, meandering through the property. The horses were over-eager at the change in routine but quickly settled into a comfortable pace, as she talked to them in a quiet voice. "Easy, Doc. Whoa now. Come on, Jethro." Kate let the surroundings calm her tangled thoughts. She gradually became immersed in the natural rhythm of being on a horse's back.

Kate had always loved the feel of late October mornings. The sun was losing its influence over even the most sensitive of earth's flora, expressing itself in exquisite sadness. In the golden wetness, the ordinary caught her eye. Dying weeds lined up in striking poses like hopeless soldiers making a last stand. Even brush adopted a Sinai-like mystery in the last of the elusive fog. *Melancholy people are drawn to dying beauty even as they yearn for the natural relief of summer's green days*, she remembered from one of her old poems.

The horses had sensed where she was going even if she didn't consciously work the reins. They stepped their way slowly along a wooded ridge above the rugged ravine, filled with rock, sand, and boulders, interspersed with branches and leaves fallen from the overhanging trees. Gradually, the ridge dropped down to a bend in the wet weather creek, where the steep walls gave way to an expansive, smooth flat rock surface, covering the bottom of the ravine.

It was several degrees cooler at the lower altitude, and Kate was thankful for her hooded, fleece-lined jacket. Isolated pools of water filled the depressions in the rock, connected by shimmering, liquid slivers, the only evidence that the water was still obeying gravity. She climbed down from Doc, leaving the horses tied to trees on an earthen ledge, knowing the rock was too slippery for them, even without shoes.

She climbed down with the help of a sycamore whose root system had given way in the loamy soil, now growing horizontally out over the creek. She swung the last few feet to the stream bed using a large hanging vine, barely avoiding a web inhabited by a sizeable yellow spider that appeared to have been tattooed with an intricate Asian pictogram. Landing neatly on the bottom, she tiptoed across the flatness of the rock to sit on the smooth edge of a boulder. It had long been a favorite spot when they had first moved here, but she hadn't visited it for more than a year. During that first year, when she was unable to write, she had come here to cleanse her senses and toss out the accumulated everyday experiences.

Filtered sun lit the vibrant green moss. She ran her fingers through the velvet strands as she peered through the calm surface of the nearest pool of water. She saw the bottom as clearly as if no water drifted above. The butterscotch algae resembled the surface of Mars; there were even canals, although unlike the planet, these cryptic symbols were actually a sign of life in the pool, trails from some aquatic life form. She slid off the rock and knelt down to peer into the water. She saw some small snails. Hmm, had the snails made the trails? Were these snail trails? Kate spontaneously starting humming and singing "snail trails, snail trails" until Jethro let out a fluttering snort above her. Doc answered with his own snort.

"Do you like my song, boys?" She climbed back on the rock ledge, closing her eyes until thoughts of Daniel returned. Her tall, dark stranger. She could have done without the darkness. But the gloom had not come until later—not until David died. The place he had gone in his mind had locked him away as if he had been imprisoned in a medieval dungeon.

It was Patti, her mother, who had first used "tall, dark stranger" to describe Daniel, but of course, she had mainly been talking about his hair. It was certainly not his eyes. They were as liquid and calm as the pool of water now before her.

His eyes were the first thing Kate had noticed about him. It had been in Ellis Library at Mizzou. She was a creature of habit even then. During her first year, she had wandered the warrens of tables among the shelves of books for a comfortable place to study, but it was a table in the wide-open vault of the Grand Reading Room that became her home. Here she came to study in the evenings to get away from the crowded, noisy dorm.

Students came and left as the weeks went by. Occasionally, guys found enough courage to flirt, if awkwardly. Faces became familiar. One tall, black-headed boy was often there, sitting two tables away, facing the other direction. She passed by him once, glancing at the titles in his pile of books, which told her he was an engineering student. Her own stack was full of the humanities. She assumed they lived in two separate worlds.

One week in November, he didn't show for three days in a row. She was surprised she had even noticed it on Monday and was annoyed on Wednesday when her mind left her reading several times to see if he had arrived. On Thursday, he appeared on crutches, stopped at his table, and balanced one crutch against the table while he pulled at his backpack. He lost the other crutch while dropping the pack on the table, hopping forward to catch himself, the casted foot held up behind him like a girl kissing in an old black and white movie. The table between them broke his fall.

"Oh, my gosh," Kate exclaimed and sprang from her chair to run around the table. She pulled a chair out for him and then retrieved his crutches and books. His face colored before he thanked her and immediately stuck his nose into one of the books. Kate sat back down at her table and tried to study, but now he was at the next table, facing her. She felt an overwhelming desire to raise her eyes, fought against it for a while, and then finally peeked his way. He immediately lowered his eyes, letting her know he had been looking at her, which somehow pleased her and made her self-conscious at the same time. The next time they both looked up at the same time, holding each other's gaze for a second. Kate tried to think of something to say to ease the awkwardness. Noticing his cast under the table, she asked, "Did you break something?"

"What?"

"Your cast. Did you break your ankle?"

"Oh. No, I fractured my leg above the ankle. Football injury," he added as if this explained everything.

She nodded and smiled, and they both returned to their books, Kate searching her mind for other ways to communicate what she wanted to say, which was simply, *Who are you and why am I so interested?*

Daniel left first, saying "Thanks again," as he struggled to rise.

"Take care," she replied as he hobbled away.

Later, in the dorm, she poured through the previous week's Mizzou Tigers game guide in one of her floor mate's rooms. She found his picture on the roster. Daniel Mitchell, junior, from St. Louis, Missouri. "What is a cornerback?" she asked Beck, her hall-mate with the guide.

"Pass defense," said Beck, as though this would mean anything to someone who knew nothing about football. Beck had a friend from high school who was on the football team. She promised Kate she would find out who he was. "I don't remember anyone getting hurt during the game last Saturday."

The next day Beck found Kate in class. "He's a backup cornerback. Broke his leg in practice at the end of last week."

On Friday evening he was already sitting at his table when she arrived—at the closer table that is—and he was facing her. *This is silly,* she thought. *If he wants to say something to me, then he should just quit being so shy and say it.* She sat down with her books, opened her 20th Century British Lit anthology, and started puzzling out William Butler Yeats. She was deep in the mystery of the lines when she read, *"Take down this book, and slowly read, and dream of the soft look your eyes had once, and of their shadows deep,"* which reminded her of the intense blue eyes at the next table. Again, they both looked up at the same time and stared at each other for a while. Kate realized and appreciated that the awkwardness was gone. Despite her determination to let him speak first, she asked him with a little smirk, "Did you perform acrobatics across the floor again tonight?"

"What?" He glanced around confused.

"Well—" Kate pointed behind him. "That used to be your table, and tonight you're at this table, so I thought that perhaps you fell again."

The smile on Daniel's face was crooked and fixed as if he was afraid to move anything for fear she would be able to see right through him. But he was no open book to Kate. She was just unable to quit searching his eyes.

"Do you want to go for a walk?" he finally asked doubtfully.

She smiled at him. "Wouldn't that be difficult for you?" she asked nodding at his crutches.

"Well, I walked here, and so... I'm going to have to walk back."

"Walk back to where?"

Kate learned several facts on that night walking across campus beside the tall young man on crutches. Daniel had known as much about her as she had known about him—which wasn't much more than her name. He had noticed her before she had noticed him. Daniel had an odd mixture of confidence about his place in the world and shyness around girls. He lived in Laws Hall, which was not far from her residence hall. And, he had chosen Mizzou because they had offered him a football scholarship.

They had never been truly apart since. As the years had passed, there had been isolated, dark moments. They began when Kate first found out Daniel had lived for years in foster care. The young man hadn't had a real family until people in his community noticed his athletic ability during junior high. The county prosecuting attorney and his wife had adopted Daniel when he entered the 7th grade. Daniel was grateful for his new surroundings and the adulation of a sports-crazed community, but he was never sure they had wanted him for any other reason than his ability to excel on the court or field. In a moment of candor, Daniel had said to her, "You know… kids without families invent themselves, and because of it are never quite sure what is real."

His core mistrust of the motives of others who took an interest in him had never included Kate, but when they began to discuss marriage and a wedding, he became tense and reluctant to discuss details. Kate finally began to understand he was self-conscious about his lack of family. In fact, other than his adoptive parents, most of the members of his "family" that came to their wedding were former teammates from college and high school. He had never wanted to talk about the multiple foster homes he had lived in—had never wanted to investigate, or even know anything about his birth father and mother.

Kate asked him about his earliest years. Daniel told her that his memories were vague. He thought he might have lived with a family that had a boy his age. He seemed puzzled. Kate prodded gently. Daniel resisted. Since that was the only way he resisted her—in all other parts of their life he held nothing back—she gave in and quit prodding.

Their attraction to each other had been intense. They were often completely satisfied to be only in the presence of the other. Kate remembered times at parties when she caught Daniel's eye, and they plotted their escape. Neither of them foresaw that they would find another love in their son, David, who somehow wiggled in to fill completely every space between them. Kate knew that her son had become the focus of her life, but it was the same for Daniel. They had camped and fished, played with their trains down in the basement— and then there was baseball. They were both crazy about America's past time. What one loved, the other loved. They must have watched "The Sandlot" and "Angels in the Outfield" a hundred times.

When a drunk driver wrenched that love from Daniel and Kate, they had lost each other as completely as if there had been an amputation. Kate, simply because of her childhood, had possessed the more fully developed sense of self that had survived. Daniel began a long and drawn-out death. Only in his work did he retain a semblance of his former identity. They tried to reconnect, but nothing felt tangible to the man who had been a great father but had lost what it meant to be a husband.

And what was worse, thought Kate, *it was in the very moments when he had tried hardest to find his way back to me that I rejected him most.* He had been so utterly pitiful. Daniel had risked showing the raw, emotional truth. He had wept, trying to talk with his head squeezed tightly in his hands as if he was trying to crush the life out of his skull. His voice had become something unnatural when he had been most desperate. It was in those moments she had glimpsed the worst of him, had somehow been unable to hold the one who now seemed to be a stranger. It was devastating to realize that she might no longer have the means of doing anything about it.

He was no longer the same man who had held their life in control. At night, he drank. Kate was afraid of who he was becoming. He had perceived her fear and misinterpreted it to be revulsion. To be honest, she had resented that his desperation seemed greater than her own—even more so, she believed, than if she had been the one who had died. She didn't know how to deal with it, and so she had turned away.

They had sold their place on the cursed highway, left behind the house haunted by images, the sound of their son's voice and laughter. Kate never got over the feeling that David was about to enter a room, to come running up the steps from the basement, or to slam the door on the way in from school. Daniel couldn't bear to look at David's room, the trains, or pick up a baseball bat. The auctioneer had packed and sold it all at auction. Kate took care of the details, and they moved to the new farm that had no memories.

A blue jay found her sitting in the creek and disturbed the peace. All at once, the morning had lost its appeal. Clouds were sweeping in low from the northwest at the edge of a cold front, and the creek altered from a place of treasured enchantment into a barren and dark gulley. She shivered and climbed the bank to the horses that were as anxious as she was to leave. The jay scolded. Kate hollered back at the loud-mouthed tattletale to shut up. Her voice sounded small in the hollow, having no effect on the bird, now joined by another heckler on the far hill.

She had a sudden, irrational, childish fear of her surroundings as if there were wolves or even something devilish about. The horses were in a hurry to go back. She had to regularly yank on Doc's reins to keep him from breaking into a trot. Jethro was more trouble, stretching the lead rope forward, back, and to the side, as tight as a guitar string. By the time they left the woods, she was mad, worn out and almost hoarse from yelling at them.

Out of the woods, within sight of the barn, the horses finally calmed enough to walk. Continuing along the ridge, they passed by a small grove of trees, mostly persimmon and walnut, and Kate noticed that almost all of the fruit was now gone. Spotting two, remaining, small, orange orbs, she stopped to shake the small trunk. Down fell one of the persimmons. She reached out and caught it, felt its soft consistency, tore off the cap, and popped it in her mouth.

The rich musky flavor was a childhood taste, arriving with a feeling of secure, confidence. She was still spitting out seeds when her cell phone rang. It was Mandy.

"Hey, what are you doing? Are you coming into town today?"

Kate considered it. "I suppose so. Do you want to have lunch?"

"Yes. What's going on? You sound out of breath."

"I'm out riding Doc, but I'm almost home. I should be in town by noon. Do you want to meet at the Lemon Tree?"

"Why don't you come get me here? I'll go with you."

"Okay. I'll see you at 12:30 then."

Everything was becoming clear; she had much to do. Might as well begin with Mandy.

If everything had been clear earlier in the morning, checking her email inbox before driving into town brought even greater clarity to the day. As Kate accessed her inbox, she saw an email with a "Daniel Mitchell" subject line. She quickly opened it and read.

Dear Kate Mitchell,

I received your letter and photographs today and decided to write to you immediately. I am instructing my Secretary to mail you a hard copy to make sure you receive it.

I met Daniel at the conference in New Orleans for the first time. I didn't spend that much time with him, but early in the week, (Tuesday, I believe it was) we happened to be in the same breakout group. It was an afternoon session. We stayed a little late to talk. I am attaching a separate list with all of our names, just in case any of them happen to remember more than I do.

There were seven people in our group. Four of us went together to eat after our session. It was Daniel, Julie Atwood, Barry Smith and me. We were all staying at the Hilton. Julie wanted to go to a restaurant someone had recommended in the French Quarter, the Des Guise Grill. It was a busy place—almost a party atmosphere. I think there were other events besides our conference.

After we were seated and had ordered, a server sat one plate in front of your husband and then looked around the table at the rest of us, evidently puzzled. It had only been a minute or two since we had put in our order, so we knew it couldn't be ours. The waitress glanced at Daniel, still perplexed, and then she turned to focus across the room and said, "I'm sorry, I brought this to the wrong table." She then said something like, "Wow, you know, you could be that other man's brother." It startled Daniel.

She took the plates to another table. It was odd, but I really didn't make anything of it. Our food came quicker than we had expected after the wait. But then later, Daniel left to walk over to this other table. I didn't have a clear view, but Barry said Daniel and the other man did resemble each other so much, they looked like they were brothers. When Daniel got back to our table, he said, "Wow. That was kind of like looking in a mirror" and then told us he was going to stay to talk to the other man for a while. He didn't want us to wait.

I know this sounds strange now, but it didn't seem odd at the time. We walked back to the hotel without him. I never saw Daniel again at the conference. I had expected to join him in at least one more session on six sigma processes because we had talked about it.

I have copied this email to Julie Atwood and Barry Smith. Perhaps they will be able to add to what I've written. I hope this information helps you in some way. If you have questions, or if there is anything else I can do for you, please do not hesitate to ask.

Best regards,

Alan Breslin

Kate read the email with growing astonishment. Who was the stranger in the restaurant? Evidently, he wasn't another attendee at the conference. Obviously, the story of Daniel meeting this other man agreed with what he had said to her over the phone, but why hadn't he mentioned that this other man resembled him? What could the two men have talked about in a few short minutes for Daniel to want to speak with him further? She quickly printed out the email and the attached list of names, grabbed her car keys, and headed into town.

Kate anxiously gauged Mandy's reaction to the email she had just handed her while they were waiting for their meals at the restaurant. Mandy read intently, her eyes widening in surprise before narrowing into a puzzled frown, then returned to astonishment before looking back at Mandy.

"What do you suppose this means?" she asked.

Kate shook her head and shrugged. "I have no idea what it means. I've been having all kinds of wild ideas. Is this other man a relative? I mean, you know Daniel was in foster care most of his childhood. He always told me he had no idea who his birth parents had been, and honestly didn't want to know. I don't know why he continued to talk to him if it was just that they looked alike. A doppelganger isn't something that would have made much of an impression on Daniel. Daniel found some reason, within just a few minutes, to stay and talk to him. Whatever they talked about must have been significant enough to keep him in New Orleans. Whatever it was, he didn't tell me."

Kate and Mandy hardly noticed when the server brought their dishes and drinks to their table. The girl disappeared, perceiving quickly that the two friends were deep into their discussion. It was after minutes of silence when Kate announced without distress or joy, but simply as a necessity, "Mandy, I have to go to New Orleans."

CHAPTER 11 – FISHING STORY
BENFORD, TN – OCTOBER 2005

The boat sat anchored in the middle of an eddy on the Duck River. Harlan and Jonas were in the swivel seats at each end of the jon boat. Jimmy Dean was sitting on the flat seat in the middle. They had motored a few miles upstream from an access ramp before stopping to float slowly back down the river. Harlan periodically anchored the boat at fishy looking holes before moving on. He expertly kept the boat positioned with the trolling motor. Jonas and Jimmy Dean hardly noticed it was ever running.

Jonas enjoyed just being on the river, soaking in the quiet, peacefulness of the water flowing under and around them.

"How did the river get the name Duck?" he asked Harlan.

Harlan spat from the side of his mouth and rolled his neck. "Well, it's like this. When Daniel Boone first made his way through Tennessee, he was traveling with a Cherokee scout down this very river. When their canoe got into Chickashaw country, they were getting out of the canoe and Boone sets eyes on a Chickashaw brave with a drawn bow. The scout was facing the other way and Boone hollers at him, 'Duck!' But it was too late. Thwack! Arrow right in the middle of his back. Of course, Daniel Boone raised his rifle and dispatched the Chickashaw, but the episode stuck in his crawl, and he named the river the Duck, 'cause the Cherokee Scout forgot to."

Jonas gave Harlan a deadpan look. "The scout forgot to *what?* Name the river?"

"He forgot to duck. Ain't you payin' attention?"

Jimmy Dean and Jonas smirked at each other. Jonas decided to egg the old man on. "That tale is taller than you are. And isn't it Chicka*saw*, not Chicka*shaw*?"

Harlan appeared right down offended by this question. "You say saw; I say shaw. And yeah, I don't know why it's called the Duck. I suppose some ancient old pilgrim saw a duck taking a break from migrating to Canada. One sighting and the river gets named the Duck. What if he'd noticed a turtle first, or a beaver, or a crawdad for heaven's sake? Then it'd be the Crawdad River. Who knows? Maybe it's short for some Indian name."

He frowned, staring at nothing. "Like the Hatchie River for instance. Hatchie means river in Chicka*shaw*," he said, emphasizing his preferred pronunciation, "So it's like the Hatchie's name is the River River."

Harlan grinned at Jimmy Dean and started singing, "Way down upon the River River, far, far away."

Jimmy Dean was sitting on a low bench seat in the middle of the boat, wearing a life jacket and a big smile. He was grinning, but it had nothing to do with the song. Jimmy Dean was actually casting well. Harlan had admitted aloud that Jonas had done a decent job of teaching him how to use the old Zebco, but the boy still hadn't figured out how to unhook the fish without impaling himself with dorsal fins, the hook, or both. Jimmy Dean had dropped the last two fish. They had tail flipped all over the boat before Jonas had grabbed them and tossed them back in the water.

"Now the bigun's ain't so easy ta catch, so be patient. Just pull it off the bottom every once in a while and reel up the slack in your line."

Harlan rigged the boy's pole with a weedless jig and a pork skin frog after complaining that he wanted to get his own line wet instead of spending the whole day getting Jimmy Dean unsnagged. Jimmy

Dean promptly cast the 'jig n pig' with a smack into the middle of an overhanging rock bluff because of the extra weight, but he caught on quickly. His second cast found open water.

"That's good," approved Harlan. "Now, slow down and stay quiet. Count to fifty before you move your jig. Fish don't take kindly to a bunch of jumpin' around and caterwaulin'."

Jimmy started counting aloud. "One, two, three—"

Harlan hissed at him, "Hey, can't you count silently?"

Jonas chuckled to himself because the boy closed his mouth and started nodding his head to keep count. It wasn't long before the nods became bigger. Jimmy Dean smiled, raised his rod tip in an exaggerated manner, glanced at the slack line for a second in panic and finally remembered he had a reel on his pole. Settling back down, he started nodding his head again. Before he got to fifty, he had opened his mouth again.

"Harlan?"

Harlan seemed to be pretending he hadn't heard.

"Harlan?" said Jimmy Dean a little louder.

"What is it?" asked Harlan, sighing.

"What's caterwaulin'?"

"It's making enough noise to wake the dead, boy. Now tend to your fishin'."

Jimmy Dean thought this was funny. He slapped a hand over his mouth to hold it in, but a snort escaped. Then he started laughing outright.

"Well, I'll be a monkey's second cousin, once-removed," Harlan said, evidently a favorite saying of his. "What is so dad-burn funny?"

Jimmy Dean tried to answer, but he couldn't. He just kept giggling and snorting while Harlan grumbled. "I'm gonna put a knot on your head, boy." He was just starting to turn back around when he hollered out, "Whoa, Jimmy Dean! Look at your line."

They stared at the spot where the monofilament fishing line was meeting the water, moving slowly upstream. Harlan started whispering excitedly, "Lower your rod tip. Reel down. That's right.

Now! Pull back hard."

Jimmy Dean set the hook like he was trying to yank the jig, frog, and fish all out of the water and into the boat at the same time, but it was like trying to pull on a concrete block. The rod bent and the fight was on. Harlan and Jonas shouted encouragement, and Harlan did everything but grab hold of the pole and begin reeling himself. The drag was set too tight, so he reached over and turned the dial with a finger. The drag started clicking when the fish pulled hard.

"It's a Kentucky," Harlan said excitedly. "Hold on. Let 'em run a bit... Now! Reel in! There you go. Keep going. Don't give up."

Jonas knew Jimmy Dean was not going to quit on this fish. The boy gripped the pole tightly and reeled with fierce determination. Jonas hoped that the fish wouldn't break the line or spit the hook. When the bass got closer, it made one last attempt to run under the boat, but the grinning boy hung on and waited until the fish gave in. Harlan netted the tired fish, lifting him out of the water.

Harlan pulled the Kentucky from the net and pulled out the jig hook that had caught the fish neatly by the mouth. He held the fish up for the other two to admire.

Harlan was clearly proud of the boy and the fish. "She's a real beaut', Jimmy Dean. I'll bet she's 17, 18" long—maybe 3 lbs."

"Is it a Kentucky Bass?" Jonas asked.

"Yep. Sure is. Notice the spots down the side? They're also called Spotted Bass. This one's a female. See how wide she is for her length? They are heavier than the males of the same length." Harlan turned the fish several times. "Well, are you going to eat her, or do you want to release her?" he asked Jimmy Dean.

This was a tough question. Jimmy Dean wanted Maggie and his mom to appreciate that he had caught a huge fish, but he wasn't sure he wanted to eat the fish either. He was taking so long to think about it, Harlan finally said, "Here. I'll put it in the live well for right now, and you can decide later."

Harlan maneuvered the boat further downstream before setting the anchor again.

"Got any more of those jigs?" Jonas asked.

"See how he is?" Harlan winked at Jimmy Dean. "Wantin' to jump on your bandwagon. This boy is outfishin' us, Jonas."

Later on in the morning, Harlan caught two smaller Kentucky and Jonas caught a Smallmouth that was large enough to keep. Jimmy Dean had Harlan put the fish back in the water. Jonas wondered if it was mostly because he thought he was going to have to eat the fish right there on the river. He didn't say anything, willing to let the boy make his own decision, but he was pleased. It made it even easier when Harlan pulled a digital camera out of a waterproof case and took his picture with the fish standing in the boat.

"Now you can come back and catch her again," said Harlan. "We'll eat the smaller fish one of these nights if we can talk Maggie into cooking them. I'll fillet 'em out so's there won't be hardly no bones."

They stopped on a gravel bar, ate lunch, and headed for home when the wind picked up.

"Ain't that somethin'?" Harlan kept saying on the way back. "First time out and he catches as big a Kentucky as I ever caught."

Back at the garage below Jonas's apartment, Harlan showed Jimmy Dean how to fillet the other fish. Maggie wasn't home, so they wrapped the fillets in plastic wrap and put them in Jonas's little refrigerator until she returned. Harlan promised to bring his fish cooker over during the next evening. Jonas agreed to supply the onions and potatoes.

"So you throw a baseball pretty well?" asked Harlan when they had finished.

"Do you wanna play catch?" asked Jimmy Dean.

"I haven't thrown a ball in years, but I reckon I'll give the ol' horsehide a toss."

"I'll meet you downstairs," hollered Jimmy Dean, already on the way out to get the gloves.

Harlan and Jonas grinned at each other. Jonas shook his head. "I actually have to keep that boy from throwing the ball too much. If I let him, he would throw hours every day."

They caught up with Jimmy Dean down by the barn where he was already throwing the ball in the air and catching it. He ran over to Harlan. "Here, you can use my new glove that Jonas got for me. I'll use the old glove 'cause I can catch just as good with it." He handed Harlan the glove with a baseball then ran back to stand in front of the barn.

Harlan turned the ball over in his hands, enjoying the smooth leather surface before tossing it in an arc toward the barn. The ball landed five feet in front of the boy, but he squatted squarely in front of it and caught it on one bounce. Harlan frowned and shook his arm and hand as if they were foreign to him. He erupted in a short cussing fit, just a little too quiet for the boy to understand. Jonas covered his smile, saying nothing.

"Are you ready?" yelled Jimmy Dean.

"I reckon so. Take it easy on an old man."

Jimmy Dean fired the ball straight at the belly button of Harlan, who couldn't decide which way to turn his glove. He caught the baseball right in the palm, and it bounced away on the ground. The ball had hit the glove with a loud pop, which made it seem even faster. Harlan threw the glove to the ground and started jumping around, this time cussin' thunderous enough for Jimmy Dean to hear, who started falling around laughing. Jonas couldn't help but laugh too.

Harlan quit cussing and started complaining. "Of all the crooked, dirty, low-down, no-good, unscrupulous cons anyone could pull on an old man who is supposed to be your friend." He glared at Jonas. "You said the boy was just learning to throw. Learning? Was Sandy Koufax just learning? Was Bob Gibson just learning?" Then he glared at Jimmy Dean. "Did I not just ask you to take it easy on an old man? Is that what you call easy?" Then he glared at the glove. "Dang it, it's still stinging! What kinda' worthless piece of dead goat hide did you buy for the boy, Jonas? What is so dad-burn funny, anyway?

Jimmy Dean and Jonas couldn't quit laughing.

That's right, have fun at the old man's expense."

Having exhausted himself of complaints, after the sting had worn off, Harlan finally chuckled to himself. Noticing an odd-looking triangular wooden frame with a pole sticking out of it over by the barn. He pointed and asked, "What sorta contraption is that?"

Jonas followed his pointing finger and motioned for Jimmy Dean to come over with them.

"Harlan wants to see the trebuchet work. Why don't you go get the sling?"

As the boy ran to the barn, Harlan hollered, "Oh yeah, I saw one of these on TV once. It was bigger, though. The throwing arm was the size of a tree itself. I think they tossed a piano with it."

Jimmy Dean came back from the barn with a nylon mesh sling and two heavy nylon strings tied to either end of it. Jonas instructed Harlan to hold the top end of the throwing arm down near the ground while he attached the sling. He then set a trigger pin in place to hold the arm, put a baseball in the sling, and placed it in front of a grooved track attached to the bottom of the wooden frame. The strings holding the sling were now taut.

"We're ready," said Jonas. "Harlan, do you see the barrel down there in the pasture tilted this way? It's about 200 ft. away."

"Are you telling me you are going to try to hit that barrel with this baseball?"

Jimmy Dean couldn't help but interrupt. "No, the baseball is going to go in the barrel. You had better stand back. This is a dangerous weapon."

Harlan staggered back as if he had been shoved. Jonas released the trigger. The weight immediately dropped, causing the other end of the pole to swivel upward, pulling the sling holding the baseball down the track until it lifted into the air in a long arc around the end of the pole. When the ball reached just the right point, the ring on the end of the string slid off a metal holder, releasing the baseball in a long arcing trajectory that ended with the baseball landing in the bottom of the barrel with a loud boom.

"Well I'll be," said Harlan. "Is it actually that accurate? Let's do it again."

They sprung the trebuchet twice more. Each time the baseball boomed into the bottom of the barrel. While Jimmy Dean retrieved the balls, Jonas explained that he had built the trebuchet to show Jimmy Dean what it meant to throw the baseball with his body, not just his arm. During the pitching motion, the pitcher's body falls as he pushes forward and the arm moves in an arc similar to the pole that propels the sling and the baseball.

Harlan's next question showed that he wasn't particularly interested in the siege engine's baseball applications. "How big would the trebuchet have to be to toss a bowling ball? I've got a neighbor in mind."

It was early evening when Harlan left to go home. Jonas took Jimmy Dean home in the pickup, relieved to see that Bo's old truck wasn't there. He was helping the boy carry his stuff back to the house when Jess came out. Jimmy Dean started talking about his big fish, and his mom replied in that sing-song, phony way parents have when they want to sound interested, but are in a hurry to get to other things. Jonas noticed she couldn't stand still, arms and head twitching, all the time avoiding looking him in the eye.

"Harlan says it was a big ol' female, mom. Over 3lbs! Ain't that right, Jonas?"

"Yeah, Bud. That's right. It was a beautiful, big fish," Jonas said, trying to get a closer look at Jess' eyes. He still suspected Bosephus might be the hitting type, but when she finally glanced at him, he knew immediately—Jess was stoned, and it wasn't just weed. That was the problem.

Jonas stood there with arms crossed, a slow fire burning inside. *How often was she using and was she using in front of Jimmy Dean?*

"Jess," he said quietly but insistently.

She gave a paranoid look somewhere to the side of him.

"Why don't we get Jimmy Dean another change of clothes? He can spend the night again. Something to wear to church with Maggie in the morning, I guess."

"Okay," Jess agreed quietly. She looked deflated.

Jimmy Dean was excited, failing to notice the tension between Jonas and his mom. Jess helped him get more clothes packed. When he ran back inside to get his forgotten toothbrush, she wouldn't face Jonas. As they were driving away, Jonas glanced back toward the house. She was still standing on the doorstep. Jonas thought he could see her eyes shining, but then he thought, maybe the only tearful eyes were his own.

Maggie was there when they got back. Jonas explained to her quietly what had just happened while Jimmy Dean was getting his gear out of the truck.

"Are you sure?" she asked quietly, and he nodded yes.

She shook her head sadly, hugging Jimmy Dean so hard when he came around the pickup, he dropped everything in the driveway. She looked down at his surprised face. "Will you stay with me tonight? I need to go to church early tomorrow to get some crafts ready. You can go with me and help if you'd like."

Jimmy Dean looked at Jonas since this wasn't quite what he had suggested. Jonas knew he was probably disappointed, but was glad to see him accept it when said he was tired and was going to eat a sandwich in his apartment before reading and going to bed. He too hugged the boy who seemed glad of the attention, yet questioning why everyone was so sad.

Jimmy Dean would have been even more perplexed if he could have witnessed Jonas hours later, huddled with head in hands in front of a computer screen. The screen cast the only light in the dark apartment, ghosting his face and lending a glow to a brown fifth of whiskey. He looked like a candle-lit alchemist with his pharmacon. If his internet browser had been allowed to accumulate a history, the list would have included an archived article from the St. Jude Record, telling about a memorial for David Mitchell. The history would also have included Google searches for *Kate Mitchell* and *St. Jude Missouri*, and several pages at the Puzzled Poet blog. The last location he accessed was a poem published by user: *quiltersleeves*. He read the words repeatedly:

I am the converse of Clark Kent,
first down, then up, then lower altitude to go.
A perfect fruit smashed by the fall.
I reach the shore, then drown—
nor will revive.
How can dawn can feel like death?
There's nothing left.
The summer's gone—bare snow will fall.
Sun will arrive but then abscond
and not return.
And though they're gone, I still go on.
I know not how or where or why
existence counts or is more real than Sisyphus.
Although I die,
I still go on.

CHAPTER 12 - PREPARING TO LEAVE
ST. JUDE, MO – OCTOBER 2005

Rain fell in sheets at the compulsion of wind and gravity, at times in drenching vertical sprays only to be twisted sideways and spun with patterns as random as nature itself. Looking out back toward the barn, Kate was glad she had hauled the horses over to her parent's farm earlier in the day. It would have been a wet and muddy chore had she waited. Her travel checklist was now almost complete. She thought back to the preparations made during the previous week, and all of the friends and family that were making it possible for her to make the trip south.

Her dad had promised to take care of the horses and drop by her house at least once a week while she was gone. He was going to come tomorrow to turn down the water heater and make sure the furnace was set and operating properly. Delbert had also promised to check on her place periodically.

Gilbert, their family attorney for years, had agreed to take care of the few business responsibilities that Kate could not handle online. Daniel's boss, Bud Kreilick, phoned her unfailingly every week. He had assured her that K&L would continue to pay Daniel's salary until the end of the year unless he was found first. He also made certain she understood that his company—and he personally—would take care of "whatever needed to be done." Kate wasn't concerned about money. Daniel had never been interested in the big toys other men seemed to enjoy, and she had always had simple tastes herself.

Kate refused to contemplate life insurance settlements or anything else remotely related to the possibility of Daniel's death. If pinned down, she would have admitted to the chance, perhaps even the likelihood that her search would not end well. But for now, there were too many possibilities—too many mysteries to solve for her to consider what might lie ahead.

Her decision to go south met with much resistance from her dad and Mandy. Her father didn't want her to go alone; Mandy didn't want her to go at all. Her decision to go anyway resulted from exchanges with former Detective Arceneaux, now known to Kate simply as Sara. She was an indispensable source of information and advice. Kate supposed that without Sara, she would be lost in her search for Daniel, and without hope of knowing where to turn to next. She discussed everything with her, including the answers she had received from convention participants from her emailed requests for information.

After having received the email from Alan Breslin, Kate checked Daniel's credit card statement once again to find out if the Des Guise Grill was one of the last recorded transactions. No such business showed on the statement, which actually didn't surprise her; Daniel always preferred to use cash and keep receipts during business trips. The last transaction was at the hotel the day he had arrived. It worried her to think of all the money he had probably been carrying. Could that have played a part in whatever had occurred?

Kate had also received follow-up emails from the other two dinner partners present when Daniel had met his look-alike. Julie Atwood remembered having dinner with Daniel and the others. Although sitting in the chair facing away from the other side of the room, she had glimpsed the other man when they left. Her experience was similar to Alan's; nothing had struck her as particularly odd at the time.

Barry Smith emailed and then phoned. He described the interior of the Des Guise Grill, explaining that his chair faced the other side of the room with a good view of the other party's table. "Your Daniel and this other guy definitely looked alike. I mean they both had dark hair. They stood like each other—very similar posture. Tall! They were both slender and tall."

Kate asked if he had noticed Daniel again any time after that night.

"You know, I don't remember him being at any of the following conference sessions, but he *was* in the hotel. I specifically remember seeing him in a hallway one evening. He appeared to have been working. Physically, I mean. He had on dirty jeans, and I wondered what he'd been doing. I thought maybe he had been helping someone work on a presentation in the manufacturer's exhibition area."

Unfortunately, Barry was unable to remember anything else about the other man in the restaurant or his companions. He suggested that Kate should contact the restaurant owner and find their server that night. Barry was confident the girl knew more. She was sharp in his memory, and he was certainly ready with *her* description: blonde, early-twenties, cute, mole on her cheek and a small diamond nose stud.

During their most recent phone conversation, Sara had cautioned Kate about raising her expectations too high. It puzzled Kate that Sara had not seemed as excited when hearing about the memories of Daniel's dinner partners.

"I wouldn't put too much hope in finding this other man. I'm sure we'll find more leads from sources we haven't even thought of yet."

"What do you have in mind?" Kate had asked.

"Oh, I don't know. When you come to Hattiesburg, you can stay in my apartment. We can work together on finding your husband."

Kate was puzzled. "But you live with your sister, right?"

"Oh, she won't mind," Sara said.

"Sara, I appreciate the offer so much, but I already have a place to stay in Hattiesburg. After telling Bud Kreilik, Daniel's boss, that I was going to use Hattiesburg as a base, he arranged a suite at a bed and breakfast inn, owned by one of his veteran friends."

Kate had perceived a distinct irritation and coldness from Sara in response to this. She had shrugged it off, realizing that Sara was undergoing difficult circumstances herself. Sara had still not found a job with law enforcement, and she was working four, late night, ten-hour shifts for a security company. It was mind-numbing work but paid the bills until she could find something better.

Sara had told Kate she was planning to go back to school to become a parole officer in January. For the time being, she promised to help Kate follow up with the leads she currently had and offered to guide her into the city.

Kate had also spoken with Lt. Grayling at the NOPD. He apologized briefly for their lack of communication with her, pleading the fact that the city was still overwhelmed with Katrina's aftermath. Almost immediately, he tried to pass her off, saying he was going to direct her call to Detective Manson, but Kate was having none of it. She told him that she didn't want to be passed around anymore.

Kate didn't feel like any of the leads she had uncovered were reliable enough to share, and so it had been a very short conversation with both promising to stay in touch. Grayling had not exactly impressed her with his competence, but she was glad to have sidestepped Manson, the dirty cop. The most positive result of the conversation in Kate's opinion was that the lieutenant had reluctantly given her his telephone extension.

The final major decision had been to trade for a new pickup. She let her dad help with the choice of the truck because she knew he wanted to feel like he was contributing. At first, she compared Jeeps and Hummers, but he convinced her that something nondescript would be better.

She finally chose a tan ¾ ton, extended cab GMC pickup with a locking bed cover. Her dad also insisted on an On Star subscription and a separate GPS system. They then filled much of the bed with bottled water and other essential supplies, not knowing what conditions might be like when she actually visited the city.

The last step in preparing for the trip had been to pack clothing and essentials. Kate planned to continue contributing to the poetry blog and perform online editing chores for the St. Jude Record, so she packed her laptop and a camera. She still needed to be able to contact people and complete research online. Kate felt that she was taking too much stuff. She pointed out to her dad that she could purchase supplies in Hattiesburg before going to New Orleans. Finally, she realized that it was easier to let her dad help as much as he wanted.

Kate and Mandy had said their goodbyes earlier in the afternoon. She was leaving early in the morning before her dad came by. All that remained was to sleep. She peered once again through the window to the outside, noticing the wind had died down. The downpour had settled to a slow and steady rain. She knew that in just a few weeks, the rain would become snow and ice, and a part of her was glad to be heading south. She had never liked the dark, coldness of winter.

Kate considered going to bed early. She had planned to leave before daylight but wasn't sleepy yet. Logging onto the computer to check her email she noticed there was a comment on her poem at The Puzzled Poet. She had posted it under a fictional username in the message area—not her usual practice—and only chosen this time to indulge a whim. Kate had wished to expose more sentiment than usual without risking consequence.

She followed the link in the email to the comment on her poem. The commenter's username was b4Isleep, obviously a reference to Robert Frost's "Stopping By Woods on a Snowy Evening". The comment itself was quoted from Walt Whitman's "Song of Myself."

"All goes onward and outward, nothing collapses. And to die is different from what anyone supposed, and luckier."

Kate scrolled up and once again read the poem she had written and posted so hastily. The last lines stared out at her from the page.

"Although I die, I still go on."

She returned to the Whitman quote once again. The commenter's presumption made her instantly angry. *He thinks he's smart*, she thought. *But why am I assuming b4Isleep is a "he"?*

She did not obey her first notion to make a cutting reply, but instead added a browser tab, and searched for the user's IP address on the statistical watchdog program site they used to monitor the blog traffic. It had originated in South Africa. *Most likely a proxy address*, she thought. Her anger somewhat defused, she was surprised to note that she was actually intrigued. It gave her something to puzzle over while falling asleep.

Kate still wanted to reply, but having posted the poem under an alias, first-time user account presented a problem. Did she want to start a conversation with someone based on an alias account she had created? A better solution finally occurred to her. She posted a comment in her own name, as a board moderator, welcoming both her alias account and the commenter to the blog. She thanked her alias for submitting the poem and asked both individuals to introduce themselves to the blog. Finally, she asked b4isleep if he/she had unique insight into the hereafter.

After finishing the comment, she almost deleted it, just as she had ripped apart the prison letter many days before. It was uncomfortably dishonest, but she posted the comment anyway, logged off the computer, and packed everything away. Kate enjoyed her first unbroken sleep in many nights.

CHAPTER 13 - HATTIESBURG
HATTIESBURG, MS – NOVEMBER 2005

Kate and Sara met at Applebees in Hattiesburg because neither one was in the mood for risk, hard decisions, or surprises. They both knew further trials were coming in the days ahead. They sat across the table from each other with a sense of relief that the person they had known only from telephone and online conversations was actually someone with whom they might enjoy spending time. Kate felt comfortable with the younger woman, although they were very different in age and background.

Kate admired the way Sara listened with dark, attentive eyes above her prominent round cheekbones. Her face was perfectly framed by lush, short, black hair with red highlights. She supposed that her intense attention was a habit born of interviewing and interrogating people as a detective. Even when Kate was merely describing some of the storm damage she had observed on the way from Missouri, Sara scrutinized her face as though she were about to disclose information which had long been held secret.

They discussed the continuing aftermath of Katrina and how widespread the damage had been. Hattiesburg had not suffered the severe catastrophic turmoil of New Orleans, but there was widespread damage to buildings that needed extensive repair. Sara told Kate she had chosen Hattiesburg because her younger sister

Belle had invited her to come and stay. Since Belle was attending the University of Southern Mississippi, it benefited both of them to share the rent and other expenses.

"Are you going back to New Orleans when things get better?" asked Kate.

Sara paused. "You know, I really don't know what my plans are beyond the immediate future. I might go back to school like Belle. I can't picture returning to the force unless it changes drastically."

"Is it that bad?"

"Manson's the worst. But it isn't just him."

"Other cops are dirty?"

Kate thought Sara seemed uncomfortable with her bluntness.

"Not just cops—government in general. I've always known corruption was a problem, but at least it wasn't in-your-face. The same water that covered the city appears to have exposed what used to be done in secret."

"Surely, there are still a lot of good—"

"You're right; there are. And I feel bad about having left. If all the decent people leave the city—"

"But you didn't have much choice."

"That's what I keep telling myself."

Kate was now reluctant to broach the subject of traveling to New Orleans the first time. Sara didn't seem like one to exaggerate the situation there. She was worried that Sara, for all of her promises to help, might not be ready to return herself, even if just for part of a day. She was mulling how to broach the idea when Sara spoke about it herself.

"Do you want to go into the city on Friday morning right after I get off work? It will only take us a couple of hours to get to the city itself, but after that, it's hard to say."

Kate was pleased with this plan. She had heard very little from the police department since Sara had left. She wanted to meet with the police—for them to have a live person to consider, and not just her voice over the telephone. Kate wanted to ensure that Daniel's case didn't slowly disappear from their long list of priorities. She also wanted to locate the restaurant server who had connected Daniel with his look-alike. Hopefully, the owner of the Des Guise Grill could provide a phone number and address. Kate had also determined to learn more about the little girl's rescue.

"Yes. You can't imagine how much I appreciate you going into the city with me," she replied. "It's still a few days until Friday. Do you think it's possible for me to meet Sicily before then?"

"Maybe. I haven't talked with Frieda, her foster care counselor for over a week. I'm sure she will be glad to arrange it after she meets you. Sicily is living with a family who already had two other foster children. When we get to New Orleans, I'll show you where Sicily's rescue took place, not that it will necessarily give us any clues."

"No, no. I understand. I want to visit the place, the whole area actually. Maybe it will give me some idea of why Daniel was there. I still have no notion of what he could have been doing."

"Okay. Come on over to the apartment after we leave here. I'll give you Frieda's number. No, wait a sec." She picked her cell phone off the table, thumbing through the contacts. "Yeah, it's on my cell."

They exchanged a few more phone numbers: Sara's sister Belle, Mandy, and Kate's parents, just in case. They agreed to meet for dinner again the next night, Kate insisting that she pay, then hugged and thanked her for all she had done.

"So if I just call Frieda?" Kate questioned as they walked out of the restaurant.

"I'll call and let her know you will be contacting her tomorrow. Unless you want to talk to her tonight?"

"No, that's fine. I'll call Frieda tomorrow. I—" Kate began, and for no reason, she was near crying. She felt the tightness in her throat, tears glazed her eyes, and a sense of hopelessness washed over her. She turned briefly to gather herself before continuing. "I guess I had better get back to the inn. I haven't even unpacked everything yet."

Sara might have noticed the moment, but if so, she didn't call attention to it. "I've heard of the Bouie Bend, but I've never been there. How do you like it?"

Kate was thankful for the reprieve. She answered, looking the other way. "It's perfect for me. I've lived in the country my whole life, except during college. Only one other couple is staying in the same lodge house, downstairs. You'll have to come out to visit."

"Okay." Sara unlocked her truck door, glancing back at Kate. "I'm glad you are here. I wish it could have been under other circumstances."

"Me too. I'll call you tomorrow evening. So, Friday morning, after you get off your graveyard shift, right?"

"Friday morning. See ya."

It was dark when Kate arrived back at the inn. She carried her bags up the outside stairs to her suite on the second floor. She was grateful that Bud had arranged for her to stay here. It wasn't a working farm or ranch, but it was peaceful and comfortably rustic. She paused on the deck in the dark, staring up at the sky. The same familiar stars pierced the blackness hundreds of miles from home. *I live on the surface of a planet.* The words came unbidden to her, just as they had since her dad had first told her about the stars and planets, riding on his shoulders under the stars on their farm. She couldn't have been more than six, or even five. The wonder of it, the sense of awe never became old. She leaned back against the rail, embracing the small joy before breathing deeply.

The Birgsons had welcomed her when she first arrived, gave her the tour and introduced her to the Smiths, a retired couple who were staying on the lower level for a week. Paul asked about Bud, letting her know that the two of them had been in the same squadron in the Air Force. His wife Mary drew her to the side, quietly telling her that Bud had explained why she was coming. She wanted Kate to know she was welcome at their place.

"We want to help. Stay as long as you need."

"I can't—"

"But you must. I'm afraid that with Bud and Paul, it is the only possible way. It's what we wish to do, hon."

There were more hugs, instructions, and advice shared before their car headed down the drive through the trees to their house.

She was alone in a strange place and yet not alone. People who had recently been strangers were making it home. She unpacked the rest of her things before sitting on the bed with her laptop. She smiled at a short email from Mandy that simply said, "I miss you, girl." Kate called her to let her know she was okay. After she had described the inn and her meeting with Sara, she could tell Mandy was relieved. Her parents would be relieved too; she made a mental note to call them in the morning.

There were no new emails from the contact list of convention-goers. She scanned quickly through the junk mail and was about to log off when another email appeared letting her know that user b4Isleep had replied to her welcome message. She followed the link to the comment and read:

> Thank you for the welcome. I have no insight into the hereafter, which is why I was relying on Whitman. I do know what it is like to be in one place when those I love are elsewhere, wherever that may be. I suppose it is only fair I introduce myself and will do that in the proper place. I hope I have not offended the writer.

Kate thought, as she often had, of the digits racing through air and wires, connecting the space between people, as separate in many ways as the stars she had just observed in the sky. An unknown person had just typed this message at a distance in the night, someone frugal with words and careful enough to use a proxy. It gave her an odd feeling she couldn't identify, almost as if she had just met someone she had known, but had forgotten existed.

She navigated to the newbie thread to read b4Isleep's introduction, evidently posted before making his comment to her:

> Hello, everyone. I'm new. I feel awkward. I'm not sure I'm prepared

to discuss poetry, but I've already learned much.

Kate was now only certain of one thing regarding b4Isleep. He was a 'he.' She could be concise as well.

"Welcome again," she wrote.

CHAPTER 14 - BUTTERFLIES & BEES
BENFORD, TN – NOVEMBER 2005

Maggie couldn't help but believe Jonas had pulled off some kind of saint-making miracle when it came to the formerly clumsy Jimmy Dean. He wasn't just showing the boy how to throw a baseball. Looking up from chopping vegetables, she could see them out there in the pasture in the late afternoon light, running a drill Jonas had recently added to their routine. They were quickly sprinting on the balls of their feet as if they were barefoot on a bed of coals. "Light on the earth," Jonas had called it. The phrase gave her the impression of something that might be part of some type of martial arts training.

She had become even surer that he knew some form of martial arts the previous Sunday evening. Jess and Bo had barreled into the drive, exhaust rattling and subwoofer beating like a marching band's bass drums on a football field. Jess had stayed in the old Ford pickup, but Bo had jumped out of the driver's seat, flaming with chemical courage. Jonas came out of the garage, looking cool and flinty-eyed like Clint Eastwood. Bo demanded that Jonas go get Jimmy Dean.

Maggie considered getting involved but instead went to the other side of the room, got the cordless phone, and went back to quietly watch out the window. Jonas's downward stare became more like a glare. He said something. Then the two went into the garage together. Maggie decided that if they came out with Jimmy Dean, she was going to call the sheriff. She knew it would cause conflict with Jess, but she wasn't going to let Jimmy Dean get into the pickup with a drunk. She wasn't going to stand by while they put the boy in danger—not without doing something.

But, only a minute later, the two men came back out of the garage alone, Jonas's hand on Bo's elbow. Bo was holding the left side of his face with one hand and was walking bent over as if he was going to be sick. Jonas led Bo over to the passenger side of the Ford before saying something through the window to Jess. She directly got out and stomped around the truck to climb into the driver's seat. Jonas helped Bo into the truck and shut the door behind him. Jess ground the gears, throwing the pickup into reverse and killed it. She got it started again, backed out of the driveway, and hurtled down the road.

Maggie came outside while Jonas was walking back to the garage.

"Where's Jimmy Dean?" she asked.

Jonas's eyes narrowed into a tight frown. "He's upstairs playing on the computer."

"What happened out here?"

Jonas glanced at the gravel, pursing his lips in an innocent shrug, "Bo must have got stung by a hornet or something. It got him right here." He pointed at his own face, right where the ball of nerves covers where the jaws connect. Maggie stepped close and stared into his eyes. He tried a deadpan look but continued talking when she kept questioning him with her eyes. "He was going down so I raised him back up with my knee. Right after that, he didn't seem to be feeling well."

"Hornets, huh? Do you know where their nest is?"

Jonas grimaced and scratched his head. "Maybe it was a wasp."

"Sounds to me like it might have floated like a butterfly and stung like a bee. I hope the idiot doesn't come back with a gun."

"He won't. He's not that ambitious."

If Jonas had been concerned about Bo, he had forgotten it quickly. Maggie watched his eyes lock onto her own teasing eyes, staying for a long drawn-out moment before continuing to her lips, and the closeness of his body left a tangible presence that lingered.

At the time, Maggie had dismissed the attraction as a passing phenomenon. Proximity to this physically powerful man had sparked a glowing ember. She was feeling the warmth once again as she looked out the window at Jonas working with Jimmy Dean. He's an attractive man. *Maybe I need to be more cautious.*

Jimmy Dean was still practicing pitching on his own down at the barn every day, even if Jonas was busy with chores. Most nights they worked on baseball skills together. To Maggie's somewhat biased eye, Jimmy Dean was looking good. She glanced back out the window after she had started browning beef for the stew. The boys had quit running and were doing a different drill. Jonas threw grounders. Jimmy Dean caught the ball, paused, and then threw back to Jonas with a very deliberate and exaggerated motion, repeating the same moves repeatedly. Repetition. It was working with baseball, and it had been working with his schoolwork as well. Something very right was happening in Jimmy Dean's life, but Jess continued to make poor choices with men. Maggie frowned. Jonas wasn't worried about Bo. Maggie, on the other hand, knew how crazy some of the boys in the county could be, especially when meth was the drug of choice.

Jonas was quiet over dinner, seemingly lost in his own thoughts.

"What do you have in mind with Jimmy Dean and baseball?" Maggie asked.

"He'll make the team next summer. I think he'll play. In fact, he'll pitch if he keeps improving as he is now." Jonas sounded like a scout, selling his prospect to a coach. "Jimmy Dean has a strong arm, and he's very accurate on both sides of the plate with his fastball. He still needs to work on a changeup, and maybe his delivery from the stretch. But he has the potential to be a good pitcher."

"That's great. It's amazing to see his progress. You've made a difference." Maggie paused and changed the subject. "So how is your job?"

"Fine."

"Busy? Plenty of work?"

"Uh-huh."

"Bill doing OK?"

Jonas nodded.

"How about Harlan? He hasn't been over here for a while."

"Helping his sister remodel her house most nights."

"Bart Simmons asked about you today."

Jonas looked puzzled.

"Remember the owner of the hardware store?"

"Oh." Jonas was surprised. "What did he want?"

"Just wondered how everything was going for you. Talked about enjoying eating lunch with you that one time."

"Oh. How's the relief effort going at the church?"

"Very well. We're just gathering and distributing certain supplies now. We're not working again until next Tuesday."

Small talk over, they ate in silence. Generally a healthy eater, Jonas was picking at his food. Finally, he raised his eyes. "I've been reading Whitman," he confessed.

Maggie was surprised, not quite sure what to say. "'Leaves of Grass?'"

"A couple of poems in an anthology. 'Song of Myself' and 'Brooklyn Ferry?' he asked, not sure of the titles.

"'Crossing Brooklyn Ferry,'" she amended. "Well, what's your verdict? What do you have questions about?"

"They are difficult, I guess. I mean, I'm not sure. I always understand Robert Frost, or at least I suppose I do. I might be missing some things," he admitted. "Just when I sense that I understand Whitman, he seems to be saying something different."

Jonas then actually blushed as he pulled the anthology out from where he had hidden it below his leg on the chair. "Here, I brought this with me. I'll read one part."

"The glories strung like beads on my smallest sights and hearings, on the walk in the street and the passage over the river—"

"What do you think he means?"

"If it was me that had written it," Jonas said, glancing at her, "I would have meant that I collect visual experiences in my memory, like beads." He held his arms out as if he was holding a string from both ends.

"But not just experiences. Moments of joy, beauty, meaning, and maybe something more—more in what I pay attention to."

Maggie smiled and replied, "Well, that is an excellent way to approach a poem, to begin by paraphrasing it."

"But is that what he meant?" Jonas asked intently. "Later in the poem, he says that he is speaking to a future reader. I guess even me possibly. And he knows I will see the same things—see as he saw." They both laughed at the inadvertent tongue twister.

Maggie was pleased with the effort he was making to express his ideas. She was careful with her reply, not wanting him to quit on his own ideas so easily. "I'm not so sure you would be satisfied with my understanding of what the poem means. It is very possible Whitman himself didn't understand completely. Sometimes the very act of writing a poem is an attempt to communicate something only vaguely understood or held so tentatively, it seems to be slipping through our fingers."

"Yes, but what do you *think*?" He stared at Maggie intently as she silently tried to think of a way to satisfy him in some small way. His eyes were so intent on her that she briefly lost concentration on what she had been thinking. Lately, unwanted adolescent emotions seemed to be infecting her body. Almost angrily, she forced herself to collect her scattered thoughts.

"I believe," she replied slowly, "and Whitman might very well disagree, that he perceived God, speaking his love through every infinitesimal fragment and essence of his creation. Still, Whitman expressed it through the context of his accepted model of existence. He was a transcendentalist." Here Kate paused and spoke very carefully. "But however and in whatever context he expressed it, what he perceived is very real."

Jonas closed his eyes and sighed. "Yes," he said. "But Maggie, he left out the darkness."

Both of them were silent.

"Jonas?"

"Yes?" Jonas didn't open his eyes. Maggie detected the wetness gather at the edge of one closed eyelid until it formed a small ball that gravity pulled down onto his face.

"What's going on with you? Can I help?"

Jonas slid his chair back and leaned forward with his head in his hands. Maggie didn't know if it was from the pain, or to hide the tears.

"I've been wrong about everything."

"I don't understand."

"I know you don't, Maggie." Jonas wiped his face and ran his hands through his hair in one motion. He looked at her with tortured eyes, speaking with practiced control, "I am sorry, but I'm not quite ready to talk about it. I am so sorry to have bothered you with this tonight."

Maggie smiled sadly at him. "I am *not* sorry," she said. "But it's okay. We can talk about it some other time."

They sat and gazed at each other until Maggie saw the tension leave his shoulders like a horse that has just given in to the rider's weight on its back. Jonas appeared to have reached some understanding. She was glad that his attention centered on what he was learning. He had seemed oblivious to her attraction to him. She was well aware that a part of her desired to see signs of a mutual attraction from Jonas. She scolded herself but it didn't stop a smile from reaching her face.

Jonas was two steps inside the apartment when he realized he was not alone. There was an extra light on, and the place smelled of herbal shampoo. He rounded the corner from the stairs to find Jimmy Dean's mom sitting at his table in front of the computer. He stopped abruptly and then walked over to sit down at the table next to her. He glanced at the screen, but it didn't appear to be on.

"Jess, what are you doing here? Where's Jimmy Dean?"

She returned his gaze evenly with a quirky little smirk as if she knew a secret and was about to use it. "He's in bed. I came over here to talk to you."

"Why didn't you come over to Maggie's?"

Her eyes didn't waver. "Because... I didn't want to talk to Maggie; I wanted to talk to you."

Jonas was puzzled. "Why? Is there something wrong? Is Jimmy Dean all right?"

"He's fine. Look, this isn't about Jimmy Dean. I want to know what you said to Bo the other day. No—actually I want to know what you said and *did* to Bo."

Jonas couldn't figure out the look on Jess' face. Was it anger—amusement? She was confident, as if she was in control, holding a trump card and intending to play it. He deliberated over what to say, and how to say it, but finally just told her the truth. "I didn't want Jimmy Dean to go with him while he was drunk, high—whatever he was that day. I just wanted to disable him temporarily. Why? He's okay, isn't he?"

Jess leaned forward and gazed even more intently. "I figured you did somethin' like that. But what did you say to him?"

"I explained that he'd better stay away from Jimmy Dean."

Fury instantly took over Jess' eyes. "That ain't up to you to say!" She huffed several loud sighs before calming down. "He claimed you threatened to kill him."

Jonas sighed. "I didn't say I was going to kill him. I just said he would be sorry if he didn't stay away. Listen. He's no good, Jess. I'm sorry." There was a short silence. "You know, actually I'm not sorry. I did what I thought was necessary to keep him from harming Jimmy Dean. I couldn't take it if something happened to that boy. And I was afraid of what he might do to you, too."

Jonas's speech had quite an effect on Jess. It was the most words he had spoken to her at one time. It was rare for him to be so expressive about caring. She surprised him by quickly kneeling in front of his chair. Leaning over his knees, she wrapped her arms around him awkwardly, laying her head in his lap, saying nothing. He was so stunned, he didn't move. Her hair spilled over his lap, head turned sidewise, eyes closed. His fingers pulled the hair back from her face and traced paths through the locks. She was a little girl, holding him tightly as he gently caressed the locks around her ears.

They said nothing for the longest time until she raised her head, stood up, and straddled him to sit in his lap, arms around his neck. She smelled of toothpaste, soap, and shampoo. Her eyes were clear. He realized that, at least for tonight, at least for this moment, she was not high. Her fingers moved around to the back of his neck. She gazed into his eyes and then at his mouth before kissing him. The soft warmth of her lips almost captured him in intensifying need.

But, as she laid her head on his shoulder with her breath washing over his neck, he felt something switch in his mind. *Unfaithful.* The thought came unbidden, and he wasn't ready for it. Then a second thought cooled his blood. It was as if he envisioned a dozen possible futures at the end of dark and twisted tunnels in time. At the end of each was Jimmy Dean, somehow diminished. Jonas couldn't bear it. He almost pushed her away as if to say, *I can't do this,* when a better idea came to him.

His touch became a father's. He held her, rocking for prolonged minutes until she was asleep. He carried her to the bed, wrapped her in a quilt and carried her home across the pasture. If she ever woke, she didn't show it. It was only on her porch that she opened her eyes. She raised her head to kiss him again, but he brushed her forehead with his lips first before carrying her to the couch inside.

Once back out of the house and into the pasture, Jonas jogged back to enter the apartment. He ran upstairs, opened a cupboard, and pulled down a bottle, stared at it, then unscrewed the lid to pour it down the sink. Dropping the empty bottle into a wastebasket, he sat in front of the computer, booted, and navigated to the Puzzled Poet.

Reading Kate's welcome to the blog, he scrolled to read the poem by *guiltersleeves* once again. He frowned in the dim light from the monitor. He read Kate's comment below his own again. He didn't know why he had thought Kate had written the poem. It just seemed to fit. Was the lack of a reply by the author a comment in itself? He must have offended or intimidated *guiltersleeves* when all he had actually wanted to do was talk to Kate. He winced and whispered quietly to himself. *So much to say and I have no idea how to say it.*

CHAPTER 15 - SICILY
HATTIESBURG, MS – NOVEMBER 2005

Kate rose before dawn. The smell of coffee brewing and bread baking let her know someone was already stirring in the common area of the Bouie Bend lodge. She dressed and walked down the hall to find Paul building a fire.

"Here's an early riser," he said.

Mary, who was puttering around in the kitchen, looked up with concern. "I hope we didn't make so much noise we woke you up."

Kate assured them she had already been awake before the pleasant aroma had drifted to her suite. Asking if she could help, Mary quickly put her to work, chopping bell pepper and onion to go in the omelets Mary was preparing to cook.

By the time the Smiths arrived, the fire was blazing. The table was laden with fruit, pitchers of juice and milk, a covered wooden bowl full of raspberry muffins just out of the oven, and plates waiting for the omelets to arrive. Jim and Vivian Smith were going to leave for Albuquerque soon after breakfast. The older couple's company made her conscious of the extent of her loneliness. She would have more freedom but was sorry they were leaving.

After helping clean up, Kate went back to her sitting room to call the foster care counselor on her cell phone, but noticing it was still before 8:00 a.m., she called her mom instead. Within five minutes, she regretted it. Risk taking was not a behavior her mother understood. Nothing Kate could say was going to reassure her. The spaces between them felt like a maze with no solution. "Is dad around?" she finally asked, sighing loud enough for her to get the hint.

Her mother set the phone down. Kate could hear her hollering in the distance. She waited until a screen door slammed and her father's out-of-breath voice came over the line. "What's up Pumpkin? I guess you made it there safely."

"Yes, Dad. Everything went smoothly. I didn't have any problems."

"Did the pickup run all right?"

Kate had anticipated his interest in the truck. She wouldn't be able to praise it enough to satisfy him.

"It's great. You were right. It's the perfect vehicle for coming down here."

"I'm glad you like it, Pumpkin. Don't forget to lock the back lid. Check the tire pressure if you have to go through water or areas with debris." He went on to remind her of advice he had already given several times. After a while, as she often did, she quit listening to his words and just listened to his calming voice and its rhythm. It reminded her of the muddy river outside her window, describing the endless flow of life that she could not stop or even grasp for a moment.

Kate finally interrupted, "Dad, Dad. Thanks for your help. I really have to go. I just… I just wanted to let you and Mom know that I'm fine. I'm not going to New Orleans until Friday. Sara is going with me. We're just going to drive there, take care of business and leave. I'll call you this weekend."

The parental pain of not being able to do anything for one's child, pain Kate knew all too well herself, resonated in her father's voice as they said goodbye. There was nothing she could do to remove it, no more than she could eliminate the guilt in her own voice.

Next, she called Bud to tell him how great the Inn and the

Birgsons had been so far. His voice expressed concern as well. She realized she might as well get used to it. It was no different with Mandy who was next on her list. People cared. Not letting them help stole the very thing that enriched their lives.

Finally, she called the Foster Care counselor who answered in an alto voice with a deep-south accent. Kate introduced herself.

"Oh hi. Sara Arceneaux said you were gonna call," Frieda Cross said. She told me you wanted to meet with Sicily."

"Yes. Did she explain why?"

"Yes, Uh-huh. I don't think it'll be a problem. I just have to talk with Sissy's foster mother. When do you want to meet with them?"

Kate didn't want to appear pushy, but she answered without hesitation. "As soon as possible, actually. I'm in Hattiesburg. Whenever it is convenient for the foster parents, and Sicily, of course."

"Okay. Mr. Jones won't be there, but I'll call Mrs. Jones this morning and then call you back. I'm sure Sissy is in school. Maybe you could meet with them tomorrow, or is this afternoon too soon?"

"This afternoon is perfect," answered Kate. "Actually, I prefer it. But whatever works for them." She paused. "Could you please give her parents my phone number? I can work it out with them—that is—unless you want to be present. Which is fine with me," she added. Kate was mentally kicking herself. She couldn't quit adding words on top of words. She wondered why she was so nervous.

She could overhear a discussion on the other end of the line. Frieda was talking to someone else, and then she was back on the phone shortly. "Okay. I'll call you back after I speak with her. I'm sorry, but I have to attend a meeting right now for about an hour. Give me your number and I'll call Gladys as soon as I get out," she said, now in a hurry.

Kate gave Frieda her cell number, and they hung up.

Now, what? She probably had at least an hour. She contemplated going for a walk but didn't want to risk walking out of range of a working cell signal. She didn't quite have four bars at the lodge.

Instead, she made a phone call to the New Orleans Police Department to let them know she was coming on Friday. After almost ten minutes of being on hold, the detective on the other end took down her information and promised nothing.

Once again, she despaired of obtaining any help from the police, logged onto her computer and checked email. There were five more replies to the Puzzled Poet newbie thread. Four were regular users. The other, Charlotte Baines, was one of the other moderators.

Kate read her response and sighed. Charlotte always gushed over a new male presence on the message board, especially if the new user wasn't knowledgeable about poetry. She loved to guide their education, trying to "put an old head on a young shoulder," but tended to smother them until they began to ignore her, or ran away.

Her reply focused on anecdotes about poets who also had other avocations, such as James Dickey. She praised b4Isleep on his introduction and was verbose with her offer to help him with any questions he might have about poetry. Charlotte had also posted a scathing review of the poem Kate had posted under the pseudonym, calling it pretentious and derivative. *Oh Charlotte, what perfect adjectives for your own poetic attempts.* The thought made her laugh. She was happy to escape from Charlotte for a while.

She then sent a short private message to b4Isleep.

If Charlotte becomes a little "too much," just ignore her. She'll soon move on to another victim.

Kate glanced outside again and carried her cell outside on the deck in front of the lodge. The Smiths were getting ready to leave, putting their luggage in the car. She walked out to say goodbye, noticing that her service was actually better. They wished her luck in her search, waving goodbye as they left.

She stood there after their car had disappeared from sight and listened. The wind whistled through the last of the leaves and the naked limbs of the trees. Occasionally a truck jake-braked down some unknown hill in the distance, like tubas providing bass contrast to the higher frequency sound of tires on pavement. A few birds were singing, but a drifting hawk cast its shadow, gliding silently over and disappearing beyond the lodge.

Her cell phone rang, startling her. Sicily's foster parent, Gladys was on the phone.

"Frieda, our foster care counselor, gave me your phone number. She told me you wanted to talk to me about meeting Sicily."

"Yes. I'm so glad you called. Did she tell you why?" Kate's cell beeped and vibrated again. "Oh, wait. She's calling me right now. May I put you on hold for a second?"

Kate switched her phone to take Frieda's call, explained that she was already on the phone with Gladys, and promised to call back later to let her know how everything had gone. She quickly switched her phone back to Gladys.

"Are you still there?"

"Yes, I'm here." Gladys' voice was not quite as pleasant.

"Okay. I'm sorry. Did Frieda tell you why I wanted to meet with Sicily?"

"I'm 'fraid I don't understand. Something to do with Sissy's rescue?"

Kate began to explain and then stopped. "You know what? It's kind of a long story. Would you mind meeting with me? I'd like to take you to lunch."

Kate looked around at the memorabilia on the wall—old sporting goods equipment and musical instruments—and smiled to herself. She had only been in Hattiesburg for 24 hours, and here she was in Applebees a second time. This time, Gladys had suggested it. Kate was simply grateful for the meeting.

Gladys had warmed to Kate within a few minutes of hearing her story over the soup and salad. She held her coffee tightly, only setting it down to twist a wedding band and a black lock of hair behind her ear as she listened. Gladys had only heard the essentials of Sicily's rescue from Frieda, who had focused on the loss of Sicily's father and the trauma she had gone through during the weeks following the hurricane.

Kate told her story while focusing on their table, unconsciously rearranging napkins and silverware, and tracing lines on the tabletop with her forefinger. Gladys only interrupted her once to ask why Daniel had stayed in New Orleans. Kate had no answer for that. She didn't want to start attempting to explain about the man who looked like Daniel.

"That's actually one reason I want to talk to Sicily. I was hoping she might remember something, anything that might help me understand."

Kate finally saw a grudging acceptance begin to transform Gladys' face. Still, it was evident that she was not a woman who necessarily followed understanding with empathy.

"I don't know what she might know or remember. I never talked to her about that day. She ain't even talked about her daddy, at least not with me. Frieda said Sicily spoke to a shrink and was okay."

Kate smiled back. "I understand. I promise not to pressure her. I just want to meet her."

Gladys nodded unenthusiastically. "Okay. She's the youngest of the kids. We have two others who have been with us for more than a year. They're all in school right now. You can come over to the house and meet her when she gets home."

Kate reached across the table to grab the other woman's hand. They sat like that for a few seconds until Gladys pulled her hand away to reach for the strand of hair behind her ear.

It was exactly as Gladys had said. The girls came home and made a lot of noise. Doors banged. Giggles and shouts rang out. Sicily appeared, looking shyly around the doorjamb into the kitchen. She was so small. Kate gazed at her with delight, completely unprepared for the leap her heart made, merely at the sight of her.

"Are you Sicily?" she asked.

Sicily smiled, but turned her eyes downward and ran bashfully to

Gladys. Only with a familiar human anchor was she confident enough to look at Kate again. Gladys turned the girl around until she was facing Kate and lifted her on her knee.

"Sissy, this is Kate. She's come all the way from Missouri to talk to you."

Kate thought that Sicily might not have any idea where Missouri was. Glancing back over her shoulder at Gladys' face, she questioned her with big eyes. Many strangers had wanted to talk with her over the last several weeks, but Sicily still wasn't quite used to it. She glanced back at Kate and then surprised both of them by hopping down and going over to climb on Kate's lap. She didn't say anything but started rearranging Kate's empty coffee cup, a spoon, and a sugar bowl.

Kate felt the warm little body sitting on her lap. She instinctively ran fingers through Sicily's hair, gathering strands together and then separating them once again.

"You're a very sweet girl, Sicily. How old are you?"

"Seven," she almost whispered, her small voice lilting upward. The sweetness of her voice tugged at Kate. Her fingers never stopped their movement, and now they had made an angle with the fork and knife—the number 7.

"Do you like school?"

"Yes."

"What grade are you in?"

"I don't know." She sang the words as if it was a jingle.

Kate looked over at Gladys who held up two fingers. She didn't know how to begin asking about the rescue. Yet, somehow, Kate wasn't particularly worried about it. She was content with holding the girl while she played with the shapes the dinnerware made. Sicily had an eye for patterns.

"Sicily, do you like to draw?" asked Kate abruptly.

The little girl smiled, nodding at Kate. Kate reached for her purse, pulled out a steno-sized notebook and pen, and put the pen in Sicily's little hand.

"Will you draw something for me?"

Kate and Gladys watched as Sicily switched the pen to her left hand and puzzled over the blank paper. She tilted her head to the right and then to the left, before drawing a square box which became a house with the addition of a triangle. Two circles became a car in front of the house, followed by billowing clouds in the sky. After outlining the clouds, she frowned. After a long pause, she finally drew two doors in the house and then stopped. Sicily was no longer a cheerful little girl.

"Is that your house, Sicily?"

She nodded but didn't say anything.

"Can you draw yourself in front of the house?"

Sicily puckered her lips, and added a small figure with a hat, holding something that might have been a purse. She paused for a second and then added another taller figure to her side.

"Is that your dad?"

She nodded slowly.

"Did anyone else live at your house, sweetheart?"

Sicily didn't answer or even nod, but she drew another figure beside the car.

Gladys scooted her chair closer, giving Kate a puzzled stare. They both focused back on the drawing.

"Who is that, hon?"

"Jonas," she said matter-of-factly.

Who was Jonas? Kate's mind reeled. She was almost afraid to ask the words which were on her mind. She held the girl's hand still. She tensed and spoke louder than she intended.

"Sicily honey, is he the man who rescued you?"

Sicily looked up with wide, worried eyes.

"What was his name?" Kate asked, choking. She heard the fear in her own voice, tears running unbidden down her face. Sicily was frightened now. She saw the terrible emotional turmoil on Kate's face; it was too much. She slid off her lap and ran from the room.

"No, no hon, I'm sorry," Kate cried out.

"Shhhh," Gladys scolded. "She'll be okay. Let me check on her. I'll be back."

Gladys disappeared through the door and down a hallway. Her voice, murmuring in low tones to Sicily, filtered out to Kate who sat at the table and rocked. She was unable to keep the tears from flowing, betraying the pent up emotions she held in check every day, always telling herself that everything was going to be okay. She quickly used all of her tissues and reached for a napkin on the table. What a disaster. Kate was determined not to put her through any more pain, even if it meant she didn't find out anything more.

Gaining control, she was about to leave when Gladys and Sicily appeared back in the doorway hand-in-hand. Gladys led her back over to the table.

"I told Sicily you were sad because you had lost someone in the hurricane too." Gladys appeared protective or annoyed—it was hard to say. Surprisingly, Sicily came back over and climbed in her lap. Kate didn't say anything. She held the little girl and felt her own reluctance to let go.

Kate could tell that Gladys was ready for her to leave. Her body was as stiff as the back of the chair she held onto, looking out through the door toward the front of the house. Kate sat Sicily down beside the chair, kissed her forehead, and said goodbye.

Kate was already on the phone filling in Mandy when she arrived back at the inn. They continued to talk as she walked a path by the river. Kate was glad to notice there was cell service even in such an out-of-the-way place. Distracted by the discussion, she almost missed the white tail of a retreating doe across the river in the growing twilight. The glassy stillness of the water and the dropping temperature broke into her awareness until her shoulders shook from a sudden chill.

She hurried back, climbing the stairs to unlock the door to her suite. She had asked the Birgsons not to wait around for her in the evenings. She wanted to be able to follow any leads as they developed. There was no longer a fire in the fireplace, but the place was still warm and inviting.

She always vented all of her doubts and frustrations to Mandy who was supportive but could be impatient if Kate was making too much of a situation. She was now stern with her advice over the phone.

"Kate, that little girl has been through a whole lot more than seeing you burst into tears. And you—think about what you may endure and witness before this is done."

"I know, but if you meet Sicily, you'll understand. She is adorable and yet so sad. She clung to me."

"You can't get attached. Doesn't she have a family?"

"Mandy, they haven't found any record of more family members in New Orleans. Frankly, the police have probably quit looking. She may be stuck in foster care for some time, although she probably wouldn't be there for long as sweet as she is."

Kate's voice trailed off as she allowed herself to consider the possibilities. Could she take care of Sicily herself?

Mandy began warning her, "Kate, what are you thinking? Don't rush into anything. I know exactly what you think because I know you."

Kate laughed at this. "Come on. I'm not going to rush into anything."

"Yeah, right."

"No, seriously; I'm sure they have laws and waiting lists down here. Who knows what else? Is it even possible?"

"Ask Gilbert. He could probably find out for you."

Kate snorted. "Now you're the one suggesting it."

"No, really I'm not. I'm just sayin'. Listen, you need to keep your priorities straight. I should have come down there with you."

"Well, I need to get off here. I barely got in the house, and I'm freezing to death. I'm going to take a bath. I'll talk to you tomorrow."

"Oh, all right. Do whatever you're gonna do. You always do no matter what I say, anyway."

"Love ya."

"Love you too. Bye."

A bath and flannels had her feeling toasty. She made a sandwich and a cup of hot chocolate in the kitchen and brought it back to eat while she checked email. Nothing. She called Sara.

"Hello Kate," Sara answered in a sleepy voice.

"Hi. Did I wake you up?"

"Yeah, but that's a good thing. Needed to get up. I didn't get to sleep right away this morning because I had a fight with my sister."

"Oh, no. What about?"

"Nothin'. Just her crap. She's irresponsible. I tell her straight, and that's all it takes."

"She's lived by herself already and doesn't need big Sis telling her what to do?"

"Yeah. 'Bout the size of it. How'd your day go?"

"I met Sicily. Totally screwed it up."

"Really? C'mon. I'll bet you didn't. What happened?"

Kate explained, leaving nothing out. Still, in the telling, she became aware that the situation didn't sound as bad as it had felt before. Sara listened without comment through most of it. She wanted Kate to explain what she had experienced while holding Sicily. Kate talked about how much she hated the thought of Sicily being stuck in the foster care system. And, she admitted that she was surprised by feelings of attachment.

"Okay, so go on," encouraged Sara.

Kate smiled. "You know, whenever I have something to tell you, I always feel like I'm being interrogated. You keep me talking."

"Oh well. Yeah, I'm sorry about that. Habit I guess."

"No, don't be sorry. It must be a useful skill for a detective. I should have had you with me the first time I met Sicily. It might have turned out quite differently." She paused. "What if I was close to finding out something about the man who rescued her? Maybe it was Daniel. I don't know. What do you think?"

Sara sounded puzzled. "It *is* interesting that she drew another man in front of her house. Was he her angel? That is the question. It hadn't even occurred to me to ask if she had met her rescuer before that day."

"What I'm concerned about," said Kate, "is that Gladys is not going to talk to me again."

"Don't worry about that." Sara was adamant. "I mean, yeah, she may be annoyed, but give it a few days. Try again next week."

"I'm not very patient. You know? Knowing something more about Sicily's angel could make a difference when we go to New Orleans on Friday morning."

"Well, call her tomorrow then. Feel your way through it."

Kate felt like Sara was trying to tell her in a polite way that she was making too much of the situation, but then Sara spoke again.

"And, Kate?"

"Yes?"

"Don't worry so much. Gladys is not Sicily's mother. Yes, she is supposed to protect her, but you haven't done anything wrong."

"Okay. Okay. Thank you. Listen, I don't want to be overly sentimental, but you make me feel better. I don't believe I could do any of this without you."

"Katie, hang in there. We'll get through it."

"Have a good night."

"See ya."

Off the phone, Kate was not sure what to do. She turned the lights down and stared out the window. TV bored her. Kate was no more alone here than she was in her own house back in Missouri, but she was acutely aware of her isolation. She read for a while before logging back on to the computer. b4Isleep had been back on. After reading his message through twice, she immediately typed out a reply.

CHAPTER 16 – ONLINE STRANGERS
BENFORD, TN – NOVEMBER 2005

Jonas had half-expected Jess to be with Jimmy Dean when he came over to Maggie's on Wednesday. He was relieved when the boy showed up on his own and had nothing to say about his mother. After completing their drills, Jimmy Dean helped Jonas pour some concrete to support a downspout extension and then went inside to tackle homework with Maggie. Jonas relaxed in a recliner with a book, frequently pausing to listen in.

Maggie was leaving soon to attend her Wednesday night small group at church, so the boys had sandwiches, chips, and an apple for dinner. Jimmy Dean gulped his down. He started to leave—only stopping at the door to mention he still had to study his lines for a Thanksgiving skit at school.

"Wait a second. When is the program, Jimmy Dean?" asked Maggie. "And why is this the first time you are telling us about it?"

Jimmy Dean's "I don't know" lingered in the air as he ran out the door.

Maggie shook her head. "That boy. I'll have to find out when the program is."

Jonas took the opportunity to leave as well. He was anxious to get back online. Thoughts of what Kate had written on the poetry blog had worried him all day. His Whitman quote had apparently been misunderstood; it bothered him to have already offended a participant. Jonas prided himself on thinking and communicating clearly. Accurately conveying his ideas concerning poetry was difficult in a way he had never encountered before.

He was beginning to have a sense of the poets' skill at conveying meaning and emotion within the constraints of the poetic form. As if those boundaries didn't complicate it enough, there was also the need to understand how a work might be a response to other writing that had come before. At this point in his understanding, he viewed poetry as a past-to-present, global conversation—a game of which he was so ignorant, he didn't even have a notion of how to break the rules.

Back inside the apartment, he brewed a pot of coffee before sitting down at the computer. He re-read two poems regarding death and studied some of the explanatory material from an anthology. Finally, he had something to say. First, a private message to Kate.

> Thanks for the warning about Charlotte. I have a mentor of sorts who is helping me understand poetry better. She refrains from giving me her own opinions, trying to help me figure it out on my own. I probably won't be posting much until I learn a little more, or at least attempt to write a poem myself.
>
> I wish I had not posted the original reply to the poem. To be frank, I was naïve enough to conclude the poem was a personal confession. I wanted to rescue the writer, I guess. I feel a bit foolish.
>
> I haven't quite had the time to navigate the site yet. Do you have any of your own work posted here? Thank you again for your welcome to the board.

After completing the private message, he went back to read the poems in the anthology that had caught his eye. Philip Larkin's "Aubade," like most of the poems concerning death, was just as adamant that nothing followed death as Whitman's Song had suggested that there was an existence afterward. He noted to himself to run this poem by Maggie. How would she react to Larkin referring to religion as "that vast moth-eaten musical brocade, created to pretend we never die?"

He frowned. He was amazed at the rhythm of the painstaking words, but Larkin's certainty annoyed him, even if he mostly agreed. But no, he actually didn't agree that everyone's ultimate fear was of life ending at death. His own greater fear was a vague, but definite unease over eternal existence. He could not imagine living forever and was convinced he didn't want to.

The computer screen showed he now had a private message reply from Kate:

> Charlotte is Charlotte. Since you already have someone assisting you with poetry, I won't worry about you succumbing to her web. I'm curious how you became interested in poetry and found someone to help. Are you attending a class, or perhaps a group? I'm always fascinated with how people come to poetry because, as you can probably imagine, it's hard to interest those who are not involved in literature. I know you have been reading Whitman... and I'm assuming Frost based on your username. Who/what else have you been reading?

> Don't worry too much about thinking yourself a fool because of what you have written on the message board. Actually, I think your instinct about the poem being confessional was probably right on. It is more common on sites like ours for the posted poetry to be confessional than the majority of published works. If you think about it, most of the posters are amateurs working out their life with the words they put down. It isn't unusual for a person to post a poem in a fit of self-revelation and then be too self-conscious to return to the board.

> I am glad to have your involvement on the site. When you are ready to post that first original work, I hope you will post it here.

She had ended the message with instructions for locating her original poems on the site.

Jonas stared at the screen with some relief. Kate was on the other end of this message. He knew this had been his goal when he first logged onto the Puzzled Poet. What had happened to his vow back in August to be reserved, to keep distance between himself and other people? It had happened much more quickly than he had anticipated. He had assumed that it would be difficult to spark the curiosity of one particular person in such a close-knit group as the poetry blog users.

Jonas started to type a response but then deleted it. He went down to the garage, looking for something to work on while he thought about Kate's message. He read his parts list for a welded wrought iron arbor to give Maggie for Christmas but decided against working on it for now. Checkmarks showed he was only about halfway through the list. At the top of the list was a reminder in his handwriting—*measure twice—cut once*. He put the list back down. He was not in a right frame of mind to make accurate cuts tonight.

Back at the apartment, he sat at the computer again, replying slowly, one point at a time.

> Hello again. I'll try to answer your questions, but I'm afraid it will be a disappointment. I became interested in poetry quite recently. My neighbor is a retired teacher with a sizeable library. I was looking through her shelves for something to read one evening. For some reason, a book of Robert Frost's poetry caught my attention.
>
> I liked his work immediately. To me, his poems are bigger on the inside than they look from the outside, and you can't quite figure out how or why. I still don't understand how he says so much with such few and simple words. I guess he hooks into your own experience. Still, his poems made me feel almost uneasy at times because they're so personal.
>
> I have been gradually reading an anthology borrowed from my neighbor. She has helped me understand types of poetry, meter and rhythm, forms, and allegory. She asks questions. I ask

questions. Then she asks more questions. I'm just beginning. I haven't been spending that much time on it.

There is much I do not understand or appreciate. Maybe someday I will be able to. Until then, it's enough when I happen on passages like the following from Richard Wilbur's "Hamlen Brook." He describes the brook and the surrounding environment and then says, "How shall I drink all this?" Then this, "Joy's trick is to supply dry lips with what can cool and slake, leaving them dumbstruck also with an ache nothing can satisfy."

I want to believe that type of joy can exist, and I recognize it somehow, even though I have never fully experienced it. My neighbor seems to have it, which might have something to do with her faith, which I do not have. Anyway, it is passages like that, you know, that keep me interested. Puzzling through poetry is like the drink, satisfying at times, yet always leaving me wanting more.

I hope that answers your questions. I still haven't had a chance to read your work yet, but will soon. Thanks again.

Maggie's faith. He could not deny it was real. What she does agrees with what she says, unlike most people, including me, he thought.

Jonas looked up. *If You're there, You've never spoken to me.* He didn't want to be profane. It was simply the truth. He could hear in his mind Maggie saying, "Have you ever truly listened?" So... Jonas sat there attending to the whole universe, dense with silence. Silence and more silence.

That's what I thought, a waste of time. He deliberated until it turned into a conversation with himself, still holding out slight hope that God was listening.

Do you believe God didn't know that you expected nothing?

Maggie says God loves us as we are. I can't help it if I'm not sure and just want to find out—to know for myself. If He were there, He would understand that I doubt. Even when I attempt to pray, I doubt. I can't seem to help that.

Is that honest?

Honest to God? I don't know if it is true. I don't know what is true. If He cared—

Whom are you talking to now?

Myself. Talking to myself. Am I only talking to myself?

Jonas was silent.

The universe was silent as well, but it no longer seemed dense and unapproachable. In fact, it no longer seemed anything. There was a real presence that didn't require his thoughts. Could it be God… was listening—even amused? He was almost certain it was so.

He finally looked down to see that he had another message from Kate.

> Don't worry about what you know or don't know. Your experience with poetry is anything but disappointing. You came to it with no pretensions. That is unusual, frankly. There is something about the act of writing poetry that makes what is real and what is phony obvious. Maybe that is what attracts people who find it difficult to attain an authentic voice.
>
> I like your neighbor's approach. She isn't pushing her own opinions or judgment on you. Your thoughts on joy are similar to what I love about poetry, although sometimes I think that it promises more than it delivers. Perhaps that's a good thing. I'll follow your neighbor's lead and leave you to your own conclusions.
>
> I've read that Frost could be severe, but I agree with you; his poems are deceptively simple. That was part of his genius. I very much enjoyed reading your perspective. Thanks for taking the time to share.

Jonas noticed the congruence of his own musings with what Kate had written. Clearly, there was no intentional irony in her "phony" comment, but it had slammed him. As much as he avoided it, he was acutely aware of how deep the gap was between what was true and what was not, at least for himself. It was like a gallery of witnesses around him pointing his direction: Frost, Maggie, and Kate—maybe even the Almighty Himself. He just didn't see any way out. The phone rang. He was afraid it was Jess, but it was Maggie.

"The Thanksgiving skit is tomorrow night."

"That soon?"

"Do you want to go?"

"No. Yes. Of course. What time does it start?"

"7:00 p.m. I talked with Jess on the phone and she wants to ride with us. Jimmy Dean has to be there at 6:15 p.m."

"Oh." Jonas's tone was doubtful.

"What? Is the time a problem?"

Jonas gritted his teeth. The problem wasn't the 'when' but the 'whom.' He didn't want to have to explain. "No, I guess not. What do people wear to these things?"

Maggie laughed. "Wear a clean pair of pants and shirt. Okay? So we'll leave here about 6:00 to pick up Jess and Jimmy Dean?"

"Sure. Okay. See you tomorrow night."

Jonas sat on the plastic bleachers between a very proud Maggie—who knew everyone around her—and Jess who was having a quarrel with the controls of a borrowed video camera. Jonas was pressed on all sides. Toddlers rode rows of parents like mosh pit surfers, and little ladies leaned on Jonas's legs and back to catch Maggie's ear. Jess used her troubles with the camera and the noise of a hundred conversations as an excuse to press her body against him and put her mouth in his ear. "I told Bo to get lost," she said—rather loudly, he thought, looking to see if Maggie had heard.

He had been introduced and explained, nodded at by Bart from the hardware store, and waved to by people he knew from the plant. The middle school gym hummed with human voices and activity. Jonas had already shed his jacket, rolling up his sleeves to get away from the crowd's combined body heat. He had to continually slide forward on the bleacher seat, contoured in a manner designed to dump him off backward into the aisle behind him. It was loud, uncomfortable, and almost claustrophobic. In spite of it all, Jonas was surprised to be having a fantastic time.

When Jimmy Dean, playing the part of Daniel Carver said his first line, Jonas was so proud, tears came to his eyes. Every person in the audience connected in some manner to at least one kid in the performance. They were as appreciative as a Broadway crowd and more involved. At one point in the performance, they had roared with laughter and pure enjoyment over the kids.

Walking out into the parking lot, Jimmy Dean had to know if they had all heard him speak his lines. He hugged his mom, Maggie, and Jonas. Then he wanted all four of them to hug. Jess took another opportunity to squeeze against Jonas. Then Jimmy Dean had to hi-five Billy Wallace who had played the part of Squanto. Billy's family joined the group.

Jonas excused himself to go warm up Maggie's car. None of them had noticed Bo staring out the window of his pickup on the outside edge of the parking lot. When Jonas walked near, Bo opened the door and rushed him. Jonas' peripheral vision registered the figure coming at him. Surprised, he whirled, trying to block the blow of a large crescent wrench.

He wasn't quite quick enough. The wrench glanced off his forearm, slowing it, before connecting with his skull. Jonas' vision starred. Bo tried to hit him again with a blow from his other fist. Jonas ducked to the side. The fist grazed his head. Still turning, he swept a leg into Bo's side. He was too close to the pickup. His balance was wrong. The weak kick missed the intended ribs but accidently connected with a better spot. Bo grunted as Jonas' boot knocked the wrench from his grasp.

"That kung fu ain't gonna help you this time. You're dead, man."

Jonas lurched across a sidewalk and into the street, trying to open space to move freely. Bo didn't pause to pick up the wrench, pressing his greater bulk, rapidly swinging fists to overpower the lighter man. Jonas methodically defended each punch, retreating with measured steps, blood trickling down into his left eye. Bo sneered, but he was breathing harder. Jonas wiped the blood from his forehead with his sleeve in between the blocks. The more labored Bo's breathing, the wilder his swings became, all hooking to miss or land uselessly on Jonas' shoulders or arms.

Realization began to worry Bo's eyes. Jonas was wearing him down without striking a blow. Now almost desperately, Bo rushed to body tackle, but Jonas threw himself to the side again, lashing out with another kick, catching him in the ribs with a crack. He had delivered this strike with power. He took a deep breath as Bo folded a bit, still standing, but favoring his side.

Neither one noticed the gathering group of onlookers. Jonas quickly jabbed as Bo approached, relieved to have restored space and balance. The hard fist connected with Bo's jaw, snapping his head back. Bo stopped, now wary. His initial strikes of surprise and power were gone. Blood still dripped from Jonas' scalp but didn't keep him from seeing.

Bo's gaze darted from Jonas to the crowd. Without warning, he charged, swinging as before, but Jonas stood ready, delaying his move to flow with the attack. Whipping his arms across his body, his right hand parried Bo's rush as his left elbow exploded back into the same ribs he had just kicked. Jonas continued his motion into a spinning kick to the back of Bo's head. The powerful kick propelled Bo forward, but his feet didn't follow as he collapsed in the street face down. Several of the crowd gasped in the silence that followed.

Jonas ignored the onlookers' stares. For the second time in a matter of days, he helped an unsteady Bo into his pickup. This time, Jess didn't drive him away. One of his more respectable cousins brought him a bottle of water and hurriedly drove Bo and his truck home while his "old lady" and the kids followed behind. Someone in the crowd called the city police, but by the time they arrived, there was nobody left with a coherent story of what had happened.

Jonas hated that so many people had witnessed the fight. He hoped they knew he hadn't started it. Jess had begun to bad mouth Bo but had stopped when she got no response from the others. He worried what Maggie's reaction had been since she hadn't mentioned it. She had quickly changed the subject to talk about the Thanksgiving program. Jimmy Dean was still excited about his performance, and Jonas' mood lifted too as they all relived the funniest parts. In his apartment that night, Jonas wrote and posted his first poem on the Puzzled Poet.

An Elementary Thanksgiving

*Sitting cross-legged on the gym floor opposite
a grinning Miles Standish, Massasoit was tickled.
Mid-sentence into his sober speech he giggled
into a microphone, carrying to the top seats,
all the way up to his mom and dad whose faces
were now more stone-faced appropriate for his part.
You'd have thought the Pilgrims had heard Massasoit fart
for all the laughter that broke out in various places
across the floor and among the parents in the bleachers.
Daniel Carver valiantly carried on, until he too relented,
his howls much stronger for having been prevented.
The very last to laugh were the supervising teachers.*

*Just as the last chortle had given way to blown
noses and sighs, Samoset jumped up, tearing
loose the last bead in a long string of beads he was wearing,
sending the rest cascading, and letting out such a moan,
the Pilgrims and parents had reason to let spill
what hilarity remained barely contained. Native Americans
chased and swarmed escaping beads like pelicans
on a school of fish, (to plant with corn in little hills).
The director grabbed the narrator and sent her in
to take charge of the mayhem and explain the gifts
of the natives, Thanksgiving correct, without any myths.
But on the way home…
Daniel Carver said he wished he'd been an Indian.*

CHAPTER 17 – INTO THE CITY
NEW ORLEANS, LA – NOVEMBER 2005

Agent Deborah Spencer informed Kate over the phone on Thursday morning that the FBI had added Daniel to the National Crime Information Missing Person database, based solely on the New Orleans Police Department's evidence. The news initially excited Kate until Agent Spencer told her that the list had hundreds of names. Agent Spencer told her that fingerprints and—in some cases—DNA from found corpses would be matched against the list of missing persons—a slow and daunting process.

She called her attorney, Gilbert, to tell him about the FBI call, and to find out if he had any news in return. Gilbert told her that Daniel's life insurance company would be interested in the FBI involvement. He said he would follow up with them.

Turning her thoughts to the upcoming trip to New Orleans the next morning, Kate tried calling the Des Guise Grill. An answering machine informed her that the restaurant had been closed temporarily until further notice. She read the contact information on the website again. She had already sent an email to the listed address with no results. She then tried a search on the restaurant manager's name, Terrance Lehan, which led to several hits, none of which gave her any contact information. She was angry with herself for waiting days before completing the research.

She considered calling Sara but didn't want to wake her. Gilbert answered the phone, amused that she was calling again so quickly until he listened to her request.

"Listen, Kate, yes I can hire a Private Investigator but are you sure you want to do this? Who is this Terrance Lehan?"

"It's a long story, Gilbert." Kate was adamant. "He's a restaurant manager that might know something about Daniel. Nothing sinister or mysterious. I just want to talk to him, and I'm in a bit of a hurry. I'm going into the city tomorrow."

Gilbert quickly sensed that Kate had little patience for any argument from him. "All right, this should be easy. I'll call you back."

Kate next dialed the NOPD and asked for Lt. Grayling's extension. She was disappointed when it was Detective Manson who answered and not Grayling. "I'm sorry," Kate said. "I asked for Lt. Grayling."

"He isn't available this afternoon. Who am I speaking with?"

Kate paused. She was reluctant to talk to Manson after all that Sara had told her about her former partner. "That's okay. I'll call back another time," she said, abruptly ending the call.

Kate went to the kitchen thinking about how difficult it had been to communicate with the NOPD. She shrugged it off to consider what she had to do to get ready for the trip the next day. While making some toast, her cell rang. She was surprised when it was Gladys, Sicily's foster mother.

"Is this Kate?"

"Hi, Gladys. How are you this morning?"

"I'm okay." "I… I just wanted to call to let you know Sicily mentioned your name several times last night."

Kate was so surprised she hardly knew what to say. Gladys sounded tentative and reluctant, not as sure of herself. "I think she was afraid. Not really afraid—just startled when you began crying. She wasn't expecting it."

"Then, she was okay?" asked Kate, relieved even if the call struck her as being odd. "Will she talk to me again?"

"That's why I called. I was wondering… We—me and my husband—may need to make room for his niece."

Now Kate was astonished. "I'm afraid I don't understand."

"I don't know. This is hard."

Kate sank into a chair near the fireplace as the idea settled on her like snow—light, pleasant, and soft. She let the silence linger. The words left her slowly with a sigh.

"Gladys, even if it is possible, do you believe Sicily will accept me?"

"Yes… I noticed something. Until she got scared, I almost felt like I was the one visiting or something. Uh huh, the two of you got along well."

Kate nodded to herself. She had felt something very like what Gladys seemed to be trying to say. The idea thrilled her, and it frightened her. Still, she always found a way through whatever obstacles got in the way. She could make it happen. She always made things happen. Except when it came to people, sometimes it went wrong. She could take in Sicily but should she?

"How soon, Gladys? How soon is this going to happen?"

"Probably next weekend. If you want, we'll talk together with the foster care counselor. I want to see Sicily go to someone who will sincerely love her—be able to take care of her."

Kate considered it. "Okay. You have to understand this is very sudden for me. I need to think about it. It's not that I don't appreciate it. I'll call you soon, okay? I need to make sure."

Kate immediately called Mandy, starting the conversation by jumping into the middle of her thoughts. "Tell me why I shouldn't become this little girl's foster parent."

Mandy didn't hesitate.

"Are you doing it for her or for you?"

"Both, I think. I'm not sure."

"Are you going to be able to commit to her? Will you have the time to keep searching for Daniel? Speaking of Daniel, what will his reaction be? What will he think?"

What will Daniel think? Kate didn't say anything for several seconds. *Why didn't I think of that? Was it because I know what his reaction will be, or was it because a part of me has already given up?*

"That's why I love you, sweetheart," Kate admitted. "You put things back into the proper perspective."

"Yeah I know," Mandy agreed. "But you're going ahead with it, aren't you?"

"I think so. Yes. I'm certain Daniel will be okay with it."

"I knew it. Somehow, I knew last night this was what you were going to do."

At the end of one conversation, the phone never left Kate's hand before she was talking again.

"Gilbert?" She heard the exasperation in his voice when he replied and pictured him rubbing his bald head.

"Kate. I don't have an answer for you. I haven't even talked to the PI yet."

"That's not why I called. I need something else."

"Maybe you should take the time to make a list and call me when you're finished." Gilbert chuckled.

"Funny, Gilbert. This will be the last call… for today anyway. I need to find out if it is possible to become a foster parent of a child who is a New Orleans refugee."

"Kate—" Gilbert sighed.

The sun had not yet peeked over the horizon when Kate picked up Sara to head for New Orleans. Having completed working a graveyard shift only minutes before, Sara crawled into the back seat of the club cab with a pillow. She fell asleep immediately and didn't wake until Kate became nervous crossing Lake Ponchartrain after driving through Slidell. Trees on the east side of I10 had hidden much of the hurricane aftermath from view, but nothing hid the expanse of water from eyes accustomed to trees and short horizons. Turning up the radio didn't wake Sara so she finally shouted her name.

Sara pulled herself up to peer over the seat and out through the windshield.

"What's wrong?" she asked, eyes blinking slowly with sleep.

"Nothing," Kate admitted. "I wanted to wake you before we got into the city."

"Those were two fast hours." Sara climbed over into the front seat. "How was the drive? Did you run into any problems?"

Kate pursed her lips, shaking her head. "You know, actually, I expected everything to be even worse. There were a lot of stripped trees, metal roofs, and piles of trash. Obviously, it was a horrific storm."

Sara pulled her feet up to lace on tactical boots. "You haven't seen anything yet. Wait until we get into the city." She climbed over the seat to join Kate in the front.

Kate continued on I10 through scrubby trees and bayou, interspersed with warehouses and anonymous businesses. It wasn't until they topped the rise on the long bridge that crossed the Industrial Canal that the city proper spread out before her eyes. She began to grasp the widespread devastation.

Television images had shocked her following Katrina. Nothing prepared her for what she was witnessing now. Water was still standing in many places. Even in the dry areas, it was evident that water had occupied the streets like an army before leaving in its own time. Her mind visualized Ponchartrain as she had just seen it—imagined it covering everything in sight, up to the eaves of the houses. *Why does anyone live in this sinking Atlantis?* It frightened her, sparking some nameless anxiety. Not even the clustered high-rises of the city center rising in the distance made her hopeful.

Kate caught Sara watching her reaction to the ruined city. It could be eye-opening to see your home through a visitor's eyes. Unlike most disasters, New Orleans was having a difficult time getting anyone in the country to keep their attention on her at all. Block after block of ruin soon became overwhelming. She soon concentrated on nothing but the road ahead.

Sara pulled a thermos of coffee out of the back seat, offered to pour some for Kate who declined, then poured her own. She told Kate to get ready to exit right onto I610. There was almost no traffic at 9:30 in the morning. A small work crew stood by a van facing the entrance to a brick school, the only visible activity from the elevated highway. After that, they passed block after block of abandoned houses. Small mountains of debris bordered the east-west section of I610, except for stretches that were elevated over city streets running north and south. Kate looked to the left as they crossed City Park to see a large group of trucks and tents in an open area between two streets, next to a football stadium.

By the time they had reached the sign for the Canal Blvd exit, Sara had finished her coffee, stored the thermos in the back and had retrieved a small nylon bag. She pulled out a small pair of binoculars and a matching black pistol, putting it into a small pocket holster on her belt. "Baby Glock," she explained to Kate before inspecting two extra magazines, putting them back in the bag and storing them under the seat.

Kate had been glad of having a former police officer for protection, had even used the fact to help persuade her father she would be safe, but Sara's weapon was sobering. "Is this legal? Carrying it in the truck?" she asked.

"Yeah. I have a concealed carry permit from Florida, which allows me to transport it across several state lines. I got it when I was making plans to leave Louisiana for Mississippi." Sara paused to examine Kate's reaction. "I'm only going to carry it on my belt under a jacket when we get out of the truck in a few areas this morning."

Kate nodded and swallowed. "Okay. Do I turn right or left on Canal?"

"Exit right and head north on Canal. We're going to West End Boulevard first, where Sicily was rescued. Maybe look around the neighborhoods to get a clue as to what they were doing in the area."

"Why go *there* first?"

"Well, everyone had left the area when we went to investigate right after it happened. I hope we meet some people who have returned. Maybe one of them might remember something."

"Okay. Yes, I wanted to go there too," agreed Kate. "I'm going to call Gilbert again this morning to ask if he has a phone number for the owner of Des Guise Grill yet. If he does, maybe we'll try to meet with him before talking to the FBI at 1:30. Have you had any other ideas since earlier in the week?"

Sara frowned. "No, not really. I wish you had received emails from more convention goers. The fact that you haven't, makes me think your husband was spending most of his time somewhere else, maybe in the area we're headed to."

After turning on Canal, Kate had to drive around mountains of trash and tree limbs through the devastated neighborhoods. South of Robert E. Lee Blvd., Kate saw an earthen mound rising in the middle of a grassy park. It was oddly out of place as if the narrow parkway was 9 months pregnant. It surprised her until she remembered Sicily's rescue. This had to be the spot. Every other piece of land she had observed crossing the bridge into New Orleans had been flat. This mound was... what? Twenty-five feet tall?

"This is the place, isn't it?" she asked Sara.

"Yep, pull into this next little drive to the left and park under the trees."

Kate parked the truck and glanced around at the strange surroundings. There was a grass-covered half circle drive leading up to the mound. Sara sat on the edge of the front seat, attached the holster, slid in the pistol, put on a jacket and grabbed the binoculars. "Let's get out," Sara said. "Lock the doors."

Climbing the rise between the trees, Kate saw a graffiti covered door in front of the mound.

"What is this place?" she asked, frowning. "It's giving me the creeps."

Sara smiled wryly. "This place *is* kind of creepy. It's an old civil defense shelter from the 50s. There are two round domed rooms underneath. The place is actually two levels deep. It had everything from stored supplies, meeting rooms, a kitchen, and a medical clinic. Nuclear strike from a Russian submarine? The government boys were ready to live in there for an extended period."

Sara stopped at the top of the circular drive, glancing back at Kate. "I guess the only life it ever saved was a little girl's; not from fallout, but from a flood."

Kate did not intend to attempt going inside. They walked around the foreboding entrance to climb to the top. Caged concrete bunkers with vent pipes and utility lines revealed the existence of the facility below. It was the only elevated ground within sight. Turning 360 degrees, Kate tried to imagine a raging flood coming at the mound and rushing around it. It was beyond her ability to visualize it. It amazed her that Sicily had ridden it out like an extreme surfer on a rogue wave.

They stood there in the quiet air for a while, surveying the surrounding neighborhood and the stretch of parkland to the south. An old pickup rumbled from the north, turning right to park in front of a two-story house part way down one of the streets running west. Sara raised the binoculars to her eyes. An older black man with salt and pepper hair eased out of the truck, limping up the steps to the house before going inside. Kate and Sara looked questioningly at each other.

"Well?" asked Sara.

Kate was adamant. "Let's go talk to him. He didn't even glance this way."

On the way to the front door, Sara zipped her jacket part way to help conceal the Glock in its holster. Kate pushed a doorbell button several times with no response, so she knocked. A male voice hollered something unintelligible from inside, and a few seconds later the door opened barely wide enough for two black eyes to peer out from under a sideways Saints cap. The young man appeared surprised to see two women standing at the door, but evidently judged them as harmless because he opened the door wider, hollering back into the house, "Pops!"

Kate looked at the gold fleur-de-lis above the bill sticking out from his ball cap while he hollered again. The meaning behind the three leaves had stuck in her head from somewhere. Those who worked, those who fought, and those who prayed. *Well, maybe two out of three wasn't bad.* When the youth turned back around, she introduced Sara and then herself. He didn't respond, so she asked if they could talk to him and his grandpa for a few minutes. He gestured indifference but hollered at his grandpa again.

Kate didn't wait. "We know the little girl who was rescued over there on the— "

Sara finished the sentence for her. "The mound above the civil defense shelter."

This set off a Rube Goldberg reaction on the young man's body. His arm swung around to the back of his head to spin his cap around which appeared to pull his eyebrows up causing his mouth to open.

"I's there. My brotha Marcus'n me. We were the ones pulled her outta the flood."

"I heard about that," Sara said. "So you were there."

"Ya, I'm Eddie. Mar stay in Houston at Aunt Em's house. He still in school." Sara's question finally registered on his face as a deepening frown. "How'd ya hear 'bout us?"

She shrugged. "I used to be NOPD, but no more. That's not why we're here. May we come in, Eddie?"

"I guess so. Ya. C'mon in. I'll get Pops." He motioned them in to sit down at a metal dining table with three chairs. The stud walls stood bare, stripped of their drywall. Obviously, they were in the process of gutting much of the interior. A rhythmic sound of scraping came from the back.

Eddie started toward the back of the room. "Hey, Pops! We got folk 'ere. C'mon out."

The salt and pepper haired gentleman they had spotted from across the street before, followed Eddie out from the back room, drywall dust and flakes of dried paint on his knees and boots. He saw

Kate and Sara sitting at the table, and asked if they were from FEMA. He didn't wait for an answer but started into a tirade on his grievances as he came over and sat down. Eddie was smiling behind his back, winking at the women while they all waited for him to run down.

"No, Pops." These ladies ain't gov'ment. They aksin 'bout the lil' girl me 'n Marcus grabbed outta the water."

"What?"

"During Katrina, Pops."

"Pops" rolled his eyes. "I know dat. What do dey—?" He focused on Kate. "What ya wanna know? And who you be?" he asked suspiciously.

Kate explained she was trying to find her husband who had been missing since Katrina. The NOPD had found his abandoned rental car a couple blocks away, near Sicily's father's car. Based on her story, they speculated that he might have put her in the inflatable pool from which she had been rescued. Kate and Sara were looking around the neighborhood for any clue to his disappearance. She pulled a small pack of pictures of Daniel from her purse, giving one to Cedric who shook his head.

"N'awlins Police," he spat in disgust. "Thugs wit a license. Not all of 'em," he grudgingly admitted. "Got a good one that lives around the corner. But most—" He shook his head.

Kate glanced at Sara whose face remained stoic. She stared back at the old man who was frowning at nothing as if he was trying to focus on something that was eluding him. In truth, he was not just thinking. He remembered the morning of the flood.

He had woken to the chaos of the storm, the flooding water, realizing the boys were not in the house after yelling for them, and then watched the water rising in the house from the top of the stairs. He and his grandsons had prepared the house as best they could, moving everything that wasn't nailed down to the second floor. He had sat there, wondering where the boys were when he remembered they often went up the street to sit on top of that old civil defense shelter.

There had been nothing to do. Cedric had sat there watching the water rise in the interior of the house. He waited until it leveled out before lying down and nodding off. He awoke again later to the sound of a motor somewhere outside, peeking out the window in time to catch sight of the craft headed away to the south. He hadn't been able to distinguish their faces. Why hadn't the boys come to get him if they were there?

He had actually considered the possibility that he was dead and didn't know it, like the guy in that scary movie the boys had made him watch. But no, it was always cold around the man in the film; it was hot and humid like it always was in New Orleans. Besides, heaven was surely not flooded. Unless this was hell? He had known the thoughts were silly and slid his bed over to watch out the window in case another boat came along.

That had been when he saw the man swimming through the rain to the mound. He hadn't told anybody about it. He had even forgotten about it after the boat came back with Eddie to pick him up. He had explained about rescuing the girl, making sure she was safe before coming back to get Pops.

"Call me Cedric, Cedric Dixon," he announced to a relieved Kate who had begun to wonder in the silence if he was going to say anything more. "I don't know nuttin' 'bout your man 'less he be the fool I saw swimmin' in the muck that day."

And so, he told them about the man swimming to the mound, too far for him to see clearly. He had figured it to be a dog until it climbed on two legs and walked off to the north.

It took a few moments for this to sink in. Kate asked quietly, "Can you describe the man?"

"I didn' see 'em good. Rainin' too hard. Didn' face this way. Tall man when he climbed out."

"What about his hair?"

"Don' remember… and like I say, didn' see 'em that well. Rain and trees in the way n' I don' see no good neither. Mighta had a navy cap on, but couldn' say much mo' fo' sho'."

"What about the picture of my husband? Was he the man you saw?"

"Maybe. I don' know. Like I say… didn' see 'em that well."

Sara glanced at Kate's stone cold face and pressed, "Do you remember anything else? Had you ever spotted anyone that looked like him around here before?"

Cedric shook his head.

Eddie seemed as interested as the women. "Why you didn't say nuttin' about a man swimmin' before, Pops?"

But they weren't able to mine any more information from Cedric. Kate asked if they needed water, and they agreed to take a case and some of the foodstuffs Kate had packed in the back of the truck. As they were leaving, Eddie leaned on the passenger window to ask about Sicily.

"That little girl was lucky."

"Except for losing her father," replied Kate.

"Yeah, 'cept fo' dat."

Kate held the boy's eyes in a steady gaze. "Be careful, Eddie. Take care of your grandpa. You have our telephone numbers, right?"

"Yeah," he said shyly.

"If you or your grandpa remember anything else, call me, okay?"

"Yeah."

They headed through the Lakeview neighborhood west, toward the broken levee. Kate stopped to let Sara drive; she knew the area, and Kate had tired of needing instructions for every turn. They drove through standing water and skirted debris, four wheeling through the sandy mud where they had to leave the streets. Sara pointed out the spot south of Hammond Highway where Daniel's rental car had been found.

Both were hoping to find someone living nearby that had

returned, but there was no sign of any occupied residences. The devastation in this area was extreme. Taking it all in, Kate couldn't help but think that rebuilding seemed utterly hopeless. A lone rocking chair on a front porch pitched back and forth in a rogue breeze. It was all too foreboding and ominous for Kate who told Sara they might as well leave the area.

CHAPTER 18 – NEW LEADS
NEW ORLEANS, LA – NOVEMBER 2005

Sara drove back east, well past Canal and City Park to Sicily and Joe's house on a street just off of Gentilly Avenue. The avenue followed a ridge, running northeast and southwest, a few feet higher than the surrounding areas. Their house was an abandoned double shotgun, with meticulously painted doors, shutters, and trim. The lack of debris and high water mark left on the houses and trees made it apparent that the flooding had not been as bad as where they had just come from in Lakeview. Here, there was not an endless succession of houses that needed to be gutted or demolished, and fewer search and rescue markings on the walls of the houses. Kate realized that, although there is no way they could have known, Sicily and her father, had left a place of relative safety for a location in the path of one of the worst levee breaks in the city.

Finding all the doors and windows on Joe and Sicily's house boarded or locked, and despairing of finding anything informative, they headed south of I610 toward downtown. Kate had been deliberating everything they had learned. She tapped the fingers on her left hand in turn, as she made her points to Sara.

"Okay, let's think about what we know. Daniel was obviously in Lakeview on the morning when the levee broke. His car was close behind Joe and Sicily's car. He left his car. Isn't that actually all we know for sure? We don't know why he was there. It's likely he abandoned his car when the levee broke, but we don't even know that for sure. Was he Sicily's angel? We don't know. Was he alone, or possibly with the other man he met at the restaurant? Maybe, but we don't know. If Sicily's angel *was* Daniel, where is he? Either Daniel didn't make it out of the flood, or something else happened afterward. I can't believe anything would keep him from coming home."

"And another thing," Kate blurted as Sara was about to answer. "Why were Joe and Sicily driving near the lake, so far from their own house? They couldn't have picked a much worse place to be. If they were going to leave, why not go south to the interstate?"

Sara opened her hands outward. "Who knows? At the time, someone suggested they were trying to get to the Causeway over Lake Pontchartrain, and then decided against it when they got to the 17th Street Canal. In reality, that never made sense. I can't imagine anyone choosing to leave by the causeway during a hurricane. Maybe something or someone was blocking their path to I610. I don't know." She shook her head. "Look, we've learned a little, and we still have leads to follow. It's okay to theorize, but sticking to what we know is smart."

The further south and east they drove, the more people and cars they met. Kate's cell rang. It was Gilbert. "Great. You finally have service. The PI found a cell number for your restaurant owner, but that is all I have. I'm still working on the adoption thing."

Kate grabbed her notebook out of the glove compartment to write down Terrance Lehan's phone number. "Okay, Gilbert. Thanks. Talk to you later."

Gilbert wasn't going to let her go quite yet. "Kate, is everything all right? Where are you right now?"

"I'm in New Orleans. Everything is fine. Listen, I guess you know that cell service is very spotty down here now. I'll be back in Hattiesburg tonight, but try my cell anytime if you find out anything more."

"Be careful, Kate. Be careful of who your trust. Don't give out too much information to anybody until you know more."

"I'm careful, Gilbert. Don't worry about me. Bye now."

"Was that your lawyer?" asked Sara, when the call ended.

Kate smiled. "Yes, that was Gilbert. I think he's worried about me, especially after I had him start looking at being a foster parent."

"Your lawyer is getting involved with that? Why? Frieda was going to—I mean Frieda could have handled—"

Sara's voice was unusually harsh. It caught Kate by surprise. She looked over at her young friend who was staring straight ahead at the street as she drove. It almost seemed as if she was angry or upset, which didn't make sense. Kate shrugged and said, "Mainly, he was just giving me Terrance Lehan's phone number."

Kate was already putting Lehan's number into her cell phone and asked Sara to pull over and park while she made the call. This was one time she didn't want a dropped call. The voice on the other end squeaked a hello, out of breath and almost drowned out by the sound of a power saw in the background.

"Mr. Lehan, I hope this isn't a bad time to call." Kate was almost shouting to make herself heard. "My name is Kate Mitchell. I am in New Orleans looking for my husband who has been missing since Katrina."

"Yes? Excuse me a second." Now distant from the phone, there was yelling in a higher octave, "Marco, turn that thing off for a second. I can't hear a blessed thing." A few seconds later, the voice was back without the saw, but still out of breath. "I'm sorry. I was unable to make out what you said. Go ahead please."

Kate repeated herself before adding, "I was hoping I might be able to meet with you. I have some questions related to my husband who is missing from Katrina."

"What is your husband's name?"

"Daniel Mitchell."

"Daniel Mitchell," he repeated. "I don't believe I have met him."

Kate answered hurriedly, "I realize you probably don't know him, or possibly never even saw him. I do have a picture of him I'd like to show you, but there is something else. Daniel was in your restaurant with a group of people a few days before Katrina. One of your servers might remember an incident that occurred. If you could give me a few minutes to explain?"

Lehan had caught his breath. "I don't meet many of the customers except for the regulars, but okay. I'm at the restaurant completing some repairs and cleaning up. I should be here for an hour or so. Are you close?"

Kate glanced at Sara. "How far are we away from the Des Guise?"

"It's in the Quarter, right?" asked Sara.

Kate nodded.

"Maybe twenty minutes," she estimated.

"We'll be there within a half hour," Kate said into the phone.

Lehan spoke with charm he reserved for customers. "I look forward to it."

Sara parked on the street behind a black Jeep, outside the restaurant. Kate was impressed with the front of the building. Two floor-to-ceiling, arched, dark-paned windows framed a wood-paneled entrance. Additional windows echoed the same design as the door. The second floor appeared similar to the first, but with a wrought iron bordered balcony, typical of many buildings in the French Quarter. Gold leaf lettering on an oval, glass door pane was the only indication this was the Des Guise.

They peered in a window before Sara knocked and opened the door. A young man with thick, spiky, dark hair smiled as he looked up from wiping off a table. Kate thought he somehow pulled off appearing simultaneously athletic and bookish.

"One of you must be Ms. Kate Mitchell, said Terrance Lehan. "And a friend?"

"I'm Kate, and this is Sara Arceneaux," introduced Kate. I'm sorry I didn't mention her on the phone. I was a bit nervous. And you are Terrance Lehan?" she asked, appreciating his laughing eyes.

Giving Sara a second look, Lehan said, "Arceneaux. I would guess you are from New Orleans or somewhere close by." To Kate, he said, "And you are not. But yes, I'm Terrance. Please call me Terry. Are the two of you hungry? How about some gumbo? Here, have a seat, and I'll be right back," before the two women could reply. "Marco, Marco. Let's eat!" he hollered as he walked toward the back of the restaurant.

Sara and Kate watched him walk away before turning to each other with delighted grins. "I was concerned about where we were going to eat lunch," said Sara. "I hardly expected this."

"Me neither, but Terrance... or Terry is exactly like I expected him to be."

"Yeah, he's metro but nice—very nice. Did you see those green eyes? I'll bet they glow in the dark. I think I like him."

Kate wasn't won over as easily, based on looks. "I suspect the feeling is mutual on his part." She smiled. "I'll form an opinion after I taste the gumbo. Well... and we'll have to see how good his answers are."

Terry wheeled out a cart from the kitchen with the Gumbo and a loaf of Italian. Marco followed with a pitcher of water. Terry offered to bring out a bottle of wine, but they all declined and dug into the Gumbo. Terry appreciated their appetite.

"How do you like it?"

Sara almost moaned her enjoyment. "Yum—I love it. It might be better than my grandma's, not that I would say so in front of her."

Kate agreed. "It's superb." She dipped the bread into a dish of oil and pepper and took a bite. "The bread is yummy, too. Did you bake it?"

Terry smiled but shook his head. "No, I have an arrangement with Leidenheimer's. Well, I *am* glad you like the Gumbo. We're going to be opening again eventually, and I'm still trying to get everything cleaned up." He included the other man in his gaze, patting him on the shoulder. "Marco's my carpenter slash accountant slash cousin. I'm lucky."

Marco smiled self-consciously, wiped his mouth with a napkin and announced, "I guess I'd better get back to it. I'm so glad to have met you both." He loaded the cart and headed back to the kitchen.

Terry gazed back earnestly at his guests. Kate noticed most of his attention seemed directed at Sara who had become so quiet, she appeared to have forgotten why they were there. His eyes were communicating enough to make her flush, but he finally spoke, "As much as I have enjoyed it, I know you came for more than lunch. Why don't you tell me your story?" he asked, looking back and forth between Kate and Sara.

Kate took a sip of her water and stared at the table. She started by explaining why Daniel was in New Orleans the week before Katrina. Kate didn't tell everything but told how she had found out about him having a meal in the restaurant with the other convention goers. When she told Terry that a server had confused Daniel with another patron who closely resembled him, his eyes opened wider in recognition.

"Oh, that was Kendra. I remember her saying something about it that night. She was extremely excited. She told everybody in the kitchen. She had two customers that appeared as if they could be twins, yet didn't know each other. We were so busy that night, I never had the chance to meet them, but I do remember her talking about it with the other staff."

Kate frowned. "That agrees completely with what Daniel's friends said, except they also said he continued to talk with this other man, and they left your restaurant together. I cannot imagine— Daniel was adopted, but he never mentioned anything about—"

Kate swept her hair back, staring hard at the table, fighting back the tears, trying to make sense once again of what had happened. Sara asked Terry quietly, "is Kendra still working for you?"

Terry frowned. "Well yes, she's still an employee, but won't be back in New Orleans until next month at the earliest. She left to stay with family in Houston two days before Katrina. I have her cell phone number. I could call—maybe explain things so you won't have to make a cold call like you did with me." He paused, smiling. "Not that I minded."

Kate's eyes showed her relief. "Thank you."

Terry pulled out his cell, and Kendra answered immediately. He smiled at everything he heard, charming all of them at the same time. He confirmed her first day back to work, explained why he had called, then handed his phone to Kate.

"Wait, can you put it on speaker so the two of you can hear too," asked Kate?"

Terrance grabbed it, punched a button, and said, "yes, but you'll need to have it close to you so Kendra can hear."

Kendra's voice sounded excited, probably surprised to find she was in the middle of a true-life mystery, and yet mature enough to be sensitive to the fact she was talking to the wife of a missing person.

"That night made a huge impression on me. Like something you watch on reality TV," she said. "I watched two long lost brothers find each other. Whether it was by accident or fate, I didn't know."

"What made you notice them in the first place?"

"I had both of their tables. I guess the other man, your husband's look-alike, was with several other men. They were celebrating being sober for at least a year. I mean, they were very open about it. That wasn't your husband, right?"

"No, Daniel was with two other men and a woman—a group of four."

"Right. So, okay. When I first asked the other group what they wanted to drink, they all grinned at each other, and then their leader or sponsor, whatever you call him, told me about the 'sober' thing, and they all ordered water."

"So, I noticed this man who looked like your husband. He didn't say much, but he was very polite, and he didn't ignore me just because I was a server. He didn't have an eye for me if you know what I mean. I liked him."

"Anyway, the other group came in with your husband. It was weird. I was so confused. It didn't occur to me that they were two separate men. Somehow, I thought they were the same person for a while. I guess I was concentrating on getting the orders, and then it hit me all at once. I was like—hey, this guy should be at the other table. So, I glanced across the room. It shocked me. Your husband noticed where I was looking, and he saw him too. He wasn't shy about it at all. He got up later and went over to the other table. I missed the first part of their conversation while I was running back to the kitchen, and waiting on other tables, but when I went back, they were talking about the possibility they might be biological brothers. It was unbelievable."

Kate was listening in awe. Questions begged for her attention, but she didn't want to miss anything, so she waited patiently until Kendra paused. "Did they really look that much alike—I mean like twins?"

"Well, not quite like identical twins, but close, ya know? Oh, and they both said they had been adopted. And they believed your husband was a year older if their ages were right."

Kate interrupted. "Wait a second. I have to write this down." She pulled her notebook and pen out of her purse. "Okay, go ahead. What else do you remember?"

"Well, they were about the same height. They were both born in Wisconsin. I guess that's what convinced them that they actually might be brothers. What are the chances? Two men that look like brothers—almost like twins. Both adopted. Both from Wisconsin?" Kendra paused for a second, remembering. "But you know… it was more than their appearance and details. They recognized something in each other. I'm probably not explaining it very well."

"No, you're doing great. I think I know what you mean," said Kate emphatically. "Please, go on."

"Jonas. The other man's name was Jonas. I just now remembered."

Kate's eyes opened wide. "Jonas? Are you sure his name was Jonas?" She looked at the other two. Terrance was grinning with excitement, but Sara's brow was furrowed in deep concentration.

"Yeah, I'm pretty sure that was his name. Now, what was your husband's name?"

"Daniel."

"Daniel! Right! So, they talked for a while before your husband's group left. Two of the guys in the sobriety group left too, except for an older black guy who was sitting next to Jonas. I can't remember his name. He said something about needing to get home because of the babysitter. Jonas must have come with the older guy because he asked your husband if he wanted to go with them. After that, they all left together, the three of them I mean."

Kate studied her notes, trying to think of more questions to ask, but her mind was buzzing with the new information, like multiple voices all vying for her attention. *The other man—the older black man Kendra had mentioned; she needed his name.*

"Did they mention the other man's name, I mean the older black guy?"

"Oh yeah," replied Kendra. "They said his name several times. I don't know why it isn't coming to me."

"Okay. I'm sure it will. Will you give me your email address? Oh, and I need your phone number if you don't mind. I'd like to send you a picture of Daniel to confirm he was there. I'm sure that I'm forgetting matters I need to ask about." Kate shook her head, glancing quizzically at Sara. She whispered to her aside. "What else do I need to ask?"

Sara leaned over and spoke into the phone, "Did you see what kind of car they left in?"

"No, I didn't see them after they left the restaurant. When they left, they thanked me, told me they would never have even noticed each other if it hadn't been for me. Your husband left a huge tip. I told everybody in the kitchen about it. I can't believe he is missing."

"Kendra, thank you so much. I guess we don't have to cover everything right now. Call my cell if you remember anything else, especially what the other man's name was." A sudden thought came to Kate. "Wait... hold on a second. Could he have been Joseph, or maybe Joe?"

"That's it!" Kendra cried on the other end. "They were calling him Joe. How did you guess that?"

"Oh, my gosh!" Kate exclaimed. "That's our link to them being together. Do you remember who paid and how they paid?" She questioned Terry with her eyes, "Can you find it in your records if they paid by credit card?"

Terry pursed his lips and nodded. "Yes, if one of the other two paid, we'll be able to get a name—perhaps more."

"Who paid for the meals?" Kate asked Kendra.

"I'm sorry Kate, but I'm sure that Daniel paid cash for the three of them."

They sat silently lost in thought on both ends of the line until finally, Kate spoke again, "You know, this is still good news. It gives us a place to start. Let's go ahead with exchanging numbers and email. I'll send you the picture tonight or tomorrow."

After the call, Kate noticed Sara appeared troubled, but she knew there was plenty of time to talk about things on the way back to Hattiesburg. She smiled at Terry and asked, "May we help with the dishes? You've been extremely helpful to us."

Terry smiled. "No, I am glad to help, ladies. Marco will take care of it. I have to meet with a community group in a half hour or so."

Kate gave him his phone back, and they all stood up. Terry hugged them, asking Kate to keep him informed. "What are you going to do next?"

Kate sighed. "I have to go talk to the NOPD and the FBI. I don't know how much of this to share."

Terry held her shoulders and looked earnestly into her eyes. "It seems to me you are doing most of their work for them."

Kate pursed her lips. "They might be overwhelmed," she said.

"Exactly... which is why they might hamper us more than help right now," added Sara.

"You don't think I should go talk to them today?"

"Well, I guess it would be okay to speak with NOPD while you're here. You can talk to the FBI anytime." She looked doubtful. "Maybe we should follow up on the leads we have first. If we can find other members of the sobriety group—AA, or some church outreach. They shouldn't be that hard to find since we already know about Joe. That would give you time to consider everything and prepare," said Sara. "I don't want to run into my old partner, Manson. I might find a use for the Glock today after all," she added as if she were only partly joking.

Kate glanced back at Terry. He was nodding again with a straight, compact little smile that she interpreted to mean that he agreed with Sara.

"Okay," she agreed. "Gilbert said something similar to me—that I should be careful who I trust."

Sara shot her a look, and Kate realized how that might have sounded. "Oh no, I don't mean he was talking about you."

Sara smiled, but it didn't reach her eyes.

Kate hurriedly continued. "I'll call Agent Spencer at the FBI first, and tell her I'm not coming. Then Grayling. By the way, when I called him the other day, it was Detective Manson who answered," she said, giving Sara a meaningful look.

Sara raised her head, eyes widening. "What did say?"

"I didn't give him much chance to say anything," Kate answered, chuckling.

On the phone, Agent Spencer seemed to have forgotten they were even supposed to meet. She did not attempt to disguise her relief that Kate wasn't coming.

Kate dialed the NOPD and asked for Lt. Grayling's extension. She was hardly surprised at her luck when Manson answered again. She stared at Sara with gritted teeth while she replied. "This is Kate Mitchell, the wife of Daniel Mitchell who is missing. Lt. Grayling asked me to call him when I was ready to meet. I seem to be having a hard time getting in contact with him. Isn't this his extension?"

Manson's reply was hesitant, but when he answered, there was no mistaking his contempt, though Kate thought he had attempted to sweeten his tone at the end. "Lt. Grayling is very busy. Do you have anything new to tell us? I'd be happy to pass it along to him."

Kate covered the phone mic and repeated what he had said to Sara.

"Don't tell that rat anything," Sara hissed.

"Kate's eyes twinkled as she uncovered the phone." Well yes, I have several things to discuss with Lt. Grayling," she said, emphasizing the other man's name. "Please tell Lt. Grayling to call me," she said sweetly before hanging up.

Kate smiled at the other two and shrugged. "I'm tired. Let's go back to Hattiesburg," she said.

Sara nodded in agreement. "I'm tired too. I guess two hours wasn't enough sleep."

Terry saw them to their truck, hugged both of them once more, gazing a little longer at Sara. There was a hint of embarrassment to both of their goodbyes. In the truck, Kate noticed Sara's cheeks were flushed. For once, the young woman looked insecure. Noticing Kate's look, she managed what might have been a smile twitching at her lips, and asked only, "What?"

CHAPTER 19 - THANKSGIVING
BENFORD, TN – NOVEMBER 2005

Jimmy Dean was passing dishes to Jonas faster than he was able to pass them on around the table to Jess and on to Maggie, then to her son James at the opposite end of the table from Jonas, to Harlan's wife Betty, Harlan, and back to Jimmy Dean.

"Slow up there, boy," growled Harlan. "You snatched the mashed potatos right out from under my spoon."

Jonas looked up from buttering his bread at the group seated around the dining table in Maggie's house. *What an odd group we are*, he thought. I am genuinely thankful for these people, God. *Whatever else I may say or think, I want you to know I am appreciative of these people.*

Maggie's son James had flown into Nashville and drove a rental car to his mom's two days before Thanksgiving. He was leaving again on Saturday. Part of his reason for visiting was to check out the stranger living at mom's and then report to his brother Rod in Minneapolis who had been unable to come.

They had talked at length. James had kept his questions innocuous enough in the beginning but eventually he became blunt. A few years of serving parishioners had taught him that confrontation was sometimes required to reveal true values. "Mom doesn't seem to know much about your background," he had said, letting the words hang in the air between them.

Jonas' answer came after a long thinking pause. "It's true that I have been slow to speak about my past."

James didn't let up. "Why is that?"

"I guess I don't like being quickly categorized and dismissed."

"Do you think I might jump to conclusions?"

Jonas shrugged. "I don't know. It seems better to leave some things unsaid, at least for a while. The people who sense that you are worth it will be patient enough to get to know you before they decide you are not worth their time."

James found that he was oddly satisfied with this answer, but He felt responsible for protecting his mother. "I want to get a sense of what your future intentions are."

Jonas nodded. "You know, I do understand why you want to know that. I'm still trying to figure it out myself. I want you to know that I didn't plan to come here in the first place. I actually didn't expect to stay the first night."

They had eyed each other frankly until Jonas finally continued, "I can tell you this; I will never do anything to harm Maggie, or take advantage of her. I'll leave at the first suggestion she is unhappy being my landlord."

James saw for himself all the work that Jonas had accomplished. The place had never looked better. Maggie was the happiest she had been since his father's death. He had tossed a baseball with Jonas and Jimmy Dean out at the barn, noticing the close and easy relationship between the man and boy. James had to admit the truth; He liked Jonas. But as a pastor, he had known many likable people with serious troubles. A few had even been dangerous.

Maggie had already made it clear to James that she would not listen to any of his misgivings. If he wasn't mistaken, she actually might be sweet on the man. The same seemed to be true of Jimmy Dean's little blonde-headed mother. Eyes peeled for their reactions, he innocently slid into the conversation, "Mother, let's see, you are now 50 years old, isn't that right?"

Maggie glared at him as if he had lost his mind. "You know perfectly well how old I am, James Edward."

James grinned as his head wigwagged. "Time flies. I forget," he lied, and almost in the same breath silently asked forgiveness. *Beg pardon, Lord.* "Well, I know Harlan here is two years older than dad. I remember seeing him in the yearbook."

"I'm 55," said Harlan matter-of-factly. Yep, Betty and I graduated in '67, so I guess your dad must have graduated in '69. I remember him from school. We were both in Vietnam, but at different times." Harlan frowned and stirred his potatoes, but had nothing more to say.

James' gaze moved on to Jimmy Dean, "We might as well go around the table. How old are you, Jimmy Dean? Let me guess—ten?"

"Yemph," mumbled the boy whose mouth was full of pumpkin pie.

"Chew with your mouth closed," Maggie and Jess said simultaneously.

"How about you, Jonas?" continued James.

"Same age as Jack Benny," quipped Jonas.

Maggie giggled. Jess seemed confused. "Thirty-nine it is," said James. He looked at Jess next. "Your turn."

"James, you know it is bad manners to ask a lady her age," Maggie scolded.

Jess appeared even more confused, but she blurted out, "I'm twenty-seven."

James did some quick math in his head. *Mom is eleven years older than Jonas unless he was joking with the Jack Benny comment, and Jess is twelve years younger.* He smiled to himself over the unspoken competition with its subtle tension. *They're both mothering Jimmy Dean, and trying to charm Jonas.* It dawned on him that his mother was staring at him. She knew something was churning in his analytical brain. He supposed, in actuality, she was almost as consciously unaware of the nature of her own feelings as was the young woman sitting by her side.

"We seem to have forgotten someone," Jonas said from the other end of the table, looking directly at James, as did the rest.

"Who, me? I'll be 32 next month."

"So you aren't much older than Jess." Jonas glanced back and forth between them. "Did the two of you know each other in school?" he asked.

James was surprised at the question. Jess answered quickly, "I didn't grow up here. I'm from Chattanooga." She gave no further explanation.

Jimmy Dean broke the short, uncomfortable silence by announcing he liked the ham almost as much as he liked Harlan's fried fish. "But not as much," he assured Harlan.

Harlan was pleased. "I've still got some of our fish in the freezer. Maybe we should have a fish fry this weekend." He glanced at James while he pointed a thumb at Jimmy Dean. "This boy out-fishes us every time we go," he admitted.

Jonas nodded in agreement. "He's getting pretty good with an electric fillet knife, too."

The boy basked in the praise from the men, but Maggie was frowning. "You're letting him use a fillet knife?"

Jonas's face gave him away. He'd been caught. "Yes, well we're keeping an eye on him every second. He's not getting his hands near the knife blades," he said quickly, trying to assure Maggie and Jess.

James rescued him. "I'm leaving Saturday, guys. How about tomorrow evening? I'd hate to miss out. I haven't been to a fish fry since I left here. Taters, onions, biscuits, right?"

"Good heavens," said Maggie. "We have a feast here today, and you men would rather have some old fish!"

"No, no!" shouted Harlan. "This is great!"

"Everything is excellent," agreed Betty.

"Oh, I'm enjoying your green bean casserole," replied Maggie. "Thanks for bringing it. I'm sure the cake will be good too."

James noticed that Harlan appeared to be ready to give a negative reply to this last statement, so he tried to divert their attention.

"Yeah, this is an unbelievable dinner. Thank you very much, ladies."

The men understood Maggie had been joking with them. When she brought in the pumpkin cheesecake, the apple pie, and the ice cream cake, they forgot all about the fish fry.

After dinner, the men were anticipating the football game on television, but Maggie had something else in mind. Marla Evans had raved about a card game called Apples to Apples until Maggie finally decided to buy it. She insisted they all gather around the table in the library to play. Harlan started complaining, but Maggie frowned at him, and he shut up.

Maggie opened the game box and started taking out the cards. "Now this is a great game for all ages. Everybody takes turns being a judge. The judge puts out an adjective card from the pile. Then everyone else plays one of his or her noun phrase cards, face down. The judge picks one, after turning them over one at a time. We'll play one round, and you'll have the hang of it."

Maggie dealt the cards. As Harlan turned over his first card, he started complaining again. "Who the— Argh. Who is Dee-mii Moore?"

"Oh for Pete's sake, Harlan," spouted Maggie. Here, give me that card back. You're not supposed to tell everybody what cards you have."

"Well, how am I supposed to—"

"You have six more cards to pick from if you don't know who they are."

Jimmy Dean was laughing. "Dee-mii Moore," he mimicked, snickering.

"Oh right. I suppose you know who he is," said Harlan to Jimmy Dean and the rest of the table laughed.

Maggie turned over the green adjective card, which read Cranky. "Okay, so you all pick a card in your hand that matches well with cranky, and then put it face down in the middle. I'll turn them over and pick which one I like best. Whoever had that card wins, but we're just practicing this round."

They all peered at their cards. Jonas spoke first, "Darn, I don't seem to have a card here with Harlan Schmidt written on it."

"What?" asked Harlan absent-mindedly as he sorted through his cards. "Are you saying I'm cranky?"

"Obviously, you understand the object of the game," Maggie said.

Harlan's wife Betty managed an ambiguous, crooked smile, like a car left alone in a parking lot because it was straddling the lines. She was never completely at ease with Harlan's kidding banter, seldom understanding his choice of words or the hilarity they conjured in other people. Despite her discomfort, she perceived one thing. People liked her husband, and this made her quietly proud.

They all pushed their cards into the middle. Maggie shuffled them before turning them over.

"Well, what do we have here? *Spiders*. Yes, I'd say spiders might be considered cranky. *Pit Bulls*. Oooh yeah, that's a good one. Okay, next is *Ear Wax*?"

"*Ear Wax*?" repeated Jess.

"*Ear Wax*," snorted Jimmy Dean.

"Believe me. Ear wax can make you cranky," Harlan said.

"Sounds like you've had experience with that," James replied.

"Hey, at my age, I've had experience with almost everything," growled Harlan.

"Wait, there are three more cards", Maggie said. "*At My Parent's House, Teachers* and *Going to Church.*" Maggie looked back and forth from Jonas to James. She started to say something to both of them when James confessed, "Well, when you have parishioners like my parishioners, going to church can make you pretty cranky."

They all laughed. Jonas asked Maggie, "So which is your choice, judge?"

Maggie returned to the cards. "I'm glad James isn't cranky at his parent's house. I was beginning to think that all three of the last cards were referring to me." She had a mock frown on her face, but it dissolved into a smile. "Just for that, I'm picking *Pitt Bulls*."

"Woo hoo!" shrieked Jess.

"Oh no!" groaned Jimmy Dean. "I knew you would pick *Spiders*. Remember how you chase them around with a magazine?"

"Oh, you're right; they do make me cranky. Well, that was only the practice round," Maggie reminded them. "From now on, whoever wins each round, keeps the green card, and whoever collects five green cards first wins. Everybody gets another card except me.

After Maggie and Betty had each won a game, the men all agreed the game favored a female perspective and decided it was football time. Maggie didn't argue after Harlan played a red *Bill Clinton* card for the green card *Flirtatious*. She was afraid of having to explain any more uncomfortable matching cards to Jimmy Dean. However, when the men saw the Falcons were destroying the Lions, they went back for a second round of dessert instead.

Jonas and James sat at the kitchen table. "Does going to church actually make you cranky, or were you joking?" Jonas asked.

James didn't answer immediately, using a bite of pumpkin cheesecake to consider his answer. "When the church becomes more business than worship, which is far more often than what I had anticipated while in Seminary, I definitely get cranky. I must admit—I'm enjoying a few days away from it."

"What kind of business?"

James rubbed out the wrinkles of his frown. "Okay, right. I don't mean *business* as in *finances*. Actually, I'm not involved with finances that much. It's the organizational issues. People disagree about the programs, the music, community involvement—it's never ending. I sometimes suspect I am spending as much time handling cultural change as I am spiritual needs."

"Why is that? Is it the age we live in, your geographical location… your denomination?"

"Wow. Actually, that's a good question," James admitted. I suppose to some extent, all of those factor in, and much more. If one compared my congregation with Mother's, for instance, the cultural differences would be evident, somewhat because of geography, but probably more so because non-denominational evangelical churches attract a very different type of parishioner, even in the same area where I live." He paused. "Have you been to Mother's church?"

Jonas grinned. "Yes, I actually went with her when I first arrived, and I went again last Sunday."

"Well, what did you think?"

Jonas glanced at Maggie who was cleaning up the dishes and putting away food with Jess. She didn't appear to be listening, but he guessed she was. "The first time I didn't like it much, but to be truthful, I didn't want to be there. On top of that, somebody in the class said something, which seemed insensitive to the people I've known in my life. I tuned out after that." Jonas smiled at James. "But my experience was entirely different this last time. I enjoyed it."

Jonas watched Maggie's back as he finished. Although it was subtle, he could tell by the way she relaxed as she exhaled—she had been listening. He also noticed the smallness of her waist and curve—

"Huh, well that begs the question; what has changed, her church or you?" asked James, interrupting his thoughts.

Jonas was embarrassed, wondering how long he had been staring and whether James had noticed. "Oh, I'm sure it's me, he said quickly. Don't get me wrong; I'm not planning to join the church. I still don't know what to believe. I've doubted God even exists most of my life and ignored or have been angry with him the rest."

"But what has changed?" James persisted.

Jonas held his chin in his hand, while his eyes swept across the room, then back at James and spoke quietly. "A couple of things. I started talking to God. I didn't expect anything. I felt awkward at first, but now I can't seem to stop. It's good to be completely honest with someone, even if I am talking to myself. Secondly, your mother is a genuine Christian, as far as I can tell. I mean, she lives it. Her reaction to difficult people and situations amazes me. She loves people, people that aren't easy to love."

He nodded and pointed with his eyes at Maggie showing Jess a recipe. "Look," he whispered. "Right now she's showing Jess how to—well, how to live, without her even realizing it, something Jess' own mother probably never had time for. She does that with Jimmy Dean too, making a difference in his life. She does it for strangers. She has done it for me."

James' eyes were shining at this honest, heartfelt appraisal of his mother. The lump in his throat made it hard to speak more than a few words. "I know."

Maggie gave the both of them a long hard look over the top of her glasses. "What are you boys talking about so seriously?"

"You," said both of them at the same time, and laughed.

That night, after everyone had left and Jonas was alone in the apartment, he logged onto the computer and saw he had a private message from Kate through the poetry blog's message board.

> I've been very busy playing amateur sleuth, so I only recently read your Thanksgiving poem. I liked it very much. It made me laugh. I enjoy narrative poems. It reminded me of something Robert Service might have written (had he been watching a play in a gymnasium), but it was based in fact, wasn't it? Must have been a fun night. Keep up the good work.

Jonas smiled for a second after reading it, but his eyes returned to the first sentence. Sleuth. What did she mean by that? He read the time signature. She had written it a few minutes before. He quickly typed back,

> Thanks. I don't know who Robert Service is but I'll look him up. Your sleuthing sounds dangerous. What kind of crime are you trying to solve?

He didn't expect her to be online, but came back to the message board after a few minutes, seeing he had a reply.

> Do an online search for "The Cremation of Sam McGee" to read

one of Service's poems. Not sure what I'm searching for is a crime. Let's just say I have found out much more than I expected. I hope I'm nearing the end of a mystery that has eluded me for a long time.

Jonas sat in the dark, wondering what Kate had meant.

CHAPTER 20 – CONNECTED BY POETRY
ST. JUDE, MO – NOVEMBER 2005

"Mandy, I'm sorry! Everything happened so fast over the last week, I couldn't get it all straight in my mind, let alone try to explain it over the phone. And then we had to go to my parents' yesterday for Thanksgiving." Kate sat at the kitchen bar in Mandy's house, trying to apologize, while Sicily sat next to her, drawing on a pad with crayons.

Mandy was leaning on the bar, drinking a cup of coffee watching Sicily color a yellow moon behind a tree, bare of leaves. "So when are you going to tell me everything that has happened?" she asked matter-of-factly, not looking up from the girl's concentrated effort. What had drawn Kate to Sicily was evident to Mandy. There was a poised sparkle escaping her dark eyes as she worked on her drawing, peeking briefly to gauge the emotions of the women. Mandy was already half in love with Sicily, herself.

"Which part? What I've found out about Daniel, or—" Mandy looked up when Kate's voice trailed off to see that she was gesturing at Sicily with her eyes.

"I need to let Knut in," Mandy said, taking Kate's cue. Opening the door, she whistled through her teeth. A chocolate lab pup bounded in the door and ran directly to Kate who jumped down from her stool to wallow the dog's head affectionately.

"Knut! Buddy!" He's my boy. Yass, he's my boy. Sit now, Knut. Sit," she said sternly.

Sicily had pulled her feet up to sit cross-legged on the stool, wide eyes on the dog. Knut inched forward, raised his nose for an exploratory sniff at Sicily's foot and ankle, and decided the little bit of skin showing was worth a lick.

Mandy made a formal introduction. "Knut, I want you to meet Sicily. Sicily, this is Knut. He might lick you, but that's it. You can come down here, Honey."

Sicily climbed down off the stool. Knut stood up and wagged his tail as she gave him a careful hug.

"Why is his name Knut?" Sicily asked, petting his head.

Mandy laughed. "People ask me that all the time. I don't know. I just like it, I guess."

Knut found a toy football near a china cabinet and pushed it against Sicily's leg, wanting her to play keep-away. The ball bounced away into the next room, and the two followed it, continuing to play. Kate turned back to Mandy.

"Yes, I actually am Sicily's foster parent now. Her last foster family had to take in more children from their own extended family because of Katrina. Things had to move quickly. Gilbert took care of residence issues. I had to complete a lot of paperwork and training. The placement counselor did whatever it took to accelerate the process. I'm taking Sicily back to Hattiesburg next week to continue the requirements, but there appears to be hope I'll be able to adopt her soon." Kate paused a second before adding, "We'll see."

Mandy gave her a knowing smile. "I knew that's what you were planning. I heard it in your voice. You do know I wasn't trying to talk you out of it, right?"

"Yes. And you would have done the same thing."

Mandy didn't seem so sure. "Maybe. It's quite a commitment." She paused to watch Sicily and Knut in the other room. "Well, what about Daniel? What have you learned?"

Kate's eyes dropped to her hands. "You know, it might help me to sort this out by starting from the beginning. Before Daniel went to New Orleans, we had settled into a routine that was mostly separate from each other. We were roommates—respectful—but apart. Daniel was lost. No doubt about that. He didn't do anything but go to work, piddle around outside and watch sports on television. I used him as a verbal punching bag when I let things build up. Still, I don't believe he was planning to leave. He went on three or four business trips a year. Nothing about him gave me the impression that anything was out of the ordinary before he went."

Kate considered her own words. "It's not like I was concerned about other women when he traveled either. You know Daniel. That's why I didn't listen carefully when he called to tell me he was staying a couple more days in New Orleans. He always made prudent, well-thought-out decisions. I don't remember him ever doing anything truly spontaneous. I assumed the extra days were somehow connected with work, you know? I know now that he met a man he sensed was his brother. Fate or accident—who knows? But that's why he stayed."

"What? Wait a second." Mandy was puzzled. "How do you know this? You're talking about the man he resembled, right? How do you know he believed this man was his brother?"

"I told you about the waitress in the restaurant where they met? Her name is Kendra. I got her phone number from the restaurant owner while I was there. In fact, Terrance called Kendra, and I was able to discuss the incident with her on his phone. She remembered his name was Jonas. While Daniel and Jonas met in the restaurant, she overheard them talking about being near the same age, both orphans, both from Wisconsin, and then they mentioned the possibility of being brothers."

"But I also haven't told you yet that Kendra said Jonas's group was celebrating at least a year of being sober. Based on that, Sara and I called around to several sobriety groups in the New Orleans area. We located another man who was celebrating with them that night. He remembered it well."

Mandy was frowning. "Wait, wait, wait! Jonas is the name of the man Daniel thought was his brother. He was with a sobriety group in the restaurant. And you talked with another member of the same group who was there with them?"

Kate nodded vigorously, biting her lower lip. "Exactly," she exclaimed. "Actually, there were five men altogether. The one we found by researching sobriety groups was the group facilitator. Charles Curtis is his name. He's a recovering alcoholic himself—been working with this faith-based group for several years. So he not only knew Jonas; he also knew Sicily's father."

Mandy's eyes grew in shock as she slapped her hands on the kitchen bar. "Sicily's father? That's the connection, right?"

"I know, Mandy." Kate threw her head back and sighed. "Oh, I'm sorry. I forgot to mention that Kendra—the waitress, right?" Kate raised questioning eyebrows to make sure Mandy was following. "Kendra remembered one of the other members of the group was a black man by the name of Joe. It was weird. When I was talking on the phone with her, I had an intuition that Sicily's dad might have been with the group at the restaurant. I must have put two-and-two together. I mean, I kept wondering who Daniel was with and why he was near Sicily during the hurricane. Anyway, when I mentioned the name Joe, Kendra remembered that was his name."

"Then when I talked with their leader, Charles, he answered many questions. Yet in some ways, I'm no closer to understanding anything. Jonas was in the same sobriety group as Sicily's father, Joe Jackson, but Charles didn't know as much about Jonas as I had hoped. Their records were destroyed when the church was flooded, so they are going to have to rebuild their contact records. Jonas hasn't been around since Katrina, and Charles doesn't know if he left New Orleans, is missing, or what."

"Didn't Charles have anything else to say about Jonas?"

"Oh yeah. He said Jonas had told the group that he was a carpenter or construction worker—something like that— and had also been a worker on an oil rig." Kate stopped to recall before continuing. "All he said about Jonas's sobriety problems were they were related to a painful past, and Jonas had been helping Joe remodel his house during the evenings. He didn't see or talk to either one of them after the dinner. Charles and his wife left to stay with family near Baton Rouge a few days before the hurricane."

Kate paused, remembering the pain and regret in Charles' voice. "He *did* say Joe's car wasn't running the night of the dinner which made them several minutes late. Jonas, Joe, and Sicily were all together when they brought her over to stay with Charles' wife. Then, Daniel, Jonas, and Joe picked Sicily back up after the dinner. The fourth man at the table? Charles doesn't know where *he* is. He's isn't in New Orleans any longer, though."

Mandy had sat there awestruck throughout the account. "So what do you suppose happened?" she asked, leaning forward to look straight into Kate's eyes.

"I think it's likely Daniel spent some time with Jonas over the following days, maybe working with him while trying to figure out if they were genuinely brothers. That would explain why one of the convention-goers saw him with work clothes on at his hotel. You know Daniel. He enjoyed working with his hands. When he called me, he must not have been sure what he was going to do. Why they stayed, I don't know. Maybe they were helping other people get ready to leave New Orleans. Maybe they were helping Joe, Sicily's dad."

Mandy considered the possibilities. "What about Sicily? Does she remember anything?"

Kate sighed. "Well, sort of." Kate paused and appeared troubled. "I showed her pictures of Daniel and her eyes seemed to show recognition, but when I asked her if he was the angel who had saved her from the flooding water. I thought she might answer, but she seemed more frightened than anything."

Mandy frowned and interrupted. "But, but—"

Kate cut her off. "It's like when she drew a picture with a man by a car in front of her house when I met her for the first time. Sicily said he was Jonas, who we have figured out was Daniel's possible brother. I also tried to ask her if Jonas was with her when the levee broke and she looked puzzled or confused... I don't know what she is thinking."

Kate shook her head at Mandy with tears welling. "I don't know what to think, Mandy. Didn't she see who was in the water with her? His face, I mean. All she does is look at me sadly every time I try to suggest anything about the angel. It seems likely the angel was either Jonas or Daniel, but which one? If it was Jonas, then where is Daniel?"

"What about the days before?" Mandy asked. "Could she have the two of them confused? She must have known Jonas if he was helping work on their house. Doesn't she remember anything else?"

Kate shook her head and closed her eyes. "Yes. Well, she talked about her dad's friend—that he was working on their car. I'm wondering now if it was confusing to her because they looked so much alike. On top of that, every time I ask about what happened during the levee break, she doesn't even give me as many details as she did the police. Maybe the experience traumatized her. At first, I assumed that she was only sensing I was upset. I'm sure that was part of it, but there has to be more to it than that."

The two sat together silently with their own thoughts until Sicily and Knut came back in the room, playing tug of war with the football. Mandy got down on the floor to play with them, but Kate's thoughts went back once again to the trip to New Orleans, to what the old man Cedric had told her about another man swimming to the mound over the old Civil Defense shelter. Why was she reluctant to tell Mandy about *that*? *It might not have anything to do with anything*, she told herself. If the man was Daniel, he might still be alive. However, if the man was Daniel and he was still alive, why had he not found his way home? Why had he not been with Sicily when their cars were abandoned so close together? She still refused to consider that he was dead, but there was one doubt that wouldn't leave her mind. She finally allowed herself to face the one possibility that she had been avoiding for so long. His unhappiness and ongoing depression over

David's death. Their separate lives. Had he impulsively taken advantage of Katrina and exited, stage left?

At home, after Sicily had fallen asleep, Kate sat with the laptop on the sofa to catch up on email. There was nothing in her inbox but junk, spam, and messages from fellow moderators on the Puzzled Poet checking on her. She quickly typed in short replies and then traveled to the site to search for new activity. Kate was annoyed at her own excitement over finding two messages from b4Isleep.

> I read The Cremation of Sam McGee. I must have read it many years ago, probably in school. I like it. Now I understand what a narrative poem is, even if I didn't know that's what I was writing. Such a great and funny way for Service to end his poem. The line, 'Since I left Plumtree, down in Tennessee, it's the first time I've been warm'? That's funny.

The second message had asked,

> How is your sleuthing coming along? Have you solved your mystery?

Kate picked up a pencil absent-mindedly and drummed the eraser on her knee as she stared at the screen. Daniel had never been a fan of the cold of winter. Abruptly, she sat it down and began to type:

> I'd like to continue our discussion, but the PMs on the message board are awkward to use. Do you have a Messenger account, ICQ, or some other chat program?

She sat for a few moments in indecision and then sent the message. This time, there was no quick reply, so she went to the kitchen to brew a cup of tea. When she came back, she checked on Sicily, watching the girl sleep for a few minutes. The tenderness she felt filled her with a combination of delight and fear. She knew she was risking awakening a painful place inside—had already done so to a certain extent. She smiled to herself and sighed.

Back at the computer, there was still no reply, so Kate grabbed a notepad and started jotting down ideas for the return to Hattiesburg and possibly another trip to New Orleans. She first wanted to concentrate on completing the adoption procedures for Sicily. Then, make a definite appointment with agent Spencer at the FBI. She wanted one more talk to Eddie Dixon, the boy who had rescued Sicily, in case he had remembered anything new. While there, she and Sara could further canvass the surrounding neighborhood to find anyone else who had returned to the city—someone who might have known Sicily and her dad or had met Daniel.

I can take care of some of this by phone, she thought. She made a note to call Charles Curtis, the sobriety group facilitator. The notes had a way of clarifying her thoughts. *We need to find out more about Jonas. If we find either Daniel or Jonas, we'll probably find the other.*

Kate glanced back at the screen to notice she had an instant message on the Puzzled Poet. It was from b4Isleep.

Hello. I haven't used Messenger, but I have a Hotmail account, so I guess I can sign up for it. What is your username?

Kate responded, and within a few minutes, she had an open chat with b4isleep. He was using the same username.

b4isleep: Hello
katedid: Hello yourself. To answer your question from before, no I have not solved my mystery … but making progress.
b4isleep: If it's too personal I understand, but will have to admit I'm curious. Love a good mystery.

Kate considered her answer for a few seconds. Don't give any details, she cautioned herself.

katedid: Don't we all? Well, there are many people still dealing with the hurricane in New Orleans. I'm one of them.
b4isleep: Oh! Sorry. It has been a terrible tragedy.
katedid: Yes. I have been working at finding someone since September. There isn't much to go on, but little facts keep popping up.

b4isleep: Are you doing all of the work on your own?

katedid: I'm lucky to have some great friends who have been helpful. I may go back to New Orleans soon to meet with law enforcement there. Hope to find out more then. But listen, I don't want to talk about that.

b4isleep: Oh, you need to be very careful about going into the city. Might be dangerous. Can't you handle everything by phone?

katedid: You know, that's funny. I was thinking the same thing. You're probably right. But I don't know… I'm sorry. Let's talk about your poem.

It was at least 5 minutes before there was an answer, enough time for Kate to doubt if he was still there, even though the chat box still showed him as being online. But then he was back.

b4isleep: Sorry 'bout that. Had a phone call. Okay. I'll have to open the poem so I'll know what we're talking about.

katedid: I mentioned before that I enjoyed your poem. And I did. But since my first reading, I've paid closer attention to it. You put some care into the structure. It appeared to me, or should I say it sounded to me as if you attempted to keep to an accentual count in the lines? Is that right?

b4isleep: Yeah, that mostly happened accidentally. I didn't even consciously intend to write a poem. I felt like writing down what had happened at a school play, and it felt like a poem, probably because I've been reading poetry. Then I worked at making it sound better gradually. I'm not even sure I'm finished with it.

katedid: The humor of the children's play comes alive. It must have been hysterical. I particularly liked 'but John Carver wished he'd been an Indian'. Kids will be kids in spite of how adults try to frame life into a teachable moment. So, it sounds like you have a little Daniel Carver you are proud of.

b4isleep: He's a great kid… and not even mine. His mother is my neighbor. I guess you could say he adopted me. We have a good time together.

katedid: Oh, is this the neighbor who is your poetry mentor?

> **b4isleep**: No. Different neighbor. Although ... Oh never mind; it's complicated.
>
> **katedid**: LOL! Okay. Well, how fascinating. I'm actually in the process of possibly adopting a little girl. She has captured my heart, and I'm not even sure how it happened. It happened so quickly. I like your way of putting it—maybe she's adopting me.
>
> **b4isleep**: Really? Wow. I'm— Wow.

More than five hundred miles apart, the two of them stared at their computer screen in astonishment, Kate at the odd, synchronous connection she was sensing—Jonas, that Kate was doing something he had completely not expected. *She was considering adopting a girl?*

> **b4isleep**: That must be a challenge, especially while trying to locate someone.

Kate noticed that the subject kept changing from poetry to her personal life. Scrolling back to read the chat history, she recognized that she had probably been as responsible as b4isleep. Still, something about his writing bothered her. In any case, being distracted off topic mirrored the story of the last several months. Her writing attempts had been short-lived, as had been involvement with the poetry blog.

> **katedid**: Life is a challenge, period. Hey, I'm curious—are you writing poetry on your computer or writing by hand?
>
> **b4isleep**: Well, remember I haven't written much yet, but so far, I've been writing in a small notebook, making corrections until it's a mess, and then typing it into the computer while I can still read my own writing. Ha.
>
> **katedid**: Okay, that's good. I was going to suggest that you keep a notebook handy, and when you notice or conceive of anything that grabs your attention, write it down. Fragments, observations—it's all good. It will eventually combine in various ways into something useful.
>
> **b4isleep**: Thanks for the advice. Anything else?
>
> **katedid**: Well, don't take this the wrong way, but work at writing

with an honest voice. Be yourself. It's harder than you may think. It's easy to slip into caring about the reader's opinion, even if that reader is yourself, or an idealized version of yourself. I had a blog participant who once said, "writing is rehabilitation for liars." It didn't make much sense to me at first, but eventually, I came to agree.

b4isleep: I get it. I considered it with the Thanksgiving poem. I didn't intend to use rhyme and then part of it accidentally fell into rhyme. I tried to take it back out, but every word I tried to change felt forced... not honest. After that, the rhyme trapped me. So did counting syllables. I tried emphasis to escape it all. I may change it again, but it feels close to being right now.

katedid: You have made a great start at writing. When you are ready, don't worry about forms or anything else when you work. Just show what is inside you. Listen, I need to get some rest, but I enjoyed chatting with you. Let's do it again. And please keep writing. Talk to you later?

b4isleep: I liked it too. I appreciate the feedback. Until next time. Take care.

CHAPTER 21 - FALLING
BENFORD, TN – DECEMBER 2005

When Jonas learned Benford Fabrication was going to lay everybody off except a skeleton crew during the week after Christmas, he asked Bill Anderson for a few days off to take care of unfinished business in New Orleans. Since Jonas had yet to miss a day, Bill told him to take as much time as he needed. Harlan busted his chops about the "poor work ethic of you kids," but then he got out a grease-stained atlas to suggest a route for him to take. Jonas put off telling Maggie about his plans until two weekends before Christmas, while he was driving her to Nashville to do some shopping.

A quiet, steady rain fell as they left in the old station wagon at daybreak. They had discussed not going, but the weatherman promised above freezing temperatures. Maggie hoped the rain would discourage Christmas shoppers, so the stores wouldn't be so crowded.

Maggie was excited about Christmas because of Jimmy Dean. She could tell that Jonas was excited as well. He told her that he had been browsing gloves and bats online and thought he might buy another dozen baseballs. Maggie wanted to buy Jimmy Dean clothes. She warned Jonas that she was going to spend most of her time in department stores, so he brought his poetry notebook. He anticipated completing shopping in about an hour.

Maggie looked out the car window at the wet, gray, monochrome winter, while Jonas explained his plans for the holidays, and asked to borrow the truck. She was disappointed in his plans, but took it in stride, especially after he explained he wasn't planning to leave for New Orleans until the Monday after Christmas day. She had been expecting him to go back south for a visit ever since he had arrived in Benford. As much as she had hinted, Jonas had remained reticent—his former life a blank page—preferring to dodge and deftly change the subject whenever his past was brought up.

Maggie's older son, Rod, had asked her weeks before to come to Minneapolis during the holidays. Her younger son's visit had been her excuse not to go at Thanksgiving. Now, after listening to Jonas's plans to be in New Orleans between Christmas and New Year's Day, she decided to fly to Minneapolis for the week. She hadn't visited Rod, his wife Julie, and her two grandsons, Geoffrey and Scotty since the previous summer. She knew Rod's career kept him busy. He often complained about the long hours, but she knew he preferred it that way. Nevertheless, the strain it had put on his marriage showed. She worried about the boys. Yes, it was time for her to visit.

They shopped in Nashville for most of the day. Their last planned stop was a sporting goods store that faced several department stores across a parking lot, allowing both of them time to shop for their preferred gifts. Jimmy Dean's pile grew into a small mountain. As they were putting the last of the packages in the back of the station wagon, their eyes met, reaching the same conclusion. Maggie asked the obvious. "Did we perhaps buy too much for Jimmy Dean?"

Jonas shut the hatch as if to hide the evidence. "Why? Do you think Jess will feel bad if we give him so much?"

Maggie nodded agreement. "It's possible. Her budget is probably as tight as a tick." She paused, thinking it over until a chill made her shiver. "Come on; I'm freezing out here. Let's eat and then go on home. We can talk about it on the way."

They stopped for Italian at a favorite of Maggie's from former days of dragging Tom to the city for shopping, a Sounds minor league baseball game or a show at the Tennessee Performing Arts Center. She talked Jonas into ordering the sirloin marsala after he ogled a steak being carried to another table. Maggie ordered the tagliarini, explaining to Jonas that she seldom ordered the same thing. She preferred to be adventurous, even if it didn't always end well.

Jonas shook his head. "I usually end up with meals I don't like when I try something completely new."

"Is my cooking too extreme for you sometimes?" Maggie asked mischievously.

Jonas started to backpedal and then saw her face. "Well, there *was* that birthday cake for Jess."

Maggie's eyes narrowed and sparked. She bit her bottom lip before speaking. "That wasn't my fault! It was either you or Jimmy Dean who couldn't keep your eyes out of the oven," she fired back.

"All I know is, that Angel Food cake looked like the devil had cooked a skateboard park. I guess that's pretty extreme."

"I should have made a hat out of it on both you and that boy. That's what I should have done."

"Hey, we ate it," Jonas countered.

"Oh, you guys will eat anything. The point is, I had to make another cake or Jess wouldn't have had a birthday cake."

Jonas and Maggie bickered back and forth, enjoying sparring with each other. The server was attentive but gave them privacy to talk. The two were so deep in conversation they hardly noticed anyone around them. Finally, the conversation returned to Jimmy Dean and their mountain of packages.

Maggie remembered Jimmy Dean was staying overnight with a friend from church, so she suggested talking with Jess when they arrived home. Jonas agreed. He had no problem with some of his gifts being tagged as if they had come from Jess. He thought how she responded would depend on how they presented the offer. Back in the car, Maggie retrieved her cell phone from her purse to call Jess, who said she could come over later. Maggie told her she hoped to be home in about an hour.

The two were quiet on the drive home, mesmerized by the swishing tires in the rain and the boat-like wandering of the old Caprice. At one point Maggie gazed at Jonas driving as if glimpsing him for the first time again.

Jonas felt her eyes on him and returned her open stare. "What?" he asked.

Maggie spoke reluctantly. "Oh, I don't know—a bit of déjà-vu, I guess. I suppose it's this old car and the rain." She dropped her eyes to stare at folded hands.

"During the early years of my marriage with Tom, especially when the boys were growing, there were days, months—" She chuckled sadly. "Actually, it was probably sometimes years between times of genuinely seeing each other—more than noticing the furniture certainly, but not quite fully aware either. And then one or the other of us would wake up, and recognize we had been living robotically, lost in a fog."

"It's a startling thing to wake up like that, you know? Seldom does the other person have the same waking experience at the same time. What can you do? You can't say it to them. You can't tell them to wake up. I sensed there were times when Tom was trying to say that we were not real with each other, but I focused on our kids, or on my children at school. Then he would be the one that drifted into his own world. Even if you recognize the other person is stuck in a rut, you resist saying much of anything about it because then they misinterpret it as unhappiness. It can't merely be *thought* about. It has to be realized inside."

Jonas drove and listened, glancing at Maggie periodically to determine if she was speaking in a general sense, or was perhaps trying to say something about him.

"Actually, we suppose we are awake, right in the middle of living in a dream, except sometimes something happens; tragedy, or even something ordinary, like just driving in the rain. You wake to the other person again, and the moment may stay for a while, but then fades. Mutual awareness *did* begin to continue for Tom and me in the later years. We began to be real for each other for extended periods, and then the dreaming fog was the unusual part of life. We laughed about it. We soaked it in. Somehow, that happened after the boys left, but even more when we both got to know God—*really* got to know God."

Maggie caught the last of Jonas rolling his eyes. "I know. I know. It's a religious cliché now, to claim a personal relationship with God. Still, that is what opened my eyes to Tom, when I began to see him a little like God might be seeing him, or at least like God wanted me to see him. It was the same way for him. It was exciting to be with each other like that. We were starting again, so aware of each other for the few years before he was gone. It was all too short. Do you know what I mean?"

Jonas's voice was vacant, as he answered, "No Maggie, I don't suppose I have ever gotten to that place with anyone. Still, for what I did have, it was far too short."

Jonas's face was expressionless and unreadable, but Maggie was instantly sorry she had asked. Jonas noticed her frozen face. "Maggie, it's alright," he assured her. "It's okay."

He continued. "I do understand being awake to what is happening in the present, and genuinely paying attention to people. Nevertheless, Tom must have had it easier than most. It's hard not to pay attention to you." This had been an unusually open and risky thing to say for Jonas. It came to him that he was right on the verge of something with Maggie. His eyes had spoken for him before he looked back to concentrate on the road.

At that moment, Maggie was tempted to slide across the mammoth front seat and sit right next to him, like a 16-year-old headed to a drive-in movie. She entertained it in her mind, first picturing it play out with Jonas being awkward and uncomfortable, and then with him putting his hand in hers. Maggie wanted it, but her body didn't obey. She couldn't move. Jonas didn't know how to interpret her lack of response, so he changed the subject. "Who is Jimmy Dean's father?" he asked quietly.

Maggie's body relaxed, and she raised her chin to look up. "We don't know. Jess and Jimmy Dean came to Benford with one of the O'Malley boys several years ago. Jimmy Dean was just a toddler, maybe 3 years old. They came from Chattanooga." She paused to recall. "Jess told me one time she didn't know where his dad was, hadn't seen him since before the boy was born, and didn't care, 'cause he didn't want nothin' to do with us anyways.'"

Jonas grinned at her spot-on impression of Jess. "And so she's been making similar brilliant choices in men ever since?" he asked.

"Yes—the latest one, Bo, who you single-handedly extracted from her life. That's a good thing," she added, noticing Jonas frown. Maggie then said something she didn't want to, knowing how it might sound. "You know she has a crush on you—probably because of that very reason, right?"

Jonas didn't try to deny it. He grimaced. "Yeah, I suppose so. I know she does. She doesn't know how to be with a man without it being something—you know—something sexual or flirting," he corrected, embarrassed. "Not that she has—" Jonas was concerned Maggie might misunderstand his uncertain chatter.

Maggie was silent. What was he saying? What was he thinking? She saw Jess as little more than an adolescent who continued to choose momentary pleasures over long-term responsibility, even over the best interest of her own son. That didn't mean Jonas necessarily saw it the same way. *Maybe he's attracted to her*, she thought. *Jess is young and cute. Men look twice at her.*

It was uncomfortably silent in the car. Both guessed that the other was thinking about Jess; they were actually thinking about each other. Jonas played with the windshield wipers, and Maggie dug in her purse. She finally broke the silence. "I saw Bo at the filling station the other day. I thought he had left town, but there he was on the other side of the pumps, staring at me like a glass eye, not a hint of a smile."

"As long as he leaves Jess and Jimmy Dean alone—"

"Watch out for him," Maggie said. "He might not be one to let a grudge go."

The sun snuck out of the clouds and below the horizon as they entered Benford, bleeding color into the dark cottony sky by the time Jonas pulled into the drive. He nodded at the brilliant sunset to Maggie as they carried bags into the house, and she stopped to enjoy it for a few moments.

"I almost sense the earth turning and leaning at this time of night and this time of year," she said. "The sun creeps during the day, but it falls like a star when it sets."

"I thought the sun *was* a star," answered Jonas.

"Exactly," Maggie said as she winked.

katedid: What have you been doing?
b4isleep: Shopping.
katedid: Seriously? Men shop?
b4isleep: Ha. Well, when we must, I guess.
katedid: Christmas shopping? Are you done?
b4isleep: Yeah, I think so. How about you?
katedid: I have my little girl's all bought, but not the rest.
b4isleep: The girl you are adopting?
katedid: Yes.
b4isleep: Okay. I rather figured that but wasn't sure.
katedid: Anything new on the poetry end?
b4isleep: No. Streaming thoughts. Sometimes enough to put lines down, but haven't finished anything.
katedid: Hey, let me ask you something...
b4isleep: Okay...
katedid: Are you married? I mean the reason I'm asking... and this may sound crazy but...
b4isleep: Yes?
katedid: if you were in the Army in Iraq, or had amnesia, and came home to a wife who had adopted someone while you were

gone? What would you think?

b4isleep: Well, if I were in Iraq, I guess I'd know about it, right? But amnesia? Has anyone ever actually had amnesia, or is that just a soap opera thing?

katedid: LOL Yeah, I know, right? They've all had amnesia. Okay, so something similar. If you didn't know about it, like Tom Hanks in that movie... what was it?

b4isleep: Shipwrecked?

katedid: That's it. Yes. So you come home from the island, and your wife has adopted a child while you were gone?

b4isleep: I don't know.

katedid: You don't know?

b4isleep: I don't know. I guess it would depend.

At that moment, the thought of Jimmy Dean broke through his uneasiness, and he hurriedly typed on.

b4isleep: You know something, though. The more I consider it? I'm okay with it... doesn't matter. If she loves this kid, then I know I will as well.

katedid: I suppose I understand why you were hesitant. Why did you change your mind?

b4isleep: You know the boy I was telling you about before? The one in the play? I thought of him and understood.

katedid: Okay. Yeah. So that's good to hear.

b4isleep: Yeah.

katedid: What did you get him for Christmas?

b4isleep: Ha. A baseball glove, among other things. Probably too much.

They chatted for a short time longer before logging off. Jonas felt like an old con with a conscience—equal parts thrill and revulsion in the middle of a scam. He told himself it wasn't a scam. He wanted to make sure Kate was going to be okay. *That's all I have wanted from this.* But even as he thought it, he knew it wasn't completely honest.

Kate pondered their discussion as she closed her laptop; *he never did say if he was married.*

Jonas picked up Jimmy Dean at his friend Billy's house on Sunday afternoon. Jess had dropped by Maggie's the night before, agreeing to share the gifts that Maggie and Jonas had bought for Jimmy Dean. Maggie had somehow made it seem like Jess was doing them all a big favor. Jonas was shy around both of them after his talk with Maggie about Jess. He circled around the kitchen table so many times to keep distance between him and the other two, he was sure they both noticed it.

As soon as they had decided which gift were to be given by each person, he excused himself, but not before agreeing to pick up Jimmy Dean the next day while Jess did some shopping herself. She hadn't made it clear where she was going, or when she intended to be back. Jonas and Jimmy Dean spent the afternoon playing games with Maggie before she demanded they quit and go over his homework.

They were deep into a math worksheet when the house phone rang. Maggie asked Jonas to answer while she kept working with Jimmy Dean.

"Young residence. This is Jonas," he spoke into the receiver.

"Jonas, this is Jess," her frightened voice, half-whispered and pleading. "I need your help."

Jonas barely understood her. She was talking quietly and not keeping her mouth near the mic end of the phone. Traffic rumbled by somewhere near.

"What Jess? I can't hear you very well." Both Jimmy Dean and Maggie looked up. Now her mouth was on top of the phone's mic, and her tight voice was a breathless panic, saying something incomprehensible, and then, "...at the Kwik Mart out on the highway. Bo saw me here and parked behind me. He's drunk. My car's trapped. I'm afraid of what he'll do."

"Jess where is he right now? What's he doing?"

A car door opened, the phone hit something hard, and Jess

shrieked from a distance. "Leave me alone! Let go of me," she screamed. Muffled noises came next, and abruptly the phone went dead.

Jonas immediately called 911, telling the operator there was an assault in progress at the Kwik Mart on the north end of town. Jimmy Dean and Maggie were frozen. Jonas maintained a neutral face, speaking quietly, "I'm leaving in the truck. I'll be back as soon as I can." He was out of the door before either one could say anything in return.

Maggie hugged Jimmy Dean. "Jonas will take care of this. Don't worry. He can take care of this." She kept trying to assure him, but Jimmy Dean pulled away to run outside, just as the pickup fired to life. The tires protested as Jonas squalled out of the driveway in reverse. Jimmy Dean came back in the house crying. Maggie collected him, and they held each other on the couch in the study while Maggie prayed. "Oh God, we need you now," she cried out and continued to pray.

Jonas knew he was at least 10 minutes away from the Kwik Mart as he sped down the road away from the house. Traffic was light on the residential streets in the twilight of a Sunday evening. He took the risk of running two stop signs on the way, turned north on the state highway, seeing the Kwik Mart and McDonald's signs in the distance.

Jonas floored the gas pedal when he saw Bo's old white Ford pass him heading south. The streetlights glared off the windshield as the truck went by, but he thought he had glimpsed Jess on the passenger side of the cab. He slammed on the brakes and jerked the steering wheel to U-turn through the soft mud of the road median to pursue Bo.

By the time Bo turned right on the road that went to Benford schools, Jonas was within 50 yards. Bo's old Ford fishtailed down the city street, straightened, and rocketed down several blocks. Jonas followed. He was gaining on Bo when the brake lights glowed, and the Ford slowed to turn into the empty football stadium parking lot, rolling slowly before coming to a halt. Jonas stopped 30 yards behind and got out.

He noticed Bo's engine wasn't running as he walked toward the truck, trying to peer through the back glass. Any number of additional details might have grabbed his attention, but Jonas focused only on seeing Jess. His brain offered a mirage-like image out of reflections and hope, ignoring everything else. Much later, odd memories resurfaced: the rust below the handle on the tailgate, the missing inside door panel behind Bo as he got out of the driver's side door, and the puddle in the gravel between them. By the time he had actualized the lack of Jess' blonde hair in the back glass, it was too late.

Bo approached, glaring back at him with an alcohol-fed, cocky smile. Something wasn't right. Still twenty yards apart, it entered his awareness that Bo's smile was far too confident and that his right arm was tucked behind him. The same arm shot forward, and a black barrel rose with an extended magazine hanging below it. Jonas began an instinctual rolling dive to the right, but the muzzle started spraying 9 mm rounds. Bullets flew wildly into the gravel, across Jonas, the old GMC, and on up into the dark evening sky. The first struck his turning right shoulder and accelerated the spin of his body. Two more rounds hit his torso from the back, and a fourth glanced off the back of his skull. He had a weightless sensation as he fell, spiraling to slam into the compressed limestone of the parking lot before everything went black.

CHAPTER 22 - ADOPTION
HATTIESBURG, MS – DECEMBER 2005

"I'll be back for Christmas. I don't intend to go to New Orleans right now," Kate replied over the phone, annoyed that Mandy was one of a long list of friends who wanted her to play things safe. "I'm concentrating on the adoption."

Kate was lying on the bed in her new place at Bayou Bend. The Birgsons had quickly arranged a lease agreement with her as soon as Gilbert had informed her of her need to establish residency. Paul and Mary were excited partners in helping Kate become Sicily's foster parent. They sought every opportunity to help and were obviously disappointed when it became apparent that Kate intended to eventually take Sicily back to Missouri.

"How is that going to work with you being a resident of a different state?" asked Mandy. "Won't that make the adoption process much more challenging?"

"No. From what I understand, it isn't that uncommon to have an adoption placement in another state. You know about my great relationship with Frieda, the foster care counselor. She had me get in touch with an interstate compact for adoption and foster care. They help with adopting across states. They provided me with information, including checklists to help understand and keep up-to-date with the process, and they promised to assist every step of the way. The fact that Sicily has no home and no known relatives is a terrible thing, but it will probably help with the adoption."

Mandy was beginning to warm to the idea, but she was a natural organizer and planner. She wanted to understand how adoption worked, and she still had questions. "Kate, I'm not trying to talk you out of this. I've always been under the impression it wasn't easy to adopt. And this continues to progress so fast."

Kate understood. "Hey girl, you're my best friend. I always want you to give me your opinion." She continued. "I know what you're saying, but this is an adoption out of the foster care system. Sicily is not a baby; she's a 7-year old without a family. There are no parents to challenge the adoption, and there is a real need because of the pressures they already have on the system in the Gulf States, mostly because of Katrina."

Sicily came in from the kitchen and climbed into Kate's lap with a new crayon drawing. Kate hugged her with one arm, turning the paper around to hold it with one hand to get a better view: a purple woman, a floppy-eared orange dog, and a spiky, yellow ball, high in the sky. Kate kissed Sicily's cheek and spoke into the phone, "And most of all, I believe it was meant to be. Wish you could see the picture Sicily drew. You and Knut, I think. It needs to be on your refrigerator. Gotta go now. I'll call you by this weekend."

Kate had not yet gotten over the thrill of the way Sicily sought out contact with her. She came to her unbidden, sitting nearby or climbing in her lap. They craved each other's touch. A kind of healing was taking place. "You are such a good artist, Sicily." Kate felt the crayon on the page, tracing the outline of the dog with her forefinger.

"Are we going back to Missouri?" asked Sicily.

"You liked Mandy and Knut, didn't you? Do you want to go back to Missouri?"

Sicily smiled, exaggerated nods showing how much she like the idea. "I want to ride the horses," she said, rocking back and forth as if she was already in the saddle.

"I have the perfect pony for you, Sissy," Kate replied. Ol' Jethro is just your size. He thinks he's the biggest horse in the world, but he knows how to take care of little girls like you."

Kate bounced her on her knee, and Sicily started to slide sideways, so Kate held her steady under her arms. "You have to grip with your legs to stay on. That's it. Like that, except Jethro has a wide, round back. He's not very tall, but he's pretty wide."

"Pretty wide," sung Sicily as she rode Kate's trotting knees. "Pretty wide. Pretty wide."

They played until Kate grew too tired to continue. Then they lay on the bed together, doodling with the crayons on a fresh sheet in the drawing pad. Kate sang "Magdalena Hagdalena," and it wasn't long before Sicily had caught on. Every time they came to "Oka Poka Noka," she sang at the top of her lungs. After three times through singing about the truck hitting Magdalena, Kate asked Sicily if she had any favorite songs.

Sicily started singing. "Jesus loves me, this I know, for the Bible tells me so." Kate listened to her sweet, solitary voice in the night. To her, it spoke of hope when there was none. Jesus loved her, but he wasn't around, and Sicily's father was gone. Kate joined in, even though she had little faith. After a while, she had forgotten her sadness. Sicily rose on her knees, waving her arms to conduct a dramatic slowdown for the ending. "The… Bible tells… me SOOO!"

They rolled around, hugged, sang and colored, and it wasn't long before Sicily's crayon had fallen from her hand onto the page, and she was asleep. Kate tucked her in and went into the kitchen to clean up. She drove Sicily to school each day and planned to continue the search for Daniel, at least as long as it took to complete the adoption. A second home study needed to be completed back in Missouri before school started again in January.

Kate checked her computer. There was only spam in her email inbox. She was disappointed. Why wasn't there anything from b4isleep on Messenger, or on the poetry blog? It had been almost a week since their last chat. Their online contact had gradually increased until there was nothing. Maybe he didn't like switching over to Messenger. Something had happened. Even as the thought came, she doubted it had anything to do with making the switch to chat. He had seemed comfortable with using Messenger. She was mystified and slightly annoyed at herself for how quickly she made attachments with people. Then it came to her; there was *one* new attachment asleep in her bed for which she would not let go. Maybe it wasn't such a bad trait. Kate found a blanket and the couch, turned out the light, and drifted into sleep.

Kate had planned to call Agent Spencer of the FBI the next day after dropping Sicily off at school, but while she was driving to meet with Frieda, the foster care counselor, a different FBI agent called on her cell. She pulled into the parking lot, sitting in the warmth of the car, looking out the windshield across the sidewalk at early morning traffic while she tried to answer his questions. They had been talking for only a minute before the agent's questions changed in character. Kate began to suspect she was being interrogated.

Agent Rasmussen claimed the life insurance company that held Daniel's policy had contacted the FBI. They had left the impression that Kate was interested in a legal declaration of Death in Absentia. He asked why Kate was confident that Daniel was dead.

"I'm not certain of that at all," Kate argued. "I have not made any such request."

"There was a call from the insurance company."

"I had nothing to do with that." Kate purposely slowed and annunciated each word. "I have been doing everything I am capable of—on my own—to find out what has happened to my husband. I'm not so sure the FBI has been doing the same."

"I'm sorry you feel that way." The agent sounded defensive. "Please understand that we are working with a vast number of missing peop—"

"That's not it," interrupted Kate. "I know you are dealing with an impossible situation. I am more concerned with the lack of communication that I have received. I have yet to talk face-to-face with anyone from the FBI. I spoke briefly on the phone with Agent Spencer before Thanksgiving. That's it. Am I right?"

There was only silence on the other end.

Kate was enjoying being on the offensive. "Well, let me be as frank and clear as I possibly can. Except for your call today, I have initiated almost all of the contact between us. Has the FBI learned anything? Do you have any new leads since I spoke with Agent Spencer?" It was as if she were listening to another voice selling anger to her other emotions. "And where is Agent Spencer, by the way?"

After piling her own questions upon questions, Kate's mind was now as silent as the telephone was silent. She watched the traffic flow by her truck, in this town that was not her own. Her anger confused her. What was she doing here? *Sicily*. The little girl had become her primary purpose.

Agent Rasmussen finally cleared his throat. "I believe Agent Spencer is in New Orleans. I am in St. Louis. We can continue our conversation in person as you suggested. Do you have time to meet with me within the next few days?"

Kate was confused until it sank in that he was in St. Louis, not New Orleans, as she had assumed. He probably didn't know where she was either. She informed him that she was in Mississippi, and briefly explained the situation with Sicily. "I plan to be back in Missouri within two weeks. Is that soon enough, Mr. Rasmussen?"

"That will be okay," said the agent agreeably, and gave her his phone number and extension. Kate smiled to herself. *Take that Mr. FBI*, she said to herself. But Agent Rasmussen had one more statement that made her wonder. "You might want to call the insurance company. We did receive a call about a legal declaration of death, and if you didn't initiate the query, it seems somewhat odd."

The only person Kate could think of that might have caused the life insurance company to call the FBI about Daniel's legal status was Gilbert, her lawyer. He had promised to talk to them about Daniel having been put on the National Crime Information Center's Missing Person database. She quickly reached him on her cell.

"Gilbert, I had a call only a minute ago from the St. Louis office of the FBI. The insurance company called and told them that I wanted a legal definition of Death In… something—"

"Death In Absentia?" Gilbert sounded surprised.

"Right. That's it. You didn't ask for that did you?"

"No, no I didn't. In fact, all I have said was that Daniel was added to the missing person database. It doesn't even make sense for them to want the legal definition declared. That would force them to pay out sooner rather than later, or even potentially not at all when we find Daniel."

Kate realized the implication of what Gilbert had just said. "No wonder the FBI thought I initiated the request. I'm the only person that would benefit. Well… and indirectly you."

Gilbert was adamant, maybe even slightly offended. "Kate, please believe me. I never—"

"No Gilbert. I'm not suggesting anything. I'm trying to understand. Will you ask them why they called the FBI?"

"Absolutely. Maybe it was purely a mistake. I'll see what I can find out."

Kate decided to make one more call before meeting with the foster care counselor.

"Des Guise Grill. How may I help you?"

"Terry! Hi! This is Kate Mitchell. How are you?"

"Kate! It's been too long. I'm well. Where are you? Are you in New Orleans?"

"No. I'm in Hattiesburg. I wish I *were* at your restaurant. It makes me happy just to hear your voice." Kate recognized how much she meant it, even as she spoke. Terrance had the gift of making a person's day brighter, even over the phone.

"I wish you were here too."

Kate laughed. "Your place has been mentioned quite often in my conversations with Sara."

"Hmm... well, I like that."

Kate thought he sounded a little unsure. "I'm sure you and Sara have kept the telephone wires hot."

Now there was complete silence on the line. Kate grimaced, scolding herself. *Yikes, what is going on?* "Well, I'm glad to have met you; at least *something* good is happening out of this horrible mess."

"Kate, you know how sorry I am you have to go through this. Have you learned anything new in the last few days?"

"Not much. My attorney has hired a private detective to find the man my husband Daniel was talking with that night. Of course, there are more than a few people named Jonas in the world. Other than that, not much is going on. Kendra was never able to remember much more. The FBI now wants to meet with me, but I'm going to meet with them in St. Louis. I'm sure my problems with contacting the NOPD were apparent to you."

"Yes, I could tell. But listen. About that. I was talking with a friend who knows Detective Manson, and when I said something about him maybe being dirty, he was like, 'huh-uh brother—no way.' So when I mentioned it to Sara, she was furious. She hasn't called me back since."

Kate knew how strongly Sara felt about Manson. Still, she was surprised that Terrance's questioning of Sara on that matter was reason enough for her to drop him. "She'll probably get over it, Terry. I wouldn't worry about it."

"I don't think so, Kate. It bothers me, but—you know what? Never mind. How is the adoption going?"

"It's going amazingly well. As confusing and frustrating as the search for Daniel has been, the adoption process has been relatively smooth so far. Every door I come to flies wide open."

"Yes! That's what I like to hear! So tell me, what else needs to happen?"

"After today, not much! Everyone has been so helpful, you know? We still have to complete a home study in Missouri. So we're only going to stay in Hattiesburg until Sicily finishes school."

Terrance's voice conveyed something other than happiness. "Really? I'm shocked!"

"Okay," Kate said. "I know this is a surprise. I hadn't intended to go back to Missouri this soon. I guess everything changed with Sicily, and I'm not sure how much more I can realistically achieve in New Orleans. Understand?"

"Hon, you need to do what it takes to make you happy and to take care of that little girl. I'm super happy for you. Just selfishly sad for myself." His voice trailed off. "And I imagine Sara is going to be sad as well, but she'll be okay. I'm sure she wants the best for you!"

"Hey! I'll be sad about it too," she replied. "But we'll be back to visit. Who knows what will happen, right?"

"Whatever happens—we will eat."

Kate laughed. "And if *you* cook, we will eat well."

Kate, Sara and Sicily took advantage of the sunny December late afternoon to wander the path by the river. The day reminded Kate of what Dickens had written about March days, "summer in the light, and winter in the shade." The sun was already dropping behind the top of the tree line across the river. A sudden chill made her shiver. She suggested they take the path back to the cabin.

Kate and Sara each had one of Sicily's hands, and they periodically counted to three and swung the giggling girl in a long jump forward. She squealed with delight each time, jumping in anticipation of the count. "I can fly," she crowed.

"You're Peter Pan," cried Kate.

"I'm Peter Pan," she repeated. Then, "Who's Peter Pan?"

"He's a boy who can fly."

Sicily scrunched her forehead and stamped the sandy path. "But I'm not a boy."

"You're not a boy?" teased Kate.

"I'm a girl."

"She's a small girl after all," sang Kate to the tune of Disney's "Small World." Sara joined in and so did Sicily. They sang all the way to the house.

"Oh no," sighed Sara. "I'll never get this song out of my head now."

"You're going back to Missouri that soon? That does it. I'm going back to New Orleans," Sara told Kate. "I don't like it here, and I'm tired of living with my sister."

"And my going back to Missouri has nothing to do with this change of plans?"

"No! Yes! I'm blaming it on you. You're leaving me to a life of skeleton crew boredom and my crazy, angry sister."

Kate laughed. "Oh, she's not that bad. At least you have a sister." Her face turned serious. "What will you do? You're the one that told me the city is still dangerous."

"Well, I hadn't mentioned it before now, but there's a good chance I have a job," announced Sara, as though she were justifying a decision to a parent. "It's a corporate security position with an oil company."

Kate knew she should not be surprised at Sara proposing any future. She nodded and smiled, imagining Sara would do very well in a corporate environment. She was independent, strong, attractive, and ambitious.

"It's actually a friend of a friend that had the idea," Sara said, smiling. "He knows a guy in charge of security at a contractor for one of the big oil companies."

"Wow! It's funny how things work out, isn't it?" Kate reflected that life was never exclusively happy or sad anymore. 'Bittersweet' had become her consistent mode of existence. People were appearing and disappearing from her life more quickly than she could consciously cope with. She reflexively put her hand on the curly, black head of Sicily who was coloring at her feet and thought, *not this one; I cannot lose this one.* She had survived the loss of her own son, David. She was somehow surviving the loss of Daniel. She didn't even want to contemplate the loss of Sicily.

Kate noticed that in all of the talk about going back to New Orleans, Sara had not bought up Terrance. "I suppose Terrance was the friend with the friend who referred you to the job." She was looking at Sicily when she noticed Sara hadn't said anything. She didn't seem to have even heard the question.

Kate shrugged, "Okay. While we are still here, let's make a couple of phone calls together. Maybe we can roll this mystery on down the road."

Kate checked the people list on her cell to verify the phone number of Charles Curtis in New Orleans, leader of the sobriety group Daniel had met with in the restaurant. Since only talk with him by phone, she had been unable to reach him. Once again, she got the same results. There was no answering machine, just an endless ring as if the phone was still active but nobody was at home.

"Let's attack this differently," said Sara. "That's his home phone number, right?" Kate nodded. "Well, what was the name of the church the sobriety group was affiliated with? Let's give them a call."

Kate appeared doubtful. "I don't know. It's already almost 5:00 o'clock. Do you suppose there will still be anybody at the church? I guess we can give it a try."

She went over to the kitchen table to access her laptop while Sara got down on the floor to help Sicily color. While she was accessing her contact manager, she opened her email and then Messenger. Nothing but junk mail in her inbox, and no instant messages. She was frowning when Sara noticed and asked her what was wrong.

"Oh, nothing," she insisted. "It's odd. I've had an ongoing discussion with a participant on my poetry blog that quit right in the middle of it. No messages in several days."

"Maybe his wife caught him," snickered Sara.

"Oh, for Pete's sake. It wasn't that kind of discussion." Kate tittered in spite of herself and felt embarrassed. It was annoying to be dropped so abruptly. "Okay, never mind that. Here's the church's number."

She keyed the number into her cell—surprised when it was

immediately answered. "Corbaine Parish. How may I help you?"

The quick answer surprised Kate—so much so—she was temporarily at a loss for words. "Yes. Hello! My name is Kate Mitchell. I am trying to contact Charles Curtis."

"Hold please."

Kate keyed the cell for the speakerphone so Sara could join the conversation. The phone made clicking noises, almost sounding dead at one point but several seconds later, Charles Curtis answered. "Addiction Triumph. This is Charles."

"Charles, this is Kate Mitchell calling again. I have you on speaker with Sara Arceneaux. I hope I'm not calling at a bad time."

Charles gave a mirthless laugh on the other end. "It's hard to imagine a good time these days." He paused. "But I'm sorry. I remember talking with you, Kate. You were trying to find out more about your husband's connection with Jonas in our sobriety group."

"Yes, exactly." Kate was relieved that he remembered her. "Actually, anything more you can tell me about Jonas or the members of the group would be great. People keep surprising me with little details that help me understand what occurred."

"Right. Right. Well, we haven't recovered any more records, but I did remember that Jonas's last name is Bays. I told you that he was working on Joe's house, but he actually shared half of their double shotgun house with Joe and his daughter. He might have been renting it from Joe, trading work for part of the rent. I'm not sure."

"Wait, you're saying he *lived* in the same house as Joe and Sicily?"

"Yes, that's right," Charles said.

Kate was overcome by the significance, but it was Sara who spoke again. "Charles, that's a crucial detail. Joe's body was discovered a few blocks south of the marina in Lakeview and Kate's husband's rental car was found in the vicinity as well."

"Oh!" Charles exclaimed. "Well, they didn't live in Lakeview. It was somewhere in Gentilly, north of I10 but on the other side of City Park from Lakeview."

"Yes, we have Joe and Sicily's address but no record of anyone else living with them. Are you sure about that? Maybe Jonas lived in Lakeview."

"No. I know they still lived in the same house at the time of the hurricane. My guess is they were going to try to leave the city together. I'm not sure why they would have been in that area. Maybe trying to take Robert E. Lee over to the Hammond Street Bridge, then shoot down and over to Causeway Avenue. That would be about 4-5 miles. With most everybody out of the city, there would have been no traffic.

"No," said Sara doubtfully. "I had a similar idea before. But it would have been crazy to cross the lake that day."

"No, I didn't mean north across the lake. South on Causeway to I10. If they were blocked from getting to I610, they might have tried Robert E. Lee... but hey, when they got to the Hammond Street Bridge, the water must have been so high it looked unsafe, so maybe they did turn back south to cut down to I610, probably right before the levee broke."

"That may be, but why did they wait?" Kate was doubtful. "Even if Joe and Sicily's car wasn't running, why wouldn't they all leave in Daniel's rental car before the hurricane hit?"

"I think I can answer that," said Charles. "Joe was a good man, but he was also a proud, stubborn man. They weren't well off. Sicily's mom died from leukemia about 5 years ago. She was quite a bit younger than him. He probably wanted to be able to take as much as possible with them, especially the car. He might have refused to leave without it."

Kate and Sara glanced at each other. A picture of what might have happened was beginning to emerge, but it never seemed to lead much closer to the truth about Daniel. Kate sighed. "Well Charles, thank you for your help. Maybe I'll be able to find this Jonas Bays. He continues to be our mystery man."

"I'm sorry. Maybe the police will help you out with this one. New Orleans is just a chaotic mess. Very few people have come back to those areas of the city."

Kate was frustrated, but she wasn't about to give up. "I'm afraid I can't count on the police. That's okay. We'll find him. Maybe he'll be able to tell us what happened." She paused. "Jonas Bays," she sighed again. "How many Jonas Bays are there are in the country, the state, or even New Orleans for that matter?"

"You know?" Charles' voice came hesitantly. "I probably shouldn't tell you this. It is privileged information, but under the circumstances, it might help you find Jonas to know he had been in trouble with the law. I don't know all of the circumstances," he added hastily. "He didn't talk about it much, but his involvement with our group was required as a part of his sentence."

Sara responded with the intensity of a detective. "It's important we find him. You need to tell us what you know—"

"That's all I'm comfortable with saying," interrupted Charles.

"No, I appreciate it so much," Kate stressed. "You have been more than helpful. Charles, is there anything else we can do for you? Is your family well?"

With a sad but unbroken voice, Charles let them know his own family was all right. His extended family at the church and in the community on the other hand—there was more loss and heartache than he was capable of articulating in a few minutes on the phone. The unique circumstances of the disaster had broken so many families and ended so many lives. That she was far from alone in not knowing if a loved one was alive or dead became apparent to Kate as he talked. "It won't be fixed," Charles said. "It will never be the same. We'll never know the actual cost. It will be months, maybe even years, before the dead are tallied."

"Hello?"

"Kate? This is Gilbert. Did I wake you?"

"I must have dozed off. Why are you calling so late?"

"I wanted to make sure you were alone. You are alone, aren't you?"

"Well sure, Gilbert. Sicily's here, but she's asleep. What's wrong?"

"Kate, I spoke with multiple people at Patriot Life. I'm persuaded that no one there called the FBI. I also can't see the FBI making it up."

"What are you saying? That someone called the FBI, pretending to be from the insurance company? Why?"

"I don't know. Someone hoping to free the money that is coming to you. I haven't figured that out."

"Why would they want to do that? Who would want to do that?"

"Again, I don't know, but Kate?"

"Yes?"

"I don't like it. Something's not right with this. You need to be on your guard. I wish you were back in Missouri."

"Just a few more days, Gilbert."

"Okay. Call me when you return. And please be careful."

CHAPTER 23 – OUT OF BODY
NASHVILLE, TN – DECEMBER 2005

Jonas became aware. His first perceptions were dreamlike and disorienting, and yet somehow tranquil. He suffered no discomfort, nor did recognition of his existence in an altered state cause him to fear. He didn't know what this reality was different from; just that *different* was the overall experience of it. His consciousness found no anchoring point, no frame of reference. He did not struggle or become anxious, largely because of an overwhelming sense of well-being mixed with curiosity. *Different* transformed into *new*. New and curious, his perceptions became purposeful and were no longer limited to sight, sound, smell, taste, and touch. All of his senses increased in amplitude and fidelity. Information flooded his being from additional unidentifiable stimuli arriving complete with understanding and a sense of knowing. He didn't feel his own body. In fact, he perceived his body lying in a hospital bed, separate from a core that he now thought of as himself. Others anxiously worked nearby. He was mildly interested, but for the moment, his interest was only passing. With his lack of attention to the hospital scene, the reality diminished simultaneously to other realities becoming available. Ideas and concepts bubbled into awareness, sharing the richness of his perceptions. Nebulous, saturated, blue and green fragrant music grabbed his attention to set off another quickly expanding reality.

A voice sounded. "You're a quick study." The figure of a man was moving toward him through a multi-hued, saturated mist, walking slowly but arriving quickly as if in a strobe light. Jonas felt disoriented again. He sought for a way to integrate the emotional complexity of the information bombarding him.

"I'm not so quick," he was able to reply. The words tasted oddly true and sad as they left his lips. They sat together on a park bench in the mist, the older man's skinny legs crossed at the knees. Jonas's attention followed the high-water khakis down to a pair of penny loafers over red and gray argyle socks, which somehow calmed his apprehensions. *Is this a lucid dream?* He doubted it; his own awareness was too intentional. He had never had a dream continue beyond the initial recognition of the fact that he was dreaming. *No, I would have woken by now.*

"I'm not a quick study. I have no idea what is happening to me." The man beside him was now clothed in grandfatherly Bermuda shorts, a striped color belt, and black socks inside of white New Balance tennis shoes. Jonas thought he looked like someone's stereotypical idea of a Florida senior. Had he always been wearing that red porkpie with a striped band that matched his belt? A laugh was conceived somewhere inside him and quickly erupted like a fountain, spreading a tsunami of tangerine flavored waves of sound that made the surrounding mist ripple in response.

"What's so funny?" asked the eccentric old man.

"Everything. Nothing. Why are you wearing a hat like that?"

"Actually, I am only appearing to you in a manner your consciousness will not fear."

Jonas questioned how consciousness was possible if he had left his body lying in a hospital bed.

The man disappeared into the mist but was obviously still somewhere in the vicinity because his voice spoke again. "You are right to question the word consciousness, but for the wrong reason. It is the closest word to my meaning you know. In your world, I am not privy to your thoughts. It is different here. What I am speaking of is certainly not tied to your body or your brain."

He is reading my mind. "Will you tell me where—whatever I am—is?" asked Jonas, and then hating his own confusing words, he made the question simpler; *where am I?*

"You don't have a sufficient frame of reference for me to answer where you are." Every time the stranger spoke, Jonas was flooded with information. Much of it was external and sensory, but part of it seemed internal, almost as if the thoughts were his own. Yet he had no difficulty in distinguishing between the two. He considered their conversation until this point. Simply existing in this place was so fluid and confusing. "In fact," the stranger explained, pausing for emphasis, "you do not have a sufficient frame of reference for existing here without my support."

"Okay. Please let me begin again." Jonas replied. "Am I dead?"

"I'm here to help you. He has required this of me. You will be returning."

Jonas considered the carefully worded response. Why wasn't he relieved? Who was the 'He' that required this stranger to assist him? Questions emerged and faded, but to understand the answers he needed to be more careful with his questions. As a result, he asked nothing. He closed his eyes, listened, and eventually the words came.

"You are a man, somewhat like another man who is with us. He was a man of the same human essence as His mother. He was also God, of the same nature as His Father, conceived by the Holy Spirit into your world. He died on a cross, rose again and ascended where He is now with us as God and man. You are a man. Do you understand this? You do not know Him, but even as I speak, you recognize the truth of it. He is both perfect God and perfect man, not two, but one. God and man together—the one whom your world knows as Jesus Christ."

"These words are also known in your world as a dusty legend in the minds of many, but as white, hot reality in the spirit of a few. Even now, he is Man sitting at the right hand of the Father, mediating for humanity. You would recognize him as a man, although his body is brilliantly transformed, much as other men's bodies have been transformed. He was the first among those many. He is still human. He is real and visible."

"Oh, but He is God, Lord of all, and heir to all. He is the way to the Father and is the advocate and guarantee for everyone who honestly believes. The most courageous and best hopes of man depend on Him. There is no other way. Salvation from the curse of man comes by believing in the Lord Jesus Christ, the only man who lived a perfect life while accepting the consequences for the rest of you. He died the death of a man but suffered the guilt of a race. He took your sins along with the rest, died and then—unlike any other man before—he woke from death, and lived, totally transformed."

"Do my words make you uncomfortable? Do you recognize the truth of it, Man? Did you know Him or did you only know your own muddled ideas? Was He your Lord when you came to me? You were stung with death, but it is not yet to be completed. You have been given a measure of grace for your measure of faith. It is for this and the prayers of those who love you that you will return."

"You have been one who lives two lives; one life lived in honesty, standing in contrast to a life that is secret. This cannot be. The hidden will destroy the open. You already knew this to be true, and yet you waited until there was no time."

Jonas did not have to consider these words. They were evident, authoritative, and tangible beyond explanation, and he wept grievously. "I would like to know all that you would have me know," he said when he regained control enough to speak.

"You wish it now. His presence, even in this place that is neither heaven nor earth, is overwhelming enough that you would one day be captive through no love of your own. He wishes you to be free. You want to follow Him now. Will you wish it when you no longer remember this experience?"

A shocked silence was all Jonas had in him. He bowed, inside and out, hoping for a grace he could not name.

"He loves you. He has always been there and will still be there in the same way. He chose you. He called you. You must choose Him from inside your own life. You will not awaken immediately, and when you do, you will not remember this until the day you and He meet face to face. On that day, you will know as you are known."

As quickly as he had arrived, Jonas slid effortlessly back into the emptiness of a brain controlled by Propofol, the drug known as the milk of amnesia.

CHAPTER 24 – DEATH & TRAUMA
BENFORD, TN – DECEMBER 2005

Maggie sat on the front row of the funeral home with Jimmy Dean at her side. He had become her one constant focus in the midst of the hazy shock surrounding her existence since the shooting. She squeezed a tissue in her hands until it became a tiny ball, and then pulled another to take its place. She worried over Jimmy Dean who had stayed close and silent through the waiting and the serious explanations and platitudes by doctors, nurses, clergy, police, and psychologists. All were well meaning, but Maggie doubted that Jimmy Dean was listening to any of them. He showed little sign he was even listening to her.

She watched him surreptitiously, but it hardly mattered. His squinting eyes followed an obsessive pattern at the front of the room. His eyes moved from the flowers on the bottom row to the top row, skirted the top of the casket to jump from the pink clamshell wall light on the left to its mate on the opposite side. His focus dropped from there to another spread of flowers, then down to a horizontal line in the tan and black Berber carpet, following it back across the floor to begin the circle all over again.

Friends from church walked down the center aisle, peered respectfully into the casket, and stopped by to embrace Maggie or grasp her hand. The women told Jimmy Dean they were sorry, and made abortive attempts at hugs, while the men reached for his hand or his unruly hair. He avoided the pats on the head, but dutifully shook their hand without meeting their eye, waiting patiently until they passed by before continuing his squint-eyed journey through the flowers.

A few of Jess's friends appeared in a blur of metal piercings, denim, tattoos, and cleavage. One girl with neon, green hair over swollen eyes knelt on the floor and tried to hug Jimmy Dean, but even green hair and running mascara could not snatch his attention. Maggie fed the girl tissues until she left, sobbing as she staggered down the outside aisle. As the first song began, Maggie didn't bother to look back to see how many had stayed.

No family attended. Jess and Jimmy Dean had been alone in the world. Bo was in jail. Jonas lay in a coma in a Nashville hospital. *Jimmy Dean has only me.* She ached for him, but then Harlan left the group of pallbearers, sat down on the other side of Jimmy Dean, and the boy finally stopped his compulsive wandering eyes, letting the older man pull him close. After all else, it was this tenderness that caused Maggie to weep.

After everyone had eaten, the women from church cleaned up what was left of the brisket, fried chicken, macaroni salad, fruit salad, rolls, scalloped potatoes and twenty desserts. They filled the refrigerator with leftovers, said their solemn goodbyes, and left. Jimmy Dean ate a few Cheetos and fell asleep on the sofa in the library.

Maggie turned on the television for the noise, but then almost immediately turned it back off. She fell into a recliner, into the silence of the room, letting her mind try to assimilate a mass of confusing and horrific images from the past days. From the time Jonas had left in answer to Jess's phone call, there had been little time to understand and accept reality.

Closing her eyes, she reflected on the previous days. It bothered her to recall that she had kept telling Jimmy Dean everything was going to be okay. Everything had *not* been okay. The boy had been inconsolable after Jonas had driven off. Something in him had known. By the time they had received the first phone call, he had withdrawn into an unhappy despondency she had never seen in him, not even during dark periods before Jonas had arrived.

Multiple sessions with law enforcement officials had left Maggie with an incomplete picture of the night's events, but she knew enough. Jess was dead, and Jonas was near death, both allegedly at the hands of Bo Donnelly, although the two fallen bodies were miles apart. There had been two eyewitnesses. A passionate weekend golfer, on his way home from 18 holes on the brisk, winter day, had stopped for gas at the Kwik Mart. He had immediately called 911 before desperately working to stop Jess' blood flow until the ambulance arrived. His statement to the police identified Bo as the man who had trapped Jess against her car and then left her lying in the parking lot, repeatedly stabbed in the abdomen. He had also thoroughly described Bo's Ford pickup and most of the license plate numbers.

The eyewitness to Jonas's shooting had been a high school freshman, jogging home from a friend's house by cutting through the school property near the football field. Dropping at the first crack of automatic gunfire, he had risen from the ground in time to watch Bo jump into the pickup and leave the parking lot. His description of the truck matched Bo's old Ford. The young man had saved Jonas's life, at least so far, by immediately calling 911 on his cell phone when he saw his crumpled body lying in the parking lot.

The license plate on Tom's old pickup had been the clue that led authorities to call Maggie. She had feared the worst when Jonas had not come home within an hour of Jess' phone call. By the time she received the phone call from the police, he had already been airlifted to a Nashville hospital. The emergency room staff resuscitated Jonas, who had come very close to bleeding out from the bullet wounds. He then began to experience seizures that doctors believed resulted from a blunt head injury, likely caused by the force of his head hitting the hard surface of the parking lot. The seizures convinced them to put him into a drug-induced coma. They were only now, after a full week, contemplating bringing him out of the coma.

Jonas had flirted with death, and yet the police told Maggie he had been lucky. The spray of 9mm bullets from Bo's Tec-9, illegally altered to full auto, had missed major organs and arteries and caused less damage than they might have because of the full metal jacket rounds. The police hadn't told her everything, but it was already common knowledge in town that possession of the Tec-9 had led to Bo ratting on his cousin Billy. The police had raided Billy Donnelly's 5-acre farm, finding a weapons stash full of stolen or illegal guns, a makeshift meth lab, and even a stolen 24' lake cabin cruiser inside a dilapidated barn with a roof falling in. The only surprise for most people had been that Billy had been so industrious with his thievery.

No one knew why Bo and Jonas had squared off in the school parking lot. Nobody remembered seeing Jonas or Maggie's old pickup at the Kwik Mart. The timeline established by the two principal witnesses didn't leave much time for anything but the drive between the two locations. The police suspected a phone conversation must have led to the confrontation, but Maggie had told them Jonas didn't have a cell phone and had not had time to call from home before he left in such a hurry. They had been skeptical, asking to look in his garage apartment, which she allowed, but they didn't find a cell phone.

The police had only completed a cursory search. Maggie had been slightly uncomfortable about letting the police in without Jonas's permission, but all they had wanted was to secure a possible phone. It was while leading them through the apartment that she noticed his laptop. She wanted to contact potential friends or relatives who needed to know about what had happened, especially if he didn't pull through at the hospital. Jonas had never talked about his past.

Maggie was disinclined to snoop, but she felt a strong temptation to get the laptop and bring it back to the house. She wrestled with conflicting thoughts. Wasn't it only right she should attempt to locate others who cared about him? *He would have told me about others if he had wanted me to know,* she answered herself. She tried to put herself in his place. What if their roles were reversed? She had nothing to hide, but did that make a difference? Given the circumstances, being so close to death, she imagined that she would welcome the intrusion.

Rationalization or not, she quickly checked on Jimmy Dean, covered him with a blanket, and walked out into cold, blackness, heading for the garage. The crisp air tasted of freedom from the stuff of sadness. The apartment felt almost as chilly to her as the outside air. Even though it was her place, what she was doing felt wrong. She almost walked out empty handed, but finally grabbed the laptop and power supply, feeling like a first-time thief.

Maggie was computer literate in a basic way. She had no problem logging in since Jonas had not bothered to change the password on the one user account. She found few files of interest, save a few Word documents, and work-related spreadsheets. Two of the Word documents were poems. One told the story of Jimmy Dean's Thanksgiving play, which Jonas had already shown her. The other was unfinished.

Finishing with the local computer files, she opened Internet Explorer. She followed a few bookmarks to news aggregate sites and online message boards for auto mechanics and handyman topics. She followed another bookmark to a site called the Puzzled Poet, which made her smile. Jonas hadn't mentioned that his interest in poetry had carried over to the internet. She spent some time browsing the site before trying the Login.

To Maggie's surprise, the user ID and password populated automatically. Navigating to the message board, she noticed Jonas had a private message from Kate Mitchell, one of the blog moderators.

> Hey, I wanted to check with you to make sure that everything is okay. Haven't seen you on the Puzzled Poet or on Messenger.

Maggie read the message history, becoming more and more perplexed. She was particularly surprised that Jonas had commented on someone else's poem. She frowned in puzzlement. It didn't appear the moderator knew Jonas, other than as a user on the blog. She was tempted to open Messenger, but had never used it before, and didn't want to take the chance that her presence would appear "live" on the chat client.

Instead, she read the short bio information on the blog, and based on the information, entered "Kate Mitchell St. Jude, MO" in a Google search. There weren't many results, but one linked to a recent online article on the website for a newspaper called the St. Jude Record. The headline read, "Local Man Still Missing From Katrina."

Maggie began to read with growing unease. Kate Mitchell's husband had been in New Orleans during Katrina and was still missing. She located the date of the article. It was scarcely weeks old. She scrolled up and down, searching for a picture in the article, but there was none. A black numbness seeped into Maggie's body. She sat staring at the computer screen with her hands on the keyboard, unable to lift a finger.

Maggie sat for the longest time, awareness closing down to a tunnel. When able to move again, she methodically shut down the computer, checked on Jimmy Dean once more, and took the laptop back to the apartment. Maggie didn't want to read anymore—didn't even want to see anything else on the computer. The tiniest of voices inside her said she was jumping to conclusions. But she knew—even her body knew—Jonas connecting with the one writer, on the one poetry site, who had lost a husband to Katrina? It was too significant to be a coincidence.

Tonight, she determined not think about what it meant or what she should do about it. She was done with thinking, worrying, managing and fixing. She had barely enough energy to get the sleepy boy up to bed and get ready for bed herself. Before falling asleep, she spoke a wordless prayer, concentrating on her God, laying it all before Him, resting in the peace she knew so well.

The next morning, Maggie dropped Jimmy Dean off at Harlan

and Betty's house. He still wasn't quite himself, but the combination of being on Christmas break and getting to spend the day with Harlan had brightened his mood enough to spawn the trace of a smile when Harlan and Betty greeted them at the door.

Harlan wasn't one to settle in the mulligrubs. "Tell Jonas, when he wakes up, to quit lollygaggin' around, and get back home. I'm tired of doin' all his work for 'em."

Maggie smiled distractedly. "Okay," she said weakly.

Harlan noticed her demeanor and asked, "Are you okay? You be careful driving."

"I'll be fine, Harlan," she replied. She smiled as Jimmy Dean noticed Betty's beckoning finger, and followed her aproned figure into the kitchen. The smell of blueberry waffles wafted through the house. She was tempted to stay herself. "You know," Maggie warned, "Jonas might not be the same when he wakes up."

Harlan frowned. "We'll deal with whatever happens," he replied gruffly. "Whatever. Don't matter. We'll be here for you, Maggie. Take care. If you need to stay there, give us a call. There's no reason why the boy cain't stay here tonight or a few more nights for that matter."

Maggie turned and left before the tears in her eyes had a chance to overflow.

On the drive to the hospital, she let her thoughts go where they may, detached for once, not trying to organize or find the best solution. She didn't understand what she knew and didn't want to guess. Without trying, she made the decision. She resolved to do nothing until Jonas regained consciousness, and even then, she would let him do what needed to be done in his own way. She owed him that. If he didn't wake up? That... she refused to contemplate.

Her problem was finding the right time and words to convey to him that she *knew*. *Suspected* a tiny voice inside argued. *Doesn't matter* she argued back. Something was there. She wouldn't be accusatory. She would not condemn. But she knew her own nature; she *would* say something, even if she didn't intend to. So it was better to plan and to know what she was going to say. Her mind drifted over the past few months: his reticence, his initial desire to move on, and his boyish delight in poetry. She smiled, recalling his admiration over Frost's ability to be so profound in such a simple fashion. Frost's poem "The Impulse" came to mind. She didn't know the words by heart but remembered they were about a young woman who had run away from her life. Had he read it? It fit so perfectly. That was it. Read the poem to him—then watch his reaction.

CHAPTER 25 – RECUPERATION
NASHVILLE, TN – DECEMBER 2005

The nurses in ICU all greeted Maggie when she arrived at the hospital. Lissa, a petite waif who had been his chief nurse since coming to the hospital, informed her that Jonas's doctor planned to be there within the hour. She led Maggie into Jonas's cubicle. The two of them stood on either side of his impassive body while Lissa explained that his wounds were healing well. They were mainly concerned now with the head injury, if and how much damage to his brain there might be, and controlling the seizures. After Lissa had left, Maggie stayed by his side, noticing his color was much better than when she had been there two days before.

Maggie pulled a chair near the bed and drew a novel out of her bag. She had purchased the book expressly to read during the long hours of waiting. Mimicking Dick Estell on NPR's Radio Reader, she announced quietly, "This morning we continue with 'The Widow of the South' by Robert Hicks." Maggie continued to read from her marked location, having no idea if Jonas comprehended anything, but it seemed like the right thing to do.

She soon trailed off, thinking of Carrie McGavock, the heroine of the novel who had dealt with so much more hardship than Maggie ever had. She was in awe of this woman who confronted the overwhelming number of civil war dead, as she had put it, "without turning her head." She did not have the same strength or Carrie's singular purpose.

Dr. Felling came into the ICU later, discussed the patients with the nursing staff, and quickly came over to check on Jonas. He informed Maggie that this morning they would begin weaning Jonas from the drugs that were keeping him in the induced coma. The reduction in drugs was to be gradual while monitoring his brain activity regularly for signs of returning seizures. If the seizures returned, they would start the drugs again to continue the induced coma.

"When?" Maggie asked.

"This morning."

Maggie was so used to waiting hours for progress, she was surprised when he directed her to the ICU waiting room as soon as she had no more questions. Lissa promised to periodically keep her informed, telling her it would be an hour before they began. After that, it might be a long, gradual process. Maggie sat in the waiting room for a few seconds before gathering her coat and bag and heading for the hospital chapel to pray.

The chapel was small and silent, all sound muted by maroon wall coverings and thick carpet, warmed by light streaming through narrow, vertical stained glass windows. Noticing no one else in the room, Maggie collapsed to kneel in the back pew. The little chapel invited her to release the emotions she had constrained in public over the preceding days.

She was no stranger to the emotions of loss. Tom had passed in the midst of a period when their love had kindled into a passion that rivaled their initial romance but still held the depth that came from years of being the only one for each other. After the boys had left, they had rediscovered each other and reveled in their love. Tom sat in the kitchen while she puttered. Maggie often caught him staring at her with an unguarded smile. She would drop in his lap, circle her arms around his neck, and kiss him frankly. She smiled, remembering his blush, embarrassed like a boy being kissed for the first time.

Maggie was suffering loss once again, but it was unlike what she had experienced with Tom. She was not afraid to express anger and confusion to her God. She believed that He valued honesty in one who honored Him entirely. She wasn't sure what emotions were sweeping over her now. There were moments of anger, certainly, but the rest were difficult to distinguish, all muddled and confused by the experience of betrayal in her life.

She cried out to God, louder than she had intended, shocking herself with the cry of raw pain in the quiet space. Maggie gave in to the release of guarded feelings, almost glad to be experiencing anything other than numbing depression. God was listening, no matter what her emotions said.

While praying for Jimmy Dean, a profound stillness flowed through her like a slow, river eddy, easing the pain. She pleaded with God not to allow him to retreat into himself. He had gained so much confidence and joy with Jonas. Could he survive losing both his mom *and* Jonas? This reminded her of who was taking care of Jimmy Dean.

"Thank you God for Harlan," she cried out. "He has genuinely stepped up." She also knew God cared more for Jimmy Dean than Harlan or anyone else in his life, even her. Jesus had always given children his full attention while he was on earth. That had not changed.

Maggie stopped praying long enough to glance at her watch. Almost an hour had passed. Rising to go back to the ICU, she was surprised to make out a figure standing at the front of the chapel, haloed by the light from the stained glass windows. She felt a chill that came from a sense of the unknown and inexplicable. But as the figure moved away from the light, down the short aisle toward her, she saw he was an ordinary, older man, dressed almost comically in pants too short, revealing argyle socks that matched an Ivy cap.

"Have you been here the whole time? I didn't know you were here," she blurted, embarrassed at the intensity of her powerful, spoken prayers.

The man sat down in the pew in front of her, turning to face her when he replied, "No need to be embarrassed. I'm here for those in need." Maggie wasn't sure what this meant. Was he a hospital chaplain? He had spoken in subdued tones, although his movements had been lively enough. Now his words took on a forceful quality. "What do you need from God today?" he asked. She was struck by the intensity of the man's gaze.

Maggie's heart became unexpectedly light. She had found peace, her distress melting as he spoke. More than this, her mind left its fuzzy confusion, and now felt swift and sharp. It was almost as if someone had impossibly opened a window in the enclosed chapel, allowing in a breeze, carrying the delicious fragrance of spring. Maggie considered his question, discarding all of the pat, easy answers that now struck her as being less than honest. "I need to know how to respond to someone who has misled me," she finally admitted.

"Someone you love?"

This she was unable to respond to immediately. Of course, she loved Jonas. She cared. Maybe even something more, but... "I'm not sure I can love someone when I don't know who he is."

Maggie was immediately second-guessing the way she had spoken freely about private matters to the stranger. There was just something about him. Perhaps it was the way he held her gaze with those intense, ageless eyes. Before she realized the oddness of their conversation and his appearance, his questions changed to knowing assertions.

"That may soon change. Shocking events accompanied by love are often pivotal. He is surely not the first person you have known to survive traumatic events by compartmentalizing his life. He will need you now more than ever."

Annoyed, Maggie was more confrontational than she intended. "You don't understand. It is much more than simply being honest, or admitting to a questionable past. He is entirely different from who he has pretended to be."

The stranger never stopped beaming. His eyes even sparkled while replying, "Things are not always what they seem. 'Not all those who wander are lost.'"

Jonas woke, amazed that he had apparently slept late into daylight hours. Light filtered through pink eyelids. There were voices in his room. Who was so inconsiderate that they came into his bedroom while he was sleeping? For the first time since he was a kid, he pretended to be asleep when he was not. He lay there trying to understand the words, but he was having a difficult time muddling through his confused mind. His throat hurt. He felt disoriented and sick. "He may be awake," he thought he heard someone say, before drifting into sleep again.

"Everything looks good," Dr. Felling told Maggie. He leaned forward in the waiting room chair, elbows on his knees, fingertips touching as his eyes peered over glasses to focus on hers. "There is no sign of returning seizures and no toxicity in his blood. His body is adapting well to the decrease of the drug in his IV. We need to be patient. He might not be able to carry on what you consider a normal conversation at first. There is the possibility of some temporary delirium or psychosis from the drugs. He may not remember much from the first few days. Don't attempt to flood him with information or questions for a while. Take your lead from what he does and says, and again, try to be patient."

Maggie nodded her way through this monolog. She had already researched medical induced comas. The nursing staff had also explained what Maggie could expect. Still, like most friends and family of patients, she didn't mind the repetition; she was hungry for information. Her questions just tended to ask for the type of guesses and forecasting that medical staff hated to give. "How long do you think it will be before he is able to speak normally? In a general sense, I mean?" she qualified.

Dr. Felling sat back, slid his glasses back up his nose and smiled. "Possibly a few hours... perhaps much longer," he admitted. "It's even very possible he will never regain what you consider normal speech and cognitive function." The doctor gave the impression of being apologetic, but Maggie appreciated the candor. She coped with most events if she knew what to expect, even if all she could expect was uncertainty.

Maggie took advantage of the available time to call the Prosecuting Attorney's office and leave a message: *Jonas is waking from the induced coma, but may not be ready to talk for hours.* She knew they were already in contact with the hospital, but wanted to make sure they had been notified. The case against Bo for Jess's murder seemed airtight, but they needed Jonas's input to understand what had led to the shooting in the high school parking lot.

She then called Harlan and Betty to ask if they would take care of Jimmy Dean overnight while she stayed at the hospital. Betty told her that her two boys would be pleased. They had been playing all day and were now sitting in the kitchen working on some milk and chocolate chip cookies. Betty asked about Jonas and then called Jimmy Dean to the phone.

Jimmy Dean was all breathy and manners. Maggie remembered he never liked talking for very long on the phone. "Yes, ma'am," he said when Maggie asked him if he had enjoyed staying with Harlan. "I been helping Harlan fix a motor off an old lawn mower."

"You have? Harlan must be a good mechanic."

"Oh, he is. Is Jonas awake yet?" he asked hopefully.

"I believe he's getting ready to wake up. The doctor has to do it just right, so they don't have to make him sleep again."

"Uhm, do you think he will be awake by Sunday?"

What was so special about Sunday? Maggie remembered—Sunday is Christmas! She was taken aback. She had actually forgotten. "I'm going to pray that he is awake by Sunday, Jimmy Dean. One way or another, we will be together for Christmas. You can count on that."

"Okay," he replied without conviction.

Maggie knew he was hurting. What must it feel like to be Jimmy

Dean? He was such a happy kid, finding joy in most situations. But losing his Mom, and possibly losing Jonas at the same time, had been a blow. No matter what else happened, she determined to be there for Jimmy Dean, whatever it took. "You take care of Harlan and Betty," she finally replied. I'll call you tomorrow. I love you."

"I love you too, Maggie." The phone clunked, probably from hitting the floor, and she smiled to picture him moving on to the next thing. Children were amazingly resilient.

Betty came back on, and Maggie promised to call the next day. "He's going to be fine, Maggie. Don't worry about him. Do what you need to do. Take care of Jonas."

Maggie laid the phone in her lap. Several people were turning the ICU waiting room into makeshift campsites by using pillows and blankets. She considered staying there but then changed her mind. She decided to check into the hotel next door for patient families, even if she only used it for a few hours.

Her conversation with Jimmy Dean somehow morphed into the melody for "I'll Be Home for Christmas." She hummed the tune to herself on the walk through the hallways and across the enclosed causeway to the hotel. The young desk clerk at the hotel seemed appalled that had presumed to walk into the hotel without calling ahead. She frowned at her cell phone vibrating on the counter. Rolling her eyes, she told Maggie she would have to wait for a room. Maggie scanned the empty lobby. "Not a problem," she said with a puzzled frown. "I wasn't planning to use the room right now anyway. If you give me the key cards, I promise not to bother you again until this evening."

The veiled sarcasm failed to find a home, but at least Maggie now had a place to stay the night. She headed back across the causeway, peering through the glass that insulated her from the busy people below. Their lives seemed somehow more real. Such cityscapes often made her melancholy and oddly unsure of herself, as though her own life were separate from the flow of humankind. *How can I be so joyful and yet so depressed within a matter of hours?* She recognized the clerk's effect on her mood, made a mental note to be kind to other people, and headed for the busy, light-hearted atmosphere of the cafeteria.

It was hours later before the ICU nurses let her go back into Jonas's room. They warned her that so far, even though he was awake and showing positive vital signs, he had not responded actively to any conversation or queries. "It's not uncommon for patients to be disoriented when they come out of an induced coma," one of the evening shift nurses reminded her. Dr. Felling had told her the same thing in the morning, but it was still disconcerting to sit in the room with Jonas awake, yet not appearing to recognize her.

She spoke to him, much as she had been reading to him, not expecting him to answer. She chatted about the weather, the clerk at the hotel, Jimmy Dean, and Harlan. She glanced at him from time to time to check if he was showing any signs of paying attention. He didn't appear to be focusing on any one thing with his eyes. She ran out of things to talk about, and sat quietly for a while, even dozing off in the chair before reading a couple more chapters of the civil war novel. She prayed aloud, standing near the bed before curling back up in her chair. No response.

Later, one of the nurses woke her to suggest she go to the hotel to rest. "Jonas is asleep now. He'll probably stay that way tonight. It's going to be awhile before the drugs have completely worn off. Come back in the morning. We'll assess where we are," she whispered, hugging Maggie.

Maggie's first thought the next morning was simply, *it's Christmas Eve*. She dreaded the coming decisions if Jonas's condition did not change. She didn't have to go back home, but she had promised Jimmy Dean they would be together for Christmas. How, if Jonas didn't wake today? Nevertheless, when the nurses gave her bright smiles upon entering the ICU, she knew it was good news.

Jonas was awake, noticeably recognizing her face immediately, smiling weakly when she walked into the room. "Hi Maggie," he was able to force out in a scratchy whisper.

"You're back," she blurted, and to her dismay, started to bawl. Maggie grabbed tissues and boohooed, alternately wiping her eyes, blowing her nose and holding his hand.

Jonas responded by holding her hand tightly when she left it there. He kept repeating a whispered, "Shh, it's okay. It's okay."

"The nurses told me I've been out for over a week," he croaked.

"You have," she sobbed. "Do you remember anything?"

"I don't know," he frowned. "They told me I might not even remember today." He gazed at her with puzzled eyes. "You know... I do remember Bo shooting at me in the parking lot. He had some kind of automatic weapon." He stopped to sip water through a straw. "I guess he must have shot me."

"He's in jail." Maggie wasn't sure whether to continue. She remembered Dr. Felling telling her not to feed Jonas too much information. He kept harping on taking everything gradually. She hardly knew what to say. Jonas was deep in thought, and then she saw recognition register in his eyes. His brow furrowed again. He slowly turned his eyes toward hers, and asked a one-word question, "Jess?"

"She didn't make it."

Her answer brought comprehension to his fuzzy brain. His eyes filled, and his voice caught and crackled like an old vinyl album. "Jimmy Dean?" he croaked.

He's okay," Maggie replied quickly. "He's had a tough time. I was afraid he was drawing into himself at first. Harlan was there for him at the funeral and has been ever since. Jimmy Dean's over at Harlan and Betty's right now. I'd better call them soon."

"You can call now," Jonas whispered, focusing his eyes away from her to a place inside, where he began organizing the new reality as if it were a crime diagram.

Maggie took the hint. She muttered something about needing to take the cell phone outside of the ICU to call. She held his hand for a second before leaving, telling the nurses she would be back soon.

Betty answered the phone when Maggie called this time. "Oh, thank you God in heaven, "she exclaimed after Maggie gave her the news, even though she wasn't particularly churchy. "Let me get the boys."

"He's awake?" Harlan was so loud on the phone; Maggie had to hold it two feet from her ear.

"Yes, he—"

"Is he all right?"

"He's weak, but he's talking."

"Is he talkin' out of his head, or is he makin' sense?"

The phone was now communicating little more than muffled voices in a discussion or an argument. Maggie wasn't sure which.

"Harlan... Harlan!"

"Maggie, hang on. We're comin'."

"Wait. When? What do you mean?"

"Maggie, don't move. We're on our way." With that, he hung up the phone, leaving her with a quizzical grin for the other visitors in the waiting room.

"Harlan doesn't want me to move. Harlan doesn't listen very well," she explained.

Despite the protestations of the ICU staff, Jonas mined Maggie for information. He appeared to gain strength and determination with each fragment she conveyed. She told him of the man at the Quick Stop who had watched in horror as Bo stabbed Jess repeatedly. He had called 911 immediately, as Jess collapsed in a bloody heap beside her car with multiple stab wounds. Bo's pickup had hurtled out of the parking lot and onto the highway.

She told him about the young witness to the shooting in the school parking lot who also called 911—how the highway patrol had quickly apprehended Bo on the state road headed south. She told him about the knife found in the dumpster in the school parking lot and the Tec-9 found in Bo's truck.

Jonas's eyes alternated between full moons of astonishment and stoic squints as he began to absorb the time and events that had continued without him. He had her explain details, and then stayed silent as they waited for whoever Harlan had meant by "we're on our way." The 'we' turned out to be Harlan and Jimmy Dean.

"I did not get lost!" Harlan argued loudly when they entered the ICU, but he cooled it as soon as one of the nurses shushed him with a reproving look. The staff was forgiving on Christmas Eve. They allowed the two new visitors to crowd in with Maggie in Jonas's cubicle of a room. "Don't listen to this boy if he tries to tell you I got lost," continued Harlan.

In other circumstances, this would have led to some good-natured ribbing and a lot of laughter at Harlan's expense. But on this day, Jimmy Dean walked around the bed and leaned over as Jonas, with bullet-riddled body, reached to pull him into a painful hug—pain he hardly noticed. The two held each other in a long, desperate embrace. Maggie let the tears flow, but Harlan had to turn away as he reached for a handkerchief.

CHAPTER 26 – TWICE BORN
BENFORD, TN – JANUARY 2012

Maggie requested and finally demanded Jonas to stay in her house when the hospital released him to recuperate at home. Caring for him in her own home promised to be easier for Maggie, as well as the nurse scheduled to come by daily to change his dressings. The stairs to the apartment would have also been difficult for him to climb.

Since waking from the coma in the hospital, he had healed quickly. He became vocally impatient, pestering the staff to let him leave. There had been no signs of infection, but Dr. Felling was still concerned about the trauma to his head. For several days, he swam in confusion with short-term memory loss. Still, Jonas had not experienced any symptoms of ICU Psychosis, so prevalent with medically induced comas. He checked out of the hospital two days after New Year's Day.

Short-term memory loss bothered him more than his wounds while the fog receded gradually. The day came when he sensed he was completely back to normal, only to recall more the next day. That repeated until he finally remembered the minutes leading up to the torrent of bullets from Bo. When Maggie told him how Jess had bled to death in the Quick Mart parking lot, he blamed himself, not for arriving too late, but for not taking Bo more seriously. Jonas gazed into nothingness for several days. After catching Jimmy Dean and Maggie watching him worriedly a few times, he resisted retreating into himself. He worked through his emotions by trying to explain his guilt to Maggie, but the need to be strong for Jimmy Dean made the difference in his recovery.

When Jimmy Dean wasn't in school, doing homework or sleeping, the two spent their hours together, playing Checkers or Cribbage, kidding each other, and talking baseball. Jonas quoted Rogers Hornsby, "People ask me what I do in winter when there's no baseball. I'll tell you what I do; I stare out the window and wait for spring". Jimmy Dean got it. He became an instant fan of Hornsby. He had to know everything there was about the old baseball player who shared a first name with his own last name.

One day after school, he asked Maggie, "Can a person get their name changed?"

Maggie noticed Jonas was listening. "Yes. Many immigrants to America changed their names. They wanted to quickly assimilate rather than have their names bring attention to their immigrant status. People still change names, sometimes for religious reasons or to hide from their past." She watched Jonas for a sign that this had bothered him. He revealed nothing. Jimmy Dean, however, smiled as though this were great news.

"Why do you ask?" she wanted to know.

"Well, I think I'm going to change my name to Rogers," he answered.

"But your name already is Rogers."

Jimmy Dean frowned, shaking his head. "Not my last name ... my first name," he explained as though this should have been obvious.

Maggie and Jonas both laughed, and then Jonas began to laugh so hard, he couldn't quit. "Oh," he groaned in pain in between guffaws. "Rogers Rogers. Now that's a baseball name if I ever heard one."

Jimmy Dean didn't seem to think it was funny. "Well, I'm changing it to Rogers, and that's that," he declared and glared at them until he too started giggling.

Maggie and Jonas enjoyed the always-surprising boy so much; they almost felt guilty about the circumstances that had led to them all living under the same roof. They were not a family and yet they *were* a family—not necessarily recognized as such by anyone else—but there was a fierce loyalty emerging quickly among them. If they had been required to articulate how they felt, no other word would have sufficed but love, an untroubled pool none of them were in a hurry to study and define. Jonas enjoyed the very act of looking at Maggie and Jimmy Dean, paying close attention to them as though he imagined they might not be there the next day.

At his age, Jimmy Dean didn't worry about personal relationships. Maggie and Jonas felt a natural reluctance to do so. They were all healing, recovering with wounds they were not ready to expose yet. Jimmy Dean wasn't exactly depressed, but he was unusually quiet at times. Maggie worried about unseen effects of Jess' death for both of her men. Jonas had refused any psychological care. She had insisted Jimmy Dean undergo counseling, and had quietly been working with the state's Division of Child Services regarding proper therapy as well as foster care and the possibility of adoption.

Her extensive network of friends had made it possible for Jimmy Dean to stay with her without him even realizing there was a world of adult activity centered on his proper placement. Maggie intended to shield him from situations and people who would bring it up until he chose to think about it on his own as an adult. She had been there for him for the last several years. Her house was his second home. It was understood that he belonged with Maggie. If there was anyone who thought differently in Benford, they didn't have the courage to speak their mind.

After Christmas break, Jimmy Dean quickly settled into a routine at Maggie's during weekdays: discuss school and homework assignments when he arrived home, eat dinner, hurry out to the barn to throw baseballs, and dawdle back in to read and do homework before going to bed. His constant questions always led to lively discussions. The two of them watched little television because Maggie seldom turned it on. Jimmy Dean never asked.

Not much had changed with this routine after Jonas came home from the hospital, except Jimmy Dean was no longer alone while throwing baseballs down at the barn. Jonas followed him and sat in a folding chair as Jimmy Dean threw baseball after baseball. They began to watch a few old baseball games on ESPN Classic since there were no live games. Jonas quietly narrated the action, and Jimmy Dean began to absorb how the game was played, as well as how to talk about it.

The three spanned the decades between them in conversation. Jonas's wide-ranging knowledge reminded Maggie of his connection with the woman from Missouri, but she pushed it out of her mind.

People dropped by; Harlan and Betty, Maggie's preacher, and Bill Anderson, the owner of the plant where Jonas worked. Even Bart Simmons from the hardware store visited. Jonas suspected some people were visiting more out of curiosity than concern. Bart's attentiveness to Maggie annoyed him until he noticed his own reaction and felt guilty. Still, Jonas had to admit, everyone had been friendly. He had noticed no veiled animosity. Harlan always made Jimmy Dean laugh. During his visits, it seemed as if nothing had changed.

After Jimmy Dean was in bed, Jonas and Maggie talked. Mostly they talked about the period while Jonas was in the coma. Like a missing tooth, he felt the need to probe for more information, hoping something would trigger parts of his memory. Jonas desperately needed the fragments of his past to be connected and make sense again.

Maggie was happy to answer Jonas's questions while he explored the missing days. She was curious about what he might have experienced internally. "Do you remember anything at all from the time you were in the coma or even before?" she asked one night.

"No—" After the abrupt answer, Jonas squinted, forehead frowning in a puzzled manner. "You know... that's not quite right. I don't remember anything specific. I can't even say that I might have been aware of anything at some point." He paused and closed his eyes, his face showing something almost akin to pleasure at the diversion. "It's an odd—

I don't know what to call it. I can't even call it a feeling. It didn't seem as if zero time passed. Do you understand?" he asked, frustrated.

"It sounds like you are saying it wasn't like blacking out and then immediately waking up."

Jonas smiled. "Yes! That's it, except I don't even remember losing consciousness. And waking up wasn't an all at once experience either. I might have been awake before I was even consciously aware that I was awake."

Maggie smiled and rolled her eyes, passing her hand over her head. "Guess you had to be there," she chuckled.

Jonas laughed outright. "The funny thing is... I'm not sure that *I* was even there."

"But you're here now."

"I suppose so. Wherever you go, there you are."

They gazed at each other until it could have been uncomfortable, and yet it somehow wasn't. Jonas's eyes broke away first, but he looked as if he had arrived at a decision and held her gaze once again. "Maggie, I *am* here now. I mean, I'm actually here and present, like you described when we were coming back from our shopping trip in Nashville. Everything has changed. I've meant to talk to you about it, but I wanted to make sure I took care of some things first, situations from my past that need to be put right. There is so much that I haven't told you. I've been less than honest."

Maggie listened thoughtfully before responding. "Sometimes we want to get everything right first. We want the circumstances to be just so, but it never happens. The unexpected always butts in. We get distracted."

"We get shot." Jonas grinned again.

"We get shot," Maggie repeated. "And we have such little time. When we are young, we deceive ourselves into thinking life lasts forever. It is a hard illusion to let go, at least on your side of 50. But don't you believe it is better to act on what we know at the time instead of waiting for everything to be perfect?"

Jonas stared at his hands and pondered her words.

Maggie continued, "I want to be here for you. I'd ask the right questions if I knew what they were, but I don't. I want you to know what you say is safe with me. I always prefer to know how things actually are as opposed to guessing." She chuckled mirthlessly, "And I keep talking on and on sometimes because all the words I've said seem to have fallen to the floor and shattered."

Jonas hesitated but then responded. "Okay. It begins with God. You know I have been uncomfortable talking about God with you. It's not that I don't believe there *is* a God. I've never quite disbelieved in His existence. When I was a boy, I thought I sensed His presence, but nothing about Him has ever made much sense to me. I've been talking to Him. I have become sure He is there. But the people who claim to speak for Him—" Jonas rolled his eyes to show his disdain. "I'm probably not being entirely fair, but it's honestly the way I feel about it."

Maggie listened with rapt attention. She felt anticipation rise inside, sensing how important this moment was, wanting to say something, but sensing she should remain quiet.

"I'll have to admit, my understanding has changed now, mostly because of you. You and God. Just because someone claims to speak for God, doesn't mean he or she actually is. I don't know why I expected that. People don't always say things well. When I think of how poets struggle with communicating spiritual matters, it seems silly to demand something more from the average person.

"But—" and here he smiled. "You always seem to do the right thing." He paused. "I'm not saying you're perfect," he added a few seconds later.

"I don't know what to say," Maggie replied.

Jonas still held her eye. "Don't say anything," he insisted almost crossly. "If that's all there was to it I'd have ignored it, or found some way to rationalize another reason for why you are unique. In fact, that's exactly what I did when I first started living here. I've always thought that some people are truly better. They find it easy to do what is right. Nevertheless, I listened to you, and even if I never admitted it, I started talking to God. I found myself talking and arguing and complaining to him about everything. And according to you, that's part of what praying is."

Jonas stood to pace slowly in front of the bookshelves, fingered a couple and pulled down an Anthology of British Literature. "I read a poem called the "Windhover" in this book. The writer's sense of awe stands out, the way he perceives beauty in the death and resurrection of Christ. And … sees it reflected in the flight of a bird." It grabbed me inside. I remember glaring up to heaven and asking, "Is this who you are? Why show yourself to this... this Hopkins and hide from most of us? Why hide?" he asked bitterly.

Maggie heard the pain and frustration in his voice, but she remained quiet. As if it were instinct, she felt God's Spirit hold her back. This man was not to be pushed or persuaded against his will. She recalled Paul's letter to the Philippians, how they were to "work out their own salvation with fear and trembling." Her own faith had come through doubt and struggle. Now her strength of faith could be a temptation for Jonas to try to use her as an intermediary with God. This should not be. He was a man who was used to heeding his own counsel. She would ask and answer questions, but he needed to come to God on his own.

Jonas pushed the book back in its place on the shelf and collapsed in a recliner. He sighed and closed his eyes. "You know, I don't even know why I'm angry. I know perfectly well that everything negative in my life has come from my own actions. Even this last thing with Bo. I read that bully wrong. I thought he was—I don't know—too weak to do much of anything. But who knows what a meth head will do.

I mean well. I do. But the people in my life always pay for my mistakes. I never get it right. I can never find the right path. There is no way God is going to accept me."

Now, Maggie could not contain herself. "Jonas, I understand. You blame yourself. I don't think you should, but I'm not going to try to talk you out of it. I know what that is like. I blamed myself for Tom's heart attack because I had not been more observant. I think you know there was no way to predict what happened. I also understand that deliberating things rationally is never quite enough. You can't help how it feels."

"The last thing you said—that you "can never get it right—can never find the right path? The truth is, you may seldom get it right. You may even be the worst at getting it right. That doesn't matter. None of us gets it right before we come to God. There isn't one perfect path that you miss, and then it's all over. The going is the path. You may think I usually do the right thing, but you didn't know me before I gave control of my heart to God. I'm glad God has changed me as much as he has, but I'm far from flawless. I have made horrible, life-damaging choices."

"Jonas, do you believe God is impressed with what we consider to be good, with people who think they are doing fine and are in control? People who think like that are more likely to ignore the very thought of God. God can't do much with people who proudly work things out on their own. He wants people to come to Him just the way they are—down and out, sick and flawed—as long as you come openly to him with an honest heart."

Jonas opened his eyes at this. "Maggie, I can be honest with God. It's everyone else I can't be honest with."

"Why? What is so terrible that you can't be honest?"

Jonas turned away. "That is the question, isn't it? We're right back where we started. I've avoided and misled you. It's obvious that I'm running, isn't it?" Glancing back, he said, "It's simple, really. If I'm not quite ready to open up to the people who know me—with my friends—how can I go to God? So, you see? In my case, there is definitely something I need to fix first." He stared at Maggie with determined eyes. "And I intend to do just that."

Maggie rose and walked across the room, pulling a ladder-back chair away from the table where they played games, and sat in it, leaning forward, her knees inches from his. She sat gazing at the pain and loneliness in his eyes, waiting as she smiled, saying nothing.

"What?" he asked.

"I'm glad your intentions are good," she said. "But you scarcely finished saying that you can never get it right. And yet you are going to fix things before you go to God?" Maggie let that sink in. They stared at each other until he closed his eyes in defeat. Jonas remained perfectly still. She instinctively reached for his hands, and he didn't resist.

"Jesus Christ was present at our creation. He became a man like us, lived among us, experienced what we go through, took our place of punishment for all we have done, died and came back to life. He said, 'I didn't come to condemn, but to save men from the consequences of their sins.'

I get the fact that you hate the mistakes that have always kept you a slave. All you have to do is admit it to Him, believe in Him and who He is, and let Him fix things. Let Him change you into the extraordinary man He intended you to be when He first contemplated you before you were even born."

Holding each other's hands, they sat there for a very long time until he quit looking through her, brought his focus back to the surface of her eyes and smiled, his eyes shimmering with something new.

"What?" she asked.

"I'm ready," Jonas replied directly. "What do I do?"

"Do you admit that you have not lived up to God's standards?"

"Yes."

"And do you believe that Jesus Christ was God's son, who took the results of your sin when He died on the cross?"

"Maggie, I don't have this all thought out, but somehow I do believe it. I believe the one who made me—the one who I've been talking to—would be willing to do this. So, yes."

Maggie stared straight at him. "Will you allow Him to take control of your life? Will you let Him be your Lord?"

The words sounded so archaic, and yet so timeless. The seriousness of the moment was not lost as Jonas considered the words. He relived the love he had received from that presence, undeniably the same love he had received from Maggie as a Christ follower. To give up control when he could never get it right now seemed wise, and he knew instinctively that it *was* right. "Yes," he said with conviction. "Yes, I will."

They sat quietly for a few moments while Jonas experienced an incredible weight leave him. He had been so accustomed to its presence that he had not comprehended how heavy it had been. "Oh," he exclaimed spontaneously. Jonas felt that he might float upward, the encounter was so intense. Now, the love that he had felt was a part of him. When he opened his eyes, a new light looked out at the world.

It was Maggie's turn to lay down the weight she had carried for him. Her face glowed. *Twice-born. There was no greater joy to experience or behold.*

CHAPTER 27 - SNOW FALLS
ST. JUDE, MO & BENFORD, TN - JANUARY 2006

Snow fell throughout the night past a full haloed moon. Kate woke after midnight, noticing the reflected light through her window. She stood to gaze at bright white pillows of snow growing on the deck furniture and the tree branches. Snow always brought the remembrance of childhood—the promise of a day away from school, sledding down hills and building snowmen. At 3:20 a.m., she woke long enough to notice large flakes still falling slowly past her bedroom window. At 6:05 a.m., the phone woke her. Mandy, on the local school's call list, told her classes were canceled.

Sicily woke an hour later. Still blinking from sleep, she wandered into the kitchen where Kate was making blueberry pancakes. Kate seldom bothered to cook breakfast since getting Sicily ready for school always left little time for much more than a bowl of cereal or oatmeal and toast. She so enjoyed the morning time with her sweet, huggable daughter, they were always flirting with being late.

When Sicily saw the snow, such a look of amazement crossed her face, Kate guessed she might be seeing snow for the first time. "No school today, little girl. As soon as we eat and get ready, we're going to go outside and play."

Kate sat places for both of them at the kitchen bar and enjoyed the child's careful manners. "Have you ever seen snow before?" she asked.

Sicily nodded. She smiled as she slowly pulled the fork from her mouth.

"Where at, honey? Do you remember?" Kate asked.

"Christmas."

Kate was puzzled at this. Surely, it hadn't snowed at Christmas in New Orleans. "Did you travel to someone else's house for Christmas?"

Sicily shook her head no and frowned. "No," she almost whispered. "It snowed on the roof on Christmas, and Santa Claus was happy because his sled had snow to slide on." She paused, smiled, and threw her arms out wide. "But it wasn't big as it is here."

"Did anyone else come to your house for Christmas?"

"I don't know," Sicily replied as she traced lines through the syrup with her fork.

Kate stopped. She had learned the signs of Sicily's reluctance whenever she began this line of questioning. There was something in her little girl that sensed Kate's tension and responded by withdrawing. Kate couldn't keep it out of her voice and gestures, or whatever it was that triggered Sicily's response. As usual, she gave up, putting it off for another day. *No, not another day. Perhaps never.* While it made her sad, she was gradually beginning to accept that it might be time to move on with her life, and concentrate on other things than her personal mystery, like being a mother to this beautiful girl.

The last few weeks had been enormously frustrating regarding finding out anything new about Daniel. Gilbert had gone with her to St. Louis to meet with FBI Agent Rasmussen. Her previous conversation with him seemed to have done some good, or perhaps it was the presence of her lawyer. He was much friendlier in person, almost eager to explain their progress. Unfortunately, his news was no better than before. The pace of finding missing people and identifying bodies was painstakingly slow.

He asked Kate what she had discovered with her own inquiries. She and Gilbert had already discussed how to handle this question at length. Ultimately, they decided not to share what they had learned about Daniel's probable movements leading up to Katrina, at least not yet. They both agreed that they knew very few actual facts. Much of what they thought might be the case was based on supposition. She told the agent she was now concentrating on caring for Sicily, something she claimed with full sincerity.

Kate certainly had turned her energy to caring for Sicily, making sure to cover every avenue with the adoption. She knew how important it was to build a life of stability for the girl, making sure Sicily could count on her to be there always. Mandy and Kate's parents were her back-ups in case she should have to be gone. Sicily had accepted Mandy. She loved Knut, her big Lab, who was always ready to return the attention.

The morning became a lazy time of drawing and playing jacks on the floor until Mandy and Knut arrived in her Jeep. They all went outside to build a snowwoman. Kate named her Rosie. She resembled Rosie the Robot, with apples for eyes, an apron, and a head shaped more like a log than a ball. Sicily liked the name. She talked about Rosie the rest of the morning, even after they went inside, peering out the window at her new friend.

After lunch, Mandy and Knut left to return to town. Sicily fell asleep to Kate reading "Harold and the Purple Crayon." Kate's morning deliberations about moving on with life led her to consider tying up loose ends. She realized she needed to relinquish involvement with the poetry blog since she had no real intention of spending much time with it; she had not reviewed posts for weeks.

Her partners didn't seem to be surprised when she called each one in turn. Even Charlotte wished her well. She surprised Kate by asking her to continue contributing when she had time. Checking online, there were no messages from board users. She had already effectively weaned her presence from the message board over the previous weeks.

It was an opportunity to clean up accumulated email. She began deleting messages methodically. Nothing new from Gilbert, Sara, her private investigator, or even the FBI. Kate almost emptied her spam folder, but at the last second, she scanned the "sender" column quickly. Most were advertisements: banks, endless tacos, insurance, and other products from websites she must have visited. She almost missed the one from a Maggie Young with a subject line that read: *Please reply concerning a personal matter.*

The email address was myoung@k12tn.net, and the message was from December, now almost three weeks old. Kate's intuition told her it was legitimate, so she transferred the message to her inbox. She then copied and pasted the address into Google search. The first link led to an advisory staff listing for Benford Schools in Tennessee. Definitely legitimate, but very puzzling since the name didn't ring a bell. She opened the email to read:

To Kate Mitchell,

I want to apologize for the fact that I am contacting you first by email. Your address was listed on the Puzzled Poet blog. I haven't even attempted to find your phone number. I struggled with whether to write to you because I first located your name by logging onto another person's computer, something I would usually never do.

This might be a terrible invasion of his privacy, but I believed it was necessary because this friend of mine has fallen into a coma, and I do not know whether he is going to live or die. I felt I should try to find his family if he has any. He hasn't lived in our area long. He is one of the refugees from New Orleans. I didn't know who to contact other than the people I have found on his computer. Actually, you are the only person I found on his computer. If you would like to contact me, either reply or please see the phone number at the end of this email.

Maggie Young

Kate's breath caught, but she dialed the phone before her body had a chance to lock her brain. She could do this. She had an ability to continue thinking and communicating even after her body had become numb.

The "hello" that came after two rings expressed a friendly voice of anticipation. Kate wondered if the friendliness would last.

"Yes. This is Kate Mitchell. May I speak with Maggie Young?"

There was a pause before Maggie answered with a voice that was pleasant, but now tentative. "Oh, Kate. Yes, this is Maggie. I suppose you are calling about my email."

"I am. I only now read it because my spam filter caught it. I was giving the spam folder a second look and almost deleted it."

"I see. I thought that maybe you had decided not to respond. I was okay with that—have been sorry several times that I even sent it. I'm still not sure it was the right thing to do."

Kate absorbed Maggie's sincerity. "That's okay, Maggie. I doubt I even know your friend. I do recognize the username from the message board. We had a short discussion about poetry."

Maggie spoke slowly, thinking as she answered, "Kate, this is awkward for me. At the time I emailed you, my friend was in a medically induced coma. I wasn't sure if he was going to make it. He had multiple gunshot wounds, and it was touch and go. He's no longer in the coma but is still recovering, so I don't know. I need to tell him about this, about emailing you, and let him choose what to do."

Kate shook her head silently as if to get rid of the confusing thoughts. As much as she instinctively liked the woman on the other end of the line, she did not intend to let her off the hook so easily. "Okay, I guess I don't expect you to tell me immediately who he is, but why did you say he was from New Orleans? Why add that piece of information?"

Maggie sighed. This was the question she had avoided thinking about herself, ever since she had learned Jonas had been messaging a woman who was missing a husband from Katrina—a woman who didn't seem to know him. She wanted to wait until he was able to deal with this. Maggie felt he would agree to speak to Kate—finally do the right thing, even if he became angry over her invading his privacy. She should wait... but then she didn't.

"The first web page I saw when I searched your name on the internet was a newspaper article saying your husband was still missing since Katrina. My friend had told me that he, himself, was a refugee from Katrina. Then he contacts you, but obviously in a manner that didn't say who he was. I hardly even allowed myself to think of the implications, but it was too much of a coincidence... just a little too convenient." Maggie paused, thinking that she was making it sound as if she had already decided Jonas was guilty. "But then I figured I was inventing a connection that wasn't there—that it *was* purely a coincidence."

Kate had kept her emotions in check to this point, but she noticed her voice trembled as she asked, "Just tell me this Maggie, did you see my husband's picture online?"

"No."

"Will you do me a favor and look?"

"Kate, I will, but the article I read was in your town newspaper's website. I don't remember there being a picture."

"Hmm... maybe the link is broken. The newspaper isn't great about keeping their archives maintained. How about if I send you a picture by email? Will that be okay?"

"Yes. I'll look at it, and then I'll let you know, even if—" Maggie paused and considered what she was trying to say. "Kate, I want to give him the chance to respond, for it to be from him either way. Okay?"

"Okay, Maggie. Let's be frank. If your friend isn't my husband, then I don't care. I didn't have a long, serious correspondence with this guy. So, if it isn't Daniel, I'm not worried about it. Let me know if it isn't him. Please? I don't think it can be him, anyway."

Maggie agreed and gave Kate her email address before hanging up. Kate sighed. There was always a "next clue," always an open end. Nothing was ever complete. She arrived at facts only to find that the road continued ever on. She stared quietly at Daniel's face as she emailed his picture. *Did you walk away? Why pretend to be someone else on my blog?* A thought took form in her mind. Kate considered the possibility of Daniel taking on a different identity before reaching out to her again. *No. But could it be him?* She was desperately tired. Remembering her resolve earlier in the day to move on, she baked a loaf of bread for Sicily to enjoy when she woke up.

The phone conversation had numbed Maggie. She moved automatically into the kitchen to brew some coffee. The pot was full before she noticed that she didn't even remember grinding the beans or measuring and putting the coffee in the filter. Maggie carried her coffee back to the computer to find a new message in her inbox. The coffee mug dropped to the floor as she stared at the picture now on her screen, an image intended for business or industry publications, a strong, lean man in a gray suit with dark hair. Apparently, the same man that was right now out in the garage puttering around, still recuperating from his injuries.

"Daniel?" Maggie asked quietly later in the evening, watching for a reaction.

Jonas didn't look up. He wasn't paying attention, his nose stuck in a newspaper. Harlan had already arrived and left with Jimmy Dean for the evening, so he was eating alone. Maggie had mumbled something about not being hungry, but now she sat down across from him on the other side of the table.

"We need to talk." Maggie's eyes stared unblinking, from a face carved in stone.

As if he sensed her laser stare through the paper, Jonas slowly lowered it to the table to meet her gaze. The slight smile at the corners of his mouth disappeared as he became aware of the coldness in her eyes.

"What's wrong, Maggie?"

"When you were in the coma—" She stopped, but he nodded for her to continue. "I didn't know what was going to happen—whether you would come out of it, or die. I did not know."

"Maggie, I underst—"

"NO! I need you to listen to me. I need you to let me finish!"

Maggie stood up and started to busy herself with wiping the counter. She quickly stopped and sighed as she sat again, wringing the cloth in her hands. "When you were in the coma, I thought I should be doing something, that I should be finding people who knew you, to let them know in case you… in case you died," she blurted out. The tears began to flow slowly down her cheeks.

"All those months," she sobbed. "All that time I waited for you to trust me enough to tell me the truth. I told myself you needed the time—that you needed people to accept you as you were. Fine. I was willing, and I trusted you. But then the coma. We didn't know whether you were going to live or die." She unconsciously stopped to wipe her face with the dishcloth, realized what it was, and got up to get a Kleenex.

Jonas was now sitting board straight, eyes wide, anticipating her next words. Maggie gathered strength and determination with his quiet attention. "I would never have done this under any other circumstances. I hope you believe me. But I logged onto your computer to find someone—anyone—a relative or friend." Maggie stared at Jonas who had yet to react. He hadn't even seemed to move. His eyes focused on her, neither in shock nor anger. If anything, he appeared to be puzzled or surprised.

"Do you understand what I'm saying to you?" she demanded. "I logged onto your computer and found Kate." she accused angrily, finally coming out with what had been torturing her ever since a few hours before, after first glimpsing the picture that had told her who he actually was. "I know you needed time, but, but… this!"

"Oh," was all he said.

They stared at each other. Maggie could not believe it. She had brought out the smoking gun, and all he had to say was, "Oh?" She was now more than angry. She was furious. She had trusted this man. She had opened her house. She had opened her heart.

Maggie huffed in frustration. She was too angry to lay it out for him. Maggie had overlooked her worst early suspicions, but they had come true. Abruptly, she remembered the poem—Robert Frost's "The Impulse".

"Where is the Frost book?" she demanded.

Jonas was at a loss. "The what?"

"The Robert Frost poem collection. Where is it?" she demanded again, and when Jonas started to rise, "No, don't get up. I'll get it."

Jonas now almost appeared to be a boy who knew he was in deep trouble but wasn't sure which of his many sins had led to his parents' current fury. He pointed to the library, and Maggie was quickly there and back. She opened to the table of contents and quickly thumbed the pages, handing Jonas the open book. He glanced down with perplexed eyes and read the poem. The last few lines had been highlighted in yellow:

. . . He never found her, though he looked
Everywhere,
And he asked at her mother's house
Was she there.

Sudden and swift and light as that
The ties gave,
And he learned of finalities
Besides the grave.

Jonas finished the poem, with no sign of recognition or admission. Maggie had expected anything but for him to have no reaction at all. She knew that his insight was subtle enough to make the connection. She shook her head slowly in disgust, stood abruptly, crumpled the tissue, and threw it down on the table. Glaring at Jonas one more time, she walked over to the kitchen door, grabbed her coat from a hook, and slammed the door on her way out. The old station wagon started up, but the engine quit almost immediately. A few seconds later, the kitchen door opened again. Maggie was back through the door hanging up her coat.

"Call Kate. Her number is by the phone," she sobbed, as she reeled by him on the way to her bedroom.

CHAPTER 28 - CONFRONTATION
BENFORD, TN – JANUARY 2006

There was no one at Kate's house to answer the ringing phone. At the very moment her answering machine recorded Jonas's call, she was already on a short flight from St. Louis to Nashville. Jonas had called because he felt like he had to, even though he had been unprepared to speak with Kate or the answering machine. He left a message consisting of three seconds of silence, followed by one broken sentence and Maggie's phone number. Kate would have also been interested in an earlier message left on her answering machine from Agent Rasmussen, stating the FBI had a new break in her husband's case.

Kate had waited for an hour after talking to Maggie on the phone, growing increasingly impatient until she decided to take matters into her own hands. The lack of a quick return call suggested strongly to her that Maggie had recognized the photograph. She thought a call to Sara would prompt her to come to Tennessee, but her friend said that she couldn't take off work on such short notice. Kate was disappointed. She was able to arrange a flight by phone.

Mandy tried to talk her out of going when Kate called her, and then gave in, volunteering to take care of Sicily. Kate agreed. It was only Wednesday. They both guessed that school would be back in session the next day since the snow was melting quickly. It was too soon for Sicily to be missing days from her new school. Kate also did not intend to take chances with any further trauma to Sicily. She was planning a surprise confrontation—hardly appropriate for her little girl to be present.

More phone calls reserved a rental car at the airport and a hotel in Benford. Kate was almost shaky with anticipation. An early morning drive into Benford might end months of uncertainty. What would she say to Daniel? What would he say?

Jonas attempted to call Kate a few more times after leaving the first message, but he ended the call each time without adding anything. Maggie was not coming out of the bedroom. For the first time since arriving in Benford, he was feeling unwelcome. Jonas packed a few things in a duffle and headed to the apartment above the garage.

Nothing had changed, but the apartment was neat and in order. He stared at the computer sitting on the table, not used by him since before the shooting. He had no desire to turn it on now.

He lay on his bed, images of all that had occurred vying for attention. Sadness enveloped him, holding him down as if to force the very breath from him. As usual, he had done everything wrong. He had warned Maggie there was much he needed to fix, but being the eternal optimist, she had concluded it wasn't that bad. There was nothing God could not fix.

Her God. Even as it came to his mind, the phrase grabbed his attention with its falseness. *But you are my God too. Why is this happening now? Are you punishing me? Just when I'm beginning to understand how my life can change? When I'm starting to see that you can make everything right? Why are you letting it fall apart now, when I needed you to show me the way?*

Jonas lay there and questioned God until he had no more words. The sadness overwhelmed him; he even had a desperate desire to run once again. Memories of the last few months with Maggie and Jimmy Dean played in his mind. He ached for the boy who had become a part of him. No, this time, he would not run. Peace permeated his soul. Everything was going to be all right. Somehow, it would work out.

There was no reason to have this confidence—no way to articulate it, but he had experienced a gift of faith from his Father who loved him. It was to be only the beginning of times of difficulty and strength, sadness and joy. He would never know what was to come, but always have what he needed—often showing up, just in time.

Kate had to wait almost 2 hours at the airport in St. Louis for the flight to Nashville. After finally arriving in Nashville, she picked up the rental car, ate on the road trip down, and reached Benford slightly before 9:00 p.m. As late as it was, she took the time to drive by Maggie's address.

No lights appeared to be on, and no vehicles were outside the garage. It appeared as if no one was at home. Maybe everyone had already gone to bed. *"What if Daniel isn't here? What if Maggie told him about my phone call and he left?"* She grew angry thinking of it. Then she remembered that Maggie said he was still recovering from gunshot wounds. It didn't seem likely that he might leave under the circumstances, especially during the winter.

The next morning, Harlan took Jimmy Dean to Maggie's to pick up a book for school he had forgotten. It was still early. They had an hour before Jimmy Dean had to be at school. Harlan had hurried the boy along because he was secretly hoping for breakfast at Maggie's instead of going to McDonald's like Jimmy Dean had kept suggesting. They were both surprised when Jonas came out of the garage door while they pulled into the drive. He wore a hoody against the early morning chill, leaning on a baseball bat as if it was a cane. The sky in the east was beginning to glow with the dawn.

"You're out and about awful early," said Harlan as he and Jimmy Dean climbed out of the truck.

"I'm not the only one. Why are you guys here?"

"I forgot my book from the library. I gotta have it today," Jimmy Dean answered. He noticed the still-open garage door. "What are you doing in the garage?"

Jonas ignored this question. He gazed at the house where Maggie had come outside, bundled against the cold. Jimmy Dean ran over to tell Maggie he needed his book while Harlan asked Jonas how his wounds were healing.

Maggie and Jimmy Dean were discussing the book the boy needed from the house. Maggie hollered something about breakfast. Harlan wasn't listening; he was distracted by Jonas looking over his shoulder at another car coming into the drive. All four of them stopped to watch as the car came to a stop, the driver's door opened, and a woman stepped out to look their way.

All sound seemed to go right out of the world except for the bell in the car complaining about the open door. Jimmy Dean and Harlan were only slightly curious until they noticed the play of emotion on the others' faces. They hardly knew who to look at first. Jonas squinted at Kate. Kate frowned at Jonas. Maggie focused on Jonas's reaction. Still, no one had said a word.

Kate, after months of uncertainty, stood in the driveway, shaking from the adrenalin rushing through her. After all these months, finally setting eyes on Daniel standing there before her, Kate's eyes grew wide, and her mouth flew open. Her heart sank. He was Daniel... but he was not Daniel. Her voice was quiet with despair. "Oh, you must be Jonas."

Kate looked as if she might sink to the driveway, but she shut the door and leaned against the car. Maggie glanced questioningly from one to the other. "You mean?" but she didn't know how to finish. The situation made no sense to her. It occurred to her that this must be Kate but— "You mean, he isn't Daniel?" she asked.

"No," Kate replied. "He looks a lot like him; they are obviously brothers. You must be Jonas," she said to the man, who now stood like the condemned before a firing squad.

Maggie didn't hide her relief, but she was still baffled.

"But how did you know his name was Jonas? I never mentioned his name."

Jonas spoke up at this. "Kate, I'm sorry. I tried to call you last night. I left a message." Then Maggie's question hit him. "How *did* you know my name was Jonas?" he asked.

"What's going on here?" shouted Harlan. "Have you people all lost your mind?"

Maggie's tears dried immediately. "Harlan Schmidt!"

Jimmy Dean was terribly confused; for once, he was speechless. Even Harlan being in trouble with Maggie didn't strike him as being funny.

Erupting emotions gripped all of them. Jonas dropped heavy eyelids and scratched the back of his head, but he knew—his time of hiding the truth was up. As usual, Maggie took charge. "Let's all go in the house. I think we all have a lot to talk about, and it is cold out here. Harlan, you and Jimmy Dean, hurry and eat so you can get to school on time."

Jimmy Dean was unhappy with this statement. He didn't want to miss any of the conversation. On top of that, as good as Maggie's cooking was, McDonalds was calling. "Do I have to go to school?" he whined. "How am I going to know what's going on?"

"You'll find out soon enough."

Maggie was patient but insistent. "You need to give us some time to sort this out. It would be boring to you anyway. You'd leave us, and be out in the barn throwing a baseball in no time."

Jimmy Dean tried to get some sympathy from Harlan and Jonas, but neither one was willing to say anything in his defense. Jonas gave him a meaningful glance, and the boy gave in, looking so mournful, Harlan had to chuckle.

Maggie was right. It took some time before they even started sorting it out. After Harlan and Jimmy Dean had left, the three busied themselves with eating Maggie's omelets. Maggie stayed busy with cooking and serving, while Kate talked about the abrupt change in weather she had experienced in Missouri, the unseasonably warm 60 degree days giving way to significant amounts of snow. There was the elephant in the room, but none of them wanted to be the first one to mention it.

Finally, Kate asked Jonas directly, "Did you say you left a message on my answering machine?" He nodded yes. Kate turned away, picked up her cell phone, and dialed her home phone along with the message access. She first listened to the message from Agent Rasmussen, eyes narrowing, then listened to Jonas's message. Without looking up, she called the FBI and asked for Agent Rasmussen. Jonas didn't know what to make of this. He dropped his eyes while he listened to her end of the conversation.

"Agent Rasmussen, this is Kate Mitchell. I only now received your message. Do you have something new?" she asked.

Kate listened intently before slowly closing her eyes as tears began to roll. She said nothing but nodded her head while Maggie handed her tissue. "Yes, I understand. Yes. Thank you for calling." She paused again. "Okay. Yes, I will be available whenever you need me. Goodbye and thank you again."

She sat with her face in her hands for a while, rocking slowly in her seat, trying to gather herself. "That was Agent Rasmussen with the FBI." Kate opened eyes full of tears. "They have found Daniel, I guess, at least a part of him. They've been able to match dental records."

"Oh Kate," exclaimed Maggie. She knelt down and hugged her as Kate began to cry openly. Maggie gestured to Jonas for the box of tissue. She empathized with the other woman's loss, even as her own mind was fully assimilating that Jonas actually was not this woman's husband.

Jonas stood by helplessly until a terrible realization came over him. *Kate was only now finding out that Daniel was dead.* "You didn't know?" he cried out. "You thought he was missing all this time?" He searched her face from across the table and read her frank stare. "Oh God!" he exclaimed. "I thought this was all about me not contacting you. If I had realized, you didn't know—"

The reality was so much worse than anything he had imagined. He had been sloppy when he first attempted to find Kate, assuming much too much. It horrified him to realize she had spent all of these months not knowing. The mystery! The mystery Kate had spoken of was not him, was not about wondering where Daniel's brother was. The mystery was Daniel himself.

"Please, believe me, Kate. If I had guessed you didn't know, I'd have told you, no matter what. I saw something about a memorial and made a terrible assumption. I thought you knew!"

Kate stared at him in disbelief. "But you were the one on the message board. I wrote that I was searching for someone on one of our messages. I'm sure I did."

Jonas nodded. "You did tell me that, but one mistaken idea led to another. I assumed Daniel had spoken about meeting me. I thought you were probably trying to find me."

"No. Well yes, I was looking for you too, but only because I was still trying to find Daniel. Daniel never told me about you." Kate sighed. "There was actually a time during our correspondence when it occurred to me that you might be ... well, what Maggie believed," Kate said, glancing over at the other woman who slid slowly into another of the dining room chairs. "I mean, not that you were Daniel specifically, but that Daniel took the opportunity to walk away. Truthfully, I guess it wouldn't have surprised me."

"Kate," he said. "This is not your fault. Daniel loved you very much. He told me so. This all rests on me. I am so, so sorry."

Kate closed her eyes and sighed. "I still don't understand. Why didn't you try to contact me afterward? Immediately? Out in the open, I mean? Why through an alias on the internet? Why the stealth?"

Jonas looked back and forth between Kate and Maggie. They were both looking back at him, waiting. It was time to confess. The enormity of it depressed him. The women were fundamentally unlike him. How to explain what it was like to be him to people whose very existence was normal? How to explain to them why you did things when you were always wrong, grew up unwanted, an accident, ignored and abandoned? Then he sought Maggie's eyes and recognized there was one who accepted him. And there was Jimmy Dean. Jimmy Dean loved him. And God. God had known and loved him before anyone else.

Understanding became radiant through him. He had not been certain God loved him until he had known God. God knew him—knew everything there was to know about him, and yet God loved him. He needed to do this. He needed to quit hiding.

Kate was waiting expectantly. She might understand. She had been married to Daniel, and Daniel had been like him in many ways. It gave him a measure of courage.

"Okay. I met Daniel in a restaurant in the Quarter. It was the week before Katrina."

Jonas sat before them, telling the story that still seemed unlikely enough to be almost impossible. He had met his brother. A brother he didn't know or remember had walked up to his table in a restaurant during a celebration of his sobriety, a success too late—a success after the fact. Yet they had both sensed they were brothers within minutes of meeting. Daniel. Daniel had accepted him without question, had accepted his past without judgment. They had been almost inseparable during the following days. They filled in missing holes for each other.

They had been born in Wisconsin. Neither knew who their father or mother was. They had no idea how or when they had been separated. Foster homes were their earliest memories. If their documented ages were correct, Daniel was a year older than Jonas was. What had separated them? They decided to work on it together, but it could wait. For now, it was enough to be together.

It was eerie how similar their experiences had been. One foster home after another until they became old enough to have their athletic ability recognized. Then—only then did the homes get better.

Daniel had even been adopted. People paid attention—had wanted them for their abilities. Daniel had kept playing sports on into college with the scholarships. Jonas got into trouble, a misdemeanor for being with some buddies who were stealing car stereos. People forgave him because he was great at baseball. He didn't even spend time in juvie like his friends. Unlike Daniel, he was finished with organized sports after high school. He went into the Navy where they tried to straighten him out.

Both men had mathematical and mechanical aptitude. Daniel went into chemical engineering. Jonas left the Navy, staying in the Northwest, picking up jobs in the shipyards when he wanted to work, finally settling in Galveston, TX to work at offshore drilling. Jonas wasn't an engineer, but his technical, problem-solving abilities were apparent in the petroleum world. He worked his way up from roughneck to a mechanic to a supervisor, and even into lower management, but always found a way to be busted down, through either insubordination or not showing up. Then, it was the drinking. But there was always the next job. He made a good first impression and sold himself well in interviews. Companies were always willing to take a chance. Daniel and Jonas had both suffered tragedy. Daniel had told Jonas about losing his son, David to a drunk driver.

At this point in the narrative, Jonas stopped to get Kate's eye. He knew Maggie was hoping and believing for the best in him. It was her way. So far, Kate had seemed sympathetic, but he was aware that he was about to lose any sympathy or compassion they were currently feeling. Despise him or pity him—they would find his confession too difficult to accept.

CHAPTER 29 - CONFESSION
BENFORD, TN – JANUARY 2006

There was no stopping now. Finally, it was almost a relief for Jonas to be confessing. "A little over three years ago, I was fired by a company in southern Texas, mostly because of drinking on the job, but I found another position with a company in Louisiana. My wife Sherry wanted to stay in Texas. She had friends. My daughters, Nicole and Emma, were 18 months and 4 years old."

"I made the drive from Texas to Louisiana and back for several months, but I hated it, only getting to be with them on weekends. I found a house in Gretna and talked Sherry into moving. I was making the last trip, bringing my family with me in a U-Haul. Sherry, Nicole, and Emma, and the last few odds-and-ends. It was night. It was raining. They were asleep."

At this point in the narrative, Jonas's words began to come in pieces. He was facing a locked door in his mind with an audience at his back. He seldom entered this place in his psyche. Showing others what was inside had so far only happened with his sobriety group. With them, it was different. They were all people revealing their own houses of horror. This was not like that at all. The people sitting before him were not broken. His eyes returned to Maggie who seemingly was unable to look at him.

His voice faltered but continued. "Morgan City. I left the highway to take a break. I was drinking... drunk. Took a wrong turn out of the gas station on a road that followed a bayou. I must have fallen asleep, although I've never been able to remember. I sometimes dream..."

The vision played behind his eyelids. Always, the legs scissoring away in the darkness, the impossibility of reaching the next breath... just before waking. He shook the vision off and continued. "The car crossed the road, over an embankment into the bayou. I woke with the truck already submerged in the water."

The room was silent. Jonas couldn't look up.

"I was the only one who survived. We were upside down in the U-Haul. I was the stereotypical drunk who somehow survives untouched, while no one else makes it. I got Nicole out, but she didn't survive. Emmy and Sherry—"

Tears flowed down Maggie's face. Kate sat in cold, silence.

"I was charged with felony vehicular manslaughter. I should have been the one to die... at least should have gone to prison. I wished for it."

Moments or minutes crawled by. Jonas looked up to focus on the room. The women were still there, but their faces were a blur. He continued. "So you see... Daniel had every reason to reject me. I was no better than the one person he despised in this world more than any other. He had already told me this. Worse than hate. Despised. That was the way he described him." Jonas gave a mirthless chuckle. "He said he should probably despise me as well, but somehow he couldn't. He didn't understand it himself."

Long moments of silence followed this statement until Kate spoke in a small, distant voice. "I don't get it. I don't see how I can accept it. The only reason I am still here is my need to know what happened with Daniel. If you care anything at all about him, please get on with it. I'd like you to explain—I don't know—maybe why you are still alive, and he is gone. Will you do that? Can you explain that?" Jonas and her son's killer had become the same person in her mind. She would not give him the satisfaction of her anger.

Jonas reacted as though Kate had kicked him in the stomach, but he continued, even if he did so without hope. He told them about staying out of prison because of one judge. He could never decide if the judge was merciful or knew that holding back the satisfaction of a prison sentence assured a personal hell with no chance for redemption. The probation terms required him to attend a sobriety group in addition to community service. "I was with my group the night I met Daniel. We met, and he came home with me. We must have talked most of that first night. I lived in a double shotgun house in midtown. The man on the other side of the house was also in my sobriety group, a single father with a little girl."

A puzzle piece dropped into place for Kate. "Joe and Sicily?" she asked.

Jonas glanced at her in surprise but continued.

"Yes. I had been helping Joe remodel his side of the house when I wasn't at work. He was having a difficult time being a single father, trying to work odd jobs while providing for Sicily." Glancing at Kate, he asked, "Do you know where Sicily is? I saw her being rescued, but couldn't follow."

Kate's face showed no indication she had even heard. She made a quick decision and answered, "Sicily is fine. She has a family who loves her and is taking care of her." Quickly moving on, she asked, "Why don't you tell us about the rescue? Tell us everything about that morning."

Kate did not appear to be ready to say anything further, so Jonas let it go. "Well, we knew Katrina was on the way, but of course we didn't know how bad it was going to be. I tried to get Daniel to go to the airport. He refused. He had been helping Joe and me make the house hurricane proof. Joe's car wasn't running. I was working on that. We were worried about Joe and Sicily, and wanted to make sure they got out of New Orleans."

"Daniel offered to fly Joe and Sicily out of the city, but Joe was having none of it. He wanted to save personal stuff. Had it packed in the car and ready to go. But we ran out of time. I never found a distributor cap for his old car. I called every parts store in New

Orleans—searched all the salvage yards. We tried to get Joe to bring Sicily with us in Daniel's car, but that man was stubborn. He decided they were going to wait out the storm."

"I kept trying to tell Daniel to go, but he wouldn't leave Sicily. It was that simple. They were like two peas in a pod. They hit it off from the get-go. Finally, I was able to get Joe's car running the day before by using epoxy. We were going to leave, but then Joe told us he didn't want to try to make it. He wasn't sure his car would keep running. He was probably right about that. It was getting nasty outside. We all huddled together in the house and waited out the leading edge of the hurricane. The wind and rain shook the house, but it seemed like everything was going to be okay."

"In the morning, Joe told us he wanted to go to a friend's place a few miles away. The winds were still high, but it was calmer because the eye was beginning to move over the city to the east of us. He told us the man who owned the house was a former firefighter who had decided to leave the city himself but told Joe that he could stay there. Joe knew where the key was. After telling us the house was two-story and elevated, we decided to make a run for it. I don't know why he waited so long to tell us about it. Joe was a proud man. He didn't like to ask for help from anyone."

"We didn't know what was going on with the hurricane. We had a hand-cranked radio that didn't work very well. And of course, no one knew the levees were going to fail. We chanced making a short trip to this other house because the foundation of our house was only about two feet tall. Joe said the main living area of the other house was at least 8 feet above the ground."

"So we grabbed the stored food and water we had prepared, with the other supplies already in the cars, and headed to this other location. Joe was afraid of his car stranding us on the elevated 610, so we headed north to Robert E. Lee before going west to Lakeview. It was only going to be a few miles. We were almost there—had turned south to head a few blocks to the other house when the 17th Street Levee failed. It was one of those small divided streets with trees down the middle."

Kate interrupted. "Was that the street the other house was on—the one you were headed to?" Jonas nodded his head, yes. There was something in the way she spoke of this, the certain familiarity perhaps, which made Jonas think that Kate might already know some of this story. He didn't know *how* she knew. Not that it made a difference in his story.

"Our timing was horrible—actually couldn't have been worse. Five minutes earlier, and we would have made it to the house. Joe and Sicily were in the lead because Joe knew the way. Daniel and I were right behind. The flood of water from the broken levee had hit Joe and Sicily broadside from the right, pushing Joe's car against the raised area in the center of the street."

"Daniel slammed on the brakes. We weren't in the center of the flow, but the water started rushing around our car too. Daniel told me not to open the passenger door. I was following him out his side even as he was leaping through the water toward Joe and Sicily. Daniel's car began to slide sideways as I was getting out. I climbed over the door onto the hood, trying to keep from being trapped. Joe's car was now wedged against a tree, but I didn't see him anywhere. So much water. An incredible rush of water."

"I saw Daniel up to his shoulders in the water, trying to hold an inflatable children's pool and push Sicily in. I jumped from the hood to help as he got her in, but the water swept them away. I tried to follow—thought I was going to drown if I got much closer to the center of the flow. So I swam to the edge of the current and tried to follow. Daniel and Sicily were in the center where it was treacherous. He went under. I lost him. The rain was picking up again. I never saw him surface again. Sicily was still in the toy pool, but she kept getting further away until I completely lost sight of her, too."

Jonas's tears began to flow. It was several seconds before he continued with his story, leaving nothing out, including his reluctance to reveal his own presence during Sicily's rescue. Kate listened intently, looking into his eyes to measure his sincerity. The story agreed with what she already knew. She remembered what Cedric, the father of the boys who had rescued Sicily had said about the man who had swum to the mound over the old civil defense shelter after the rescue. It had not been Daniel, as she had feared. It had been Jonas.

"After Sicily was rescued by those boys on top of the mound, I swam over there to look around. Eventually, I made my way back to the car. I don't know how long it took because I wasn't thinking straight. I was hoping that maybe I had missed something—that maybe I'd find Joe or Daniel, but the water was well over the roof of the cars. It reached the eaves of the one-story houses by this time. I remembered the house Joe was taking us to, and having nowhere else to go, I went there until I could decide what to do. It was a few more blocks south. Fortunately, the porch was high enough that even though it was covered with water, I was able to find the key under the porch roof."

"I slept on the second floor through the rest of the storm that night, and used it as a base, the next day, searching for Daniel and Joe, but it was useless. The water wasn't receding. I can hardly describe how horrible it was. I guess everyone knows only too well now," he said. "On Wednesday I found a dinghy roped to a sailboat, blown on its side. I cut it loose, got it back on top of the water, and returned to where we abandoned the cars to have another look. The water hadn't receded much. I gave up—had to paddle the dinghy with a wooden plank all the way down to I610. Helicopters were plucking people from the tops of houses, but I didn't want to wait for them to find me. I was finally picked up from the elevated road, and then left the city several days later with other evacuees."

"Quite a story, and understandable," Kate said. "That is if it's all true. It must have been a horrific experience. But it doesn't make sense to me."

"Okay," Jonas said. "What doesn't make sense?"

Kate looked at him with disgust. "Why didn't you follow up with Sicily? You lived next to her? You saw her get rescued, and didn't care what happened to her afterward? That doesn't make sense to me."

Jonas nodded. "Okay. I understand what you are thinking. Why didn't I holler to let them know I was there? I've pretended to myself that I was too exhausted." He closed his eyes and lowered his head. "But the truth is... I was a coward. I couldn't face Sicily, and tell her that her dad had probably drowned. I hesitated, and then their boat left, and it was too late."

Jonas quickly continued insistently. "But I did care. I still do. When the rescuers picked me up, I asked about her. I spoke with a detective who said she knew all about Sicily's rescue—that she had already been evacuated out of New Orleans. I also told her what had happened with Joe and Daniel, even where to find the rental cars. Basically, I told her the same story I just told you, although I'll admit, I didn't tell anyone about actually seeing Sicily's rescue."

Kate was so stunned her mouth flew open. "The cop you talked to? What did she look like?" Kate demanded. She looked like she was in shock.

Jonas was aware that what he had said was distressing Kate. "Well, she had dark features—seemed like a little ball of fire."

"Do you remember her name?"

"No. Why? Should I?"

"Are you certain it was a female detective that you talked to about Daniel and Sicily? Could you have talked to another cop, and then spoke with the detective?"

Jonas was almost afraid to answer. Something crucial hinged on this one fact, but he had no idea what it was. He replied quietly. "I'm quite sure. It's why I was confident that Sicily was okay. The detective talked like she was the one who would follow through with the investigation."

Kate shook her head and stood, telling Maggie and Jonas she was going outside to think things over and get a breath of air. Maggie busied herself with making coffee in the kitchen, leaving Jonas alone. He sat there thinking about Sicily, wondering where she was. Kate had said that she was in a good home. *How did she know, and why was she was so upset about the detective?*

When Kate came back in the house, Maggie called them into the kitchen. "I made coffee, but do either of you want something else to drink? I'm going to fix lunch soon."

"Coffee's fine. Maybe some ice water too, if you don't mind," said Kate. She leaned on the table. "To be candid with both of you, the story Jonas has just told is tough for me to believe. I can't seem to bring myself to see all of the implications."

Maggie brought the drinks over to the table, and they all sat down. Kate continued, "You see, I know the detective Jonas says he talked to. Her name is Sara Arceneaux. She's been helping, or pretending to help me for months, but—" With this she broke into tears, unable to continue.

"She didn't tell you about Sicily and Joe? Wait! She didn't tell you about Daniel?" Jonas was almost shouting. Like Kate, he couldn't comprehend why the detective would not have told her.

Kate was sobbing as she answered. "No, she told Sicily's story, but nothing about Joe—and certainly said nothing about Daniel."

Jonas was frowning. "I think I may know why she didn't say anything." He paused, thinking. "Listen. I told her where the cars were, and that Daniel had put cash in one of his bags in the car. She was extremely helpful, maybe even in a big hurry for me to get out of New Orleans. I don't know how much cash it was, but I know Daniel was relying on it to help us leave the city. When I went back the day after the levee break to recover stuff from the car, the water was too deep and nasty to dive down to get anything out. I didn't just tell her about Daniel and Joe. I mentioned the money as well, worried about looters after the water receded. I didn't want to leave it either, but she said she would make sure that search and rescue got to it first."

"I hate to say it, but if she took the money herself, it would have suited her purposes if Daniel's body wasn't found until later, or not found at all."

Kate nodded in resignation. "I told her that Daniel carried cash instead of using cards." Kate thought back to how Sara had tried to keep her from Detective Manson, and how Terrance's friend didn't believe that Manson was dirty. Sara had quit seeing Terrance as soon as he had suggested otherwise. She thought about the phone call, supposedly from Daniel's life insurance company to the FBI to have Daniel declared dead. Was Sara trying to set up a scam with Kate to get even more money? Why else would she have been so helpful? Then, it came to mind that her information had never actually led to Daniel or Jonas.

Sara had even been upset when Gilbert had taken over Sicily's adoption process. Kate remembered that she had wanted Frieda the social worker to handle it. Had they been planning to take money from her for the adoption?

Finally, she had given a weak excuse for not coming with Kate to Nashville. She could have taken a day off. She intended to quit soon anyway. Even though the puzzle was still incomplete, reality was beginning to set in. Never in her life had her trust in people been so shaken.

I think we have a lot to talk about with the FBI," she said. "Are you willing to talk with them—tell your story to the FBI?" Kate asked Jonas.

Jonas nodded. He knew it was time to expose his past by bringing it into the light—the only way he would ever have peace. He was aware that God required it as well. He bowed his head as it became more and more apparent what Kate had gone through, not knowing. Then Jonas thought of Sicily. "Oh no!" he exclaimed. "Was Sara lying about Sicily? What has happened to her?"

For the first time, Kate was able to smile. She punched a number into her cell phone, asking Jonas, "Do you want to talk with her? She's my daughter."

CHAPTER 30 - CLOSURE
BENFORD, TN – JANUARY 2006

While Kate was talking to Mandy first, and then Sicily on the phone, Jonas remained quiet and listening, letting her words carry him along. He noticed her watching him at one point—opened his mouth to say something about it not being necessary for him to talk to Sicily—and snapped it back shut when she turned away.

In moments like these, he felt like giving up. He didn't fit in with Maggie and Kate. To them, he must be a symbol of everything wrong with the world. He had come to the same conclusion himself after he had been responsible for the loss of his family, and even more recently after Katrina. He had no expectations of a real life until he met Maggie.

Maggie, with her incessant optimism. Maggie, who saw the best in everyone and made them think it was possible to be more than they were. He found her across the room, noticing the delight in her eyes while listening to Kate talk to her daughter. That was Maggie, enjoying other people's happiness, wanting the best for them—always willing to put them before her own desires.

Maggie was the one who had made him want more from life, to have expectations again. Maggie and Jimmy Dean. She tugged and pulled and prodded, showing him what he could be through her eyes. He marveled at the brightness of her face now, the characteristic wave in her hair, haloed by the light behind her. *She is a beautiful woman*, he thought. *She's far too good for me.* Then the most important realization of all: *I love her. I don't care if she's older. But a part of me will always know that she is too good for me.*

As if she were privy to his mind, her eyes turned his way. Their eyes met and locked. Maggie then turned her head entirely his way, their eyes still holding, and she gave him a look as if to ask, *what?* For once, Jonas didn't turn. He didn't hold back or shrink away. Now that he was bringing everything into the light, he didn't want to leave it ever again. He held her gaze from across the room, and told her, without speaking, what was in his heart. *I hope you will forgive me.* At the same time, he felt another pleased presence inside. What made it even better was that he knew the Holy Spirit was also smiling inside of her, confirming.

Maggie knew Jonas wanted to say something to her. She rose to go sit by him just as Kate called him over to answer the phone. Jonas started to get up himself, in tiredness and pain, but Maggie passed the phone to him on her way across the room.

"I turned on the speaker phone," Kate said, as Jonas was turning it around, trying to make sure he had it right side up.

"Sicily, this is Jonas," he began. "Do you remember me?"

He melted when her sweet little voice sang out of the small speaker, yet somehow filled the room. "Yes."

"I'm so glad you are okay. And you have a mommy now."

"Kate," Sicily sang out. "My mommy is Kate."

"That's right, Sicily," replied Jonas. "She is very nice. Do you like your new house?"

"Uh-huh."

A dog barked in the background, and Sicily giggled into the phone. "That's Knut," Kate explained. "He's my friend Mandy's dog."

"Do you like Knut, Sicily? Is he a friendly dog?"

"Yes, but sometimes he's a bad dog," she added. "He got into the trash 'cause he's a bad dog."

"Oh well, you'll have to teach him to be a good dog. You can do that, Sicily. You're such a good girl."

There was more giggling before Kate came over to get the phone, just as Sicily abruptly asked, "Is Angel there?"

Kate froze as Jonas sighed sadly. "No honey." Jonas held Kate's gaze as he continued. "We'll see him again someday. Okay?"

"Okay."

"Sicily?" Jonas asked gently. "I think Angel came to rescue you. I think he'll always be watching to make sure you're okay."

"Me too," she said sweetly.

Kate came over to the phone and said goodbye to Sicily and Mandy.

"Daniel was Sicily's angel?" Kate asked Jonas. "Why did she call Daniel 'Angel'? You don't know how long I've been trying to figure out who 'the angel' is."

Jonas blinked at how simple the answer was. He stood to meet her eyes. He wanted her to know that this, at least, was the truth. "She called him 'Angel,' not 'the Angel.' When Sicily first met Daniel, he had a California Angels baseball cap on. He was an Angels fan, right?"

Unexpected understanding flooded Kate who nodded her agreement. "Oh, why didn't I think of that? He's always wearing that cap. She teared again at the thought. He and our son David were big fans. I believe that it started with the movie "Angels in the Outfield."

"Daniel taught Sicily to read his cap," said Jonas. "She loved it." Jonas smiled as he remembered. "She liked to sit on his lap raising the bill up and down. She kept calling him Angel. It stuck, and we started calling him that too. That's all there was to it."

Kate sighed, unexpectedly hugging Jonas. He winced but held on as he told her, "Kate, I am so sorry. If I had it all to do again, I would have contacted you as soon as I was able, even—well, even if, if you decided not to accept me. Daniel told me so much about you. That's why I used the poetry blog. I didn't want to be a peeping Tom; I just wanted to make sure you were okay and trying to think of a way to eventually—"

"Be honest?" Kate asked.

Jonas sighed and nodded. "Honest to God and man. I have finally understood that I cannot have one without the other."

There were so many gaps to fill from both directions. Jonas was overwhelmed with the story of how Kate had come to adopt Sicily. They all marveled at the unexplained connection both Daniel and Kate had made with the little girl. When Jonas's nurse came to examine his healing wounds, Maggie explained how Jonas had become a mentor to Jimmy Dean. She also told the story of how Bo had killed Jess and almost killed Jonas. They all talked until Kate had to leave for the airport in Nashville to make the return flight to Missouri, but not before making promises to stay in contact and meet again.

The three stood by Kate's rental car as she was preparing to leave. Jonas was suddenly afraid he might never see her again. "There is so much I want to say about Daniel." His throat tightened with the effort to find words.

Kate gazed from one of his eyes to the other, eyes so much like Daniel's, grasping that this man had come to love her husband. She too needed to hear all that he could tell her about Daniel during those last days in New Orleans. Where had his heart been? Had Daniel given up on her? "He talked about me?" she asked, afraid, but needing to hear the answer.

"Kate, when he wasn't asking questions about me, he was talking about you. He became my big brother so quickly, telling me how important it was that I find someone to love and never let anything come between us."

Jonas looked at Maggie. "It's like you told me before Christmas. Do you remember? How we sometimes "wake up" and realize what is important? I knew he was telling himself the same thing. He couldn't wait to get home."

"And yet he did wait," Kate said.

Jonas shook his head slowly in sorrow. "I'm afraid that was for me." He brightened. "But it wasn't only for me. It was mostly for Sicily. Maybe that's one reason he could hardly wait to get back home—to tell you about Sicily. She made him realize that he was ready to open his heart to a child once again. So, when you adopted her—"

Kate marveled. "It's like a miracle, isn't it?"

"It *is* a miracle. It is precisely what Daniel would have wanted—I mean... if Joe had to die, of course."

"I believe that," she said, sighing at the bitter sweetness of it. She smiled and looked back at Jonas. "So, what about you?" Jonas wasn't sure what she was asking, so he didn't know how to reply. Looking back and forth between them, Kate smiled and winked, "You do know you can find love and life again, right?"

Kate laughed when neither Jonas nor Maggie spoke. "I want you to know that no matter what, I consider you to be family now. I need to hear from you—for you to stay in touch."

Her words moved Jonas. Family was priceless. He also realized Kate was demonstrating her willingness to forgive, and in so doing, overcoming long-held emotions to reach out to him. Finally, he found his voice to say he would call and email. They hugged. Jonas was surprised at how difficult it was to say goodbye.

"We'll talk again soon," she promised.

Standing together alone in the driveway, Maggie and Jonas watched the rental car until it was out of sight. Without looking, Jonas reached for and squeezed her hand

Once she was back at the airport in Missouri, Kate called Sara's cell, only to listen to a recorded message telling her the number was no longer in service. She thought about calling the FBI but decided the call could wait a day. What couldn't wait was a little girl named Sicily.

EPILOGUE
BENFORD, TN – JUNE 2006

Jonas drove Jimmy Dean to the ballpark. He refused to miss any part of the first game of the season, even the players warming up. One of the first parents there, he found a place on the bleachers, while a few boys started tossing balls back and forth. Resting his arms on the seat behind him, he watched the whole field without obviously focusing on just one boy. He didn't want to make Jimmy Dean nervous by only paying attention to him.

A baseball flew over the fence beyond first base. Checking to see if anyone was going to go after it, Jonas noticed one of the mothers in his line of sight. She was smiling at him from the other end of the same section of bleachers. He instinctively smiled back. After a few minutes, she called over to ask if his boy was playing.

Jonas pointed out toward the field. "I'm here for Jimmy Dean." The woman turned back to glance at where he was pointing, looked back at him with puzzlement, stood up, and walked the bleacher seat like a balance beam to where Jonas was standing.

"I'm Julie," she announced, sitting beside him.

Jonas thought he might have seen her at an earlier practice. Under her short, wavy auburn hair, her bright blue-green eyes gradually opened wider until she blinked, only to expand again. He recognized her as someone who probably attracted second looks from men, and had come to expect it, but he only had eyes for Jimmy Dean. He realized he had let an uncomfortable period go by without saying anything.

"Yes. I mean— I'm sorry. My name is Jonas."

"Ooooh... okay. You're Jonas," she repeated. "I should have known. I worked with Maggie as a volunteer last year before she uh, well, before we— I haven't talked with her since. I'm Julie—Julie Seifert," she blurted, not finding any satisfactory finishes to her sentences. Her face warmed considerably, but again, Jonas had no response, so she continued. "We left here last November when my ex-husband got a job in Memphis. It didn't work out like we planned, so Corey and I came back a few weeks ago. I'm working at Simmons Hardware."

"Oh, so I guess Bart's niece didn't work out very well."

"So I've heard from Bart... many times," she said rolling her eyes and smiling.

Jonas and Julie watched Jimmy Dean and another boy run toward a makeshift bullpen beyond the dugout after finishing their infield drill.

"You've done wonders with him," she said, returning Jonas's smile, even as he shrugged. "I mean it. Jimmy Dean has been on my son Corey's team since they were in toss ball." She returned her gaze to the field and pointed. "That's Corey on first base." Jonas followed her eyes out to a tall boy stretched out, with his foot on the bag.

"It certainly wasn't Jimmy Dean's fault," she continued, still looking out at the field. "He never had anyone to work with him or show him anything. It's horrible what happened to his mom." Her eyes abruptly shone with tears. "Maggie told me last fall you had been spending a lot of time with him. That's great—really a nice thing you've done."

Jonas didn't know what to say. "Thank you, but it's easy with Jimmy Dean. He's a great kid. I've noticed your son Corey at practices. He's perfect for first base," he added.

Jonas was dividing his attention between Julie and the team, when

Maggie arrived, walking hand-in-hand with a little curly black-headed girl, and one other woman walking behind. Jonas stood up, waving for them to come over.

"Julie! It's good to see you," exclaimed Maggie. "Is Corey playing?"

"Oh yes," she said, pointing at her boy. "I was talking to Jonas about Jimmy Dean."

The women climbed the bleachers, Maggie stopping to introduce the others.

"Julie Seifert, this is Kate Mitchell, and this beautiful little girl is Kate's daughter, Sicily." But I'm tempted to take her home with me, and keep her." Maggie teased and winked at Sicily, the two of them sitting down a couple of rows below. Sicily looked tremendously cute, holding Maggie's hand. Kate sat down behind them, and Jonas stepped down to join Maggie.

Unable to keep the puzzlement from her face, Julie asked politely, "So, are you all here to watch Jimmy Dean play ball?"

Kate laughed. "Well yes, but not just for that. Like Maggie said, Sicily is my daughter, and she wanted to come see Jonas and Jimmy Dean." Sicily stepped around Maggie to sit by Jonas who gave her a hug.

Maggie turned around to explain further. "Jonas owns one side of a house that also belonged to Sicily's father in New Orleans. Jonas and Jimmy Dean are also co-owners of the house that his mom rented. Jonas lives there now. Jimmy Dean lives with me, but he stays with Jonas too. And let's see, I don't think I mentioned that Kate is Jonas's sister-in-law. So, if you have followed all of that, you would be right to think that this is one of the most unconventional families you will ever meet."

Julie responded with a nervous giggle that made them all laugh.

Harlan and Betty climbed the bleachers to sit by Kate, and Bart Simmons from the hardware store wasn't too far behind, deciding to sit by his new employee, Julie. All of the arrivals launched another round of introductions.

Julie leaned over to Bart to question him quietly, but it still carried down to the bleacher below. "So, are Jonas and Maggie— I mean, are they a couple?"

Bart grumbled in annoyance, "Nah, just friends. Surrogate parents."

Betty turned her head to whisper, "more than that, and you know it."

Harlan's brow furrowed as he leaned back to rest his arm on the bleacher above. "What did she say?"

"She wants to know if Jonas and Maggie are in a relationship," Betty whispered again.

"Why do you want to know? Are you interested in him?" Harlan addressed this directly to Julie, loudly enough for Maggie to look back to see what they were talking about.

Julie blushed. Betty shushed Harlan.

They all waited for Maggie to turn back around, and then Julie whispered to Kate, "What do you think?"

Kate furrowed an expressive forehead, considering her answer before look intently into Julie's eyes. "I know they love each other. I can't speak for them, but one thing is certain—they both put Jimmy Dean before the other. But if I had to guess—it won't be long before they see that is no longer necessary. The three of them belong together."

Harlan gave a spirited nod and then wanted to know if Jimmy Dean was going to be pitching. None of them needed to answer because, when they looked out at the field, he was walking over to the pitcher's mound.

After several warm-up pitches and a toss down to second base, the ball returned to Jimmy Dean. He held his glove under his arm, rubbed the baseball in his hands, and looked up to find Jonas in the crowd. A calm, confidence passed between them.

Jimmy Dean put the glove back on, stepped onto the rubber, peered in at the catcher's mitt, and repeated a motion he had performed thousands of times since the past September. The ball left his fingers, sizzling to its target, with a pop that could be heard all the way out past the center field fence.

"Steeeerike!" called the umpire.

Made in the USA
Charleston, SC
10 December 2016